S0-AQG-223

TONO-BUNGAY

TONO-BUNGAY

BY

H. G. WELLS

THE
MODERN LIBRARY
NEW YORK

Random House IS THE PUBLISHER OF

THE MODERN LIBRARY

BENNETT A. CERF · DONALD S. KLOPFER · ROBERT K. HAAS

Manufactured in the United States of America

By H. Wolff

CONTENTS

BOOK THE FIRST

THE DAYS BEFORE TONO-BUNGAY WAS INVENTED

BOOK THE SECOND

THE RISE OF TONO-BUNGAY

BOOK THE THIRD

THE GREAT DAYS OF TONO-BUNGAY

[xii]

BOOK THE FIRST

THE DAYS BEFORE TONO-BUNGAY WAS INVENTED

CHAPTER THE FIRST

Of Bladesover House, and My Mother; and the Constitution of Society

I

MOST people in this world seem to live "in character"; they have a beginning, a middle and an end, and the three are congruous one with another and true to the rules of their type. You can speak of them as being of this sort of people or that. They are, as theatrical people say, no more (and no less) than "character actors." They have a class, they have a place, they know what is becoming in them and what is due to them, and their proper size of tombstone tells at last how properly they have played the part. But there is also another kind of life that is not so much living as a miscellaneous tasting of life. One gets hit by some unusual transverse force, one is jerked out of one's stratum and lives crosswise for the rest of the time, and, as it were, in a succession of samples. That has been my lot, and that is what has set me at last writing something in the nature of a novel. I have got an unusual series of impressions that I want very urgently to tell. I have seen life at very different levels, and at all these levels I have seen it with a sort of intimacy and in good faith. I have been a native in many social countries. I have been the unwelcome guest of a working baker, my cousin, who has since died in the Chatham infirmary; I have eaten illegal snacks—the unjustifiable gifts of footmen—in pantries, and been despised for my want of style (and subsequently married and divorced) by the daughter of a gasworks clerk; and—to go to my other extreme—I was once—oh, glittering days!—an item in the house-party of a countess. She was, I admit, a countess with a financial aspect, but still, you know, a countess. I've seen these people at various angles. At the dinner-table I've met not simply the titled but the great. On one occasion—it is my brightest memory—I upset my champagne over the trousers of the greatest statesman in the empire—Heaven forbid I should be so invidious as to name him!—in the warmth of our mutual admiration.

And once (though it is the most incidental thing in my life) I murdered a man. . . .

Yes, I've seen a curious variety of people and ways of living altogether. Odd people they all are, great and small, very much alike at bottom and curiously different on their surfaces. I wish I had ranged just a little further both up and down, seeing I have ranged so far. Royalty must be worth knowing and very great fun. But my contacts with princes have been limited to quite public occasions, nor at the other end of the scale have I had what I should call an inside acquaintance with that dusty but attractive class of people who go about on the high-roads drunk but *en famille* (so redeeming the minor lapse), in the summer-time, with a perambulator, lavender to sell, sun-brown children, a smell, and ambiguous bundles that fire the imagination. Navvies, farm-labourers, sailormen and stokers, all such as sit in 1834 beer-houses, are beyond me also, and I suppose must remain so now for ever. My intercourse with the ducal rank too has been negligible; I once went shooting with a duke, and in an outburst of what was no doubt snobbishness, did my best to get him in the legs. But that failed.

I'm sorry I haven't done the whole lot though. . . .

You will ask by what merit I achieved this remarkable social range, this extensive cross-section of the British social organism. It was the Accident of Birth. It always is in England. Indeed, if I may make the remark so cosmic, everything is. But that is by the way. I was my uncle's nephew, and my uncle was no less a person than Edward Ponderevo, whose comet-like transit of the financial heavens happened—it is now ten years ago! Do you remember the days of

Ponderevo, the *great* days, I mean, of Ponderevo? Perhaps you had a trifle in some world-shaking enterprise! Then you know him only too well. Astraddle on Tono-Bungay, he flashed athwart the empty heavens—like a comet—rather, like a stupendous rocket!—and overawed investors spoke of his star. At his zenith he burst into a cloud of the most magnificent promotions. What a time that was! The Napoleon of domestic conveniences! . . .

I was his nephew, his peculiar and intimate nephew. I was hanging on to his coat-tails all the way through. I made pills with him in the chemist's shop at Wimblehurst before he began. I was, you might say, the stick of his rocket; and after our tremendous soar, after he had played with millions, a golden rain in the sky, after my bird's-eye view of the modern world, I fell again, a little scarred and blistered perhaps, two and twenty years older, with my youth gone, my manhood eaten in upon, but greatly edified, into this Thames-side yard, into these white heats and hammerings, amidst the fine realities of steel—to think it all over in my leisure and jot down the notes and inconsecutive observations that make this book. It was more, you know, than a figurative soar. The zenith of that career was surely our flight across the channel in the Lord Roberts β. . . .

I warn you this book is going to be something of an agglomeration. I want to trace my social trajectory (and my uncle's) as the main line of my story, but as this is my first novel and almost certainly my last, I want to get in, too, all sorts of things that struck me, things that amused me and impressions I got—even although they don't minister directly to my narrative at all. I want to set out my own queer love experiences too, such as they are, for they troubled and distressed and swayed me hugely, and they still seem to me to contain all sorts of irrational and debatable elements that I shall be the clearer-headed for getting on paper. And possibly I may even flow into descriptions of people who are really no more than people seen in transit, just because it amuses me to recall what they said and did to us, and more particularly how they behaved in the brief but splendid glare of Tono-Bungay and its still more glaring offspring. It lit some of them up, I can assure you! Indeed, I want to get in all sorts of things. My ideas of a novel all through are comprehensive rather than austere. . . .

Tono-Bungay still figures on the hoardings, it stands in rows in every chemist's storeroom, it still assuages the coughs of age and brightens the elderly eye and loosens the elderly tongue; but its social glory, its financial illumination, have faded from the world for ever. And I, sole scorched survivor from the blaze, sit writing of it here in an air that is never still for the clang and thunder of machines, on a table littered with working drawings, and amid fragments of models and notes about velocities and air and water pressures and trajectories—of an altogether different sort from that of Tono-Bungay.

II

I write that much and look at it, and wonder whether, after all, this is any fair statement of what I am attempting in this book. I've given, I see, an impression that I want to make simply a hotch-potch of anecdotes and experiences with my uncle swimming in the middle as the largest lump of victual. I'll own that here, with the pen already started, I realise what a fermenting mass of things learnt and emotions experienced and theories formed I've got to deal with, and how, in a sense, hopeless my book must be from the very outset. I suppose what I'm really trying to render is nothing more nor less than Life—as one man has found it. I want to tell—*myself,* and my impressions of the thing as a whole, to say things I have come to feel intensely of the laws, traditions, usages, and ideas we call society, and how we poor individuals get driven and lured and stranded among these windy, perplexing shoals and channels. I've got, I suppose, to a time of life when things begin to take on shapes that have an air of reality, and become no longer material for dreaming, but interesting in themselves. I've reached the criticising, novel-writing age, and here I am writing mine—my one novel—without having any of the discipline to refrain and omit that I suppose the regular novel-writer acquires.

I've read an average share of novels and made some starts before this beginning, and I've found the restraints and rules of the art (as I made them out) impossible for me. I like to write, I am keenly interested in writing, but it is not my technique. I'm an engineer with a patent or two and a set of ideas; most of whatever artist there is in me has been given to turbine machines and boat building and the problem of flying, and do what I will I fail to see how I can be other than a lax, undisciplined story-teller. I must sprawl and flounder, comment and theorise, if I am to get the thing out I have in mind. And it isn't a constructed tale I have to tell, but unmanageable realities. My love-story—and if only I can keep up the spirit of truth-telling all through as strongly as I have now, you shall have it all—falls into no sort of neat scheme of telling. It involves three separate feminine persons. It's all mixed up with the other things. . . .

But I've said enough, I hope, to excuse myself for the method or want of method in what follows, and I think I had better tell without further delay of my boyhood and my early impressions in the shadow of Bladesover House.

III

There came a time when I realised that Bladesover House was not all it seemed, but when I was a little boy I took the place with the entirest faith as a complete authentic microcosm. I believed that the Bladesover system was a little working-model—and not so very little either—of the whole world.

Let me try and give you the effect of it.

Bladesover lies up on the Kentish Downs, eight miles perhaps from Ashborough; and its old pavilion, a little wooden parody of the temple of Vesta at Tibur, upon the hill crest behind the house, commands in theory at least a view of either sea, of the Channel southward and the Thames to the northeast. The park is the second largest in Kent, finely wooded with well-placed beeches, many elms and some sweet chestnuts, abounding in little valleys and hollows of bracken, with springs and a stream and three fine ponds and multitudes of fallow deer. The house was built in the eighteenth century, it is of pale red brick in the style of a French château, and save for one pass among the crests which opens to blue distances, to minute, remote, oast-set farmhouses and copses and wheat fields and the occasional gleam of water, its hundred and seventeen windows look on nothing but its own wide and handsome territories. A semi-circular screen of great beeches masks the church and village, which cluster picturesquely about the high road along the skirts of the great park. Northward, at the remotest corner of that enclosure, is a second dependent village, Ropedean, less fortunate in its greater distance and also on account of a rector. This divine was indeed rich, but he was vindictively economical because of some shrinkage of his tithes; and by reason of his use of the word Eucharist for the Lord's Supper he had become altogether estranged from the great ladies of Bladesover. So that Ropedean was in the shadows through all that youthful time.

Now the unavoidable suggestion of that wide park and that fair large house, dominating church, village and the country side, was that they represented the thing that mattered supremely in the world, and that all other things had significance only in relation to them. They represented the Gentry, the Quality, by and through and for whom the rest of the world, the farming folk and the labouring folk, the trades-people of Ashborough, and the upper servants and the lower servants and the servants of the estate, breathed and lived and were permitted. And the Quality did it so quietly and thoroughly, the great house mingled so solidly and effectually with earth and sky, the contrast of its spacious hall and saloon and galleries, its airy housekeeper's room and warren of offices with the meagre dignities of the vicar, and the pinched and stuffy rooms of even the post-office people and the grocer, so enforced these suggestions, that it was only when I was a boy of thirteen or fourteen and some queer inherited strain of scepticism had set me doubting whether Mr. Bartlett, the vicar, did really know with certainty all about God, that as a further and deeper step in doubting I began to question the final rightness of the gentlefolks, their primary necessity in the scheme of things. But once that scepticism had awakened it took me fast and far. By fourteen I had achieved terrible blasphemies and sacrilege; I had resolved to marry a viscount's daughter, and I had blacked the left eye—I think it was the left—of her half-brother, in open and declared rebellion.

But of that in its place.

The great house, the church, the village, and the labourers and the servants in their stations and degrees, seemed to me, I say, to be a closed and complete social system. About us were other villages and great estates, and from house to house, interlacing, correlated, the Gentry, the fine Olympians, came and went. The country towns seemed mere collections of shops, marketing places for the tenantry, centres for such education as they needed, as entirely dependent on the gentry as the village and scarcely less directly so. I thought this was the order of the whole world. I thought London was only a greater country town where the gentlefolk kept town-houses and did their greater shopping under the magnificent shadow of the greatest of all fine gentlewomen, the Queen. It seemed to be in the divine order. That all this fine appearance was already sapped, that there were forces at work that might presently carry all this elaborate social system in which my mother instructed me so carefully that I might understand my "place," to Limbo, had scarcely dawned upon me even by the time that Tono-Bungay was fairly launched upon the world.

There are many people in England to-day upon whom it has not yet dawned. There are times when I doubt whether any but a very inconsiderable minority of English people realise how extensively this ostensible order has even now passed away. The great houses stand in the parks still, the cottages cluster respectfully on their borders, touching their eaves with their creepers, the English countryside—you can range through Kent from Bladesover northward and see— persists obstinately in looking what it was. It is like an early day in a fine October. The hand of change rests on it all, unfelt, unseen; resting for awhile, as it were half reluctantly, before it grips and ends the thing for ever. One frost and the whole face of things will be bare, links snap, patience end, our fine foliage of pretences lie glowing in the mire.

For that we have still to wait a little while. The new order may have gone far towards shaping itself, but just as in that sort of lantern show that used to be known in the village as the "Dissolving Views," the scene that is going remains upon the mind, traceable and evident, and the newer picture is yet enigmatical long after the lines that are to replace those former ones have grown bright and strong, so that the new England of our children's children is still a riddle to me. The ideas of democracy, of equality, and above all of promiscuous fraternity have certainly never really entered into the English mind. But what *is* coming into it? All this book, I hope, will bear a little on that. Our people never formulates; it keeps words for jests and ironies. In the meanwhile the old shapes, the old attitudes remain, subtly changed and changing still, sheltering strange tenants. Bladesover House is now let furnished to Sir Reuben Lichtenstein, and has been since old Lady Drew died; it was my odd experience to visit there, in the house of which my mother had been housekeeper, when my uncle was at the climax of Tono-Bungay. It was curious to notice then the little differences that had come to things with this substitution. To borrow an image from my mineralogical days, these Jews were not so much a new British gentry as "pseudomorphous" after the gentry. They are a very clever people, the Jews, but not clever enough to suppress their cleverness. I wished I could have gone downstairs to savour the tone of the pantry. It would have been very different I know. Hawksnest, over beyond, I noted, had its pseudomorph too; a newspaper proprietor of the type that hustles along with stolen ideas from one loud sink-or-swim enterprise to another, had bought the place outright; Redgrave was in the hands of brewers.

But the people in the villages, so far as I could detect, saw no difference in their world. Two little girls bobbed and an old labourer touched his hat convulsively as I walked through the village. He still thought he knew his place—and mine. I did not know him, but I would have liked dearly to have asked him if he remembered my mother, if either my uncle or old Lichtenstein had been man enough to stand being given away like that.

In that English countryside of my boyhood every human being had a "place." It belonged to you from your birth like the colour of your eyes, it was inextricably your destiny. Above you were your betters, below you were your inferiors, and there were even an unstable questionable few, cases so disputable that you might for the rough purposes of every day at least, regard them as your equals. Head and centre of our system was Lady Drew, her "leddyship," shrivelled, garrulous, with a wonderful memory for genealogies and very, very old, and beside her and nearly as old, Miss Somerville, her cousin and companion. These two old souls lived like dried-up kernels in the great shell of Bladesover House, the shell that had once been gaily full of fops, of fine ladies in powder and patches and courtly gentlemen with swords; and when there was no company they spent whole days in the corner parlour just over the housekeeper's room, between reading and slumber and caressing their two pet dogs. When I was a boy I used always to think of these two poor old creatures as superior beings living, like God, somewhere through the ceiling. Occasionally they bumped about a bit and one even heard them overhead, which gave them a greater effect of reality without mitigating their vertical predominance. Sometimes too I saw them. Of course if I came upon them in the park or in the shrubbery (where I was a trespasser) I hid or fled in pious horror, but I was upon due occasion taken into the Presence by request. I remember her "leddyship" then as a thing of black silks and a golden chain, a quavering injunction to me to be a good boy, a very shrunken loose-skinned face and neck, and a ropy hand that trembled a halfcrown into mine. Miss Somerville hovered behind, a paler thing of broken lavender and white and black, with screwed up, sandy-lashed eyes. Her hair was yellow and her colour bright, and when we sat in the housekeeper's room of a winter's night warming our toes and sipping elder wine, her maid would tell us the simple secrets of that belated flush. . . . After my fight with young Garvell I was of course banished, and I never saw those poor old painted goddesses again.

Then there came and went on these floors over our respectful heads, the Company; people I rarely saw, but whose tricks and manners were imitated and discussed by their maids and valets in the housekeeper's room and the steward's room—so that I had them through a medium at second hand. I gathered that none of the company were really Lady Drew's equals, they were greater and lesser—after the manner of all things in our world. Once I remember there was a Prince, with a real live gentleman in attendance, and that was a little above our customary levels and excited us all, and perhaps raised our expectations unduly. Afterwards, Rabbits, the butler, came into my mother's room downstairs, red with indignation and with tears in his eyes. "Look at *that!*" gasped Rabbits. My mother was speechless with horror. *That* was a sovereign, a mere sovereign, such as you might get from any commoner!

After Company, I remember, came anxious days, for the poor old women upstairs were left tired and cross and vindictive, and in a state of physical and emotional indigestion after their social efforts. . . .

On the lowest fringe of these real Olympians hung the vicarage people, and next to them came those ambiguous beings who are neither quality nor subjects. The vicarage people certainly hold a place by themselves in the typical English scheme; nothing is more remarkable than the progress the

Church has made—socially—in the last two hundred years. In the early eighteenth century the vicar was rather under than over the house-steward, and was deemed a fitting match for the housekeeper or any not too morally discredited discard. The eighteenth century literature is full of his complaints that he might not remain at table to share the pie. He rose above these indignities because of the abundance of younger sons. When I meet the large assumptions of the contemporary cleric, I am apt to think of these things. It is curious to note that to-day that down-trodden, organ-playing creature, the Church of England village Schoolmaster, holds much the same position as the seventeenth century parson. The doctor in Bladesover ranked below the vicar but above the "vet," artists and summer visitors squeezed in above or below this point according to their appearance and expenditure, and then in a carefully arranged scale came the tenantry, the butler and housekeeper, the village shopkeeper, the head keeper, the cook, the publican, the second keeper, the blacksmith (whose status was complicated by his daughter keeping the post-office—and a fine hash she used to make of telegrams too!) the village shopkeeper's eldest son, the first footman, younger sons of the village shopkeeper, his first assistant, and so forth. . . .

All these conceptions and applications of a universal precedence and much else I drank in at Bladesover, as I listened to the talk of valets, ladies'-maids, Rabbits the butler and my mother in the much-cupboarded, white-painted, chintz-brightened housekeeper's room where the upper servants assembled, or of footmen and Rabbits and estate men of all sorts among the green baize and Windsor chairs of the pantry—where Rabbits, being above the law, sold beer without a license or any compunction—or of housemaids and still-room maids in the bleak, matting-carpeted still-room, or of the cook and her kitchen maids and casual friends among the bright copper and hot glow of the kitchens.

Of course their own ranks and places came by implication to these people, and it was with the ranks and places of the Olympians that the talk mainly concerned itself. There was an old peerage and a Crockford together with the books of recipes, the Whitaker's Almanack, the Old Moore's Almanack, and the eighteenth century dictionary, on the little dresser that broke the cupboards on one side of my mother's room; there was another peerage, with the covers off, in the pantry; there was a new peerage in the billiard-room, and I seem to remember another in the anomalous apartment that held the upper servants' bagatelle board, and in which, after the Hall dinner, they partook of the luxury of sweets. And if you had asked any of those upper servants how such and such a Prince of Battenberg was related to, let us say, Mr. Cunninghame Graham or the Duke of Argyle, you would have been told upon the nail. As a boy, I heard a great deal of that sort of thing, and if to this day I am still a little vague about courtesy titles and the exact application of honorifics, it is, I can assure you, because I hardened my heart, and not from any lack of adequate opportunity of mastering these succulent particulars.

Dominating all these memories is the figure of my mother —my mother who did not love me because I grew liker my father every day—and who knew with inflexible decision her place and the place of every one in the world— except the place that concealed my father—and in some details mine. Subtle points were put to her. I can see and hear her saying now, "No, Miss Fison, peers of England go in before peers of the United Kingdom, and he is merely a peer of the United Kingdom." She had much exercise in placing people's servants about her tea-table, where the etiquette was very strict. I wonder sometimes if the etiquette of housekeepers' rooms is as strict to-day, and what my mother would have made of a *chauffeur*. . . .

On the whole I am glad that I saw so much as I did of Bladesover—if for no other reason than because seeing it when I did, quite naïvely, believing in it thoroughly, and then coming to analyse it, has enabled me to understand much that would be absolutely incomprehensible in the structure of English society. Bladesover is, I am convinced, the clue to almost all that is distinctively British and perplexing to the foreign inquirer in England and the English-speaking peoples. Grasp firmly that England was all Bladesover two hundred years ago; that it has had Reform Acts indeed, and such-like changes of formula, but no essential revolution since then; that all that is modern and different has come in as a thing intruded or as a gloss upon this predominant formula, either impertinently or apologetically; and you will perceive at once the reasonableness, the necessity, of that snobbishness which is the distinctive quality of English thought. Everybody who is not actually in the shadow of a Bladesover is as it were perpetually seeking after lost orientations. We have never broken with our tradition, never even symbolically hewed it to pieces, as the French did in quivering fact in the Terror. But all the organizing ideas have slackened, the old habitual bonds have relaxed or altogether come undone. And America too, is, as it were, a detached, outlying part of that estate which has expanded in queer ways. George Washington, Esquire, was of the gentlefolk, and he came near being a King. It was Plutarch, you know, and nothing intrinsically American that prevented George Washington being a King. . . .

IV

I hated teatime in the housekeeper's room more than anything else at Bladesover. And more particularly I hated it when Mrs. Mackridge and Mrs. Booch and Mrs. Latude-Fernay were staying in the house. They were, all three of them, pensioned-off servants. Old friends of Lady Drew's had rewarded them posthumously for a prolonged devotion to their minor comforts, and Mrs. Booch was also trustee for a favourite Skye terrier. Every year Lady Drew gave them an invitation—a reward and encouragement of virtue with especial reference to my mother and Miss Fison, the maid. They sat about in black and shiny and flouncey clothing adorned with gimp and beads, eating great quantities of cake, drinking much tea in a stately manner and reverberating remarks.

I remember these women as immense. No doubt they were of negotiable size, but I was only a very little chap and they have assumed nightmare proportions in my mind. They loomed, they bulged, they impended. Mrs. Mackridge was large and dark; there was a marvel about her head, inasmuch as she was bald. She wore a dignified cap, and in front of that upon her brow, hair was *painted*. I have never seen the like since. She had been maid to the widow of Sir Roderick Blenderhasset Impey, some sort of governor or such-like portent in the East Indies, and from her remains— in Mrs. Mackridge—I judge Lady Impey was a very stupendous and crushing creature indeed. Lady Impey had been of the Juno type, haughty, unapproachable, given to irony and a caustic wit. Mrs. Mackridge had no wit, but she had acquired the caustic voice and gestures along with the old satins and trimmings of the great lady. When she told you it was a fine morning, she seemed also to be telling you you were a fool and a low fool to boot; when she was spoken to, she had a way of acknowledging your poor tinkle of utterance with a voluminous, scornful "Haw!" that made you want to burn her alive. She also had a way of saying "Indade!" with a droop of the eyelids.

Mrs. Booch was a smaller woman, brown haired, with queer little curls on either side of her face, large blue eyes and a small set of stereotyped remarks that constituted her entire mental range. Mrs. Latude-Fernay has left, oddly enough, no memory at all except her name and the effect of a green-grey silk dress, all set with gold and blue buttons. I fancy she was a large blonde. Then there was Miss Fison, the maid who served both Lady Drew and Miss Somerville, and at the end of the table opposite my mother, sat Rabbits the butler. Rabbits, for a butler, was an unassuming man, and at tea he was not as you know butlers, but in a morning coat and a black tie with blue spots. Still, he was large, with side whiskers, even if his clean-shaven mouth was weak and little. I sat among these people on a high, hard, early

Gregorian chair, trying to exist, like a feeble seedling amidst great rocks, and my mother sat with an eye upon me, resolute to suppress the slightest manifestation of vitality. It was hard on me, but perhaps it was also hard upon these rather over-fed, ageing, pretending people, that my youthful restlessness and rebellious unbelieving eyes should be thrust in among their dignities.

Tea lasted for nearly three-quarters of an hour, and I sat it out perforce; and day after day the talk was exactly the same.

"Sugar, Mrs. Mackridge?" my mother used to ask. "Sugar, Mrs. Latude-Fernay?"

The word sugar would stir the mind of Mrs. Mackridge. "They say," she would begin, issuing her proclamation—at least half her sentences began "they say"—"sugar is fatt-an-ing, nowadays. Many of the best people do not take it at all."

"Not with their tea, ma'am," said Rabbits, intelligently.

"Not with anaything," said Mrs. Mackridge, with an air of crushing repartee, and drank.

"What won't they say next?" said Miss Fison.

"They do say such things!" said Mrs. Booch.

"They say," said Mrs. Mackridge, inflexibly, "the doctors are not recomm-an-ding it now."

MY MOTHER: "No, ma'am?"

MRS. MACKRIDGE: "No, ma'am."

Then, to the table at large: "Poor Sir Roderick, before he died, consumed great quan-ta-ties of sugar. I have sometimes fancied it may have hastened his end."

This ended the first skirmish. A certain gloom of manner and a pause was considered due to the sacred memory of Sir Roderick.

"George," said my mother, "don't kick the chair!"

Then, perhaps, Mrs. Booch would produce a favourite piece from her repertoire. "The evenings are drawing out nicely," she would say, or if the season was decadent, "How the evenings draw in!" It was an invaluable remark to her; I do not know how she would have got along without it.

My mother, who sat with her back to the window, would always consider it due to Mrs. Booch to turn about and regard the evening in the act of elongation or contraction, whichever phase it might be.

A brisk discussion of how long we were to the longest or shortest day would ensue, and die away at last exhausted.

Mrs. Mackridge, perhaps, would reopen. She had many intelligent habits; among others she read the paper—*The Morning Post*. The other ladies would at times tackle that sheet, but only to read the births, marriages, and deaths on the front page. It was, of course, the old *Morning Post* that cost threepence, not the brisk coruscating young thing of to-day. "They say," she would open, "that Lord Tweedums is to go to Canada."

"Ah!" said Mr. Rabbits; "dew they?"

"Isn't he," said my mother, "the Earl of Slumgold's cousin?" She knew he was; it was an entirely irrelevant and unnecessary remark, but still, something to say.

"The same, ma'am," said Mrs. Mackridge. "They say he was extremely popular in New South Wales. They looked up to him greatlay. I knew him, ma'am, as a young man. A very nice pleasant young fella."

Interlude of respect.

" 'Is predecessor," said Rabbits, who had acquired from some clerical model a precise emphatic articulation without acquiring at the same time the aspirates that would have graced it, "got into trouble at Sydney."

"Haw!" said Mrs. Mackridge, scornfully, "so I am tawled."

" 'E came to Templemorton after 'e came back, and I remember them talking 'im over after 'e'd gone again."

"Haw?" said Mrs. Mackridge, interrogatively.

" 'Is fuss was quotin' poetry, ma'am. 'E said—what was it 'e said—'They lef' their country for their country's good,' which in some way was took to remind them of their being originally convic's, though now reformed. Every one I 'eard speak, agreed it was takless of 'im."

"Sir Roderick used to say," said Mrs. Mackridge, "that

[18]

the First Thing,"—here Mrs. Mackridge paused and looked dreadfully at me—"and the Second Thing"—here she fixed me again—"and the Third Thing"—now I was released—"needed in a colonial governor is Tact." She became aware of my doubts again, and added predominantly, "It has always struck me that that was a Singularly True Remark."

I resolved that if ever I found this polypus of Tact growing up in my soul, I would tear it out by the roots, throw it forth and stamp on it.

"They're queer people—colonials," said Rabbits, "very queer. When I was at Templemorton I see something of 'em. Queer fellows, some of 'em. Very respectful of course, free with their money in a spasammy sort of way, but—— Some of 'em, I must confess, make me nervous. They have an eye on you. They watch you—as you wait. They let themselves appear to be lookin' at you . . ."

My mother said nothing in that discussion. The word colonies always upset her. She was afraid, I think, that if she turned her mind in that direction my errant father might suddenly and shockingly be discovered, no doubt conspicuously bigamic and altogether offensive and revolutionary. She did not want to rediscover my father at all.

It is curious that when I was a little listening boy I had such an idea of our colonies that I jeered in my heart at Mrs. Mackridge's colonial ascendency. These brave emancipated sunburnt English of the open, I thought, suffer these aristocratic invaders as a quaint anachronism, but as for being gratified——!

I don't jeer now. I'm not so sure.

V

It is a little difficult to explain why I did not come to do what was the natural thing for any one in my circumstances to do, and take my world for granted. A certain innate scepticism, I think, explains it—and a certain inaptitude for sympathetic assimilation. My father, I believe, was a sceptic; my mother was certainly a hard woman.

I was an only child, and to this day I do not know

whether my father is living or dead. He fled my mother's virtues before my distincter memories began. He left no traces in his flight, and she, in her indignation, destroyed every vestige that she could of him. Never a photograph nor a scrap of his handwriting have I seen; and it was, I know, only the accepted code of virtue and discretion that prevented her destroying her marriage certificate and me, and so making a clean sweep of her matrimonial humiliation. I suppose I must inherit something of the moral stupidity that could enable her to make a holocaust of every little personal thing she had of him. There must have been presents made by him as a lover, for example—books with kindly inscriptions, letters perhaps, a flattened flower, a ring, or such-like gage. She kept her wedding-ring, of course, but all the others she destroyed. She never told me his Christian name or indeed spoke a word to me of him, though at times I came near daring to ask her: and what I have of him—it isn't much—I got from his brother, my hero, my Uncle Ponderevo. She wore her ring; her marriage certificate she kept in a sealed envelope in the very bottom of her largest trunk, and me she sustained at a private school among the Kentish hills. You must not think I was always at Bladesover—even in my holidays. If at the time these came round, Lady Drew was vexed by recent Company, or for any other reason wished to take it out of my mother, then she used to ignore the customary reminder my mother gave her, and I "stayed on" at the school.

But such occasions were rare, and I suppose that between ten and fourteen I averaged fifty days a year at Bladesover.

Don't imagine I deny that was a fine thing for me. Bladesover, in absorbing the whole countryside, had not altogether missed greatness. The Bladesover system has at least done one good thing for England, it has abolished the peasant habit of mind. If many of us still live and breathe pantry and housekeeper's room, we are quit of the dream of living by economising parasitically on hens and pigs. . . . About that park there were some elements of a liberal education; there was a great space of greensward not given over to manure and food grubbing; there was mystery, there was matter for the imagination. It was still a park of deer. I saw something of the life of these dappled creatures, heard the belling of stags, came upon young fawns among the bracken, found bones, skulls, and antlers in lonely places. There were corners that gave a gleam of meaning to the word forest, glimpses of unstudied natural splendour. There was a slope of bluebells in the broken sunlight under the newly green beeches in the west wood that is now precious sapphire in my memory; it was the first time that I knowingly met Beauty.

And in the house there were books. The rubbish old Lady Drew read I never saw; stuff of the Maria Monk type, I have since gathered, had a fascination for her; but back in the past there had been a Drew of intellectual enterprise, Sir Cuthbert, the son of Sir Matthew who built the house; and thrust away, neglected and despised, in an old room upstairs, were books and treasures of his that my mother let me rout among during a spell of wintry wet. Sitting under a dormer window on a shelf above great stores of tea and spices, I became familiar with much of Hogarth in a big portfolio, with Raphael,—there was a great book of engravings from the stanzas of Raphael in the Vatican—and with most of the capitals of Europe as they had looked about 1780, by means of several big iron-moulded books of views. There was also a broad eighteenth century atlas with huge wandering maps that instructed me mightily. It had splendid adornments about each map title; Holland showed a fisherman and his boat; Russia a Cossack; Japan, remarkable people attired in pagodas—I say it deliberately, "pagodas." There were Terrae Incognitae in every continent then, Poland, Sarmatia, lands since lost; and many a voyage I made with a blunted pin about that large, incorrect and dignified world. The books in that little old closet had been banished, I suppose, from the saloon during the Victorian revival of good taste and emasculated orthodoxy, but my mother had no suspicion of their character. So I read and understood the good sound rhetoric of Tom Paine's

"Rights of Man," and his "Common Sense," excellent books, once praised by bishops and since sedulously lied about. Gulliver was there unexpurgated, strong meat for a boy perhaps, but not too strong I hold—I have never regretted that I escaped niceness in these affairs. The satire of Traldragdubh made my blood boil as it was meant to do, but I hated Swift for the Houyhnhnms and never quite liked a horse afterwards. Then I remember also a translation of Voltaire's "Candide," and "Rasselas"; and, vast book though it was, I really believe I read, in a muzzy sort of way of course, from end to end, and even with some reference now and then to the Atlas, Gibbon—in twelve volumes.

These readings whetted my taste for more, and surreptitiously I raided the bookcases in the big saloon. I got through quite a number of books before my sacrilegious temerity was discovered by Ann, the old head-housemaid. I remember that among others I tried a translation of Plato's "Republic" then, and found extraordinarily little interest in it; I was much too young for that; but "Vathek" —"Vathek" was glorious stuff. That kicking affair! When everybody *had* to kick!

The thought of "Vathek" always brings back with it my boyish memory of the big saloon at Bladesover.

It was a huge long room with many windows opening upon the park, and each window—there were a dozen or more reaching from the floor up—had its elaborate silk or satin curtains, heavily fringed, a canopy (is it?) above, its complex white shutters folding into the deep thickness of the wall. At either end of that great still place was an immense marble chimney-piece; the end by the bookcase showed the wolf and Romulus and Remus, with Homer and Virgil for supporters; the design of the other end I have forgotten. Frederick, Prince of Wales, swaggered flatly over the one, twice life-size, but mellowed by the surface gleam of oil; and over the other was an equally colossal group of departed Drews as sylvan deities, scantily clad, against a storm-rent sky. Down the centre of the elaborate ceiling were three chandeliers, each bearing some hundreds of dangling glass lustres, and over the interminable carpet—it impressed me as about as big as Sarmatia in the store-room Atlas—were islands and archipelagoes of chintz-covered chairs and couches, tables, great Sèvres vases on pedestals, a bronze man and horse. Somewhere in this wilderness one came, I remember, upon a big harp beside a lyre-shaped music-stand, and a grand piano. . . .

The book-borrowing raid was one of extraordinary dash and danger. One came down the main service stairs—that was legal, and illegality began in a little landing when, very cautiously, one went through a red baize door. A little passage led to the hall, and here one reconnoitred for Ann, the old head-housemaid—the younger housemaids were friendly and did not count. Ann located, came a dash across the open space at the foot of that great staircase that has never been properly descended since powder went out of fashion, and so to the saloon door. A beast of an oscillating China-man in china, as large as life, grimaced and quivered to one's lightest steps. That door was the perilous place; it was double, with the thickness of the wall between, so that one could not listen beforehand for the whisk of the feather-brush on the other side. Oddly rat-like, is it not, this darting into enormous places in pursuit of the abandoned crumbs of thought?

And I found Langhorne's "Plutarch" too, I remember, on those shelves. It seems queer to me now to think that I acquired pride and self-respect, the idea of a state and the germ of public spirit, in such a furtive fashion; queer, too, that it should rest with an old Greek, dead these eighteen hundred years, to teach me that.

VI

The school I went to was the sort of school the Blades-over system permitted. The public schools that had come into existence in the brief glow of the Renascence had been taken possession of by the ruling class; the lower classes were not supposed to stand in need of schools, and our middle stratum got the schools it deserved, private schools, schools any unqualified pretender was free to establish. Mine was kept by a man who had had the energy to get himself a College of Preceptors diploma, and considering how cheap his charges were, I will readily admit the place might have been worse. The building was a dingy yellow-brick residence outside the village, with the schoolroom as an outbuilding of lath and plaster.

I do not remember that my school-days were unhappy—indeed I recall a good lot of fine mixed fun in them—but I cannot without grave risk of misinterpretation declare that we were at all nice and refined. We fought much, not sound formal fighting, but "scrapping" of a sincere and murderous kind, into which one might bring one's boots—it made us tough at any rate—and several of us were the sons of London publicans, who distinguished "scraps" where one meant to hurt from ordered pugilism, practising both arts, and having, moreover, precocious linguistic gifts. Our cricket-field was bald about the wickets, and we played without style and disputed with the umpire; and the teaching was chiefly in the hands of a lout of nineteen, who wore ready-made clothes and taught despicably. The head-master and proprietor taught us arithmetic, algebra, and Euclid, and to the older boys even trigonometry, himself; he had a strong mathematical bias, and I think now that by the standard of a British public school he did rather well by us.

We had one inestimable privilege at that school, and that was spiritual neglect. We dealt with one another with the forcible simplicity of natural boys, we "cheeked," and "punched" and "clouted"; we thought ourselves Red Indians and cowboys and such-like honourable things, and not young English gentlemen; we never felt the strain of "On-ward, Christian Soldiers," nor were swayed by any premature piety in the cold oak pew of our Sunday devotions. All that was good. We spent our rare pennies in the uncensored reading matter of the village dame's shop, on the *Boys of England* and honest penny dreadfuls—ripping stuff, stuff

[24]

that anticipated Haggard and Stevenson, badly printed and queerly illustrated, and very, very good for us. On our half-holidays we were allowed the unusual freedom of rambling in twos and threes wide and far about the land, talking experimentally, dreaming wildly. There was much in those walks! To this day the landscape of the Kentish weald, with its low broad distances, its hop gardens and golden stretches of wheat, its oasts and square church towers, its background of downland and hangers, has for me a faint sense of adventure added to the pleasure of its beauty. We smoked on occasion, but nobody put us up to the proper "boyish" things to do; we never "robbed an orchard" for example, though there were orchards all about us, we thought stealing was sinful, we stole incidental apples and turnips and strawberries from the fields indeed, but in a criminal inglorious fashion, and afterwards we were ashamed. We had our days of adventure, but they were natural accidents, our own adventures. There was one hot day when several of us, walking out towards Maidstone, were incited by the devil to despise ginger beer, and we fuddled ourselves dreadfully with ale; and a time when our young minds were infected to the pitch of buying pistols, by the legend of the Wild West. Young Roots from Highbury came back with a revolver and cartridges, and we went off six strong to live a free wild life one holiday afternoon. We fired our first shot deep in the old flint mine at Chiselstead, and nearly burst our ear drums; then we fired in a primrose studded wood by Pickthorn Green, and I gave a false alarm of "keeper," and we fled in disorder for a mile. After which Roots suddenly shot at a pheasant in the high road by Chiselstead, and then young Barker told lies about the severity of the game laws and made Roots sore afraid, and we hid the pistol in a dry ditch outside the school field. A day or so after we got it again, and ignoring a certain fouling and rusting of the barrel, tried for a rabbit at three hundred yards. Young Roots blew a molehill at twenty paces into a dust cloud, burnt his fingers, and scorched his face; and the weapon having once displayed this strange disposition to flame back upon the shooter, was not subsequently fired.

One main source of excitement for us was "cheeking" people in vans and carts upon the Goudhurst road; and getting myself into a monstrous white mess in the chalk pits beyond the village, and catching yellow jaundice as a sequel to bathing stark naked with three other Adamites, old Ewart leading that function, in the rivulet across Hickson's meadows, are among my *memorabilia*. Those free imaginative afternoons! how much they were for us! how much they did for us! All streams came from the then undiscovered "sources of the Nile" in those days, all thickets were Indian jungles, and our best game, I say it with pride, I invented. I got it out of the Bladesover saloon. We found a wood where "Trespassing" was forbidden, and did the "Retreat of the Ten Thousand" through it from end to end, cutting our way bravely through a host of nettle beds that barred our path, and not forgetting to weep and kneel when at last we emerged within sight of the High Road Sea. So we have burst at times, weeping and rejoicing, upon startled wayfarers. Usually I took the part of that distinguished general Xenōphen—and please note the quantity of the ō. I have all my classical names like that,—Socrates rhymes with Bates for me, and except when the bleak eye of some scholar warns me of his standards of judgment, I use those dear old mispronunciations still. The little splash into Latin made during my days as a chemist washed off nothing of the habit. Well,—if I met those great gentlemen of the past with their accents carelessly adjusted I did at least meet them alive, as an equal, and in a living tongue. Altogether my school might easily have been worse for me, and among other good things it gave me a friend who has lasted my life out.

This was Ewart, who is now a monumental artist at Woking, after many vicissitudes. Dear chap, how he did stick out of his clothes to be sure! He was a long-limbed lout, ridiculously tall beside my more youthful compactness, and, except that there was no black moustache under his nose blob, he had the same round knobby face as he has to-day, the same bright and active hazel brown eyes, the stare, the meditative moment, the insinuating reply. Surely no boy ever played the fool as Bob Ewart used to play it, no boy had a readier knack of mantling the world with wonder. Commonness vanished before Ewart, at his expository touch all things became memorable and rare. From him I first heard tell of love, but only after its barbs were already sticking in my heart. He was, I know now, the bastard of that great improvident artist, Rickmann Ewart; he brought the light of a lax world that at least had not turned its back upon beauty, into the growing fermentation of my mind.

I won his heart by a version of Vathek, and after that we were inseparable yarning friends. We merged our intellectual stock so completely that I wonder sometimes how much I did not become Ewart, how much Ewart is not vicariously and derivatively me. . . .

VII

And then when I had newly passed my fourteenth birthday, came my tragic disgrace.

It was in my midsummer holidays that the thing happened, and it was through the Honourable Beatrice Normandy. She had "come into my life," as they say, before I was twelve.

She descended unexpectedly into a peaceful interlude that followed the annual going of those Three Great Women. She came into the old nursery upstairs, and every day she had tea with us in the housekeeper's room. She was eight, and she came with a nurse called Nannie; and to begin with, I did not like her at all.

Nobody liked this irruption into the downstairs rooms; the two "gave trouble,"—a dire offence; Nannie's sense of duty to her charge led to requests and demands that took my mother's breath away. Eggs at unusual times, the re-boiling of milk, the rejection of an excellent milk pudding— not negotiated respectfully but dictated as of right. Nannie was a dark, long-featured, taciturn woman in a grey dress; she had a furtive inflexibility of manner that finally dismayed and crushed and overcame. She conveyed she was "under orders"—like a Greek tragedy. She was that strange product of the old time, a devoted, trusted servant; she had, as it were, banked all her pride and will with the greater, more powerful people who employed her, in return for a life-long security of servitude—the bargain was none the less binding for being implicit. Finally they were to pension her, and she would die the hated treasure of a boarding-house. She had built up in herself an enormous habit of reference to these upstairs people, she had curbed down all discordant murmurings of her soul, her very instincts were perverted or surrendered. She was sexless, her personal pride was all transferred, she mothered another woman's child with a hard, joyless devotion that was at least entirely compatible with a stoical separation. She treated us all as things that counted for nothing save to fetch and carry for her charge. But the Honourable Beatrice could condescend.

The queer chances of later years come between me and a distinctly separated memory of that childish face. When I think of Beatrice, I think of her as I came to know her at a later time, when at last I came to know her so well that indeed now I could draw her, and show a hundred little delicate things you would miss in looking at her. But even then I remember how I noted the infinite delicacy of her childish skin and the fine eyebrow, finer than the finest feather that ever one felt on the breast of a bird. She was one of those elfin, rather precocious little girls, quick coloured, with dark hair, naturally curling dusky hair that was sometimes astray over her eyes, and eyes that were sometimes impishly dark, and sometimes a clear brown yellow. And from the very outset, after a most cursory attention to Rabbits, she decided that the only really interesting thing at the tea-table was myself.

The elders talked in their formal dull way—telling Nannie the trite old things about the park and the village that they told every one, and Beatrice watched me across the table with a pitiless little curiosity that made me uncomfortable.

"Nannie," she said, pointing, and Nannie left a question of my mother's disregarded to attend to her; "is he a servant boy?"

"S-s-sh," said Nannie. "He's Master Ponderevo."

"Is he a servant boy?" repeated Beatrice.

"He's a schoolboy," said my mother.

"Then may I talk to him, Nannie?"

Nannie surveyed me with brutal inhumanity. "You mustn't talk too much," she said to her charge, and cut cake into fingers for her. "No," she added decisively, as Beatrice made to speak.

Beatrice became malignant. Her eyes explored me with unjustifiable hostility. "He's got dirty hands," she said, stabbing at the forbidden fruit. "And there's a fray to his collar."

Then she gave herself up to cake with an appearance of entire forgetfulness of me that filled me with hate and a passionate desire to compel her to admire me. . . . And the next day before tea, I did for the first time in my life, freely, without command or any compulsion, wash my hands.

So our acquaintance began, and presently was deepened by a whim of hers. She had a cold and was kept indoors, and confronted Nannie suddenly with the alternative of being hopelessly naughty, which in her case involved a generous amount of screaming unsuitable for the ears of an elderly, shaky, rich aunt, or having me up to the nursery to play with her all the afternoon. Nannie came downstairs and borrowed me in a careworn manner; and I was handed over to the little creature as if I was some large variety of kitten. I had never had anything to do with a little girl before, I thought she was more beautiful and wonderful and bright than anything else could possibly be in life, and she found me the gentlest of slaves—though at the same time, as I made evident, fairly strong. And Nannie was amazed to find the afternoon slip cheerfully and rapidly away. She praised my manners to Lady Drew and to my mother, who said she was glad to hear well of me, and after that I played with Beatrice several times. The toys she had remain in my memory still as great splendid things, gigantic to all my previous experience of toys, and we even went to the great doll's house on the nursery landing to play discreetly with that, the great doll's house that the Prince Regent had given Sir Harry Drew's first-born (who died at five), that was a not ineffectual model of Bladesover itself, and contained eighty-five dolls and had cost hundreds of pounds. I played under imperious direction with that toy of glory.

I went back to school when that holiday was over, dreaming of beautiful things, and got Ewart to talk to me of love; and I made a great story out of the doll's house, a story that, taken over into Ewart's hands, speedily grew to an island doll's city all our own.

One of the dolls, I privately decided, was like Beatrice.

One other holiday there was when I saw something of her—oddly enough my memory of that second holiday in which she played a part is vague—and then came a gap of a year, and then my disgrace.

VIII

Now I sit down to write my story and tell over again things in their order, I find for the first time how inconsecutive and irrational a thing the memory can be. One recalls acts and cannot recall motives; one recalls quite vividly moments that stand out inexplicably—things adrift, joining on to nothing, leading nowhere. I think I must have seen Beatrice and her half-brother quite a number of times in my last holiday at Bladesover, but I really cannot recall more than a little of the quality of the circumstances. That great crisis of my boyhood stands out very vividly as an effect, as a sort of cardinal thing for me, but when I look for details—particularly details that led up to the crisis —I cannot find them in any developing order at all. This half-brother, Archie Garvell, was a new factor in the affair. I remember him clearly as a fair-haired, supercilious-looking, weedily-lank boy, much taller than I, but I should imagine very little heavier, and that we hated each other by a sort of instinct from the beginning; and yet I cannot remember my first meeting with him at all.

Looking back into these past things—it is like rummaging in a neglected attic that has experienced the attentions of some whimsical robber—I cannot even account for the presence of these children at Bladesover. They were, I know, among the innumerable cousins of Lady Drew, and according to the theories of downstairs, candidates for the ultimate possession of Bladesover. If they were, their candidature was unsuccessful. But that great place, with all its faded splendour, its fine furniture, its large traditions, was entirely at the old lady's disposition; and I am inclined to think it is true that she used this fact to torment and dominate a number of eligible people. Lord Osprey was among the number of these, and she showed these hospitalities to his motherless child and step-child, partly, no doubt, because he was poor, but quite as much, I nowadays imagine, in the dim hope of finding some affectionate or imaginative outcome of contact with them. Nannie had dropped out of the world this second time, and Beatrice was in the charge of an extremely amiable and ineffectual poor army-class young woman whose name I never knew. They were, I think, two remarkably ill-managed and enterprising children. I seem to remember too, that it was understood that I was not a fit companion for them, and that our meetings had to be as unostentatious as possible. It was Beatrice who insisted upon our meeting.

I am certain I knew quite a lot about love at fourteen, and that I was quite as much in love with Beatrice then as any impassioned adult could be, and that Beatrice was, in her way, in love with me. It is part of the decent and useful pretences of our world that children of the age at which we were, think nothing, feel nothing, know nothing of love. It is wonderful what people the English are for keeping up

[31]

pretences. But indeed I cannot avoid telling that Beatrice and I talked of love and kissed and embraced one another.

I recall something of one talk under the overhanging bushes of the shrubbery—I on the park side of the stone wall, and the lady of my worship a little inelegantly astride thereon. Inelegantly do I say? You should have seen the sweet imp as I remember her. Just her poise on the wall comes suddenly clear before me, and behind her the light various branches of the bushes of the shrubbery that my feet might not profane, and far away and high behind her, dim and stately, the cornice of the great façade of Blades-over rose against the dappled sky. Our talk must have been serious and business-like, for we were discussing my social position.

"I don't love Archie," she had said, *apropos* of nothing; and then in a whisper, leaning forward with the hair about her face, "I love *you!*"

But she had been a little pressing to have it clear that I was not and could not be a servant.

"You'll never be a servant—ever!"

I swore that very readily, and it is a vow I have kept by nature.

"What will you be?" said she.

I ran my mind hastily over the professions.

"Will you be a soldier?" she asked.

"And be bawled at by duffers? No fear!" said I. "Leave that to the plough-boys."

"But an officer?"

"I don't know," I said, evading a shameful difficulty. "I'd rather go into the navy."

"Wouldn't you like to fight?"

"I'd like to fight," I said. "But a common soldier—it's no honour to have to be told to fight and to be looked down upon while you do it, and how could I be an officer?"

"Couldn't you be?" she said, and looked at me doubt-fully; and the spaces of the social system opened between us.

Then, as became a male of spirit, I took upon myself to

brag and lie my way through this trouble. I said I was a poor man, and poor men went into the navy; that I "knew" mathematics, which no army officer did; and I claimed Nelson for an exemplar, and spoke very highly of my outlook upon blue water. "He loved Lady Hamilton," I said, "although she *was* a lady—and I will love you."

We were somewhere near that when the egregious governess became audible, calling "Beeee-âtrice! Beeee-e-e-âtrice!"

"Snifty beast!" said my lady, and tried to get on with the conversation; but that governess made things impossible.

"Come here!" said my lady suddenly, holding out a grubby hand; and I went very close to her, and she put her little head down upon the wall until her black fog of hair tickled my cheek.

"You are my humble, faithful lover," she demanded in a whisper, her warm flushed face near touching mine, and her eyes very dark and lustrous.

"I am your humble, faithful lover," I whispered back.

And she put her arm about my head and put out her lips, and we kissed, and boy though I was, I was all atremble. So we two kissed for the first time.

"*Beeee-e-e-â*-trice!" fearfully close.

My lady had vanished, with one wild kick of her black-stockinged leg. A moment after, I heard her sustaining the reproaches of her governess, and explaining her failure to answer with an admirable lucidity and disingenuousness.

I felt it was unnecessary for me to be seen just then, and I vanished guiltily round the corner into the West Wood, and so to love-dreams and single-handed play, wandering along one of those meandering bracken valleys that varied Bladesover park. And that day and for many days that kiss upon my lips was a seal, and by night the seed of dreams.

Then I remember an expedition we made—she, I, and her half-brother—into those West Woods—they two were supposed to be playing in the shrubbery—and how we were

Indians there, and made a wigwam out of a pile of beech logs, and how we stalked deer, crept near and watched rabbits feeding in a glade, and almost got a squirrel. It was play seasoned with plentiful disputing between me and young Garvell, for each firmly insisted upon the leading *rôles*, and only my wider reading—I had read ten stories to his one—gave me the ascendency over him. Also I scored over him by knowing how to find the eagle in a bracken stem. And somehow—I don't remember what led to it at all—I and Beatrice, two hot and ruffled creatures, crept in among the tall bracken and hid from him. The great fronds rose above us, five feet or more, and as I had learnt how to wriggle through that undergrowth with the minimum of betrayal by tossing greenery above, I led the way. The ground under bracken is beautifully clear and faintly scented in warm weather; the stems come up black and then green; if you crawl flat, it is a tropical forest in miniature. I led the way and Beatrice crawled behind, and then as the green of the further glade opened before us, stopped. She crawled up to me, her hot little face came close to mine; once more she looked and breathed close to me, and suddenly she flung her arm about my neck and dragged me to earth beside her, and kissed me and kissed me again. We kissed, we embraced and kissed again, all without a word; we desisted, we stared and hesitated—then in a suddenly damped mood and a little perplexed at ourselves, crawled out, to be presently run down and caught in the tamest way by Archie.

That comes back very clearly to me, and other vague memories—I know old Hall and his gun, out shooting at jackdaws, came into our common experiences, but I don't remember how; and then at last abruptly, our fight in the Warren stands out. The Warren, like most places in England that have that name, was not particularly a warren it was a long slope of thorns and beeches through which a path ran, and made an alternative route to the downhill carriage road between Bladesover and Ropedean. I don't know how we three got there, but I have an uncertain fancy it was connected with a visit paid by the governess to the Ropedean vicarage people. But suddenly Archie and I, in discussing a game, fell into a dispute for Beatrice. I had made him the fairest offer: I was to be a Spanish nobleman, she was to be my wife, and he was to be a tribe of Indians trying to carry her off. It seems to me a fairly attractive offer to a boy to be a whole tribe of Indians with a chance of such a booty. But Archie suddenly took offence.

"No," he said; "we can't have that!"

"Can't have what?"

"You can't be a gentleman, because you aren't. And you can't play Beatrice is your wife. It's—it's impertinent."

"But——" I said, and looked at her.

Some earlier grudge in the day's affairs must have been in Archie's mind. "We let you play with us," said Archie; "but we can't have things like that."

"What rot!" said Beatrice. "He can if he likes."

But he carried his point. I let him carry it, and only began to grow angry three or four minutes later. Then we were still discussing play and disputing about another game. Nothing seemed right for all of us.

"We don't want you to play with us at all," said Archie.

"Yes, we do," said Beatrice.

"He drops his aitches like anything."

"No, 'e doesn't," said I, in the heat of the moment.

"There you go!" he cried. "E, he says. E! E! E!"

He pointed a finger at me. He had struck to the heart of my shame. I made the only possible reply by a rush at him. "Hello!" he cried, at my black-a-vised attack. He dropped back into an attitude that had some style in it, parried my blow, got back at my cheek, and laughed with surprise and relief at his own success. Whereupon I became a thing of murderous rage. He could box as well or better than I—he had yet to realise I knew anything of that at all—but I had fought once or twice to a finish with bare fists, I was used to inflicting and enduring savage hurting, and I doubt if he had ever fought. I hadn't fought ten seconds before I felt this softness in him, realised all that quality of modern upper-class England that never goes to the quick, that hedges about rules and those petty points of honour that are the ultimate comminution of honour, that claims credit for things demonstrably half done. He seemed to think that first hit of his and one or two others were going to matter, that I ought to give in when presently my lip bled and dripped blood upon my clothes. So before we had been at it a minute he had ceased to be aggressive except in momentary spurts, and I was knocking him about almost as I wanted to do, and demanding breathlessly and fiercely, after our school manner, whether he had had enough, not knowing that by his high code and his soft training it was equally impossible for him to either buck-up and beat me, or give in.

I have a very distinct impression of Beatrice dancing about us during the affair in a state of unladylike appreciation, but I was too preoccupied to hear much of what she was saying. But she certainly backed us both, and I am inclined to think now—it may be the disillusionment of my ripened years—whichever she thought was winning.

Then young Garvell, giving way before my slogging, stumbled and fell over a big flint, and I, still following the tradition of my class and school, promptly flung myself on him to finish him. We were busy with each other on the ground when we became aware of a dreadful interruption.

"Shut up, you *fool!*" said Archie.

"Oh, Lady Drew!" I heard Beatrice cry. "They're fighting! They're fighting something awful!"

I looked over my shoulder. Archie's wish to get up became irresistible, and my resolve to go on with him vanished altogether.

I became aware of the two old ladies, presences of black and purple silk and fur and shining dark things; they had walked up through the Warren, while the horses took the hill easily, and so had come upon us. Beatrice had gone to them at once with an air of taking refuge, and stood beside and a little behind them. We both rose dejectedly. The two old ladies were evidently quite dreadfully shocked.

and peering at us with their poor old eyes; and never had I seen such a tremblement in Lady Drew's lorgnettes.

"You've never been fighting?" said Lady Drew. "You have been fighting."

"It wasn't proper fighting," snapped Archie, with accusing eyes on me.

"It's Mrs. Ponderevo's George!" said Miss Somerville, so adding a conviction for ingratitude to my evident sacrilege.

"How could he *dare?*" cried Lady Drew, becoming very awful.

"He broke the rules," said Archie, sobbing for breath. "I slipped, and—he hit me while I was down. He knelt on me."

"How could you *dare?*" said Lady Drew.

I produced an experienced handkerchief rolled up into a tight ball, and wiped the blood from my chin, but I offered no explanation of my daring. Among other things that prevented that, I was too short of breath.

"He didn't fight fair," sobbed Archie. . . .

Beatrice, from behind the old ladies, regarded me intently and without hostility. I am inclined to think the modification of my face through the damage to my lip interested her. It became dimly apparent to my confused intelligence that I must not say these two had been playing with me. That would not be after the rules of their game. I resolved in this difficult situation upon a sulky silence, and to take whatever consequences might follow.

IX

The powers of justice in Bladesover made an extraordinary mess of my case.

I have regretfully to admit that the Honourable Beatrice Normandy did, at the age of ten, betray me, abandon me, and lie most abominably about me. She was, as a matter of fact, panic-stricken about me, conscience-stricken too; she bolted from the very thought of my being her affianced lover and so forth, from the faintest memory of kissing; she was indeed altogether disgraceful and human in her betrayal. She and her half-brother lied in perfect concord, and I was presented as a wanton assailant of my social betters. They were waiting about in the Warren, when I came up and spoke to them, etc.

On the whole, I now perceive Lady Drew's decisions were, in the light of the evidence, reasonable and merciful.

They were conveyed to me by my mother, who was, I really believe, even more shocked by the grossness of my social insubordination than Lady Drew. She dilated on her ladyship's kindnesses to me, on the effrontery and wickedness of my procedure, and so came at last to the terms of my penance. "You must go up to young Mr. Garvell, and beg his pardon."

"I won't beg his pardon," I said, speaking for the first time.

My mother paused, incredulous.

I folded my arms on her table-cloth, and delivered my wicked little ultimatum. "I won't beg his pardon nohow," I said. "See?"

"Then you will have to go off to your uncle Frapp at Chatham."

"I don't care where I have to go or what I have to do, I won't beg his pardon," I said.

And I didn't.

After that I was one against the world. Perhaps in my mother's heart there lurked some pity for me, but she did not show it. She took the side of the young gentleman; she tried hard, she tried very hard, to make me say I was sorry I had struck him. Sorry!

"I couldn't explain.

So I went into exile in the dog-cart to Redwood station, with Jukes the coachman, coldly silent, driving me, and all my personal belongings in a small American-cloth portmanteau behind.

I felt I had much to embitter me; the game had not the beginnings of fairness by any standards I knew. . . . But the thing that embittered me most was that the Honourable Beatrice Normandy should have repudiated and fled from me as though I was some sort of leper, and not even have taken a chance or so, to give me a good-bye. She might have done that anyhow! Supposing I had told on her! But the son of a servant counts as a servant. She had forgotten and now remembered. . . .

I solaced myself with some extraordinary dream of coming back to Bladesover, stern, powerful, after the fashion of Coriolanus. I do not recall the details, but I have no doubt I displayed great magnanimity. . . .

Well, anyhow I never said I was sorry for pounding young Garvell, and I am not sorry to this day.

CHAPTER THE SECOND

Of My Launch into the World and the Last I Saw of Bladesover

I

WHEN I was thus banished from Bladesover House, as it was then thought for good and all, I was sent by my mother in a vindictive spirit, first to her cousin Nicodemus Frapp, and then, as a fully indentured apprentice, to my uncle Ponderevo.

I ran away from the care of my cousin Nicodemus back to Bladesover House.

My cousin Nicodemus Frapp was a baker in a back street —a slum rather—just off that miserable narrow mean high road that threads those exquisite beads, Rochester and Chatham. He was, I must admit, a shock to me, much dominated by a young, plump, prolific, malingering wife; a bent, slow-moving, unwilling dark man, with flour in his hair and eyelashes, in the lines of his face and the seams of his coat. I've never had a chance to correct my early impression of him, and he still remains an almost dreadful memory, a sort of caricature of incompetent simplicity. As I remember him, indeed, he presented the servile tradition perfected. He had no pride in his person; fine clothes and dressing up wasn't "for the likes of" him, so that he got his wife, who was no artist at it, to cut his black hair at irregular intervals, and let his nails become disagreeable to the fastidious eye; he had no pride in his business nor any initiative; his only virtues were not doing certain things and hard work. "Your uncle," said my mother—all grown-up cousins were uncles by courtesy among the Victorian middle-class—"isn't much to look at or talk to, but he's a Good Hard-Working Man." There was a sort of base honourableness about toil, however needless, in that system of inversion. Another point of honour was to rise at or before dawn, and then laboriously muddle about. It was very distinctly impressed on my mind that the Good Hard-Working Man would have thought it "fal-lallish" to own a pocket-handkerchief. Poor old Frapp—dirty and crushed by, product of, Bladesover's magnificence! He made no fight against the world at all, he was floundering in small debts that were not so small but that finally they overwhelmed him, whenever there was occasion for any exertion his wife fell back upon pains and her "condition," and God sent them many children, most of whom died, and so, by their coming and going, gave a double exercise in the virtues of submission.

Resignation to God's will was the common device of these people in the face of every duty and every emergency. There were no books in the house; I doubt if either of them had retained the capacity for reading consecutively for more than a minute or so, and it was with amazement that day after day, over and above stale bread, one beheld food and again more food amidst the litter that held permanent session on the living-room table.

One might have doubted if either of them felt discomfort in this dusty darkness of existence, if it was not that they did visibly seek consolation. They sought this and found it of a Sunday, not in strong drink and raving, but in imaginary draughts of blood. They met with twenty or thirty other darkened and unclean people, all dressed in dingy colours that would not show the dirt, in a little brick-built chapel equipped with a spavined roarer of a harmonium, and there solaced their minds on the thought that all that was fair and free in life, all that struggled, all that planned and made, all pride and beauty and honour, all fine and enjoyable things, were irrevocably damned to everlasting torments. They were the self-appointed confidants of God's mockery of his own creation. So at any rate they stick in my mind. Vaguer, and yet hardly less agreeable than this cosmic jest, this coming "Yah, clever!" and general serving out and "showing up" of the lucky, the bold, and the cheerful, was their own predestination to Glory.

> "There is a Fountain, filled with Blood
> Drawn from Emmanuel's Veins,"

so they sang. I hear the drone and wheeze of that hymn now. I hated them with the bitter uncharitable condemnation of boyhood, and a twinge of that hate comes back to me. As I write the words, the sounds and then the scene return, these obscure, undignified people, a fat woman with asthma, an old Welsh milk-seller with a tumour on his bald head, who was the intellectual leader of the sect, a huge-voiced haberdasher with a big black beard, a white-faced, extraordinarily pregnant woman, his wife, a spectacled rate collector with a bent back. . . . I hear the talk about souls, the strange battered old phrases that were coined ages ago in the seaports of the sun-dry Levant, of balm of Gilead and manna in the desert, of gourds that give shade and water in a thirsty land; I recall again the way in which at the conclusion of the service the talk remained pious in form but became medical in substance, and how the women got together for obstetric whisperings. I, as a boy, did not matter, and might overhear. . . .

If Bladesover is my key for the explanation of England, I think my invincible persuasion that I understand Russia was engendered by the circle of Uncle Frapp.

I slept in a dingy sheeted bed with the two elder survivors of Frapp fecundity, and spent my week days in helping in the laborious disorder of the shop and bakehouse, in incidental deliveries of bread and so forth, and in parrying the probings of my uncle into my relations with the Blood, and his confidential explanations that ten shillings a week—which was what my mother paid him—was not enough to cover my accommodation. He was very anxious to keep that, but also he wanted more. There were neither books nor any seat nor corner in that house where reading was possible, no newspaper ever brought the clash of worldly things into its heavenward seclusion; horror of it all grew in me daily, and whenever I could I escaped into the streets and tramped about Chatham. The news shops appealed to me particularly. One saw there smudgy illustrated sheets, the *Police News* in particular, in which vilely drawn pictures brought home to the dullest intelligence an interminable succession of squalid crimes, women murdered and put into boxes, buried under floors, old men bludgeoned at midnight by robbers, people thrust suddenly out of trains, happy lovers shot, vitrioled and so forth by rivals. I got my first glimpse of the life of pleasure in foully drawn pictures of "police raids" on this and that. Interspersed with these sheets were others in which Sloper, the urban John Bull, had his fling with gin bottle and obese umbrella, or the kindly empty faces of the Royal Family appeared and reappeared, visiting this, opening that, getting married, getting offspring, lying in state, doing everything but anything, a wonderful, good-meaning, impenetrable race apart. . . .

I have never revisited Chatham; the impression it has left on my mind is one of squalid compression, unlit by any gleam of a maturer charity. All its effects arranged themselves as antithetical to the Bladesover effects. They confirmed and intensified all that Bladesover suggested. Bladesover declared itself to be the land, to be essentially England; I have already told how its airy spaciousness, its wide dignity, seemed to thrust village, church, and vicarage into corners, into a secondary and conditional significance. Here one gathered the corollary of that. Since the whole wide country of Kent was made up of contiguous Bladesovers and for the gentlefolk, the surplus of population, all who were not good tenants nor good labourers, Church of England, submissive and respectful, were necessarily thrust together, jostled out of sight, to fester as they might in this place that had the colours and even the smells of a well-packed dustbin. They should be grateful even for that; that, one felt, was the theory of it all.

And I loafed about this wilderness of crowded dinginess, with young, receptive, wide-open eyes, and through the blessing (or curse) of some fairy godmother of mine, asking and asking again: "But after all, *why——?*"

I wandered up through Rochester once, and had a glimpse of the Stour valley above the town, all horrible with cement works and foully smoking chimneys and rows of workmen's cottages, minute, ugly, uncomfortable, and grimy. So I had my first intimation of how industrialism must live in a landlord's land. I spent some hours, too, in the streets that give upon the river, drawn by the spell of the sea. But I saw barges and ships stripped of magic and mostly devoted to cement, ice, timber, and coal. The sailors looked to me gross and slovenly men, and the shipping struck me as clumsy, ugly, old, and dirty. I discovered that most sails don't fit the ships that hoist them, and that there may be as pitiful and squalid a display of poverty with a vessel as with a man. When I saw colliers unloading, watched the workers in the hold filling up silly little sacks and the succession of blackened, half-naked men that ran to and fro with these along a plank over a thirty-foot drop into filth and mud, I was first seized with admiration of their courage and toughness and then, "But after all, *why*—?" and the stupid ugliness of all this waste of muscle and endurance came home to me. Among other things it obviously wasted and deteriorated the coal. . . . And I had imagined great things of the sea! . . .

Well, anyhow, for a time that vocation was stilled.

But such impressions came into my leisure, and of that I had no excess. Most of my time was spent doing things for Uncle Frapp, and my evenings and nights perforce in the company of the two eldest of my cousins. One was errand boy at an oil shop and fervently pious, and of him I saw nothing until the evening except at meals; the other was enjoying the midsummer holidays without any great elation; a singularly thin and abject, stunted creature he was, whose chief liveliness was to pretend to be a monkey, and who I am now convinced had some secret disease that drained his vitality away. If I met him now I should think him a pitiful little creature and be extremely sorry for him. Then I felt only a wondering aversion. He sniffed horribly, he was tired out by a couple of miles of loafing, he never started any conversation, and he seemed to prefer his own company to mine. His mother, poor woman, said he was the "thoughtful one."

Serious trouble came suddenly out of a conversation we held in bed one night. Some particularly pious phrase of my elder cousin's irritated me extremely, and I avowed outright my entire disbelief in the whole scheme of revealed religion. I had never said a word about my doubts to any one before, except to Ewart, who had first evolved them. I had never settled my doubts until at this moment when I spoke. But it came to me then that the whole scheme of salvation of the Frapps was not simply doubtful, but impossible. I fired this discovery out into the darkness with the greatest promptitude.

My abrupt denials certainly scared my cousins amazingly.

At first they could not understand what I was saying, and when they did I fully believe they expected an instant answer in thunderbolts and flames. They gave me more room in the bed forthwith, and then the elder sat up and expressed his sense of my awfulness. I was already a little frightened at my temerity, but when he asked me categorically to unsay what I had said, what could I do but confirm my repudiation?

"There's no hell," I said, "and no eternal punishment. No God would be such a fool as that."

My elder cousin cried aloud in horror, and the younger lay scared, but listening.

"Then you mean," said my elder cousin, when at last he could bring himself to argue, "you might do just as you liked?"

"If you were cad enough," said I.

Our little voices went on interminably, and at one stage my cousin got out of bed and made his brother do likewise, and knelt in the night dimness and prayed at me. That I found trying, but I held out valiantly. "Forgive him," said my cousin, "he knows not what he sayeth."

"You can pray if you like," I said, "but if you're going to cheek me in your prayers I draw the line."

The last I remember of that great discussion was my cousin deploring the fact that he "should ever sleep in the same bed with an Infidel!"

The next day he astonished me by telling the whole business to his father. This was quite outside all my codes. Uncle Nicodemus sprang it upon me at the midday meal.

"You been sayin' queer things, George," he said abruptly. "You better mind what you're saying."

"What did he say, father?" said Mrs. Frapp.

"Things I couldn' repeat," said he.

"What things?" I asked hotly.

"Ask *'im*," said my uncle, pointing with his knife to his informant, and making me realise the nature of my offence. My aunt looked at the witness. "Not——?" she framed a question.

"Wuss," said my uncle. "Blarsphemy."

My aunt couldn't touch another mouthful. I was already a little troubled in my conscience by my daring, and now I began to feel the black enormity of the course upon which I had embarked.

"I was only talking sense," I said.

I had a still more dreadful moment when presently I met my cousin in the brick alley behind the yard, that led back to his grocer's shop.

"You sneak!" I said, and smacked his face hard forth-

[45]

with. "Now then," said I.

He started back, astonished and alarmed. His eyes met mine, and I saw a sudden gleam of resolution. He turned his other cheek to me.

" 'It it," he said. " 'It it. *I'll* forgive you."

I felt I had never encountered a more detestable way of evading a licking. I shoved him against the wall and left him there, forgiving me, and went back into the house.

"You better not speak to your cousins, George," said my aunt, "till you're in a better state of mind."

I became an outcast forthwith. At supper that night a gloomy silence was broken by my cousin saying, " 'E 'it me for telling you, and I turned the other cheek, muvver."

" 'E's got the evil one be'ind 'im now, a ridin' on 'is back," said my aunt, to the grave discomfort of the eldest girl, who sat beside me.

After supper my uncle, in a few ill-chosen words, prayed me to repent before I slept.

"Suppose you was took in your sleep, George," he said; "where'd you be then? You jest think of that, me boy." By this time I was thoroughly miserable and frightened, and this suggestion unnerved me dreadfully, but I kept up an impenitent front. "To wake in 'ell," said Uncle Nicodemus, in gentle tones. "You don't want to wake in 'ell, George, burnin' and screamin' for ever, do you? You wouldn't like that?"

He tried very hard to get me to "jest 'ave a look at the bake'ouse fire" before I retired. "It might move you," he said.

I was awake longest that night. My cousins slept the sleep of faith on either side of me. I decided I would whisper my prayers, and stopped midway because I was ashamed, and perhaps also because I had an idea one didn't square God like that.

"No," I said, with a sudden confidence, "damn me if you're coward enough. . . . But you're not. . . . No! You couldn't be!"

I woke my cousins up with emphatic digs, and told them

as much, triumphantly, and went very peacefully to sleep with my act of faith accomplished.

I slept not only through that night, but for all my nights since then. So far as any fear of Divine injustice goes, I sleep soundly, and shall, I know, to the end of things. That declaration was an epoch in my spiritual life.

II

But I didn't expect to have the whole meeting on Sunday turned on to me.

It was. It all comes back to me, that convergence of attention, even the faint leathery smell of its atmosphere returns, and the coarse feel of my aunt's black dress beside me in contact with my hand. I see again the old Welsh milkman "wrestling" with me—they all wrestled with me, by prayer or exhortation. And I was holding out stoutly, though convinced now by the contagion of their universal conviction that by doing so I was certainly and hopelessly damned. I felt that they were right, that God was probably like them, and that on the whole it didn't matter. And to simplify the business thoroughly I had declared I didn't believe anything at all. They confuted me by texts from Scripture which I now perceive was an illegitimate method of reply. When I got home, still impenitent and eternally lost and secretly very lonely and miserable and alarmed, Uncle Nicodemus docked my Sunday pudding.

One person only spoke to me like a human being on that day of wrath, and that was the younger Frapp. He came up to me in the afternoon while I was confined upstairs with a Bible and my own thoughts.

" 'Ello," he said, and fretted about.

"D'you mean to say there isn't—no one," he said, funking the word.

"No one?"

"No one watching yer—always."

"Why should there be?" I asked.

"You can't 'elp thoughts," said my cousin, "any'ow. . . . You mean——" He stopped hovering. "I s'pose I oughtn't to be talking to you."

He hesitated and flitted away with a guilty back glance over his shoulder. . . .

The following week made life quite intolerable for me; these people forced me at last into an Atheism that terrified me. When I learnt that next Sunday the wrestling was to be resumed, my courage failed me altogether.

I happened upon a map of Kent in a stationer's window on Saturday, and that set me thinking of one form of release. I studied it intently for half an hour perhaps, on Saturday night, got a route list of villages well fixed in my memory, and got up and started for Bladesover about five on Sunday morning while my two bed mates were still fast asleep.

III

I remember something, but not so much of it as I should like to recall, of my long tramp to Bladesover House. The distance from Chatham is almost exactly seventeen miles, and it took me until nearly one. It was very interesting and I do not think I was over-fatigued, though I got rather pinched by one boot.

The morning must have been very clear, because I remember that near Itchinstow Hall I looked back and saw the estuary of the Thames, that river that has since played so large a part in my life. But at the time I did not know it was the Thames, I thought this great expanse of mud flats and water was the sea, which I had never yet seen nearly. And out upon it stood ships, sailing ships and a steamer or so, going up to London or down out into the great seas of the world. I stood for a long time watching these and thinking whether after all I should not have done better to have run away to sea.

The nearer I drew to Bladesover, the more doubtful I grew of the quality of my reception, and the more I regretted that alternative. I suppose it was the dirty clumsiness of the shipping I had seen nearly, that put me out of mind of that. I took a short cut through the Warren across the corner of the main park to intercept the people from the

[48]

church. I wanted to avoid meeting any one before I met my mother, and so I went to a place where the path passed between banks, and without exactly hiding, stood up among the bushes. This place among other advantages eliminated any chance of seeing Lady Drew, who would drive round by the carriage road.

Standing up to waylay in this fashion I had a queer feeling of brigandage, as though I was some intrusive sort of bandit among these orderly things. It is the first time I remember having that outlaw feeling distinctly, a feeling that has played a large part in my subsequent life. I felt there existed no place for me—that I had to drive myself in.

Presently, down the hill, the servants appeared, straggling by twos and threes, first some of the garden people and the butler's wife with them, then the two laundry maids, odd inseparable old creatures, then the first footman talking to the butler's little girl, and at last, walking grave and breathless beside old Ann and Miss Fison, the black figure of my mother.

My boyish mind suggested the adoption of a playful form of appearance. "Coo-ee, mother!" said I, coming out against the sky, "Coo-ee!"

My mother looked up, went very white, and put her hand to her bosom. . . .

I suppose there was a fearful fuss about me. And of course I was quite unable to explain my reappearance. But I held out stoutly, "I won't go back to Chatham; I'll drown myself first." The next day my mother carried me off to Wimblehurst, took me fiercely and aggressively to an uncle I had never heard of before, near though the place was to us. She gave me no word as to what was to happen, and I was too subdued by her manifest wrath and humiliation at my last misdemeanour to demand information. I don't for one moment think Lady Drew was "nice" about me. The finality of my banishment was endorsed and underlined and stamped home. I wished very much now that I had run away to sea, in spite of the coally dust and squalor Rochester had revealed to me. Perhaps overseas one came to different lands.

IV

I do not remember much of my journey to Wimblehurst with my mother except the image of her as sitting bolt upright, as rather disdaining the third-class carriage in which we travelled, and how she looked away from me out of the window when she spoke of my uncle. "I have not seen your uncle," she said, "since he was a boy. . . ." She added grudgingly, "Then he was supposed to be clever."

She took little interest in such qualities as cleverness.

"He married about three years ago, and set up for himself in Wimblehurst. . . . So I suppose she had some money."

She mused on scenes she had long dismissed from her mind. "Teddy," she said at last in the tone of one who has been feeling in the dark and finds. "He was called Teddy . . . about your age. . . . Now he must be twenty-six or seven."

I thought of my uncle as Teddy directly I saw him; there was something in his personal appearance that in the light of that memory phrased itself at once as Teddiness—a certain Teddidity. To describe it in any other terms is more difficult. It is nimbleness without grace, and alertness without intelligence. He whisked out of his shop upon the pavement, a short figure in grey and wearing grey carpet slippers; one had a sense of a young fattish face behind gilt glasses, wiry hair that stuck up and forward over the forehead, an irregular nose that had its aquiline moments, and that the body betrayed an equatorial laxity, an incipient "bow window" as the image goes. He jerked out of the shop, came to a stand on the pavement outside, regarded something in the window with infinite appreciation, stroked his chin, and, as abruptly, shot sideways into the door again, charging through it as it were behind an extended hand.

"That must be him," said my mother, catching at her breath.

We came past the window whose contents I was presently

[50]

to know by heart, a very ordinary chemist's window except that there was a frictional electrical machine, an air pump and two or three tripods and retorts replacing the customary blue, yellow, and red bottles above. There was a plaster of Paris horse to indicate veterinary medicines among these breakables, and below were scent packets and diffusers and sponges and soda-water syphons and such-like things. Only in the middle there was a rubricated card, very neatly painted by hand, with these words—

Buy Ponderevo's Cough Linctus *Now*.

NOW!

WHY?

Twopence Cheaper than in Winter.
You Store Apples! why not the Medicine
You are Bound to Need?

---

in which appeal I was to recognise presently my uncle's distinctive note.

My uncle's face appeared above a card of infants' comforters in the glass pane of the door. I perceived his eyes were brown, and that his glasses creased his nose. It was manifest he did not know us from Adam. A stare of scrutiny allowed an expression of commercial deference to appear in front of it, and my uncle flung open the door.

"You don't know me?" panted my mother.

My uncle would not own he did not, but his curiosity was manifest. My mother sat down on one of the little chairs before the soap and patent medicine-piled counter, and her lips opened and closed.

"A glass of water, madam," said my uncle, waved his hand in a sort of curve, and shot away.

My mother drank the water and spoke. "That boy," she said, "takes after his father. He grows more like him every day. . . . And so I have brought him to you."

"His father, madam?"

"George."

For a moment the chemist was still at a loss. He stood behind the counter with the glass my mother had returned to him in his hand. Then comprehension grew.

"By Gosh!" he said. "Lord!" he cried. His glasses fell off. He disappeared, replacing them, behind a pile of boxed-up bottles of blood mixture. "Eleven thousand virgins!" I heard him cry. The glass was banged down. "O-riental Gums!"

He shot away out of the shop through some masked door. One heard his voice. "Susan! Susan!"

Then he reappeared with an extended hand. "Well, how *are* you?" he said. "I was never so surprised in my life. Fancy! . . . *You!*"

He shook my mother's impassive hand and then mine very warmly, holding his glasses on with his left forefinger.

"Come right in!" he cried—"come right in! Better late than never!" and led the way into the parlour behind the shop.

After Bladesover that apartment struck me as stuffy and petty, but it was very comfortable in comparison with the Frapp living-room. It had a faint, disintegrating smell of meals about it, and my most immediate impression was of the remarkable fact that something was hung about or wrapped round or draped over everything. There was bright-patterned muslin round the gas-bracket in the middle of the room, round the mirror over the mantel, stuff with ball-fringe along the mantel and casing in the fireplace,—I first saw ball-fringe here—and even the lamp on the little bureau wore a shade like a large muslin hat. The table-cloth had ball-fringe and so had the window curtains, and the carpet was a bed of roses. There were little cupboards on either side of the fireplace, and in the recesses, ill-made shelves packed with books, and enriched with pinked American cloth. There was a dictionary lying face downward on the table, and the open bureau was littered with foolscap paper and the evidences of recently abandoned toil. My eye caught, "The Ponderevo Patent Flat, a Machine you can Live in," written in large firm letters. My uncle opened a little door like a cupboard door in the corner of this room, and revealed the narrowest twist of staircase I had ever set eyes upon. "Susan!" he bawled again. "Wantje. Some one to see you. Surprisin'."

There came an inaudible reply, and a sudden loud bump over our heads as of some article of domestic utility pettishly flung aside, then the cautious steps of some one descending the twist, and then my aunt appeared in the doorway with her hand upon the jamb.

"It's Aunt Ponderevo," cried my uncle. "George's wife—and she's brought over her son!" His eye roved about the room. He darted to the bureau with a sudden impulse, and turned the sheet about the patent flat face down. Then he waved his glasses at us, "*You* know, Susan, my elder brother George. I told you about 'im lots of times."

He fretted across to the hearthrug and took up a position there, replaced his glasses and coughed.

My aunt Susan seemed to be taking it in. She was then rather a pretty slender woman of twenty-three or four, I suppose, and I remember being struck by the blueness of her eyes and the clear freshness of her complexion. She had little features, a button nose, a pretty chin and a long graceful neck that stuck out of her pale blue cotton morning dress. There was a look of half-assumed perplexity on her face, a little quizzical wrinkle of the brow that suggested a faintly amused attempt to follow my uncle's mental operations, a vain attempt and a certain hopelessness that had in succession become habitual. She seemed to be saying, "Oh Lord! What's he giving me *this* time?" And as I came to know her better I detected, as a complication of her effort of apprehension, a subsidiary riddle to "What's he giving me?" and that was—to borrow a phrase from my schoolboy language—"Is it keeps?" She looked at my mother and me, and back to her husband again.

"You know," he said. "George."

"Well," she said to my mother, descending the last three steps of the staircase and holding out her hand, "you're

[53]

welcome. Though it's a surprise. . . . I can't ask you to *have* anything, I'm afraid, for there isn't anything in the house." She smiled, and looked at her husband banteringly. "Unless he makes up something with his old chemicals, which he's quite equal to doing."

My mother shook hands stiffly, and told me to kiss my aunt. . . .

"Well, let's all sit down," said my uncle, suddenly whistling through his clenched teeth, and briskly rubbing his hands together. He put up a chair for my mother, raised the blind of the little window, lowered it again, and returned to his hearthrug. "I'm sure," he said, as one who decides, "I'm very glad to see you."

V

As they talked I gave my attention pretty exclusively to my uncle.

I noted him in great detail. I remember now his partially unbuttoned waistcoat, as though something had occurred to distract him as he did it up, and a little cut upon his chin. I liked a certain humour in his eyes. I watched, too, with the fascination these things have for an observant boy, the play of his lips—they were a little oblique, and there was something "slipshod," if one may strain a word so far, about his mouth, so that he lisped and sibilated ever and again—and the coming and going of a curious expression, triumphant in quality it was, upon his face as he talked. He fingered his glasses, which did not seem to fit his nose, fretted with things in his waistcoat pockets or put his hands behind him, looked over our heads, and ever and again rose to his toes and dropped back on his heels. He had a way of drawing air in at times through his teeth that gave a whispering zest to his speech. It's a sound I can only represent as a soft Zzzz.

He did most of the talking. My mother repeated what she had already said in the shop, "I have brought George over to you," and then desisted for a time from the real business in hand. "You find this a comfortable house?" she

asked; and this being affirmed: "It looks—very convenient.
. . . Not too big to be a trouble—no. You like Wimblehurst, I suppose?"

My uncle retorted with some inquiries about the great
people of Bladesover, and my mother answered in the character of a personal friend of Lady Drew's. The talk hung
for a time, and then my uncle embarked upon a disserta-
tion upon Wimblehurst.

"This place," he began, "isn't of course quite the place
I ought to be in."

My mother nodded as though she had expected that.

"It gives me no Scope," he went on. "It's dead-and-alive.
Nothing happens."

"He's always wanting something to happen," said my
aunt Susan. "Some day he'll get a shower of things and
they'll be too much for him."

"Not they," said my uncle, buoyantly.

"Do you find business—slack?" asked my mother.

"Oh! one rubs along. But there's no Development—no
Growth. They just come along here and buy pills when
they want 'em—and a horseball or such. They've got to be
ill before there's a prescription. That sort they are. You
can't get 'em to launch out, you can't get 'em to take up
anything new. F'rinstance, I've been trying lately—induce
them to buy their medicines in advance, and in larger quantities. But they won't look at it! Then I tried to float a
little notion of mine, sort of an insurance scheme for colds;
you pay so much a week, and when you've got a cold you
get a bottle of Cough Linctus so long as you can produce
a substantial sniff. See? But Lord! they've no capacity for
ideas, they don't catch on; no Jump about the place, no
Life! Live!—they trickle, and what one has to do here is
to trickle too—Zzzz."

"Ah!" said my mother.

"It doesn't suit me," said my uncle. "I'm the cascading
sort."

"George was that," said my mother after a pondering
moment.

My aunt Susan took up the parable with an affectionate glance at her husband.

"He's always trying to make his old business jump," she said. "Always putting fresh cards in the window, or getting up to something. You'd hardly believe. It makes *me* jump sometimes."

"But it does no good," said my uncle.

"It does no good," said his wife. "It's not his *miloo*. . . ."

Presently they came upon a wide pause.

From the beginning of their conversation there had been the promise of this pause, and I pricked my ears. I knew perfectly what was bound to come; they were going to talk of my father. I was enormously strengthened in my persuasion when I found my mother's eyes resting thoughtfully upon me in the silence, and then my uncle looked at me and then my aunt. I struggled unavailingly to produce an expression of meek stupidity.

"I think," said my uncle, "that George will find it more amusing to have a turn in the market-place than to sit here talking with us. There's a pair of stocks there, George —very interesting. Old-fashioned stocks."

"I don't mind sitting here," I said.

My uncle rose and in the most friendly way led me through the shop. He stood on his doorstep and jerked amiable directions to me.

"Ain't it sleepy, George, eh? There's the butcher's dog over there, asleep in the road—half an hour from midday! If the last Trump sounded I don't believe it would wake. Nobody would wake! The chaps up there in the churchyard—they'd just turn over and say: 'Naar—you don't catch us, you don't! See?' . . . Well, you'll find the stocks just round that corner."

He watched me out of sight.

So I never heard what they said about my father after all.

VI

When I returned, my uncle had in some remarkable way become larger and central. "Tha'chu, George?" he cried, when the shop-door bell sounded. "Come right through", and I found him, as it were, in the chairman's place before the draped grate.

The three of them regarded me.

"We have been talking of making you a chemist, George," said my uncle.

My mother looked at me. "I had hoped," she said, "that Lady Drew would have done something for him——" She stopped.

"In what way?" said my uncle.

"She might have spoken to some one, got him into something perhaps. . . ." She had the servant's invincible persuasion that all good things are done by patronage.

"He is not the sort of boy for whom things are done," she added, dismissing these dreams. "He doesn't accommodate himself. When he thinks Lady Drew wishes a thing, he seems not to wish it. Towards Mr. Redgrave, too, he has been—disrespectful—he is like his father."

"Who's Mr. Redgrave?"

"The Vicar."

"A bit independent?" said my uncle, briskly.

"Disobedient," said my mother. "He has no idea of his place. He seems to think he can get on by slighting people and flouting them. He'll learn perhaps before it is too late."

My uncle stroked his cut chin and regarded me. "Have you learnt any Latin?" he asked abruptly.

I said I had not.

"He'll have to learn a little Latin," he explained to my mother, "to qualify. H'm. He could go down to the chap at the grammar school here—it's just been routed into existence again by the Charity Commissioners—and have lessons."

"What, me learn Latin!" I cried, with emotion.

"A little," he said.

"I've always wanted——" I said and; *"Latin!"*

I had long been obsessed by the idea that having no

Latin was a disadvantage in the world, and Archie Garvell had driven the point of this pretty earnestly home. The literature I had read at Bladesover had all tended that way. Latin had had a quality of emancipation for me that I find it difficult to convey. And suddenly, when I had supposed all learning was at an end for me, I heard this!

"It's no good to you, of course," said my uncle, "except to pass exams with, but there you are!"

"You'll have to learn Latin because you have to learn Latin," said my mother, "not because you *want* to. And afterwards you will have to learn all sorts of other things. . . ."

The idea that I was to go on learning, that to read and master the contents of books was still to be justifiable as a duty, overwhelmed all other facts. I had had it rather clear in my mind for some weeks that all that kind of opportunity might close to me for ever. I began to take a lively interest in this new project.

"Then shall I live here?" I asked, "with you, and study . . . as well as work in the shop?"

"That's the way of it," said my uncle.

I parted from my mother that day in a dream, so sudden and important was this new aspect of things to me. I was to learn Latin! Now that the humiliation of my failure at Bladesover was past for her, now that she had a little got over her first intense repugnance at this resort to my uncle and contrived something that seemed like a possible provision for my future, the tenderness natural to a parting far more significant than any of our previous partings crept into her manner.

She sat in the train to return, I remember, and I stood at the open door of her compartment, and neither of us knew how soon we should cease for ever to be a trouble to one another.

"You must be a good boy, George," she said. "You must learn. . . . And you mustn't set yourself up against those who are above you and better than you. . . . Or envy them."

"No, mother," I said.

I promised carelessly. Her eyes were fixed upon me. I was wondering whether I could by any means begin Latin that night.

Something touched her heart then, some thought, some memory; perhaps some premonition. . . . The solitary porter began slamming carriage doors.

"George," she said hastily, almost shamefully, "kiss me!"

I stepped up into her compartment as she bent forward. She caught me in her arms quite eagerly, she pressed me to her—a strange thing for her to do. I perceived her eyes were extraordinarily bright, and then this brightness burst along the lower lids and rolled down her cheeks.

For the first and last time in my life I saw my mother's tears. Then she had gone, leaving me discomforted and perplexed, forgetting for a time even that I was to learn Latin, thinking of my mother as of something new and strange.

The thing recurred though I sought to dismiss it, it stuck itself into my memory against the day of fuller understanding. Poor, proud, habitual, sternly narrow soul! poor difficult and misunderstanding son! it was the first time that ever it dawned upon me that my mother also might perhaps feel.

VII

My mother died suddenly and, it was thought by Lady Drew, inconsiderately, the following spring. Her ladyship instantly fled to Folkestone with Miss Somerville and Fison, until the funeral should be over and my mother's successor installed.

My uncle took me over to the funeral. I remember there was a sort of prolonged crisis in the days preceding this because, directly he heard of my loss, he had sent a pair of check trousers to the Judkins people in London to be dyed black, and they did not come back in time. He became very excited on the third day, and sent a number of increasingly fiery telegrams without any result whatever, and succumbed next morning with a very ill grace to my aunt Susan's insistence upon the resources of his dress-suit. In my memory those black legs of his, in a particularly thin and shiny black cloth—for evidently his dress-suit dated from adolescent and slenderer days—straddle like the Colossus of Rhodes over my approach to my mother's funeral. Moreover, I was inconvenienced and distracted by a silk hat he had bought me, my first silk hat, much ennobled, as his was also, by a deep mourning band.

I remember, but rather indistinctly, my mother's white panelled housekeeper's room and the touch of oddness about it that she was not there, and the various familiar faces made strange by black, and I seem to recall the exaggerated self-consciousness that arose out of their focussed attention. No doubt the sense of the new silk hat came and went and came again in my emotional chaos. Then something comes out clear and sorrowful, rises out clear and sheer from among all these rather base and inconsequent things, and once again I walk before all the other mourners close behind her coffin as it is carried along the church-yard path to her grave, with the old vicar's slow voice saying regretfully and unconvincingly above me, triumphant solemn things.

"I am the resurrection and the life, saith the Lord; he that believeth in me, though he were dead, yet shall he live: and whosoever liveth and believeth in me shall never die."

Never die! The day was a high and glorious morning in spring, and all the trees were budding and bursting into green. Everywhere there were blossoms and flowers; the pear trees and cherry trees in the sexton's garden were sunlit snow, there were nodding daffodils and early tulips in the graveyard beds, great multitudes of daisies, and everywhere the birds seemed singing. And in the middle was the brown coffin end, tilting on men's shoulders and half occluded by the vicar's Oxford hood.

And so we came to my mother's waiting grave. . . .

[60]

For a time I was very observant, watching the coffin lowered, hearing the words of the ritual. It seemed a very curious business altogether.

Suddenly as the service drew to its end, I felt something had still to be said which had not been said, realised that she had withdrawn in silence, neither forgiving me nor hearing from me—those now lost assurances. Suddenly I knew I had not understood. Suddenly I saw her tenderly; remembered not so much tender or kindly things of her as her crossed wishes and the ways in which I had thwarted her. Surprisingly I realised that behind all her hardness and severity she had loved me, that I was the only thing she had ever loved and that until this moment I had never loved her. And now she was there and deaf and blind to me, pitifully defeated in her designs for me, covered from me so that she could not know. . . .

I dug my nails into the palms of my hands, I set my teeth, but tears blinded me, sobs would have choked me had speech been required of me. The old vicar read on, there came a mumbled response—and so on to the end. I wept as it were internally, and only when we had come out of the churchyard could I think and speak calmly again.

Stamped across this memory are the little black figures of my uncle and Rabbits, telling Avebury, the sexton and undertaker, that "it had all passed off very well—very well indeed."

VIII

That is the last I shall tell of Bladesover. The drop-scene falls on that, and it comes no more as an actual presence into this novel. I did indeed go back there once again, but under circumstances quite immaterial to my story. But in a sense Bladesover has never left me; it is, as I said at the outset, one of those dominant explanatory impressions that make the framework of my mind. Bladesover illuminates England; it has become all that is spacious, dignified, pretentious, and truly conservative in English life. It is my social datum. That is why I have drawn it here on so large a scale.

When I came back at last to the real Bladesover on an inconsequent visit, everything was far smaller than I could have supposed possible. It was as though everything had shivered and shrivelled a little at the Lichtenstein touch. The harp was still in the saloon, but there was a different grand piano with a painted lid and a metrostyle pianola, and an extraordinary quantity of artistic litter and *bric-à-brac* scattered about. There was the trail of the Bond Street showroom over it all. The furniture was still under chintz, but it wasn't the same sort of chintz although it pretended to be, and the lustre-dangling chandeliers had passed away. Lady Lichtenstein's books replaced the brown volumes I had browsed among—they were mostly presentation copies of contemporary novels and the *National Review* and the *Empire Review,* and the *Nineteenth Century and After* jostled current books on the tables—English new books in gaudy catchpenny "artistic" covers, French and Italian novels in yellow, German art handbooks of almost incredible ugliness. There were abundant evidences that her ladyship was playing with the Keltic renascence, and a great number of ugly cats made of china—she "collected" china and stoneware cats—stood about everywhere—in all colours, in all kinds of deliberately comic, highly glazed distortion. . . .

It is nonsense to pretend that finance makes any better aristocrats than rent. Nothing can make an aristocrat but pride, knowledge, training, and the sword. These people were no improvement on the Drews, none whatever. There was no effect of a beneficial replacement of passive unintelligent people by active intelligent ones. One felt that a smaller but more enterprising and intensely undignified variety of stupidity had replaced the large dulness of the old gentry, and that was all. Bladesover, I thought, had undergone just the same change between the seventies and the new century that had overtaken the dear old *Times,* and heaven knows how much more of the decorous British fabric. These Lichtensteins and their like seem to have no promise in them at all of any fresh vitality for the kingdom.

I do not believe in their intelligence or their power—they have nothing new about them at all, nothing creative nor rejuvenescent, no more than a disorderly instinct of acquisition; and the prevalence of them and their kind is but a phase in the broad slow decay of the great social organism of England. They could not have made Bladesover, they cannot replace it; they just happen to break out over it— saprophytically.

Well,—that was my last impression of Bladesover.

CHAPTER THE THIRD

The Wimblehurst Apprenticeship

I

So far as I can remember now, except for that one emotional phase by the graveside, I passed through all these experiences rather callously. I had already, with the facility of youth, changed my world, ceased to think at all of the old school routine and put Bladesover aside for digestion at a latter stage. I took up my new world in Wimblehurst with the chemist's shop as its hub, set to work at Latin and materia medica, and concentrated upon the present with all my heart. Wimblehurst is an exceptionally quiet and grey Sussex town, rare among south of England towns in being largely built of stone. I found something very agreeable and picturesque in its clean cobbled streets, its odd turnings and abrupt corners, and in the pleasant park that crowds up one side of the town. The whole place is under the Eastry dominion, and it was the Eastry influence and dignity that kept its railway station a mile and three-quarters away. Eastry House is so close that it dominates the whole; one goes across the market-place (with its old lock-up and stocks), past the great pre-reformation church, a fine grey shell, like some empty skull from which the life has fled, and there at once are the huge wrought-iron gates.

and one peeps through them to see the façade of this place, very white and large and fine, down a long avenue of yews. Eastry was far greater than Bladesover and an altogether completer example of the eighteenth century system. It ruled not two villages, but a borough, that had sent its sons and cousins to parliament almost as a matter of right so long as its franchise endured. Every one was in the system, every one—except my uncle. He stood out and complained.

My uncle was the first real breach I found in the great front of Bladesovery the world had presented me, for Chatham was not so much a breach as a confirmation. But my uncle had no respect for Bladesover and Eastry—none whatever. He did not believe in them. He was blind even to what they were. He propounded strange phrases about them, he exfoliated and wagged about novel and incredible ideas.

"This place," said my uncle, surveying it from his open doorway in the dignified stillness of a summer afternoon, "wants Waking Up!"

I was sorting up patent medicines in the corner.

"I'd like to let a dozen young Americans loose into it," said my uncle. "Then we'd see."

I made a tick against Mother Shipton's Sleeping Syrup. We had cleared our forward stock.

"Things must be happening *somewhere*, George," he broke out in a querulously rising note as he came back into the little shop. He fiddled with the piled dummy boxes of fancy soap and scent and so forth that adorned the end of the counter, then turned about petulantly, stuck his hands deeply into his pockets and withdrew one to scratch his head. "I must do *something*," he said. "I can't stand it.

"I must invent something. And shove it. . . . I could.

"Or a play. There's a deal of money in a play, George. What would you think of me writing a play—eh? . . . There's all sorts of things to be done.

"Or the stog-igschange."

He fell into that meditative whistling of his.

"Sac-ramental wine!" he swore, "this isn't the world—it's Cold Mutton Fat! That's what Wimblehurst is! Cold

Mutton Fat!—dead and stiff! And I'm buried in it up to the arm pits. Nothing ever happens, nobody wants things to happen 'scept me! Up in London, George, things happen. America! I wish to Heaven, George, I'd been born American—where things hum.

"What can one do here? How can one grow? While we're sleepin' here with our Capital oozing away—into Lord Eastry's pockets for rent—men are up there. . . ." He indicated London as remotely over the top of the dispensing counter, and then as a scene of great activity by a whirl of the hand and a wink and a meaning smile at me.

"What sort of things do they do?" I asked.

"Rush about," he said. "Do things! Somethin' glorious. There's cover gambling. Ever heard of that, George?" He drew the air in through his teeth. "You put down a hundred say, and buy ten thousand pounds worth. See? That's a cover of one per cent. Things go up one, you sell, realise cent per cent; down, whiff, it's gone! Try again! Cent per cent, George, every day. Men are made or done for in an hour. And the shoutin'! Zzzz. . . . Well, that's one way, George. Then another way—there's Corners!"

"They're rather big things, aren't they?" I ventured.

"Oh, if you go in for wheat or steel—yes. But suppose you tackled a little thing, George. Just some leetle thing that only needed a few thousands. Drugs, for example. Shoved all you had into it—staked your liver on it, so to speak. Take a drug—take ipecac, for example. Take a lot of ipecac. Take all there is! See? There you are! There aren't unlimited supplies of ipecacuanha—can't be!—and it's a thing people *must* have. Then quinine again! You watch your chance, wait for a tropical war breaking out, let's say, and collar all the quinine. Where *are* they? Must have quinine, you know. Eh? Zzzz.

"Lord! there's no end of things—no end of *little* things. Dill-water—all the suff'ring babes yowling for it. Eucalyptus again—cascara—witch hazel—menthol—all the tooth ache things. Then there's antiseptics, and curare, cocaine. . . ."

"Rather a nuisance to the doctors," I reflected.

"They got to look out for themselves. By Jove, yes. They'll do you if they can, and you do them. Like brigands. That makes it romantic. That's the Romance of Commerce, George. You're in the mountains there! Think of having all the quinine in the world, and some millionaire's pampud wife gone ill with malaria, eh? That's a squeeze, George, eh? Eh? Millionaire on his motor car outside, offering you any price you liked. That 'ud wake up Wimblehurst. . . . Lord! You haven't an Idea down here. Not an idea. Zzzz."

He passed into a rapt dream, from which escaped such fragments as: "Fifty per cent. advance, sir; security—tomorrow. Zzzz."

The idea of cornering a drug struck upon my mind then as a sort of irresponsible monkey trick that no one would ever be permitted to do in reality. It was the sort of nonsense one would talk to make Ewart laugh and set him going on to still odder possibilities. I thought it was part of my uncle's way of talking. But I've learnt differently since. The whole trend of modern money-making is to foresee something that will presently be needed and put it out of reach, and then to haggle yourself wealthy. You buy up land upon which people will presently want to build houses, you secure rights that will bar vitally important developments, and so on, and so on. Of course the naïve intelligence of a boy does not grasp the subtler developments of human inadequacy. He begins life with a disposition to believe in the wisdom of grown-up people, he does not realise how casual and disingenuous has been the development of law and custom, and he thinks that somewhere in the state there is a power as irresistible as a head master's to check mischievous and foolish enterprises of every sort. I will confess that when my uncle talked of cornering quinine, I had a clear impression that any one who contrived to do that would pretty certainly go to jail. Now I know that any one who could really bring it off would be much more ilkely to go to the House of Lords!

My uncle ranged over the gilt labels of his bottles and drawers for a while, dreaming of corners in this and that. But at last he reverted to Wimblehurst again.

"You got to be in London when these things are in hand. Down here——!

"Jee-rusalem!" he cried. "Why did I plant myself here? Everything's done. The game's over. Here's Lord Eastry, and he's got everything, except what his lawyers get, and before you get any more change this way you'll have to dynamite him—and them. *He* doesn't want anything more to happen. Why should he? Any change 'ud be a loss to him. He wants everything to burble along and burble along and go on as it's going for the next ten thousand years, Eastry after Eastry, one parson down another come, one grocer dead, get another! Any one with any ideas better go away. They *have* gone away! Look at all these blessed people in this place! Look at 'em! All fast asleep, doing their business out of habit—in a sort of dream. Stuffed men would do just as well—just. They've all shook down into their places. *They* don't want anything to happen either. They're all broken in. There you are! Only what are they all alive for? . . .

"Why can't they get a clockwork chemist?"

He concluded as he often concluded these talks. "I must invent something,—that's about what I must do. Zzzz. Some convenience. Something people want. . . . Strike out. . . . You can't think, George, of anything everybody wants and hasn't got? I mean something you could turn out retail under a shilling, say? Well, *you* think, whenever you haven't got anything better to do. See?"

II

So I remember my uncle in that first phase, young, but already a little fat, restless, fretful, garrulous, putting in my fermenting head all sorts of discrepant ideas. Certainly he was educational. . . .

For me the years at Wimblehurst were years of pretty active growth. Most of my leisure and much of my time in

[67]

the shop I spent in study. I speedily mastered the modicum of Latin necessary for my qualifying examinations, and—a little assisted by the Government Science and Art Department classes that were held in the Grammar School—went on with my mathematics. There were classes in physics, in chemistry, in mathematics and machine drawing, and I took up all these subjects with considerable avidity. Exercise I got chiefly in the form of walks. There was some cricket in the summer and football in the winter sustained by young men's clubs that levied a parasitic blackmail on the big people and the sitting member, but I was never very keen at these games. I didn't find any very close companions among the youths of Wimblehurst. They struck me, after my cockney schoolmates, as loutish and slow, servile and furtive, spiteful and mean. *We* used to swagger, but these countrymen dragged their feet and hated an equal who didn't; we talked loud, but you only got the real thoughts of Wimblehurst in a knowing undertone behind its hand. And even then they weren't much in the way of thoughts.

No, I didn't like those young countrymen, and I'm no believer in the English countryside under the Bladesover system as a breeding ground for honourable men. One hears a frightful lot of nonsense about the Rural Exodus and the degeneration wrought by town life upon our population. To my mind, the English townsman, even in the slums, is infinitely better spiritually, more courageous, more imaginative and cleaner, than his agricultural cousin. I've seen them both when they didn't think they were being observed, and I know. There was something about my Wimblehurst companions that disgusted me. It's hard to define. Heaven knows that at that cockney boarding-school at Goudhurst we were coarse enough; the Wimblehurst youngsters had neither words nor courage for the sort of thing we used to do—for our bad language, for example; but, on the other hand, they displayed a sort of sluggish, real lewdness,—lewdness is the word—a baseness of attitude. Whatever we exiled urbans did at Goudhurst was touched with something, however coarse, of romantic imagination. We had read the *Boys of England,* and told each other stories. In the English countryside there are no books at all, no songs, no drama, no valiant sin even; all these things have never come or they were taken away and hidden generations ago, and the imagination aborts and bestialises. That, I think, is where the real difference against the English rural man lies. It is because I know this that I do not share in the common repinings because our countryside is being depopulated, because our population is passing through the furnace of the towns. They starve, they suffer, no doubt, but they come out of it hardened, they come out of it with souls. . . .

Of an evening the Wimblehurst blade, shiny-faced from a wash and with some loud finery, a coloured waistcoat or a vivid tie, would betake himself to the Eastry Arms billiard-room, or to the bar parlour of some minor pub where nap could be played. One soon sickened of his slow knowingness, the cunning observation of his deadened eyes, his idea of a "good story," always, always told in undertones, poor dirty worm! his shrewd, elaborate manœuvres for some petty advantage, a drink to the good or such-like deal. There rises before my eyes as I write, young Hopley Dodd, the son of the Wimblehurst auctioneer, the pride of Wimblehurst, its finest flower, with his fur waistcoat and his bulldog pipe, his riding breeches—he had no horse—and his gaiters, as he used to sit, leaning forward and watching the billiard-table from under the brim of his artfully tilted hat. A half-dozen phrases constituted his conversation: "Hard lines!" he used to say, and "Good baazness," in a bass bleat. Moreover, he had a long slow whistle that was esteemed the very cream of humorous comment. Night after night he was there. . . .

Also you knew he would not understand that *I* could play billiards, and regarded every stroke I made as a fluke. For a beginner I didn't play so badly, I thought. I'm not so sure now; that was my opinion at the time. But young Dodd's scepticism and the "good baazness" finally cured me of my disposition to frequent the Eastry Arms, and so these noises had their value in my world.

I made no friends among the young men of the place at all, and though I was entering upon adolescence I have no love-affair to tell of here. Not that I was not waking up to that aspect of life in my middle teens. I did, indeed, in various slightly informal ways scrape acquaintance with casual Wimblehurst girls; with a little dressmaker's apprentice I got upon shyly speaking terms, and a pupil teacher in the National School went further and was "talked about" in connection with me; but I was not by any means touched by an reality of passion for either of these young people; love—love as yet came to me only in my dreams. I only kissed these girls once or twice. They rather disconcerted than developed those dreams. They were so clearly not "it." I shall have much to say of love in this story, but I may break it to the reader now that it is my *rôle* to be a rather ineffectual lover. Desire I knew well enough—indeed, too well; but love I have been shy of. In all my early enterprises in the war of the sexes, I was torn between the urgency of the body and a habit of romantic fantasy that wanted every phase of the adventure to be generous and beautiful. And I had a curiously haunting memory of Beatrice, or her kisses in the bracken and her kiss upon the wall, that somehow pitched the standard too high for Wimblehurst's opportunities. I will not deny I did in a boyish way attempt a shy, rude adventure or so in love-making at Wimblehurst; but through these various influences, I didn't bring things off to any extent at all. I left behind me no devastating memories, no splendid reputation. I came away at last, still inexperienced and a little thwarted, with only a natural growth of interest and desire in sexual things.

If I fell in love with any one in Wimblehurst it was with my aunt. She treated me with a kindliness that was only half maternal—she petted my books, she knew about my certificates, she made fun of me in a way that stirred my heart to her. Quite unconsciously I grew fond of her. . . .

My adolescent years at Wimblehurst were on the whole

laborious, uneventful years that began in short jackets and left me in many ways nearly a man, years so uneventful that the Calculus of Variations is associated with one winter, and an examination in Physics for Science and Art Department Honours marks an epoch. Many divergent impulses stirred within me, but the master impulse was a grave young disposition to work and learn and thereby in some not very clearly defined way get out of the Wimblehurst world into which I had fallen. I wrote with some frequency to Ewart, self-conscious, but, as I remember them, not unintelligent letters, dated in Latin and with lapses into Latin quotation that roused Ewart to parody. There was something about me in those days more than a little priggish. But it was, to do myself justice, something more than the petty pride of learning. I had a very grave sense of discipline and preparation that I am not ashamed at all to remember. I was serious. More serious than I am at the present time. More serious, indeed, than any adult seems to be. I was capable then of efforts—of nobilities. . . . They are beyond me now. I don't see why, at forty, I shouldn't confess I respect my own youth. I had dropped being a boy quite abruptly. I thought I was presently to go out into a larger and quite important world and do significant things there. I thought I was destined to do something definite to a world that had a definite purpose. I did not understand then, as I do now, that life was to consist largely in the world's doing things to me. Young people never do seem to understand that aspect of things. And, as I say, among my educational influences my uncle, all unsuspected, played a leading part, and perhaps among other things gave my discontent with Wimblehurst, my desire to get away from that clean and picturesque emptiness, a form and expression that helped to emphasise it. In a way that definition made me patient. "Presently I shall get to London," I said, echoing him.

I remember him now as talking, always talking, in those days. He talked to me of theology, he talked of politics, of the wonders of science and the marvels of art, of the passions and the affections, of the immortality of the soul and the peculiar actions of drugs; but predominantly and constantly he talked of getting on, of enterprises, of inventions and great fortunes, of Rothschilds, silver kings, Vanderbilts, Goulds, flotations, realisations and the marvellous ways of Chance with men—in all localities, that is to say, that are not absolutely sunken to the level of Cold Mutton Fat.

When I think of those early talks, I figure him always in one of three positions. Either we were in the dispensing lair behind a high barrier, he pounding up things in a mortar perhaps, and I rolling pill-stuff into long rolls and cutting it up with a sort of broad, fluted knife, or he stood looking out of the shop door against the case of sponges and spray-diffusers, while I surveyed him from behind the counter, or he leant against the little drawers behind the counter, and I hovered dusting in front. The thought of those early days brings back to my nostrils the faint smell of scent that was always in the air, marbled now with streaks of this drug and now of that, and to my eyes the rows of jejune glass bottles with gold labels, mirror-reflected, that stood behind him. My aunt, I remember, used sometimes to come into the shop in a state of aggressive sprightliness, a sort of connubial ragging expedition, and get much fun over the abbreviated Latinity of those gilt inscriptions. "Ol Amjig, George," she would read derisively, "and he pretends it's almond oil! Snap!—and that's mustard. Did you *ever*, George?

"Look at him, George, looking dignified. I'd like to put an old label on to *him* round the middle like his bottles are, with Ol Pondo on it. That's Latin for Impostor, George— *must* be. He'd look lovely with a stopper."

"*You* want a stopper," said my uncle, projecting his face. . . .

My aunt, dear soul, was in those days quite thin and slender, with a delicate rosebud complexion and a disposition to connubial badinage, to a sort of gentle skylarking. There was a silvery ghost of lisping in her speech. She was a great humourist, and as the constraint of my presence at meals wore off, I became more and more aware of a filmy but extensive net of nonsense she had woven about her domestic relations until it had become the reality of her life. She affected a derisive attitude to the world at large and applied the epithet "old" to more things than I have ever heard linked to it before or since. "Here's the old newspaper," she used to say to my uncle. "Now don't go and get it in the butter, you silly old Sardine!"

"What's the day of the week, Susan?" my uncle would ask.

"Old Monday, Sossidge," she would say, and add, "I got all my Old Washing to do. Don't I *know* it!" . . .

She had evidently been the wit and joy of a large circle of schoolfellows, and this style had become a second nature with her. It made her very delightful to me in that quiet place. Her customary walk even had a sort of hello! in it. Her chief preoccupation in life was, I believe, to make my uncle laugh, and when by some new nickname, some new quaintness or absurdity, she achieved that end, she was, behind a mask of sober amazement, the happiest woman on earth. My uncle's laugh when it did come, I must admit was, as Baedeker says, "rewarding." It began with gusty blowings and snortings, and opened into a clear "Ha ha!" but in its fullest development it included, in those youthful days, falling about anyhow and doubling up tightly, and whackings of the stomach, and tears and cries of anguish. I never in my life heard my uncle laugh to his maximum except at her; he was commonly too much in earnest for that, and he didn't laugh much at all, to my knowledge, after those early years. Also she threw things at him to an enormous extent in her resolve to keep things lively in spite of Wimblehurst; sponges out of stock she threw, cushions, balls of paper, clean washing, bread; and once up the yard when they thought that I and the errand boy and the diminutive maid of all work were safely out of the way, she smashed a boxful of eight-ounce bottles I had left to drain, assaulting my uncle with a new soft broom. Sometimes she would shy things at me—but not often. There seemed always laughter round and about her—all three of us would share hysterics at times—and on one occasion the two of them came home from church shockingly ashamed of themselves, because of a storm of mirth during the sermon. The vicar, it seems, had tried to blow his nose with a black glove as well as the customary pocket-handkerchief. And afterwards she had picked up her own glove by the finger, and looking innocently but intently sideways, had suddenly by this simple expedient exploded my uncle altogether. We had it all over again at dinner.

"But it shows you," cried my uncle, suddenly becoming grave, "what Wimblehurst is, to have us all laughing at a little thing like that! We weren't the only ones that giggled. Not by any means! And, Lord! it *was* funny!"

Socially, my uncle and aunt were almost completely isolated. In places like Wimblehurst the tradesmen's wives always are isolated socially, all of them, unless they have a sister or a bosom friend among the other wives, but the husbands met in various bar-parlours or in the billiard-room of the Eastry Arms. But my uncle, for the most part, spent his evenings at home. When first he arrived in Wimblehurst I think he had spread his effect of abounding ideas and enterprise rather too aggressively; and Wimblehurst, after a temporary subjugation, had rebelled and done its best to make a butt of him. His appearance in a public-house led to a pause in any conversation that was going on.

"Come to tell us about everything, Mr. Pond'revo?" some one would say politely.

"You wait," my uncle used to answer, disconcerted, and sulk for the rest of his visit.

Or some one with an immense air of innocence would remark to the world generally, "They're talkin' of rebuildin' Wimblehurst all over again, I'm told. Anybody heard anything of it? Going to make it a reg'lar smart-goin', enterprisin' place—kind of Crystal Pallas."

"Earthquake and a pestilence before you get *that*," my

uncle would mutter, to the infinite delight of every one, and add something inaudible about "Cold Mutton Fat." . . .

III

We were torn apart by a financial accident to my uncle of which I did not at first grasp the full bearings. He had developed what I regarded as an innocent intellectual recreation which he called stock-market meteorology. I think he got the idea from the use of curves in the graphic presentation of associated variations that he saw me plotting. He secured some of my squared paper and, having cast about for a time, decided to trace the rise and fall of certain mines and railways. "There's something in this, George," he said, and I little dreamt that among other things that were in it, was the whole of his spare money and most of what my mother had left to him in trust for me.

"It's as plain as can be," he said. "See, here's one system of waves and here's another! These are prices for Union Pacifics—extending over a month. Now next week, mark my words, they'll be down one whole point. We're getting near the steep part of the curve again. See? It's absolutely scientific. It's verifiable. Well, and apply it! You buy in the hollow and sell on the crest, and—there you are!"

I was so convinced of the triviality of this amusement that to find at last that he had taken it in the most disastrous earnest overwhelmed me.

He took me for a long walk to break it to me, over the hills towards Yare and across the great gorse commons by Hazelbrow.

"There are ups and downs in life, George," he said—halfway across that great open space, and paused against the sky. . . . "I left out one factor in the Union Pacific analysis."

"*Did* you?" I said, struck by the sudden change in his voice. "But you don't mean——?"

I stopped and turned on him in the narrow sandy rut of pathway and he stopped likewise.

"I do, George. I *do* mean. It's bust me! I'm a bankrupt here and now."

"Then——?"

"The shop's bust too. I shall have to get out of that."

"And me?"

"Oh, you!—*you're* all right. You can transfer your apprenticeship, and—er—well, I'm not the sort of man to be careless with trust funds, you can be sure. I kept that aspect in mind. There's some of it left, George—trust me!— quite a decent little sum."

"But you and aunt?"

"It isn't *quite* the way we meant to leave Wimblehurst, George; but we shall have to go. Sale; all the things shoved about and ticketed—lot a hundred and one. Ugh! . . . It's been a larky little house in some ways. The first we had. Furnishing—a spree in its way. . . . Very happy . . ." His face winced at some memory. "Let's go on, George," he said shortly, near choking, I could see.

I turned my back on him, and did not look round again for a little while.

"That's how it is, you see, George," I heard him after a time.

When we were back in the high road again he came alongside, and for a time we walked in silence.

"Don't say anything home yet," he said presently. "Fortunes of War. I got to pick the proper time with Susan— else she'll get depressed. Not that she isn't a first-rate brick whatever comes along."

"All right," I said, "I'll be careful"; and it seemed to me for the time altogether too selfish to bother him with any further inquiries about his responsibility as my trustee. He gave a little sigh of relief at my note of assent, and was presently talking quite cheerfully of his plans. . . . But he had, I remember, one lapse into moodiness that came and went suddenly. "Those others!" he said, as though the thought had stung him for the first time.

"What others?" I asked.

"Damn them!" said he.

"But what others?"

"All those damned stick-in-the-mud-and-die-slowly trades-people: Ruck, the butcher, Marbel, the grocer. Snape! Gord! George, *how* they'll grin!" . . .

I thought him over in the next few weeks, and I remember now in great detail the last talk we had together before he handed over the shop and me to his successor. For he had the good luck to sell his business, "lock, stock, and barrel"—in which expression I found myself and my indentures included. The horrors of a sale by auction of the furniture even were avoided.

I remember that either coming or going on that occasion, Ruck, the butcher, stood in his doorway and regarded us with a grin that showed his long teeth.

"You half-witted hog!" said my uncle. "You grinning hyaena"; and then, "Pleasant day, Mr. Ruck."

"Goin' to make your fortun' in London, then?" said Mr. Ruck, with slow enjoyment.

That last excursion took us along the causeway to Beeching, and so up the downs and round almost as far as Steadhurst, home. My moods, as we went, made a mingled web. By this time I had really grasped the fact that my uncle had, in plain English, robbed me; the little accumulations of my mother, six hundred pounds and more, that would have educated me and started me in business, had been eaten into and was mostly gone into the unexpected hollow that ought to have been a crest of the Union Pacific curve, and of the remainder he still gave no account. I was too young and inexperienced to insist on this or know how to get it, but the thought of it all made streaks of decidedly black anger in that scheme of interwoven feelings. And you know, I was also acutely sorry for him—almost as sorry as I was for my aunt Susan. Even then I had quite found him out. I knew him to be weaker than myself; his incurable, irresponsible childishness was as clear to me then as it was on his deathbed, his redeeming and excusing imaginative silliness. Through some odd mental twist perhaps I was disposed to exonerate him even at the cost of blaming my poor old mother who had left things in his untrustworthy hands.

I should have forgiven him altogether, I believe, if he had been in any manner apologetic to me; but he wasn't that. He kept reassuring me in a way I found irritating. Mostly, however, his solicitude was for Aunt Susan and himself.

"It's these Crises, George," he said, "try Character. Your aunt's come out well, my boy."

He made meditative noises for a space.

"Had her cry of course,"—the thing had been only too painfully evident to me in her eyes and swollen face—"who wouldn't? But now—buoyant again! . . . She's a Corker.

"We'll be sorry to leave the little house of course. It's a bit like Adam and Eve, you know. Lord! what a chap old Milton was!

" 'The world was all before them, where to choose
Their place of rest, and Providence their guide.'

It sounds, George. . . . Providence their guide! . . . Well —thank goodness there's no imeedgit prospect of either Cain or Abel!

"After all, it won't be so bad up there. Not the scenery, perhaps, or the air we get here, but—*Life!* We've got very comfortable little rooms, very comfortable considering, and I shall rise. We're not done yet, we're not beaten; don't think that, George. I shall pay twenty shillings in the pound before I've done—you mark my words, George,— twenty-five to you. . . . I got this situation within twenty-four hours—others offered. It's an important firm—one of the best in London. I looked to that. I might have got four or five shillings a week more—elsewhere. Quarters I could name. But I said to them plainly, wages to go on with, but opportunity's my game—development. We understood each other."

He threw out his chest, and the little round eyes behind his glasses rested valiantly on imaginary employers.

We would go on in silence for a space while he revised

and restated that encounter. Then he would break out abruptly with some banal phrase.

"The Battle of Life, George, my boy," he would cry, or "Ups and Downs!"

He ignored or waived the poor little attempts I made to ascertain my own position. "That's all right," he would say; or, "Leave all that to me. *I'll* look after them." And he would drift away towards the philosophy and moral of the situation. What was I to do?

"Never put all your resources into one chance, George; that's the lesson I draw from this. Have forces in reserve. It was a hundred to one, George, that I was right—a hundred to one. I worked it out afterwards. And here we are spiked on the off-chance. If I'd have only kept back a little, I'd have had it on U. P. next day, like a shot, and come out on the rise. There you are!"

His thoughts took a graver turn.

"It's when you bump up against Chance like this, George, that you feel the need of religion. Your hard-and-fast scientific men—your Spencers and Huxleys—they don't understand that. I do. I've thought of it a lot lately—in bed and about. I was thinking of it this morning while I shaved. It's not irreverent for me to say it, I hope—but God comes in on the off-chance, George. See? Don't you be too cocksure of anything, good or bad. That's what I make out of it. I could have sworn. Well, do you think I—particular as I am—would have touched those Union Pacifics with trust-money at all, if I hadn't thought it a thoroughly good thing —good without spot or blemish? . . . And it was bad!

"It's a lesson to me. You start in to get a hundred per cent. and you come out with that. It means, in a way, a reproof for Pride. I've thought of that, George—in the Night Watches. I was thinking this morning when I was shaving, that that's where the good of it all comes in. At the bottom I'm a mystic in these affairs. You calculate you're going to do this or that, but at bottom who knows at all *what* he's doing? When you most think you're doing things, they're being done right over your head. *You're* being done—in a sense. Take a hundred-to-one chance, or one to a hundred—what does it matter? You're being Led."

It's odd that I heard this at the time with unutterable contempt, and now that I recall it—well, I ask myself, what have I got better?

"I wish," said I, becoming for a moment outrageous, "*you* were being Led to give me some account of my money, uncle."

"Not without a bit of paper to figure on, George, I can't. But you trust me about that, never fear. You trust me."

And in the end I had to.

I think the bankruptcy hit my aunt pretty hard. There was, so far as I can remember now, a complete cessation of all those cheerful outbreaks of elasticity—no more skylarking in the shop nor scampering about the house. But there was no fuss that I saw, and only little signs in her complexion of the fits of weeping that must have taken her. She didn't cry at the end, though to me her face with its strain of self-possession was more pathetic than any weeping. "Well," she said to me as she came through the shop to the cab, "here's old orf, George! Orf to Mome number two! Good-bye!" And she took me in her arms and kissed me and pressed me to her. Then she dived straight for the cab before I could answer her.

My uncle followed, and he seemed to me a trifle too valiant and confident in his bearing for reality. He was unusually white in the face. He spoke to his successor at the counter. "Here we go!" he said. "One down, the other up. You'll find it a quiet little business so long as you run it on quiet lines—a nice, quiet little business. There's nothing more? No? Well, if you want to know anything write to me. I'll always explain fully. Anything—business, place, or people. You'll find Pil Antibil. a little overstocked, by-the-by. I found it soothed my mind the day before yesterday making 'em, and I made 'em all day. Thousands! And where's George? Ah! there you are! I'll write to you, George, *fully*, about all that affair. Fully!"

It became clear to me, as if for the first time, that I was

really parting from my aunt Susan. I went out on to the pavement and saw her head craned forward, her wide-open blue eyes and her little face intent on the shop that had combined for her all the charms of a big doll's house and a little home of her very own. "Good-bye!" she said to it and to me. Our eyes met for a moment—perplexed. My uncle bustled out and gave a few totally unnecessary directions to the cabman and got in beside her. "All right?" asked the driver. "Right," said I; and he woke up the horse with a flick of his whip. My aunt's eyes surveyed me again. "Stick to your old science and things, George, and write and tell me when they make you a Professor," she said cheerfully.

She stared at me for a second longer with eyes growing wider and brighter and a smile that had become fixed, glanced again at the bright little shop still saying "Ponderevo" with all the emphasis of its fascia, and then flopped back hastily out of sight of me into the recesses of the cab. Then it had gone from before me, and I beheld Mr. Snape, the hairdresser, inside his shop regarding its departure with a quiet satisfaction and exchanging smiles and significant headshakes with Mr. Marbel.

IV

I was left, I say, as part of the lock, stock, and barrel, at Wimblehurst with my new master, a Mr. Mantell; who plays no part in the progress of this story except in so far as he effaced my uncle's traces. So soon as the freshness of this new personality faded, I began to find Wimblehurst not only a dull but a lonely place, and to miss my aunt Susan immensely. The advertisements of the summer terms for Cough Linctus were removed; the bottles of coloured water—red, green, and yellow—restored to their places; the horse announcing veterinary medicine, which my uncle, sizzling all the while, had coloured in careful portraiture of a Goodwood favourite, rewhitened; and I turned myself even more resolutely than before to Latin (until the passing of my preliminary examination enabled me to drop that), and then to mathematics and science.

There were classes in Electricity and Magnetism at the Grammar School. I took a little "elementary" prize in that in my first year and a medal in my third; and in Chemistry and Human Physiology and Sound, Light and Heat, I did well. There was also a lighter, more discursive subject called Physiography, in which one ranged among the sciences and encountered Geology as a process of evolution from Eozoon to Eastry House, and Astronomy as a record of celestial movements of the most austere and invariable integrity. I learnt out of badly-written, condensed little textbooks, and with the minimum of experiment, but still I learnt. Only thirty years ago it was, and I remember I learnt of the electric light as an expensive, impracticable toy, the telephone as a curiosity, electric traction as a practical absurdity. There was no argon, no radium, no phagocytes—at least to my knowledge, and aluminum was a dear, infrequent metal. The fastest ships in the world went then at nineteen knots, and no one but a lunatic here and there ever thought it possible that men might fly.

Many things have happened since then, but the last glance I had of Wimblehurst two years ago remarked no change whatever in its pleasant tranquillity. They had not even built any fresh houses—at least not actually in the town, though about the station there had been some building. But it was a good place to do work in, for all its quiescence. I was soon beyond the small requirements of the Pharmaceutical Society's examination, and as they do not permit candidates to sit for that until one and twenty, I was presently filling up my time and preventing my studies becoming too desultory by making an attack upon the London University degree of Bachelor of Science, which impressed me then as a very splendid but almost impossible achievement. The degree in mathematics and chemistry appealed to me as particularly congenial—albeit giddily inaccessible. I set to work. I had presently to arrange a holiday and go to London to matriculate, and so it was I came upon my aunt and uncle again. In many ways that visit marked an epoch. It was my first impression of London at all. I was then nineteen, and by a conspiracy of chances my nearest approach to that human wilderness had been my brief visit to Chatham. Chatham too had been my largest town. So that I got London at last with an exceptional freshness of effect, as the sudden revelation of a whole unsuspected other side to life.

I came to it on a dull and smoky day by the South Eastern Railway, and our train was half an hour late, stopping and going on and stopping again. I marked beyond Chiselhurst the growing multitude of villas, and so came stage by stage through multiplying houses and diminishing interspaces of market garden and dingy grass to regions of interlacing railway lines, big factories, gasometers and wide reeking swamps of dingy little homes, more of them and more and more. The number of these and their dinginess and poverty increased, and here rose a great public house and here a Board School and here a gaunt factory; and away to the east there loomed for a time a queer, incongruous forest of masts and spars. The congestion of houses intensified and piled up presently into tenements; I marvelled more and more at this boundless world of dingy people; whiffs of industrial smell, of leather, of brewing, drifted into the carriage; the sky darkened, I rumbled thunderously over bridges, van-crowded streets, peered down on and crossed the Thames with an abrupt eclat of sound. I got an effect of tall warehouses, of grey water, barge crowded, of broad banks of indescribable mud, and then I was in Cannon Street Station—a monstrous dirty cavern with trains packed across its vast floor and more porters standing along the platform than I had ever seen in my life before. I alighted with my portmanteau and struggled along, realising for the first time just how small and weak I could still upon occasion feel. In this world, I felt, an Honours medal in Electricity and Magnetism counted for nothing at all.

Afterwards I drove in a cab down a cañon of rushing street between high warehouses, and peeped up astonished at the blackened greys of Saint Paul's. The traffic of Cheapside—it was mostly in horse omnibuses in those days—seemed stupendous, its roar was stupendous; I wondered where the money came from to employ so many cabs, what industry could support the endless jostling stream of silk-hatted, frock-coated, hurrying men. Down a turning I found the Temperance Hotel Mr. Mantell had recommended to me. The porter in a green uniform who took over my portmanteau, seemed, I thought, to despise me a good deal.

V

Matriculation kept me for four full days and then came an afternoon to spare, and I sought out Tottenham Court Road through a perplexing network of various and crowded streets. But this London was vast! it was endless! it seemed the whole world had changed into packed frontages and hoardings and street spaces. I got there at last and made inquiries, and I found my uncle behind the counter of the pharmacy he managed, an establishment that did not impress me as doing a particularly high-class trade. "Lord!" he said at the sight of me, "I was wanting something to happen!"

He greeted me warmly. I had grown taller, and he, I thought, had grown shorter and smaller and rounder, but otherwise he was unchanged. He struck me as being rather shabby, and the silk hat he produced and put on, when, after mysterious negotiations in the back premises he achieved his freedom to accompany me, was past its first youth; but he was as buoyant and confident as ever.

"Come to ask me about all *that?*" he cried. "I've never written yet."

"Oh! among other things," said I, with a sudden regrettable politeness, and waived the topic of his trusteeship to ask after my aunt Susan.

"We'll have her out of it," he said suddenly; "we'll go somewhere. We don't get you in London every day."

"It's my first visit," I said, "I've never seen London before"; and that made him ask me what I thought of it, and the rest of the talk was London, London, to the exclu-

sion of all smaller topics. He took me up the Hampstead
Road almost to the Cobden statue, plunged into some back
streets to the left, and came at last to a blistered front door
that responded to his latch-key, one of a long series of
blistered front doors with fanlights and apartment cards
above. We found ourselves in a drab-coloured passage that
was not only narrow and dirty but desolatingly empty, and
then he opened a door and revealed my aunt sitting at the
window with a little sewing-machine on a bamboo occasional table before her, and "work"—a plum-coloured walking dress I judged at its most analytical stage—scattered
over the rest of the apartment.

At the first glance I judged my aunt was plumper than
she had been, but her complexion was just as fresh and
her China blue eye as bright as in the old days.

"London," she said, didn't "get blacks" on her.

She still "cheeked" my uncle, I was pleased to find.
"What are you old Poking in for at *this* time,—*Gubbitt?*"
she said when he appeared, and she still looked with a
practised eye for the facetious side of things. When she
saw me behind him, she gave a little cry and stood up
radiant. Then she became grave.

I was surprised at my own emotion in seeing her. She
held me at arm's length for a moment, a hand on each
shoulder, and looked at me with a sort of glad scrutiny. She
seemed to hesitate, and then pecked a little kiss off my
cheek.

"You're a man, George," she said, as she released me,
and continued to look at me for a while.

Their *ménage* was one of a very common type in London. They occupied what is called the dining-room floor
of a small house, and they had the use of a little inconvenient kitchen in the basement that had once been a
scullery. The two rooms, bedroom behind and living-room
in front, were separated by folding-doors that were never
now thrown back, and indeed, in the presence of a visitor,
not used at all. There was of course no bathroom or anything of that sort available, and there was no water supply

[85]

except to the kitchen below. My aunt did all the domestic work, though she could have afforded to pay for help if the build of the place had not rendered that inconvenient to the pitch of impossibility. There was no sort of help available except that of indoor servants, for whom she had no accommodation. The furniture was their own; it was partly second-hand, but on the whole it seemed cheerful to my eye, and my aunt's bias for cheap, gay-figured muslin had found ample score. In many ways I should think it must have been an extremely inconvenient and cramped sort of home, but at the time I took it, as I was taking everything, as being there and in the nature of things. I did not see the oddness of solvent decent people living in a habitation so clearly neither designed nor adapted for their needs, so wasteful of labour and so devoid of beauty as this was, and it is only now as I describe this that I find myself thinking of the essential absurdity of an intelligent community living in such makeshift homes. It strikes me now as the next thing to wearing second-hand clothes.

You see it was a natural growth, part of that system to which Bladesover, I hold, is the key. There are wide regions of London, miles of streets of houses, that appear to have been originally designed for prosperous middle-class homes of the early Victorian type. There must have been a perfect fury of such building in the thirties, forties, and fifties. Street after street must have been rushed into being, Campden Town way, Pentonville way, Brompton way, West Kensington way in the Victoria region and all over the minor suburbs of the south side. I am doubtful if many of these houses had any long use as the residences of single families, if from the very first almost their tenants did not makeshift and take lodgers and sublet. They were built with basements, in which their servants worked and lived— servants of a more submissive and troglodytic generation who did not mind stairs. The dining-room (with folding doors) was a little above the ground level, and in that the wholesome boiled and roast with damp boiled potatoes and then pie to follow, was consumed, and the numerous family

[86]

read and worked in the evening, and above was the drawing-room (also with folding doors), where the infrequent callers were received. That was the vision at which those industrious builders aimed. Even while these houses were being run up, the threads upon the loom of fate were shaping to abolish altogether the type of household that would have fitted them. Means of transit were developing to carry the moderately prosperous middle-class families out of London, education and factory employment were whittling away at the supply of rough, hardworking, obedient girls who would stand the subterranean drudgery of these places, new classes of hard-up middle-class people such as my uncle, employees of various types, were coming into existence, for whom no homes were provided. None of these classes have ideas of what they ought to be, or fit in any legitimate way into the Bladesover theory that dominates our minds. It was nobody's concern to see them housed under civilised conditions, and the beautiful laws of supply and demand had free play. They had to squeeze in. The landlords came out financially intact from their blundering enterprise. More and more these houses fell into the hands of married artisans, or struggling widows or old servants with savings, who became responsible for the quarterly rent and tried to sweat a living by sub-letting furnished or unfurnished apartments.

I remember now that a poor grey-haired old woman who had an air of having been roused from a nap in the dust bin, came out into the area and looked up at us as we three went out from the front door to "see London" under my uncle's direction. She was the sub-letting occupier; she squeezed out a precarious living by taking the house whole and sub-letting it in detail, and she made her food and got the shelter of an attic above and a basement below by the transaction. And if she didn't chance to "let" steadily, out she went to pauperdom and some other poor, sordid old adventurer tried in her place. . . .

It is a foolish community that can house whole classes, useful and helpful, honest and loyal classes, in such squal·

idly unsuitable dwellings. It is by no means the social economy it seems, to use up old women's savings and inexperience in order to meet the landlord's demands. But any one who doubts this thing is going on right up to to-day need only spend an afternoon in hunting for lodgings in any of the regions of London I have named.

But where has my story got to? My uncle, I say, decided I must be shown London, and out we three went as soon as my aunt had got her hat on, to catch all that was left of the day.

VI

It pleased my uncle extremely to find I had never seen London before. He took possession of the metropolis forthwith. "London, George," he said, "takes a lot of understanding. It's a great place. Immense. The richest town in the world, the biggest port, the greatest manufacturing town, the Imperial city—the centre of civilisation, the heart of the world! See those sandwich men down there! That third one's hat! Fair treat! You don't see poverty like that in Wimblehurst, George! And many of them high Oxford honour men too. Brought down by drink! It's a wonderful place, George—a whirlpool, a maelstrom! whirls you up and whirls you down."

I have a very confused memory of that afternoon's inspection of London. My uncle took us to and fro showing us over his London, talking erratically, following a route of his own. Sometimes we were walking, sometimes we were on the tops of great staggering horse omnibuses in a heaving jumble of traffic, and at one point we had tea in an Aerated Bread Shop. But I remember very distinctly how we passed down Park Lane under an overcast sky, and how my uncle pointed out the house of this child of good fortune and that with succulent appreciation.

I remember, too, that as he talked I would find my aunt watching my face as if to check the soundness of his talk by my expression.

"Been in love yet, George?" she asked suddenly, over a bun in the tea-shop.

[88]

"Too busy, aunt," I told her.

She bit her bun extensively, and gesticulated with the remnant to indicate that she had more to say.

"How are *you* going to make your fortune?" she said so soon as she could speak again. "You haven't told us that."

" 'Lectricity," said my uncle, taking breath after a deep draught of tea.

"If I make it at all," I said. "For my part I think I shall be satisfied with something less than a fortune."

"We're going to make ours—suddenly," she said. "So *he* old says." She jerked her head at my uncle. "He won't tell me when—so I can't get anything ready. But it's coming. Going to ride in our carriage and have a garden. Garden—like a bishop's."

She finished her bun and twiddled crumbs from her fingers. "I shall be glad of the garden," she said. "It's going to be a real big one with rosaries and things. Fountains in it. Pampas grass. Hothouses."

"You'll get it all right," said my uncle, who had reddened a little.

"Grey horses in the carriage, George," she said. "It's nice to think about when one's dull. And dinners in restaurants often and often. And theatres—in the stalls. And money and money and money."

"You may joke," said my uncle, and hummed for a moment.

"Just as though an old Porpoise like him would ever make money," she said, turning her eyes upon his profile with a sudden lapse to affection. "He'll just porpoise about."

"I'll do something," said my uncle, "you bet! Zzzz!" and rapped with a shilling on the marble table.

"When you do you'll have to buy me a new pair of gloves," she said, "anyhow. That finger's past mending. Look! you Cabbage—you." And she held the split under his nose, and pulled a face of comical fierceness.

My uncle smiled at these sallies at the time, but afterwards, when I went back with him to the Pharmacy—the low-class business grew brisker in the evening and they kept open late—he reverted to it in a low expository tone. "Your aunt's a bit impatient, George. She gets at me. It's only natural. . . . A woman doesn't understand how long it takes to build up a position. No. . . . In certain directions now—I am—quietly—building up a position. Now here. . . . I get this room. I have my three assistants. Zzzz. It's a position that, judged by the criterion of immeedjit income, isn't perhaps so good as I deserve, but strategically —yes. It's what I want. I make my plans. I rally my attack."

"What plans," I said, "are you making?"

"Well, George, there's one thing you can rely upon. I'm doing nothing in a hurry. I turn over this idea and that, and I don't talk—indiscreetly. There's—— No! I don't think I can tell you that. And yet, why *not?*"

He got up and closed the door into the shop. "I've told no one," he remarked, as he sat down again. "I owe you something."

His face flushed slightly, he leant forward over the little table towards me.

"Listen!" he said.

I listened.

"Tono-Bungay," said my uncle very slowly and distinctly.

I thought he was asking me to hear some remote, strange noise. "I don't hear anything," I said reluctantly to his expectant face.

He smiled undefeated. "Try again," he said, and repeated, "Tono-Bungay."

"Oh, *that!*" I said.

"Eh?" said he.

"But what is it?"

"Ah!" said my uncle, rejoicing and expanding. "What *is* it? That's what you got to ask? What *won't* it be?" He dug me violently in what he supposed to be my ribs. "George," he cried—"George, watch this place! There's more to follow."

And that was all I could get from him.

That, I believe, was the very first time that the words

Tono-Bungay were heard on earth—unless my uncle indulged in monologues in his chamber—a highly probable thing. Its utterance certainly did not seem to me at the time to mark any sort of epoch, and had I been told this word was the Open Sesame to whatever pride and pleasure the grimy front of London hid from us that evening, I should have laughed aloud.

"Coming now to business," I said after a pause, and with a chill sense of effort; and I opened the question of his trust.

My uncle sighed, and leant back in his chair. "I wish I could make all this business as clear to you as it is to me," he said. "However—— Go on! Say what you have to say."

VII

After I left my uncle that evening I gave way to a feeling of profound depression. My uncle and aunt seemed to me to be leading—I have already used the word too often, but I must use it again—*dingy* lives. They seemed to be adrift in a limitless crowd of dingy people, wearing shabby clothes, living uncomfortably in shabby second-hand houses, going to and fro on pavements that had always a thin veneer of greasy, slippery mud, under grey skies that showed no gleam of hope of anything for them but dinginess until they died. It seemed absolutely clear to me that my mother's little savings had been swallowed up and that my own prospect was all too certainly to drop into and be swallowed up myself sooner or later by this dingy London ocean. The London that was to be an adventurous escape from the slumber of Wimblehurst, had vanished from my dreams. I saw my uncle pointing to the houses in Park Lane and showing a frayed shirt-cuff as he did so. I heard my aunt: "I'm to ride in my carriage then. So he old says."

My feelings towards my uncle were extraordinarily mixed. I was intensely sorry not only for my aunt Susan but for him—for it seemed indisputable that as they were living then so they must go on—and at the same time I was angry with the garrulous vanity and silliness that had clipped all my chance of independent study, and imprisoned her in those grey apartments. When I got back to Wimblehurst I allowed myself to write him a boyishly sarcastic and sincerely bitter letter. He never replied. Then, believing it to be the only way of escape for me, I set myself far more grimly and resolutely to my studies than I had ever done before. After a time I wrote to him in more moderate terms, and he answered me evasively. And then I tried to dismiss him from my mind and went on working.

Yes, that first raid upon London under the moist and chilly depression of January had an immense effect upon me. It was for me an epoch-making disappointment. I had thought of London as a large, free, welcoming, adventurous place, and I saw it slovenly and harsh and irresponsive.

I did not realise at all what human things might be found behind those grey frontages, what weakness that whole forbidding façade might presently confess. It is the constant error of youth to over-estimate the Will in things. I did not see that the dirt, the discouragement, the discomfort of London could be due simply to the fact that London was a witless old giantess of a town, too slack and stupid to keep herself clean and maintain a brave face to the world. No! I suffered from the sort of illusion that burnt witches in the seventeenth century. I endued her grubby disorder with a sinister and magnificent quality of intention.

And my uncle's gestures and promises filled me with doubt and a sort of fear for him. He seemed to me a lost little creature, too silly to be silent, in a vast implacable condemnation. I was full of pity and a sort of tenderness for my aunt Susan, who was doomed to follow his erratic fortunes mocked by his grandiloquent promises.

I was to learn better. But I worked with the terror of the grim underside of London in my soul during all my last year at Wimblehurst.

BOOK THE SECOND

THE RISE OF TONO-BUNGAY

CHAPTER THE FIRST

How I Became a London Student and Went Astray

I

I CAME to live in London, as I shall tell you, when I was nearly twenty-two. Wimblehurst dwindles in perspective, is now in this book a little place far off, Bladesover no more than a small pinkish speck of frontage among the distant Kentish hills; the scene broadens out, becomes multitudinous and limitless, full of the sense of vast irrelevant movement. I do not remember my second coming to London as I do my first, nor my early impressions, save that an October memory of softened amber sunshine stands out, amber sunshine falling on grey house fronts, I know not where. That, and a sense of a large tranquillity. . . .

I could fill a book, I think, with a more or less imaginary account of how I came to apprehend London, how first in one aspect and then in another it grew in my mind. Each day my accumulating impressions were added to and qualified and brought into relationship with new ones; they fused inseparably with others that were purely personal and accidental. I find myself with a certain comprehensive perception of London, complex indeed, incurably indistinct in places and yet in some way a whole that began with my first visit and is still being mellowed and enriched.

London!

At first, no doubt, it was a chaos of streets and people and buildings and reasonless going to and fro. I do not remember that I ever struggled very steadily to understand it, or explored it with any but a personal and adventurous intention. Yet in time there has grown up in me a kind of theory of London; I do think I see lines of an ordered structure out of which it has grown, detected a process that is something more than a confusion of casual accidents, though indeed it may be no more than a process of disease.

I said at the outset of my first book that I find in Bladesover the clue to all England. Well, I certainly imagine it is the clue to the structure of London. There have been no revolutions, no deliberate restatements or abandonments of opinion in England since the days of the fine gentry, since 1688 or thereabouts, the days when Bladesover was built; there have been changes, dissolving forces, replacing forces, if you will; but then it was that the broad lines of the English system set firmly. And as I have gone to and fro in London, in certain regions constantly the thought has recurred, this is Bladesover House, this answers to Bladesover House. The fine gentry may have gone; they have indeed largely gone, I think; rich merchants may have replaced them, financial adventurers or what not. That does not matter; the shape is still Bladesover.

I am most reminded of Bladesover and Eastry by all those regions round about the West End parks, for example, estate parks, each more or less in relation to a palace or group of great houses. The roads and back ways of Mayfair and all about St. James's again, albeit perhaps of a later growth in point of time, were of the very spirit and architectural texture of the Bladesover passages and yards; they had the same smells, the space, the large cleanness, and always going to and fro there one met unmistakable Olympians, and even more unmistakable valets, butlers, footmen in mufti. There were moments when I seemed to glimpse down areas the white panelling, the very chintz of my mother's room again.

I could trace out now on a map what I would call the Great-House region; passing south-westward into Belgravia, becoming diffused and sporadic westward, finding its last systematic outbreak round and about Regent's Park. The Duke of Devonshire's place in Piccadilly, in all its insolent ugliness, pleases me particularly; it is the quintessence of the thing; Apsley House is all in the manner of my theory, Park Lane has its quite typical mansions, and they run along the border of the Green Park and St. James's. And I struck out a truth one day in Cromwell Road quite suddenly, as I looked over the Natural History Museum: "By Jove," said I, "but this is the little assemblage of cases of stuffed birds and animals upon the Bladesover staircase grown enormous, and yonder as the corresponding thing to the Bladesover curios and porcelain is the Art Museum, and there in the little observatories in Exhibition Road is old Sir Cuthbert's Gregorian telescope that I hunted out in the storeroom and put together." And diving into the Art Museum under this inspiration, I came to a little reading-room and found, as I had inferred, old brown books!

It was really a good piece of social comparative anatomy I did that day; all these museums and libraries that are dotted over London between Piccadilly and West Kensington, and indeed the museum and library movement throughout the world, sprang from the elegant leisure of the gentlemen of taste. Theirs were the first libraries, the first houses of culture; by my ratlike raids into the Bladesover saloon I became, as it were, the last dwindled representative of such a man of letters as Swift. But now these things have escaped out of the Great House altogether, and taken on a strange independent life of their own.

It is this idea of escaping parts from the seventeenth century system of Bladesover, of proliferating and over-growing elements from the Estates, that to this day seems to me the best explanation, not simply of London, but of all England. England is a country of great Renascence landed gentlefolk who have been unconsciously outgrown and overgrown. The proper shops for Bladesover custom were still to be found in Regent Street and Bond Street in my early London days—in those days they had been but lightly touched by the American's profaning hand—and in Piccadilly. I found the doctor's house of the country village or country town up and down Harley Street, multiplied but not otherwise different, and the family solicitor (by the hundred) further eastward in the abandoned houses of a previous generation of gentlepeople, and down in Westminster, behind Palladian fronts, the public offices sheltered in large Bladesoverish rooms and looked out on St. James's Park. The Parliament Houses of lords and gentlemen, the parliament house that was horrified when merchants and brewers came thrusting into it a hundred years ago, stood out upon its terrace gathering the whole system together into a head.

And the more I have parallelled these things with my Bladesover-Eastry model, the more evident it has become to me that the balance is not the same, and the more evident is the presence of great new forces, blind forces of invasion, of growth. The railway termini on the north side of London have been kept as remote as Eastry had kept the railway-station from Wimblehurst; they stop on the very outskirts of the estates, but from the south, the South Eastern railway had butted its great stupid rusty iron head of Charing Cross station—that great head that came smashing down in 1905—clean across the river, between Somerset House and Whitehall. The south side had no protecting estates. Factory chimneys smoke right over against Westminster with an air of carelessly not having permission, and the whole effect of industrial London and of all London east of Temple Bar and of the huge dingy immensity of London port, is to me of something disproportionately large, something morbidly expanded, without plan or intention, dark and sinister toward the clean clear social assurance of the West End. And south of this central London, south-east, south-west, far west, north-west, all round the northern hills, are similar disproportionate growths, endless streets of undistinguished houses, undistinguished industries, shabby families, second-rate shops, inexplicable people who in a once fashionable phrase do not "exist." All these aspects have suggested to my mind at times, do suggest to this day, the unorganised, abundant substance of some tumorous growth-process, a process which indeed bursts all the outlines of the affected carcass and protrudes such masses as ignoble comfortable Croydon, as tragic impoverished West Ham. To this day I ask myself will those masses ever become structural, will they indeed shape into anything new whatever, or is that cancerous image their true and ultimate diagnosis? . . .

Moreover, together with this hypertrophy there is an immigration of elements that have never understood and never will understand the great tradition, wedges of foreign settlement embedded in the heart of this yeasty English expansion. One day I remember wandering eastward out of pure curiosity—it must have been in my early student days —and discovering a shabbily bright foreign quarter, shops displaying Hebrew placards and weird, unfamiliar commodities, and a concourse of bright-eyed, eagle-nosed people talking some incomprehensible gibberish between the shops and the barrows. And soon I became quite familiar with the devious, vicious, dirtily-pleasant exoticism of Soho. I found those crowded streets a vast relief from the dull grey exterior of Brompton where I lodged and lived my daily life. In Soho, indeed, I got my first inkling of the factor of replacement that is so important in both the English and the American process.

Even in the West End, in Mayfair and the squares about Pall Mall, Ewart was presently to remind me the face of the old aristocratic dignity was fairer than its substance; here were actors and actresses, here moneylenders and Jews, here bold financial adventurers, and I thought of my uncle's frayed cuff as he pointed out this house in Park Lane and that. That was so and so's who made a corner in borax, and that palace belonged to that hero among modern adventurers, Barmentrude, who used to be an I.D.B.,—an illicit diamond buyer that is to say. A city of Bladesovers, the capital of a kingdom of Bladesovers, all much shaken and many altogether in decay, parasitically occupied, insiduously replaced by alien, unsympathetic and irresponsible elements;—and withal ruling an adventitious and miscellaneous empire of a quarter of this dædal earth. Complex laws, intricate social necessities, disturbing insatiable suggestions, followed from this. Such was the world into which I had come, into which I had in some way to thrust myself and fit my problem, my temptations, my efforts, my patriotic instinct, all my moral instincts, my physical appetites, my dreams and my vanity.

London! I came up to it, young and without advisers, rather priggish, rather dangerously open-minded and very open-eyed, and with something—it is, I think, the common gift of imaginative youth, and I claim it unblushingly—fine in me, finer than the world and seeking fine responses. I did not want simply to live or simply to live happily or well; I wanted to serve and do and make—with some nobility. It was in me. It is in half the youth of the world.

II

I had come to London as a scholar. I had taken the Vincent Bradley scholarship of the Pharmaceutical Society, but I threw this up when I found that my work of the Science and Art Department in mathematics, physics and chemistry had given me one of the minor Technical Board Scholarships at the Consolidated Technical Schools at South Kensington. This latter was in mechanics and metallurgy; and I hesitated between the two. The Vincent Bradley gave me £70 a year and quite the best start-off a pharmaceutical chemist could have; the South Kensington thing was worth about twenty-two shillings a week, and the prospects it opened were vague. But it meant far more scientific work than the former, and I was still under the impulse of that great intellectual appetite that is part of the adolescence of men of my type. Moreover, it seemed to lead towards engineering, in which I imagined—I imagine to this day— my particular use is to be found. I took its greater uncertainty as a fair risk. I came up very keen, not doubting that the really hard and steady industry that had carried me through Wimblehurst would go on still in the new surroundings.

Only from the very first it didn't. . . .

When I look back now at my Wimblehurst days, I still

find myself surprised at the amount of steady grinding study, of strenuous self-discipline that I maintained through-out my apprenticeship. In many ways I think that time was the most honourable period in my life. I wish I could say with a certain mind that my motives in working so well were large and honourable too. To a certain extent they were so; there was a fine sincere curiosity, a desire for the strength and power of scientific knowledge and a passion for intellectual exercise; but I do not think those forces alone would have kept me at it so grimly and closely if Wimblehurst had not been so dull, so limited and so ob-servant. Directly I came into the London atmosphere, tast-ing freedom, tasting irresponsibility and the pull of new forces altogether, my discipline fell from me like a garment. Wimblehurst to a youngster in my position offered no temp-tations worth counting, no interests to conflict with study, no vices—such vices as it offered were coarsely stripped of any imaginative glamour—dull drunkenness, clumsy leering shameful lust, no social intercourse even to waste one's time, and on the other hand it would minister greatly to the self-esteem of a conspicuously industrious student. One was marked as "clever," one played up to the part, and one's little accomplishment stood out finely in one's private reckoning against the sunlit small ignorance of that agree-able place. One went with an intent rush across the market square, one took one's exercise with as dramatic a sense of an ordered day as an Oxford don, one burnt the midnight oil quite consciously at the rare, respectful, benighted passer-by. And one stood out finely in the local paper with one's unapproachable yearly harvest of certificates. Thus I was not only a genuinely keen student, but also a little of a prig and poseur in those days—and the latter kept the former at it, as London made clear. Moreover, Wimblehurst had given me no outlet in any other direction.

But I did not realise all this when I came to London, did not perceive how the change of atmosphere began at once to warp and distribute my energies. In the first place I became invisible. If I idled for a day, no one except my fellow-students (who evidently had no awe for me) remarked it. No one saw my midnight taper; no one pointed me out as I crossed the street as an astonishing intellectual phenomenon. In the next place I became inconsiderable. In Wimblehurst I felt I stood for Science; nobody there seemed to have so much as I and to have it so fully and completely. In London I walked ignorant in an immensity, and it was clear that among my fellow-students from the midlands and the north I was ill-equipped and under-trained. With the utmost exertion I should only take a secondary position among them. And finally, in the third place, I was distracted by voluminous new interests; London took hold of me, and Science, which had been the universe, shrank back to the dimensions of tiresome little formulæ compacted in a book. I came to London in late September, and it was a very different London from that great greyly-overcast, smoke-stained house-wilderness of my first impressions. I reached it by Victoria and not by Cannon Street, and its centre was now in Exhibition Road. It shone, pale amber, blue-grey and tenderly spacious and fine under clear autumnal skies, a London of hugely handsome buildings and vistas and distances, a London of gardens and labyrinthine tall museums, of old trees and remote palaces and artificial waters. I lodged near by in West Brompton at a house in a little square.

So London faced me the second time, making me forget altogether for a while the grey, drizzling city visage that had first looked upon me. I settled down and went to and fro to my lectures and laboratory; in the beginning I worked hard, and only slowly did the curiosity that presently possessed me to know more of this huge urban province arise, the desire to find something beyond mechanism that I could serve, some use other than learning. With this was a growing sense of loneliness, a desire for adventure and intercourse. I found myself in the evenings poring over a map of London I had bought, instead of copying out lecture notes—and on Sundays I made explorations, taking omnibus rides east and west and north and south, and so enlarging and broadening the sense of great swarming hinterlands of humanity with whom I had no dealings, of whom I knew nothing. . . .

The whole illimitable place teemed with suggestions of indefinite and sometimes outrageous possibility, of hidden but magnificent meanings.

It wasn't simply that I received a vast impression of space and multitude and opportunity; intimate things also were suddenly dragged from neglected, veiled and darkened corners into an acute vividness of perception. Close at hand in the big art museum I came for the first time upon the beauty of nudity, which I had hitherto held to be a shameful secret, flaunted and gloried in; I was made aware of beauty as not only permissible, but desirable and frequent, and of a thousand hitherto unsuspected rich aspects of life. One night in a real rapture, I walked round the upper gallery of the Albert Hall and listened for the first time to great music; I believe now that it was a rendering of Beethoven's Ninth Symphony. . . .

My apprehension of spaces and places was reinforced by a quickened apprehension of persons. A constant stream of people passed by me, eyes met and challenged mine and passed—more and more I wanted them to stay—if I went eastward towards Piccadilly, women who seemed then to my boyish inexperience softly splendid and alluring, murmured to me as they passed. Extraordinarily life unveiled. The very hoardings clamoured strangely at one's senses and curiosities. One bought pamphlets and papers full of strange and daring ideas transcending one's boldest; in the parks one heard men discussing the very existence of God, denying the rights of property, debating a hundred things that one dared not think about in Wimblehurst. And after the ordinary overcast day, after dull mornings, came twilight, and London lit up and became a thing of white and yellow and red jewels of light and wonderful floods of golden illumination and stupendous and unfathomable shadows— and there were no longer any mean or shabby people—but a great mysterious movement of unaccountable beings. . . .

Always I was coming on the queerest new aspects. Late one Saturday night I found myself one of a great slow-moving crowd between the blazing shops and the flaring barrows in the Harrow Road; I got into conversation with two bold-eyed girls, bought them boxes of chocolate, made the acquaintance of father and mother and various younger brothers and sisters, sat in a public-house hilariously with them all, standing and being stood drinks, and left them in the small hours at the door of "home," never to see them again. And once I was accosted on the outskirts of a Salvation Army meeting in one of the parks by a silk-hatted young man of eager and serious discourse, who argued against scepticism with me, invited me home to tea into a clean and cheerful family of brothers and sisters and friends, and there I spent the evening singing hymns to the harmonium (which reminded me of half-forgotten Chatham) and wishing all the sisters were not so obviously engaged. . . .

Then on the remote hill of this boundless city-world, I found Ewart.

III

How well I remember the first morning, a bright Sunday morning in early October, when I raided in upon Ewart! I found my old schoolfellow in bed in a room over an oil-shop in a back street at the foot of Highgate Hill. His land-lady, a pleasant, dirty young woman with soft brown eyes, brought down his message for me to come up; and up I went. The room presented itself as ample and interesting in detail and shabby with a quite commendable shabbiness. I had an impression of brown walls—they were papered with brown paper—of a long shelf along one side of the room, with dusty plaster casts and a small cheap lay figure of a horse, of a table and something of grey wax partially covered with a cloth, and of scattered drawings. There was a gas stove in one corner, and some enamelled ware that had been used for overnight cooking. The oilcloth on the floor was streaked with a peculiar white dust. Ewart himself was not in the first instance visible, but only a fourfold canvas screen at the end of the room from which shouts proceeded of "Come on!" then his wiry black hair, very much rumpled, and a staring red-brown eye and his stump of a nose came round the edge of this at a height of about three feet from the ground. "It's old Ponderevo!" he said, "the Early Bird! And he's caught the worm! By Jove, but it's cold this morning! Come round here and sit on the bed!"

I walked round, wrung his hand, and we surveyed one another.

He was lying on a small wooden fold-up bed, the scanty covering of which was supplemented by an overcoat and an elderly but still cheerful pair of check trousers, and he was wearing pyjamas of a virulent pink and green. His neck seemed longer and more stringy than it had been even in our schooldays, and his upper lip had a wiry black moustache. The rest of his ruddy, knobby countenance, his erratic hair and his general hairy leanness had not even—to my perceptions—grown.

"By Jove!" he said, "you've got quite decent-looking, Ponderevo! What do you think of me?"

"You're all right. What are you doing here?"

"Art, my son—sculpture! And incidentally——" He hesitated. "I ply a trade. Will you hand me that pipe and those smoking things? So! You can't make coffee, eh? Well, try your hand. Cast down this screen—no—fold it up and so we'll go into the other room. I'll keep in bed all the same. The fire's a gas stove. Yes. Don't make it bang too loud as you light it—I can't stand it this morning. You won't smoke? . . . Well, it does me good to see you again, Ponderevo. Tell me what you're doing, and how you're getting on."

He directed me in the service of his simple hospitality, and presently I came back to his bed and sat down and smiled at him there, smoking comfortably, with his hands under his head, surveying me.

"How's Life's Morning, Ponderevo? By Jove, it must be nearly six years since we met! We've got moustaches. We've fleshed ourselves a bit, eh? And you——?"

I felt a pipe was becoming after all, and that lit, I gave him a favourable sketch of my career.

"Science! And you've worked like that! While I've been potting round doing odd jobs for stone-masons and people, and trying to get to sculpture. I've a sort of feeling that the chisel—— I began with painting, Ponderevo, and found I was colour-blind, colour-blind enough to stop it. I've drawn about and thought about—thought more particularly. I give myself three days a week as an art student, and the rest of the time—I've a sort of trade that keeps me. And we're still in the beginning of things, young men starting. Do you remember the old times at Goudhurst, our doll's-house island, the Retreat of the Ten Thousand, Young Holmes and the rabbits, eh? It's surprising, if you think of it, to find we are still young. And we used to talk of what we would be, and we used to talk of love! I suppose you know all about that now, Ponderevo?"

I flushed and hesitated on some vague foolish lie. "No," I said, a little ashamed of the truth. "Do you? I've been too busy."

"I'm just beginning—just as we were then. Things happen——"

He sucked at his pipe for a space and stared at the plaster cast of a flayed hand that hung on the wall.

"The fact is, Ponderevo, I'm beginning to find life a most extraordinary queer set-out; the things that pull one, the things that don't. The wants—— This business of sex. It's a net. No end to it, no way out of it, no sense in it. There are times when women take possession of me, when my mind is like a painted ceiling at Hampton Court with the pride of the flesh sprawling all over it. *Why?* . . . And then again sometimes when I have to encounter a woman, I am overwhelmed by a terror of tantalising boredom—I fly, I hide, I do anything. You've got your scientific explanations perhaps; what's Nature and the universe up to in that matter?"

"It's her way, I gather, of securing the continuity of the species."

[106]

'But it doesn't," said Ewart. "That's just it! No. I have succumbed to—dissipation—down the hill there. Euston Road way. And it was damned ugly and mean, and I hate having done it. And the continuity of the species—Lord! . . . And why does Nature make a man so infernally ready for drinks? There's no sense in that anyhow." He sat up in bed, to put this question with the greater earnestness. "And why has she given me a most violent desire towards sculpture and an equally violent desire to leave off work directly I begin it, eh? . . . Let's have some more coffee. I put it to you, these things puzzle me, Ponderevo. They dishearten me. They keep me in bed."

He had an air of having saved up these difficulties for me for some time. He sat with his chin almost touching his knees, sucking at his pipe.

"That's what I mean," he went on, "when I say life is getting on to me as extraordinarily queer. I don't see my game, nor why I was invited. And I don't make anything of the world outside either. What do *you* make of it?"

"London," I began. "It's—so enormous!"

"Isn't it! And it's all up to nothing. You find chaps keeping grocers' shops—why the *devil*, Ponderevo, do they keep grocers' shops? They all do it very carefully, very steadily, very meanly. You find people running about and doing the most remarkable things—being policemen, for example, and burglars. They go about these businesses quite gravely and earnestly. I—somehow—can't go about mine. Is there any sense in it at all—anywhere?"

"There must be sense in it," I said. "We're young."

"We're young—yes. But one must inquire. The grocer's a grocer because, I suppose, he sees he comes in there. Feels that on the whole it amounts to a call. . . . But the bother is I don't see where I come in at all. Do you?"

"Where *you* come in?"

"No, where *you* come in."

"Not exactly, yet," I said. "I want to do some good in the world—something—something effectual, before I die. I have a sort of idea my scientific work—— I don't know."

"Yes," he mused. "And I've got a sort of idea my sculpture,—but *how* it is to come in and *why*,—I've no idea at all." He hugged his knees for a space. "That's what puzzles me, Ponderevo, no end."

He became animated. "If you will look in that cupboard," he said, "you will find an old respectable-looking roll on a plate and a knife somewhere and a gallipot containing butter. You give them me and I'll make my breakfast, and then if you don't mind watching me paddle about at my simple toilet I'll get up. Then we'll go for a walk and talk about this affair of life further. And about Art and Literature and anything else that crops up on the way. . . . Yes, that's the gallipot. Cockroach got in it? Chuck him out—damned interloper. . . ."

So in the first five minutes of our talk, as I seem to remember it now, old Ewart struck the note that ran through all that morning's intercourse. . . .

To me it was a most memorable talk because it opened out quite new horizons of thought. I'd been working rather close and out of touch with Ewart's free gesticulating way. He was pessimistic that day and sceptical to the very root of things. He made me feel clearly, what I had not felt at all before, the general adventurousness of life, particularly of life at the stage we had reached, and also the absence of definite objects, of any concerted purpose in the lives that were going on all round us. He made me feel, too, how ready I was to take up commonplace assumptions. Just as I had always imagined that somewhere in social arrangements there was certainly a Head-Master who would intervene if one went too far, so I had always had a sort of implicit belief that in our England there were somewhere people who understood what we were all, as a nation, about. That crumpled into his pit of doubt and vanished. He brought out, sharply cut and certain, the immense effect of purposelessness in London that I was already indistinctly feeling. We found ourselves at last returning through Highgate Cemetery and Waterlow Park—and Ewart was talking.

"Look at it there," he said, stopping and pointing to the

great vale of London spreading wide and far. "It's like a sea—and we swim in it. And at last down we go, and then up we come—washed up here." He swung his arms to the long slopes about us, tombs and headstones in long perspectives, in limitless rows.

"We're young, Ponderevo, but sooner or later our whitened memories will wash up on one of these beaches, on some such beach as this. George Ponderevo, F.R.S., Sidney Ewart, R.I.P. Look at the rows of 'em!"

He paused. "Do you see that hand? The hand, I mean, pointing upward, on the top of a blunted obelisk. Yes. Well, that's what I do for a living—when I'm not thinking, or drinking, or prowling, or making love, or pretending I'm trying to be a sculptor without either the money or the morals for a model. See? And I do those hearts afire and those pensive angel guardians with the palm of peace. Damned well I do 'em and damned cheap! I'm a sweated victim, Ponderevo . . ."

That was the way of it, anyhow. I drank deep of talk that day; we went into theology, into philosophy; I had my first glimpse of socialism. I felt as though I had been silent in a silence since I and he had parted. At the thought of socialism Ewart's moods changed for a time to a sort of energy. "After all, all this confounded vagueness *might* be altered. If you could get men to work together . . ."

It was a good talk that rambled through all the universe. I thought I was giving my mind refreshment, but indeed it was dissipation. All sorts of ideas, even now, carry me back as it were to a fountain-head, to Waterlow Park and my resuscitated Ewart. There stretches away south of us long garden slopes and white gravestones and the wide expanse of London, and somewhere in the picture is a red old wall, sun-warmed, and a great blaze of Michaelmas daisies set off with late golden sunflowers and a drift of mottled, blood-red, fallen leaves. It was with me that day as though I had lifted my head suddenly out of dull and immediate things and looked at life altogether. . . . But it played the very devil with the copying up of my arrears of notes to which I had vowed the latter half of that day.

After that reunion Ewart and I met much and talked much, and in our subsequent encounters his monologue was interrupted and I took my share. He had exercised me so greatly that I lay awake at nights thinking him over, and discoursed and answered him in my head as I went in the morning to the College. I am by nature a doer and only by the way a critic; his philosophical assertion of the incalculable vagueness of life which fitted his natural indolence roused my more irritable and energetic nature to active protests. "It's all so pointless," I said, "because people are slack and because it's in the ebb of an age. But you're a socialist. Well, let's bring that about! And there's a purpose. There you are!"

Ewart gave me all my first conceptions of socialism; in a little while I was an enthusiastic socialist and he was a passive resister to the practical exposition of the theories he had taught me. "We must join some organisation," I said. "We ought to do things. . . . We ought to go and speak at street corners. People don't know."

You must figure me a rather ill-dressed young man in a state of great earnestness, standing up in that shabby studio of his and saying these things, perhaps with some gesticulations, and Ewart with a clay-smudged face, dressed perhaps in a flannel shirt and trousers, with a pipe in his mouth, squatting philosophically at a table, working at some chunk of clay that never got beyond suggestion.

"I wonder why one doesn't want to," he said. . . .

It was only very slowly I came to gauge Ewart's real position in the scheme of things, to understand how deliberate and complete was this detachment of his from the moral condemnation and responsibilities that played so fine a part in his talk. His was essentially the nature of an artistic appreciator; he could find interest and beauty in endless aspects of things that I marked as evil, or at least as not negotiable; and the impulse I had towards self-deception, to sustained and consistent self-devotion, disturbed and detached and pointless as it was at that time, he had indeed a sort of admiration for but no sympathy. Like many fantastic and ample talkers he was at bottom secretive, and he gave me a series of little shocks of discovery throughout our intercourse. The first of these came in the realisation that he quite seriously meant to do nothing in the world at all towards reforming the evils he laid bare in so easy and dexterous a manner. The next came in the sudden appearance of a person called "Milly"—I've forgotten her surname—whom I found in his room one evening, simply attired in a blue wrap—the rest of her costume behind the screen—smoking cigarettes and sharing a flagon of an amazingly cheap and self-assertive grocer's wine Ewart affected, called "Canary Sack." "Hullo!" said Ewart, as I came in. "This is Milly, you know. She's been being a model—she *is* a model really. . . . (Keep calm, Ponderevo!) Have some sack?"

Milly was a woman of thirty, perhaps, with a broad, rather pretty face, a placid disposition, a bad accent and delightful blond hair that waved off her head with an irrepressible variety of charm; and whenever Ewart spoke she beamed at him. Ewart was always sketching this hair of hers and embarking upon clay statuettes of her that were never finished. She was, I know now, a woman of the streets, whom Ewart had picked up in the most casual manner, and who had fallen in love with him, but my inexperience in those days was too great for me to place her then, and Ewart offered no elucidations. She came to him, he went to her, they took holidays together in the country when certainly she sustained her fair share of their expenditure. I suspect him now even of taking money from her. Odd old Ewart! It was a relationship so alien to my orderly conceptions of honour, to what I could imagine any friend of mine doing, that I really hardly saw it with it there under my nose. But I see it and I think I understand it now. . . .

Before I fully grasped the discursive manner in which Ewart was committed to his particular way in life, I did, I say, as the broad constructive ideas of socialism took hold of me, try to get him to work with me in some definite fashion as a socialist.

"We ought to join on to other socialists," I said. "They've got something."

"Let's go and look at some first."

After some pains we discovered the office of the Fabian Society, lurking in a cellar in Clement's Inn; and we went and interviewed a rather discouraging secretary who stood astraddle in front of a fire and questioned us severely and seemed to doubt the integrity of our intentions profoundly. He advised us to attend the next open meeting in Clifford's Inn and gave us the necessary data. We both contrived to get to the affair, and heard a discursive gritty paper on Trusts and one of the most inconclusive discussions you can imagine. Three-quarters of the speakers seemed under some jocular obsession which took the form of pretending to be conceited. It was a sort of family joke, and as strangers to the family we did not like it. . . . As we came out through the narrow passage from Clifford's Inn to the Strand, Ewart suddenly pitched upon a wizened, spectacled little man in a vast felt hat and a large orange tie.

"How many members are there in this Fabian Society of yours?" he asked.

The little man became at once defensive in his manner.

"About seven hundred," he said; "perhaps eight."

"Like—like the ones here?"

The little man gave a nervous self-satisfied laugh. "I suppose they're up to sample," he said.

The little man dropped out of existence and we emerged upon the Strand. Ewart twisted his arm into a queerly eloquent gesture that gathered up all the tall façades of the banks, the business places, the projecting clock and towers of the Law Courts, the advertisements, the luminous signs, into one social immensity, into a capitalistic system gigantic and invincible.

"These socialists have no sense of proportion," he said. "What can you expect of them?"

[112]

Ewart, as the embodiment of talk, was certainly a leading factor in my conspicuous failure to go on studying. Social theory in its first crude form of Democratic Socialism gripped my intelligence more and more powerfully. I argued in the laboratory with the man who shared my bench until we quarrelled and did not speak. And also I fell in love.

The ferment of sex had been creeping into my being like a slowly advancing tide through all my Wimblehurst days, the stimulus of London was like the rising of a wind out of the sea that brings the waves in fast and high. Ewart had his share in that. More and more acutely and unmistakably did my perception of beauty in form and sound, my desire for adventure, my desire for intercourse, converge on this central and commanding business of the individual life. I had to get me a mate.

I began to fall in love faintly with girls I passed in the street, with women who sat before me in trains, with girl fellow-students, with ladies in passing carriages, with loiterers at the corners, with neat-handed waitresses in shops and tea-rooms, with pictures even of girls and women. On my rare visits to the theatre I always became exalted, and found the actresses and even the spectators about me mysterious, attractive, creatures of deep interest and desire. I had a stronger and stronger sense that among these glancing, passing multitudes there was somewhere one who was for me. And in spite of every antagonistic force in the world, there was something in my very marrow that insisted: "Stop! Look at this one! Think of her! Won't she do? This signifies—this before all things signifies! Stop! Why are you hurrying by? This may be the predestined person—before all others."

It is odd that I can't remember when first I saw Marion, who became my wife—whom I was to make wretched, who was to make me wretched, who was to pluck that fine generalised possibility of love out of my early manhood and make it a personal conflict. I became aware of her as one of a number of interesting attractive figures that moved about in my world, that glanced back at my eyes, that flitted by with a kind of averted watchfulness. I would meet her coming through the Art Museum, which was my short cut to the Brompton Road, or see her sitting, reading as I thought, in one of the bays of the Education Library. But really, as I found out afterwards, she never read. She used to come there to eat a bun in quiet. She was a very gracefully-moving figure of a girl then, very plainly dressed, with dark brown hair I remember, in a knot low on her neck behind that confessed the pretty roundness of her head and harmonised with the admirable lines of ears and cheek, the grave serenity of mouth and brow.

She stood out among the other girls very distinctly because they dressed more than she did, struck emphatic notes of colour, startled one by novelties in hats and bows and things. I've always hated the rustle, the disconcerting colour boundaries, the smart unnatural angles of women's clothes. Her plain black dress gave her a starkness. . . .

I do remember, though, how one afternoon I discovered the peculiar appeal of her form for me. I had been restless with my work and had finally slipped out of the Laboratory and come over to the Art Museum to lounge among the pictures. I came upon her in an odd corner of the Sheepshanks gallery, intently copying something from a picture that hung high. I had just been in the gallery of casts from the antique, my mind was all alive with my newly awakened sense of line, and there she stood with face upturned, her body drooping forward from the hips just a little—memorably graceful—feminine.

After that I know I sought to see her, felt a distinctive emotion at her presence, began to imagine things about her. I no longer thought of generalised womanhood or of this casual person or that. I thought of her.

An accident brought us together. I found myself one Monday morning in an omnibus staggering westward from Victoria—I was returning from a Sunday I'd spent at Wimblehurst in response to a unique freak of hospitality on the part of Mr. Mantell. She was the sole other inside passenger. And when the time came to pay her fare, she became an extremely scared, disconcerted and fumbling young woman; she had left her purse at home.

Luckily I had some money.

She looked at me with startled, troubled brown eyes; she permitted my proffered payment to the conductor with a certain ungraciousness that seemed a part of her shyness, and then as she rose to go, she thanked me with an obvious affectation of ease.

"Thank you so much," she said in a pleasant soft voice; and then less gracefully, "Awfully kind of you, you know."

I fancy I made polite noises. But just then I wasn't disposed to be critical. I was full of the sense of her presence; her arm was stretched out over me as she moved past me, the gracious slenderness of her body was near me. The words we used didn't seem very greatly to matter. I had vague ideas of getting out with her—and I didn't.

That encounter, I have no doubt, exercised me enormously. I lay awake at night rehearsing it, and wondering about the next phase of our relationship. That took the form of the return of my twopence. I was in the Science Library, digging something out of the *Encyclopædia Britannica,* when she appeared beside me and placed on the open page an evidently premeditated thin envelope, bulgingly confessing the coins within.

"It was so very kind of you," she said, "the other day. I don't know what I should have done, Mr. ——"

I supplied my name. "I knew," I said, "you were a student here."

"Not exactly a student. I——"

"Well, anyhow, I knew you were here frequently. And I'm a student myself at the Consolidated Technical Schools."

I plunged into autobiography and questionings, and so entangled her in a conversation that got a quality of intimacy through the fact that, out of deference to our fellow-readers, we were obliged to speak in undertones. And I have no doubt that in substance it was singularly banal. Indeed I have an impression that all our early conversations were incredibly banal. We met several times in a manner half-accidental, half-furtive and wholly awkward. Mentally I didn't take hold of her. I never did take hold of her mentally. Her talk, I now know all too clearly, was shallow, pretentious, evasive. Only—even to this day—I don't remember it as in any way vulgar. She was, I could see quite clearly, anxious to overstate or conceal her real social status, a little desirous to be taken for a student in the art school and a little ashamed that she wasn't. She came to the museum to "copy things," and this, I gathered, had something to do with some way of partially earning her living that I wasn't to inquire into. I told her things about myself, vain things that I felt might appeal to her, but that I learnt long afterwards made her think me "conceited." We talked of books, but there she was very much on her guard and secretive, and rather more freely of pictures. She "liked" pictures. I think from the outset I appreciated and did not for a moment resent that hers was a commonplace mind, that she was the unconscious custodian of something that had gripped my most intimate instinct, that she embodied the hope of a possibility, was the careless proprietor of a physical quality that had turned my head like strong wine. I felt I had to stick to our acquaintance, flat as it was. Presently we should get through these irrelevant exterior things, and come to the reality of love beneath.

I saw her in dreams released, as it were, from herself, beautiful, worshipful, glowing. And sometimes when we were together, we would come on silences through sheer lack of matter, and then my eyes would feast on her, and the silence seemed like the drawing back of a curtain—her superficial self. Odd, I confess. Odd, particularly, the enormous hold of certain things about her upon me, a certain slight rounded duskiness of skin, a certain perfection of modelling in her lips, her brow, a certain fine flow about the shoulders. She wasn't indeed beautiful to many people—these things are beyond explaining. She had manifest defects of form and feature, and they didn't matter at all. Her complexion was bad, but I don't think it would have mattered if it had been positively unwholesome. I had extraordinarily limited, extraordinarily painful, desires. I longed intolerably to kiss her lips.

V

The affair was immensely serious and commanding to me. I don't remember that in these earlier phases I had any thought of turning back at all. It was clear to me that she regarded me with an eye entirely more critical than I had for her, that she didn't like my scholarly untidiness, my want of even the most commonplace style. "Why do you wear collars like that?" she said, and sent me in pursuit of gentlemanly neckwear. I remember when she invited me a little abruptly one day to come to tea at her home on the following Sunday and meet her father and mother and aunt, that I immediately doubted whether my hitherto un suspected best clothes would create the impression she de- sired me to make on her belongings. I put off the en counter until the Sunday after, to get myself in order. I had a morning coat made and I bought a silk hat, and had my reward in the first glance of admiration she ever gave me. I wonder how many of my sex are as preposterous. I was, you see, abandoning all my beliefs—all my conventions un- asked. I was forgetting myself—immensely. And there was a conscious shame in it all. Never a word did I breathe to Ewart—to any living soul—of what was going on.

Her father and mother and aunt struck me as the dis- malest of people, and her home in Walham Green was chiefly notable for its black and amber tapestry carpets and curtains and table-cloths, and the age and irrelevance of its books, mostly books with faded gilt on the covers. The windows were fortified against the intrusive eye by cheap lace curtains and an "art pot" upon an unstable octagonal table. Several framed Art School drawings of Marion's, bearing official South Kensington marks of ap- proval, adorned the room, and there was a black and gilt

[117]

piano with a hymn-book on the top of it. There were draped mirrors over all the mantels, and above the sideboard in the dining-room in which we sat at tea was a portrait of her father, villainously truthful after the manner of such works. I couldn't see a trace of the beauty I found in her in either parent, yet she somehow contrived to be like them both.

These people pretended in a way that reminded me of the Three Great Women in my mother's room, but they had not nearly so much social knowledge and did not do it nearly so well. Also, I remarked, they did it with an eye on Marion. They had wanted to thank me, they said, for the kindness to their daughter in the matter of the 'bus fare, and so accounted for anything unusual in their invitation. They posed as simple gentlefolk, a little hostile to the rush and gadding-about of London, preferring a secluded and unpretentious quiet.

When Marion got out the white table-cloth from the sideboard-drawer for tea, a card bearing the word "APARTMENTS" fell to the floor. I picked it up and gave it to her before I realised from her quickened colour that I should not have seen it; that probably it had been removed from the window in honour of my coming.

Her father spoke once in a large remote way of the claims of business engagements, and it was only long afterwards I realised that he was a supernumerary clerk in the Walham Green Gas Works and otherwise a useful man at home. He was a large, loose, fattish man with unintelligent brown eyes magnified by spectacles; he wore an ill-fitting frock-coat and a paper collar, and he showed me, as his great treasure and interest, a large Bible which he had grangerised with photographs of pictures. Also he cultivated the little garden-yard behind the house, and he had a small greenhouse with tomatoes. "I wish I 'ad 'eat," he said. "One can do such a lot with 'eat. But I suppose you can't 'ave everything you want in this world."

Both he and Marion's mother treated her with a deference that struck me as the most natural thing in the world.

Her own manner changed, became more authoritative and watchful, her shyness disappeared. She had taken a line of her own I gathered, draped the mirror, got the second-hand piano, and broken her parents in. Her mother must once have been a pretty woman; she had regular features and Marion's hair without its lustre, but she was thin and careworn. The aunt, Miss Ramboat, was a large, abnormally shy person very like her brother, and I don't recall anything she said on this occasion.

To begin with there was a good deal of tension—Marion was frightfully nervous and every one was under the necessity of behaving in a mysteriously unreal fashion until I plunged, became talkative and made a certain ease and interest. I told them of the schools, of my lodgings, of Wimblehurst and my apprenticeship days. "There's a lot of this Science about nowadays," Mr. Ramboat reflected; "but I sometimes wonder a bit what good it is?"

I was young enough to be led into what he called "a bit of a discussion," which Marion truncated before our voices became unduly raised. "I dare say," she said, "there's much to be said on both sides."

I remember Marion's mother asked me what church I attended, and that I replied evasively. After tea there was music and we sang hymns. I doubted if I had a voice when this was proposed, but that was held to be a trivial objection, and I found sitting close beside the sweep of hair from Marion's brow had many compensations. I discovered her mother sitting in the horsehair armchair and regarding us sentimentally. I went for a walk with Marion towards Putney Bridge, and then there was more singing and a supper of cold bacon and pie, after which Mr. Ramboat and I smoked. During that walk, I remember, she told me the import of her sketchings and copyings in the museum. A cousin of a friend of hers whom she spoke of as Smithie, had developed an original business in a sort of tea-gown garment which she called a Persian Robe, a plain sort of wrap with a gaily embroidered yoke, and Marion went there and worked in the busy times. In the times that weren't busy she designed novelties in yokes by an assiduous use of eyes and note-book in the museum, and went home and traced out the captured forms on the foundation material. "I don't get much," said Marion, "but it's interesting, and in the busy times we work all day. Of course the workgirls are dreadfully common, but we don't say much to them. And Smithie talks enough for ten."

I quite understood the workgirls were dreadfully common.

I don't remember that the Walham Green *ménage* and the quality of these people, nor the light they threw on Marion, detracted in the slightest degree at that time from the intent resolve that held me to make her mine. I didn't like them. But I took them as part of the affair. Indeed, on the whole, I think they threw her up by an effect of contrast; she was so obviously controlling them, so consciously superior to them.

More and more of my time did I give to this passion that possessed me. I began to think chiefly of ways of pleasing Marion, of acts of devotion, of treats, of sumptuous presents for her, of appeals she would understand. If at times she was manifestly unintelligent, if her ignorance became indisputable, I told myself her simple instincts were worth all the education and intelligence in the world. And to this day I think I wasn't really wrong about her. There was something extraordinarily fine about her, something simple and high, that flickered in and out of her ignorance and commonness and limitations like the tongue from the mouth of a snake. . . .

One night I was privileged to meet her and bring her home from an entertainment at the Birkbeck Institute. We came back on the underground railway and we travelled first-class—that being the highest class available. We were alone in the carriage, and for the first time I ventured to put my arm about her.

"You mustn't," she said feebly.

"I love you," I whispered suddenly with my heart beating wildly, drew her to me, drew all her beauty to me and kissed her cool and unresisting lips.

"Love me?" she said, struggling away from me. "Don't!" and then, as the train ran into a station, "You must tell no one. . . . I don't know. . . . You shouldn't have done that. . . ."

Then two other people got in with us and terminated my wooing for a time.

When we found ourselves alone together, walking towards Battersea, she had decided to be offended. I parted from her unforgiven and terribly distressed.

When we met again, she told me I must never do "that" again.

I had dreamt that to kiss her lips was ultimate satisfaction. But it was indeed only the beginning of desires. I told her my one ambition was to marry her.

"But," she said, "you're not in a position—— What's the good of talking like that?"

I stared at her. "I mean to," I said.

"You can't," she answered. "It will be years——"

"But I love you," I insisted.

I stood not a yard from the sweet lips I had kissed; I stood within arm's length of the inanimate beauty I desired to quicken, and I saw opening between us a gulf of years, toil, waiting, disappointments and an immense uncertainty.

"I love you," I said. "Don't you love me?"

She looked me in the face with grave irresponsive eyes.

"I don't know," she said. "I *like* you, of course. . . . One has to be sensible . . ."

I can remember now my sense of frustration by her unresilient reply. I should have perceived then that for her my ardour had no quickening fire. But how was I to know? I had let myself come to want her, my imagination endowed her with infinite possibilities. I wanted her and wanted her, stupidly and instinctively. . . .

"But," I said. "Love——!"

"One has to be sensible," she replied. "I like going about with you. Can't we keep as we are?"

[121]

VI

Well, you begin to understand my breakdown now. I have been copious enough with these apologia. My work got more and more spiritless, my behaviour degenerated, my punctuality declined; I was more and more outclassed in the steady grind by my fellow-students. Such supplies of moral energy as I still had at command shaped now in the direction of serving Marion rather than science.

I fell away dreadfully, more and more I shirked and skulked; the humped men from the north, the pale men with thin, clenched minds, the intent, hard-breathing students I found against me, fell at last from keen rivalry to moral contempt. Even a girl got above me upon one of the lists. Then indeed I made it a point of honour to show by my public disregard of every rule that I really did not even pretend to try. . . .

So one day I found myself sitting in a mood of considerable astonishment in Kensington Gardens, reflecting on a recent heated interview with the school Registrar in which I had displayed more spirit than sense. I was astonished chiefly at my stupendous falling away from all the militant ideals of unflinching study I had brought up from Wimblehurst. I had displayed myself, as the Registrar put it, "an unmitigated rotter." My failure to get marks in the written examination had only been equalled by the insufficiency of my practical work.

"I ask you," the Registrar had said, "what will become of you when your scholarship runs out?"

It certainly was an interesting question. What *was* going to become of me?

It was clear there would be nothing for me in the schools as I had once dared to hope; there seemed, indeed, scarcely anything in the world except an ill-paid assistantship in some provincial organized Science School or grammar school. I knew that for that sort of work, without a degree or any qualification, one earned hardly a bare living and had little leisure to struggle up to anything better. If only

I had even as little as fifty pounds I might hold out in London and take my B.Sc. degree, and quadruple my chances! My bitterness against my uncle returned at the thought. After all, he had some of my money still, or ought to have. Why shouldn't I act within my rights, threaten to "take proceedings"? I meditated for a space on the idea, and then returned to the Science Library and wrote him a very considerable and occasionally pungent letter.

That letter to my uncle was the nadir of my failure. Its remarkable consequences, which ended my student days altogether, I will tell in the next chapter.

I say "my failure." Yet there are times when I can even doubt whether that period was a failure at all, when I become defensively critical of those exacting courses I did not follow, the encyclopædic process of scientific exhaustion from which I was distracted. My mind was not inactive, even if it fed on forbidden food. I did not learn what my professors and demonstrators had resolved I should learn, but I learnt many things. My mind learnt to swing wide and to swing by itself.

After all, those other fellows who took high places in the College examinations and were the professor's model boys haven't done so amazingly. Some are professors themselves, some technical experts; not one can show things done such as I, following my own interest, have achieved. For I have built boats that smack across the water like whiplashes; no one ever dreamt of such boats until I built them; and I have surprised three secrets that are more than technical discoveries, in the unexpected hiding-places of Nature. I have come nearer flying than any man has done. Could I have done as much if I had had a turn for obeying those rather mediocre professors at the college who proposed to train my mind? If I had been *trained* in research—that ridiculous contradiction in terms—should I have done more than produce additions to the existing store of little papers with blunted conclusions, of which there are already too many? I see no sense in mock modesty upon this matter. Even by the standards of worldly success I am, by the side of my fellow-students, no failure. I had my F.R.S. by the time I was thirty-seven, and if I am not very wealthy, poverty is as far from me as the Spanish Inquisition. Suppose I had stamped down on the head of my wandering curiosity, locked my imagination in a box just when it wanted to grow out to things, worked by so-and-so's excellent method and so-and-so's indications, where should I be now? . . .

I may be all wrong in this. It may be I should be a far more efficient man than I am if I had cut off all those divergent expenditures of energy, plugged up my curiosity about society with more currently acceptable rubbish or other, abandoned Ewart, evaded Marion instead of pursuing her, concentrated. But I don't believe it!

However, I certainly believed it completely and was filled with remorse on that afternoon when I sat dejectedly in Kensington Gardens and reviewed, in the light of the Registrar's pertinent questions, my first two years in London.

CHAPTER THE SECOND

The Dawn Comes, and My Uncle Appears in a New Silk Hat

I

THROUGHOUT my student days I had not seen my uncle. I refrained from going to him in spite of an occasional regret that in this way I estranged myself from my aunt Susan, and I maintained a sulky attitude of mind towards him. And I don't think that once in all that time I gave a thought to that mystic word of his that was to alter all the world for us. Yet I had not altogether forgotten it. It was with a touch of memory, dim transient perplexity if no more—why did this thing seem in some way personal?—that I read a new inscription upon the hoardings:

That was all. It was simple and yet in some way arresting. I found myself repeating the word after I had passed; it roused one's attention like the sound of distant guns. "Tono"—what's that? and deep, rich, unhurrying;—"*Bun*—gay!*"

Then came my uncle's amazing telegram, his answer to my hostile note: *"Come to me at once you are wanted three hundred a year certain tono-bungay."*

"By Jove!" I cried, "of course!

"It's something——. A patent-medicine! I wonder what he wants with me."

In his Napoleonic way my uncle had omitted to give an address. His telegram had been handed in at Farringdon Road, and after complex meditations I replied to Ponderevo, Farringdon Road, trusting to the rarity of our surname to reach him.

"Where are you?" I asked.

His reply came promptly:

"192A, Raggett Street, E.C."

The next day I took an unsanctioned holiday after the morning's lecture. I discovered my uncle in a wonderfully new silk hat—oh, a splendid hat! with a rolling brim that went beyond the common fashion. It was decidedly too big for him—that was its only fault. It was stuck on the back of his head, and he was in a white waistcoat and shirt sleeves. He welcomed me with a forgetfulness of my bitter satire and my hostile abstinence that was almost divine. His glasses fell off at the sight of me. His round inexpressive eyes shone brightly. He held out his plump short hand.

"Here we are, George! What did I tell you? Needn't whisper it now, my boy. Shout it—*loud!* spread it about! Tell every one! Tono—ToNo,—TONO-BUNGAY!"

Raggett Street, you must understand, was a thoroughfare over which some one had distributed large quantities of cabbage stumps and leaves. It opened out of the upper end of Farringdon Street, and 192A was a shop with the plate-glass front coloured chocolate, on which several of the same bills I had read upon the hoardings had been stuck. The floor was covered by street mud that had been brought in on dirty boots, and three energetic young men of the hooligan type, in neck-wraps and caps, were packing wooden cases with papered-up bottles, amidst much straw and confusion. The counter was littered with these same swathed bottles, of a pattern then novel but now amazingly familiar in the world, the blue paper with the coruscating figure of a genially nude giant, and the printed directions of how under practically all circumstances to take Tono-Bungay. Beyond the counter on one side opened a staircase down which I seem to remember a girl descending with a further consignment of bottles, and the rest of the background was a high partition, also chocolate, with "Temporary Laboratory" inscribed upon it in white letters, and over a door that pierced it, "Office." Here I rapped, inaudible amid much hammering, and then entered unanswered to find my uncle, dressed as I have described, one hand gripping a sheath of letters, and the other scratching his head as he dictated to one of three toiling typewriter girls. Behind him was a further partition and a door inscribed "ABSO-LUTELY PRIVATE—NO ADMISSION," thereon. This partition was of wood painted the universal chocolate, up to about eight feet from the ground, and then of glass. Through the glass I saw dimly a crowded suggestion of crucibles and glass retorts, and—by Jove!—yes!—the dear old Wimblehurst air-pump still! It gave me quite a little thrill—that air-pump! And beside it was the electrical machine—but something—some serious trouble—had happened to that. All these were evidently placed on a shelf just at the level to show.

"Come right into the sanctum," said my uncle, after he had finished something about "esteemed consideration," and whisked me through the door into a room that quite amazingly failed to verify the promise of that apparatus. It was papered with dingy wall-paper that had peeled in places; it contained a fireplace, an easy-chair with a cushion, a table on which stood two or three big bottles, a number of cigar-boxes on the mantel, a whisky Tantalus and a row of soda syphons. He shut the door after me carefully.

"Well, here we are!" he said. "Going strong! Have a whisky, George? No!—Wise man! Neither will I! You see me at it! At it—hard!"

"Hard at what?"

"Read it," and he thrust into my hand a label—that label that has now become one of the most familiar objects of the chemist's shop, the greenish-blue rather old-fashioned bordering, the legend, the name in good black type, very clear, and the strong man all set about with lightning flashes above the double column of skilful lies in red—the label of Tono-Bungay. "It's afloat," he said, as I stood puzzling at this. "It's afloat. I'm afloat!" And suddenly he burst out singing in that throaty tenor of his—

"I'm afloat, I'm afloat on the fierce flowing tide,
The ocean's my home and my bark is my bride!

"Ripping song that is, George. Not so much a bark as a solution, but still—it does! Here we are at it! By-the-by! Half a mo'! I've thought of a thing." He whisked out, leaving me to examine this nuclear spot at leisure, while his voice became dictatorial without. The den struck me as in its large grey dirty way quite unprecedented and extraordinary. The bottles were all labelled simply A, B, C, and so forth, and that dear old apparatus above, seen from this side, was even more patently "on the shelf" than when it had been used to impress Wimblehurst. I saw nothing for it but to sit down in the chair and await my uncle's explanations. I remarked a frock-coat with satin lapels behind the door; there was a dignified umbrella in the corner and a clothes-brush and a hat-brush stood on a side-table. My uncle returned in five minutes looking at his watch—a gold watch—"Gettin' lunch-time, George," he said. "You'd better come and have lunch with me!"

"How's Aunt Susan?" I asked.

"Exuberant. Never saw her so larky. This has bucked her up something wonderful—all this."

"All what?"

"Tono-Bungay."

"What *is* Tono-Bungay?" I asked.

My uncle hesitated. "Tell you after lunch, George," he said. "Come along!" and having locked up the sanctum after himself, led the way along a narrow dirty pavement, lined with barrows and swept at times by avalanche-like porters bearing burthens to vans, to Farringdon Street. He hailed a passing cab superbly, and the cabman was infinitely respectful. "Schäfer's," he said, and off we went side by side—and with me more and more amazed at all these things—to Schäfer's Hotel, the second of the two big places with huge lace curtain-covered windows, near the corner of Blackfriars Bridge.

I will confess I felt a magic charm in our relative proportions as the two colossal, pale-blue-and-red liveried porters of Schäfer's held open the inner doors for us with a respectful salutation that in some manner they seemed to confine wholly to my uncle. Instead of being about four inches taller, I felt at least the same size as he, and very much slenderer. Still more respectful waiters relieved him of the new hat and the dignified umbrella, and took his orders for our lunch. He gave them with a fine assurance.

He nodded to several of the waiters.

"They know me, George, already," he said. "Point me out. Live place! Eye for coming men!"

The detailed business of the lunch engaged our attention for a while, and then I leant across my plate. "And *now?*" said I.

"It's the secret of vigour. Didn't you read that label?"

"Yes, but——"

"It's selling like hot cakes."

"And what is it?" I pressed.

"Well," said my uncle, and then leant forward and spoke

softly under cover of his hand, "it's nothing more or less than . . ."

(But here an unfortunate scruple intervenes. After all, Tono-Bungay is still a marketable commodity and in the hands of purchasers, who bought it from—among other vendors—me. No! I am afraid I cannot give it away.)

"You see," said my uncle in a slow confidential whisper, with eyes very wide and a creased forehead, "it's nice because of the" (here he mentioned a flavouring matter and an aromatic spirit), "it's stimulating because of" (here he mentioned two very vivid tonics, one with a marked action on the kidney). "And the" (here he mentioned two other ingredients) "makes it pretty intoxicating. Cocks their tails. Then there's" (but I touch on the essential secret). "And there you are. I got it out of an old book of recipes—all except the" (here he mentioned the more virulent substance, the one that assails the kidneys), "which is my idea Modern touch! There you are!"

He reverted to the direction of our lunch.

Presently he was leading the way to the lounge—a sumptuous place in red morocco and yellow glazed crockery, with incredible vistas of settees and sofas and things, and there I found myself grouped with him in two excessively upholstered chairs with an earthenware Moorish table between us bearing coffee and Benedictine, and I was tasting the delights of a tenpenny cigar. My uncle smoked a similar cigar in an habituated manner, and he looked energetic and knowing and luxurious and most unexpectedly a little bounder, round the end of it. It was just a trivial flaw upon our swagger, perhaps, that we both were clear our cigars had to be "mild." He got obliquely across the spaces of his great armchair so as to incline confidentially to my ear, he curled up his little legs, and I, in my longer way, adopted a corresponding receptive obliquity. I felt that we should strike an unbiassed observer as a couple of very deep and wily and developing and repulsive persons.

"I want to let you into this"—puff—"George," said my uncle round the end of his cigar. "For many reasons."

His voice grew lower and more cunning. He made explanations that to my inexperience did not completely explain. I retain an impression of a long credit and a share with a firm of wholesale chemists, of a credit and a prospective share with some pirate printers, of a third share for a leading magazine and newspaper proprietor.

"I played 'em off one against the other," said my uncle. I took his point in an instant. He had gone to each of them in turn and said the others had come in.

"I put up four hundred pounds," said my uncle, "myself and my all. And you know——"

He assumed a brisk confidence. "I hadn't five hundred pence. At least——"

For a moment he really was just a little embarrassed. "I *did*," he said, "produce capital. You see, there was that trust affair of yours—I ought, I suppose—in strict legality —to have put that straight first. Zzzz. . . .

"It was a bold thing to do," said my uncle, shifting the venue from the region of honour to the region of courage. And then with a characteristic outburst of piety, "Thank God it's all come right!

"And now, I suppose, you ask where do *you* come in? Well, fact is I've always believed in you, George. You've got—it's a sort of dismal grit. Bark your shins, rouse you, and you'll go! You'd rush any position you had a mind to rush. I know a bit about character, George—trust me. You've got——" He clenched his hands and thrust them out suddenly, and at the same time said, with explosive violence, "Wooosh! Yes. You have! The way you put away that Latin at Wimblehurst; I've never forgotten it. Wo-oo-oo-osh! Your science and all that! Wo-oo-oo-osh! I know my limitations. There's things I can do, and" (he spoke in a whisper, as though this was the first hint of his life's secret) "there's things I can't. Well, I can create this business, but I can't make it go. I'm too voluminous—I'm a boiler-over, not a simmering stick-at-it. *You* keep on *hotting up and hotting up*. Papin's digester. That's you, steady and long and piling up,—then, wo-oo-oo-oo-osh. Come in and stiffen these niggers. Teach them that wo-oo-oo-oo-osh. There you are! That's what I'm after. You! Nobody else believes you're more than a boy. Come right in with me and be a man. Eh, George? Think of the fun of it—a thing on the go—a Real Live Thing! Wooshing it up! Making it buzz and spin! Whoo-oo-oo."—He made alluring expanding circles in the air with his hand. "Eh?"

His proposal, sinking to confidential undertones again, took more definite shape. I was to give all my time and energy to developing and organising. "You shan't write a single advertisement, or give a single assurance," he declared. "I can do all that." And the telegram was no flourish; I was to have three hundred a year. Three hundred a year. ("That's nothing," said my uncle, "the thing to freeze on to, when the time comes, is your tenth of the vendor's share.")

Three hundred a year certain, anyhow! It was an enormous income to me. For a moment I was altogether staggered. Could there be that much money in the whole concern? I looked about me at the sumptuous furniture of Schäfer's Hotel. No doubt there were many such incomes.

My head was spinning with unwonted Benedictine and Burgundy.

"Let me go back and look at the game again," I said. "Let me see upstairs and round about."

I did.

"What do you think of it all?" my uncle asked at last.

"Well, for one thing," I said, "why don't you have those girls working in a decently ventilated room? Apart from any other consideration, they'd work twice as briskly. And they ought to cover the corks before labelling round the bottle——"

"Why?" said my uncle.

"Because—they sometimes make a mucker of the cork job, and then the label's wasted."

"Come and change it, George," said my uncle, with sudden fervour. "Come here and make a machine of it. You

can. Make it all slick, and then make it woosh. I know you
can. Oh! I know you can."

II

I seem to remember very quick changes of mind after
that lunch. The muzzy exaltation of the unaccustomed stim-
ulants gave way very rapidly to a model of pellucid and
impartial clairvoyance which is one of my habitual mental
states. It is intermittent; it leaves me for weeks together,
I know, but back it comes at last like justice on circuit,
and calls up all my impressions, all my illusions, all my
wilful and passionate proceedings. We came downstairs
again into that inner room which pretended to be a scientific laboratory through its high glass lights, and indeed was
a lurking place. My uncle pressed a cigarette on me, and I
took it and stood before the empty fireplace while he
propped his umbrella in the corner, deposited the new silk
hat that was a little too big for him on the table, blew
copiously and produced a second cigar.

It came into my head that he had shrunken very much
in size since the Wimblehurst days, that the cannon ball he
had swallowed was rather more evident and shameless than
it had been, his skin less fresh and the nose between his
glasses, which still didn't quite fit, much redder. And just
then he seemed much laxer in his muscles and not quite
as alertly quick in his movements. But he evidently wasn't
aware of the degenerative nature of his changes as he sat
there, looking suddenly quite little under my eyes.

"Well, George!" he said, quite happily unconscious of
my silent criticism, "what do you think of it all?"

"Well," I said, "in the first place—it's a damned
swindle!"

"Tut! tut!" said my uncle. "It's as straight as——— It's
fair trading!"

"So much the worse for trading," I said.

"It's the sort of thing everybody does. After all, there's
no harm in the stuff—and it may do good. It might do a
lot of good—giving people confidence, f'rinstance, against

[132]

an epidemic. See? Why not? I don't see where your swindle comes in."

"H'm," I said. "It's a thing you either see or don't see."

"I'd like to know what sort of trading isn't a swindle in its way. Everybody who does a large advertised trade is selling something common on the strength of saying it's uncommon. Look at Chickson—they made him a baronet. Look at Lord Radmore, who did it on lying about the alkali in soap! Rippin' ads those were of his too!"

"You don't mean to say you think doing this stuff up in bottles and swearing it's the quintessence of strength and making poor devils buy it at that, is straight?"

"Why not, George? How do we know it mayn't be the quintessence to them so far as they're concerned?"

"Oh!" I said, and shrugged my shoulders.

"There's Faith. You put Faith in 'em. . . . I grant our labels are a bit emphatic. Christian Science, really. No good setting people against the medicine. Tell me a solitary trade nowadays that hasn't to be—emphatic. It's the modern way! Everybody understands it—everybody allows for it."

"But the world would be no worse and rather better, if all this stuff of yours was run down a conduit into the Thames."

"Don't see that, George, at all. 'Mong other things, all our people would be out of work. Unemployed! I grant you Tono-Bungay *may* be—not *quite* so good a find for the world as Peruvian bark, but the point is, George—it *makes trade!* And the world lives on trade. Commerce! A romantic exchange of commodities and property. Romance. 'Magination. See? You must look at these things in a broad light. Look at the wood—and forget the trees! And hang it, George! we got to do these things! There's no way unless you do. What do *you* mean to do—anyhow?"

"There's ways of living," I said, "without either fraud or lying."

"You're a bit stiff, George. There's no fraud in this affair, I'll bet my hat. But what do you propose to do? Go as chemist to some one who *is* running a business, and draw a salary without a share like I offer you. Much sense in that! It comes out of the swindle—as you call it—just the same."

"Some businesses are straight and quiet, anyhow; supply a sound article that is really needed, don't shout advertisements."

"No, George. There you're behind the times. The last of that sort was sold up 'bout five years ago."

"Well, there's scientific research."

"And who pays for that? Who put up that big City and Guilds place at South Kensington? Enterprising business men! They fancy they'll have a bit of science going on, they want a handy Expert ever and again, and there you are! And what do you get for research when you've done it? Just a bare living and no outlook. They just keep you to make discoveries, and if they fancy they'll use 'em they do."

"One can teach."

"How much a year, George? How much a year? I suppose you must respect Carlyle! Well,—you take Carlyle's test—solvency. (Lord! what a book that French Revolution of his is!) See what the world pays teachers and discoverers and what it pays business men! That shows the ones it really wants. There's a justice in these big things, George, over and above the apparent injustice. I tell you it wants trade. It's Trade that makes the world go round! Argosies! Venice! Empire!"

My uncle suddenly rose to his feet.

"You think it over, George. You think it over! And come up on Sunday to the new place—we got rooms in Gower Street now—and see your aunt. She's often asked for you, George—often and often, and thrown it up at me about that bit of property—though I've always said and always will, that twenty-five shillings in the pound is what I'll pay you and interest up to the nail. And think it over. It isn't me I ask you to help. It's yourself. It's your aunt Susan. It's the whole concern. It's the commerce of your country. And we want you badly. I tell you straight, I know my limitations. You could take this place, you could make it go! I can see you at it—looking rather sour. Woosh is the word, George."

And he smiled endearingly.

"I got to dictate a letter," he said, ending the smile, and vanished into the outer room.

III

I didn't succumb without a struggle to my uncle's allurements. Indeed, I held out for a week while I contemplated life and my prospects. It was a crowded and muddled contemplation. It invaded even my sleep.

My interview with the Registrar, my talk with my uncle, my abrupt discovery of the hopeless futility of my passion for Marion, had combined to bring me to a sense of crisis. What was I going to do with life?

I remember certain phases of my indecisions very well.

I remember going home from our talk. I went down Farringdon Street to the Embankment because I thought to go home by Holborn and Oxford Street would be too crowded for thinking. . . . That piece of Embankment from Blackfriars to Westminster still reminds me of that momentous hesitation.

You know, from first to last, I saw the business with my eyes open, I saw its ethical and moral values quite clearly. Never for a moment do I remember myself faltering from my persuasion that the sale of Tono-Bungay was a thoroughly dishonest proceeding. The stuff was, I perceived, a mischievous trash, slightly stimulating, aromatic and attractive, likely to become a bad habit and train people in the habitual use of stronger tonics and insidiously dangerous to people with defective kidneys. It would cost about sevenpence the large bottle to make, including bottling, and we were to sell it at half a crown plus the cost of the patent medicine stamp. A thing that I will confess deterred me from the outset far more than the sense of dishonesty in this affair, was the supreme silliness of the whole concern. I still clung to the idea that the world of men was or should be a sane and just organisation, and the idea that I should set myself gravely, just at the fine springtime of my life, to developing a monstrous bottling and packing warehouse, bottling rubbish for the consumption of foolish, credulous and depressed people, had in it a touch of insanity. My early beliefs still clung to me. I felt assured that somewhere there must be a hitch in the fine prospect of ease and wealth under such conditions; that somewhere, a little overgrown, perhaps, but still traceable, lay a neglected, wasted path of use and honour for me.

My inclination to refuse the whole thing increased rather than diminished at first as I went along the Embankment. In my uncle's presence there had been a sort of glamour that had prevented an outright refusal. It was a revival of affection for him I felt in his presence, I think, in part, and in part an instinctive feeling that I must consider him as my host. But much more was it a curious persuasion he had the knack of inspiring—a persuasion not so much of his integrity and capacity as of the reciprocal and yielding foolishness of the world. One felt that he was silly and wild, but in some way silly and wild after the fashion of the universe. After all, one must live somehow. I astonished him and myself by temporising.

"No," said I, "I'll think it over!"

And as I went along the Embankment, the first effect was all against my uncle. He shrank—for a little while he continued to shrink—in perspective until he was only a very small shabby little man in a dirty back street, sending off a few hundred bottles of rubbish to foolish buyers. The great buildings on the right of us, the Inns and the School Board place—as it was then—Somerset House, the big hotels, the great bridges, Westminster's outlines ahead, had an effect of grey largeness that reduced him to the proportions of a busy black beetle in a crack in the floor.

And then my eye caught the advertisements on the south side of "Sorber's Food," of "Cracknell's Ferric Wine," very bright and prosperous signs, illuminated at night, and I realised how astonishingly they looked at home there, how evidently part they were in the whole thing.

I saw a man come charging out of Palace Yard—the policeman touched his helmet to him— with a hat and a bearing astonishingly like my uncle's. After all,—didn't Cracknell himself sit in the House? . . .

Tono-Bungay shouted at me from a hoarding near Adelphi Terrace; I saw it afar off near Carfax Street; it cried out again upon me in Kensington High Street, and burst into a perfect clamour; six or seven times I saw it as I drew near my diggings. It certainly had an air of being something more than a dream. . . .

Yes, I thought it over—thoroughly enough. . . . Trade rules the world. Wealth rather than trade! The thing was true, and true too was my uncle's proposition that the quickest way to get wealth is to sell the cheapest thing possible in the dearest bottle. He was frightfully right after all. *Pecunia non olet,*—a Roman emperor said that. Perhaps my great heroes in Plutarch were no more than such men, fine now only because they are distant; perhaps after all this Socialism to which I had been drawn was only a foolish dream, only the more foolish because all its promises were conditionally true. Morris and these others played with it wittingly; it gave a zest, a touch of substance, to their æsthetic pleasures. Never would there be good faith enough to bring such things about. They knew it; every one, except a few young fools, knew it. As I crossed the corner of St. James's Park wrapped in thought, I dodged back just in time to escape a prancing pair of greys. A stout, common-looking woman, very magnificently dressed, regarded me from the carriage with a scornful eye. "No doubt," thought I, "a pill-vendor's wife. . . ."

Running through all my thoughts, surging out like a refrain, was my uncle's master-stroke, his admirable touch of praise: "Make it all slick—and then make it Woosh. I know you can! Oh! I *know* you can!"

Ewart as a moral influence was unsatisfactory. I had made up my mind to put the whole thing before him, partly to see how he took it, and partly to hear how it sounded when it was said. I asked him to come and eat with me in an Italian place near Panton Street where one could get a curious, interesting, glutting sort of dinner for eighteen-pence. He came with a disconcerting black-eye that he wouldn't explain. "Not so much a black-eye," he said, "as the aftermath of a purple patch. . . . What's your difficulty?"

"I'll tell you with the salad," I said.

But as a matter of fact I didn't tell him. I threw out that I was doubtful whether I ought to go into trade, or stick to teaching in view of my deepening socialist proclivities; and he, warming with the unaccustomed generosity of a sixteen-penny Chianti, ran on from that without any further inquiry as to my trouble.

His utterances roved wide and loose.

"The reality of life, my dear Ponderevo," I remember him saying very impressively and punctuating with the nutcrackers as he spoke, "is Chromatic Conflict . . . and Form. Get hold of that and let all these other questions go. The Socialist will tell you one sort of colour and shape is right, the Individualist another. What does it all amount to? What *does* it all amount to? *Nothing!* I have no advice to give any one, none,—except to avoid regrets. Be yourself,—seek after such beautiful things as your own sense determines to be beautiful. And don't mind the headache in the morning. . . . For what, after all, *is* a morning, Ponderevo? It isn't like the upper part of a day!"

He paused impressively.

"What Rot!" I cried, after a confused attempt to apprehend him.

"Isn't it! And it's my bedrock wisdom in the matter! Take it or leave it, my dear George; take it or leave it."
. . . He put down the nut-crackers out of my reach and

[138]

lugged a greasy-looking note-book from his pocket. "I'm going to steal this mustard pot," he said.

I made noises of remonstrance.

"Only as a matter of design. I've got to do an old beast's tomb. Wholesale grocer. I'll put it on his corners,—four mustard pots. I dare say he'd be glad of a mustard plaster now to cool him, poor devil, where he is. But anyhow,— here goes!"

V

It came to me in the small hours that the real moral touchstone for this great doubting of mind was Marion. I lay composing statements of my problem and imagined myself delivering them to her—and she, goddess-like and beautiful; giving her fine, simply-worded judgment.

"You see, it's just to give one's self over to the Capitalistic System," I imagined myself saying in good Socialist jargon; "it's surrendering all one's beliefs. We *may* succeed, we *may* grow rich, but where would the satisfaction be?"

Then she would say, "No! That wouldn't be right."

"But the alternative is to wait!"

Then suddenly she would become a goddess. She would turn upon me frankly and nobly, with shining eyes, with arms held out. "No," she would say, "we love one another. Nothing ignoble shall ever touch us. We love one another. Why wait to tell each other that, dear? What does it matter that we are poor and may keep poor?" . . .

But indeed the conversation didn't go at all in that direction. At the sight of her my nocturnal eloquence became preposterous and all the moral values altered altogether. I had waited for her outside the door of the Persian-robe establishment in Kensington High Street and walked home with her thence. I remember how she emerged into the warm evening light and that she wore a brown straw hat that made her, for once, not only beautiful but pretty.

"I like that hat," I said by way of opening; and she smiled her rare delightful smile at me.

[139]

"I love you," I said in an undertone, as we jostled closer on the pavement.

She shook her head forbiddingly, but she still smiled. Then—

"Be sensible!"

The High Street pavement is too narrow and crowded for conversation and we were some way westward before we spoke again.

"Look here," I said; "I want you, Marion. Don't you understand? I want you."

"Now!" she cried warningly.

I do not know if the reader will understand how a passionate lover, an immense admiration and desire, can be shot with a gleam of positive hatred. Such a gleam there was in me at the serene self-complacency of that *"Now!"* It vanished almost before I felt it. I found no warning in it of the antagonisms latent between us.

"Marion," I said, "this isn't a trifling matter to me. I love you. I would die to get you. . . . Don't you care?"

"But what is the good?"

"You don't care," I cried. "You don't care a rap!"

"You know I care," she answered. "If I didn't—— If I didn't like you very much, should I let you come and meet me—go about with you?"

"Well then," I said, "promise to marry me!"

"If I do, what difference will it make?"

We were separated by two men carrying a ladder who drove between us unawares.

"Marion," I asked when we got together again, "I tell you I want you to marry me."

"We can't."

"Why not?"

"We can't marry—in the street."

"We could take our chance!"

"I wish you wouldn't go on talking like this. What *is* the good?"

She suddenly gave way to gloom. "It's no good marrying," she said. "One's only miserable. I've seen other girls.

When one's alone one has a little pocket-money anyhow, one can go about a little. But think of being married and no money, and perhaps children—you can't be sure. . . ."

She poured out this concentrated philosophy of her class and type in jerky uncompleted sentences, with knitted brows, with discontented eyes towards the westward glow—forgetful, it seemed, for a moment even of me.

"Look here, Marion," I said abruptly, "what would you marry on?"

"What *is* the good?" she began.

"Would you marry on three hundred a year?"

She looked at me for a moment. "That's six pounds a week," she said. "One could manage on that,—easily. Smithie's brother—— No, he only gets two hundred and fifty. He married a typewriting girl."

"Will you marry me if I get three hundred a year?"

She looked at me again, with a curious gleam of hope. *"If!"* she said.

I held out my hand and looked her in the eyes. "It's a bargain," I said.

She hesitated and touched my hand for an instant. "It's silly," she remarked as she did so. "It means really we're——" She paused.

"Yes?" said I.

"Engaged. You'll have to wait years. What good can it do you?"

"Not so many years," I answered.

For a moment she brooded.

Then she glanced at me with a smile, half-sweet, half-wistful, that has stuck in my memory for ever.

"I like you," she said. "I shall like to be engaged to you."

And, faint on the threshold of hearing, I caught her ventured "dear!" It's odd that in writing this down my memory passes over all that intervened and I feel it all again, and once again I'm Marion's boyish lover taking great joy in such rare and little things.

At last I went to the address my uncle had given me in Gower Street, and found my aunt Susan waiting tea for him.

Directly I came into the room I appreciated the change in outlook that the achievement of Tono-Bungay had made almost as vividly as when I saw my uncle's new hat. The furniture of the room struck upon my eye as almost stately. The chairs and sofa were covered with chintz which gave it a dim, remote flavour of Bladesover; the mantel, the cornice, the gas pendant were larger and finer than the sort of thing I had grown accustomed to in London. And I was shown in by a real housemaid with real tails to her cap, and great quantities of reddish hair. There was my aunt too, looking bright and pretty, in a blue-patterned tea-wrap with bows that seemed to me the quintessence of fashion. She was sitting in a chair by the open window with quite a pile of yellow-labelled books on the occasional table beside her. Before the large, paper-decorated fireplace stood a three-tiered cake-stand displaying assorted cakes, and a tray with all the tea equipage except the teapot, was on the large centre-table. The carpet was thick, and a spice of adventure was given it by a number of dyed sheep-skin mats.

"Hel-*lo!*" said my aunt as I appeared. "It's George!"

"Shall I serve the tea now, Mem?" said the real housemaid, surveying our greeting coldly.

"Not till Mr. Ponderevo comes, Meggie," said my aunt, and grimaced with extraordinary swiftness and virulence as the housemaid turned her back.

"Meggie she calls herself," said my aunt as the door closed, and left me to infer a certain want of sympathy.

"You're looking very jolly, aunt," said I.

"What do you think of all this old Business he's got?" asked my aunt.

"Seems a promising thing," I said.

"I suppose there is a business somewhere?"

"Haven't you seen it?"

" 'Fraid I'd say something *at* it, George, if I did. So he won't let me. It came on quite suddenly. Brooding he was and writing letters and sizzling something awful—like a chestnut going to pop. Then he came home one day saying Tono-Bungay till I thought he was clean off his onion, and singing—what was it?"

" 'I'm afloat, I'm afloat,' " I guessed.

"The very thing. You've heard him. And saying our fortunes were made. Took me out to the Ho'burn Restaurant, George,—dinner, and we had champagne, stuff that blows up the back of your nose and makes you go *So,* and he said at last he'd got things worthy of me—and we moved here next day. It's a swell house, George. Three pounds a week for the rooms. And he says the Business'll stand it."

She looked at me doubtfully.

"Either do that or smash," I said profoundly.

We discussed the question for a moment mutely with our eyes. My aunt slapped the pile of books from Mudie's.

"I've been having such a Go of reading, George. You never did!"

"What do you think of the business?" I asked.

"Well, they've let him have money," she said, and thought and raised her eyebrows.

"It's been a time," she went on. "The flapping about! Me sitting doing nothing and him on the go like a rocket. He's done wonders. But he wants you, George—he wants you. Sometimes he's full of hope—talks of when we're going to have a carriage and be in society—makes it seem so natural and topsy-turvy, I hardly know whether my old heels aren't up here listening to him, and my old head on the floor. . . . Then he gets depressed. Says he wants restraint. Says he can make a splash but can't keep on. Says if you don't come in everything will smash—— But you *are* coming in?"

She paused and looked at me.

"Well——"

"You don't say you won't come in!"

"But look here, aunt," I said, "do you understand quite? . . . It's a quack medicine. It's trash."

"There's no law against selling quack medicine that I know of," said my aunt. She thought for a minute and became unusually grave. "It's our only chance, George," she said. "If it doesn't go . . ."

There came the slamming of a door, and a loud bellowing from the next apartment through the folding doors. "Here—er Shee *Rulk* lies *Poo* Tom Bo—oling."

"Silly old Concertina! Hark at him, George!" She raised her voice. "Don't sing that, you old Walrus, you! Sing 'I'm afloat!' "

One leaf of the folding doors opened and my uncle appeared.

"Hullo, George! Come along at last? Gossome tea-cake, Susan?"

"Thought it over, George?" he said abruptly.

"Yes," said I.

"Coming in?"

I paused for a last moment and nodded yes.

"Ah!" he cried. "Why couldn't you say that a week ago?"

"I've had false ideas about the world," I said. . . . "Oh! they don't matter now! Yes, I'll come, I'll take my chance with you, I won't hesitate again."

And I didn't. I stuck to that resolution for seven long years.

CHAPTER THE THIRD

How We Made Tono-Bungay Hum

I

So I made my peace with my uncle, and we set out upon this bright enterprise of selling slightly injurious rubbish at one-and-three-halfpence and two-and-nine a bottle, including the Government stamp. We made Tono-Bungay hum! It brought us wealth, influence, respect, the confidence of endless people. All that my uncle promised me proved truth and understatement; Tono-Bungay carried me to freedoms and powers that no life of scientific research, no passionate service of humanity could ever have given me. . . . .

It was my uncle's genius that did it. No doubt he needed me,—I was, I will admit, his indispensable right hand; but his was the brain to conceive. He wrote every advertisement; some of them even he sketched. You must remember that his were the days before the *Times* took to enterprise and the vociferous hawking of that antiquated *Encyclopædia*. That alluring, button-holing, let-me-just-tell-you-quite-soberly-something-you-ought-to-know style of newspaper advertisement, with every now and then a convulsive jump of some attractive phrase into capitals, was then almost a novelty. "Many people who are MODERATELY well think they are QUITE well," was one of his early efforts. The jerks in capitals were, "DO NOT NEED DRUGS OR MEDICINE," and "SIMPLY A PROPER REGIMEN TO GET YOU IN TONE." One was warned against the chemist or druggist who pushed "much-advertised nostrums" on one's attention. That trash did more harm than good. The thing needed was regimen— and Tono-Bungay!

Very early, too, was that bright little quarter column, at least it was usually a quarter column in the evening papers: "HILARITY—TONO-BUNGAY. Like Mountain Air in the Veins." The penetrating trio of questions: "Are you bored with your Business? Are you bored with your Dinner? Are you bored with your Wife?"—that, too, was in our Gower Street days. Both these we had in our first campaign when we worked London south, central, and west; and then, too, we had our first poster,—the HEALTH, BEAUTY, AND STRENGTH one. That was his design; I happen still to have got by me the first sketch he made for it. I have reproduced it here with one or two others to enable the reader to understand the mental quality that initiated these familiar ornaments of London. (The second one is about eighteen months later, the germ of the well-known "Fog" poster; the third was designed for an influenza epidemic, but never issued.)

These things were only incidental in my department. I had to polish them up for the artist and arrange the business of printing and distribution, and after my uncle had had a violent and needless quarrel with the advertising manager of the *Daily Regulator* about the amount of display given to one of his happy thoughts, I also took up the negotiations of advertisements for the press.

We discussed and worked out distribution together—first in the drawing-room floor in Gower Street with my aunt sometimes helping very shrewdly, and then, with a steadily improving type of cigar and older and older whisky, in his snuggery at their first house, the one in Beckenham. Often we worked far into the night—sometimes until dawn.

We really worked infernally hard, and, I recall, we worked with a very decided enthusiasm, not simply on my uncle's part but mine. It was a game, an absurd but absurdly interesting game, and the points were scored in cases of bottles. People think a happy notion is enough to make a man rich, that fortunes can be made without toil. It's a dream, as every millionaire (except one or two lucky gamblers) can testify; I doubt if J. D. Rockefeller in the early days of Standard Oil, worked harder than we did. We worked far into the night—and we also worked all day. We made a rule to be always dropping in at the factory unannounced to keep things right—for at first we could afford no properly responsible underlings—and we travelled London, pretending to be our own representatives and making all sorts of special arrangements.

But none of this was my special work, and as soon as we could get other men in, I dropped the travelling, though my uncle found it particularly interesting and kept it up for years. "Does me good, George, to see the chaps behind their counters like I was once," he explained. My special and distinctive duty was to give Tono-Bungay substance and an outward and visible bottle, to translate my uncle's

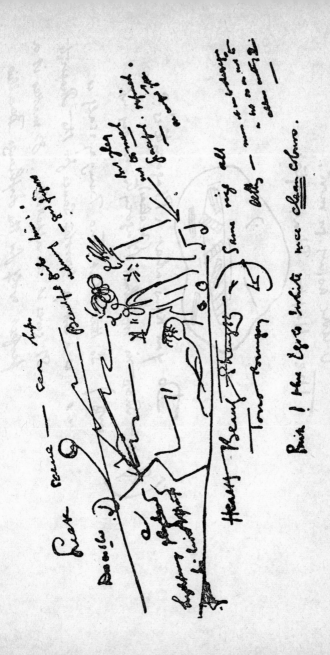

Others asking for more.
— The Happy Phagocyte.

(Says — Stick in not about Phagocytes wonder what
mf).

Do you know what a Phagocyte is? (be clean)

.. So that what Tono Bungay itself is
is a sort of Worcester Sauce for the Phagocyte
It gives it an appetite. It makes it a
perfect nosh for the Influenza Bacillis —

great imaginings into the creation of case after case of labelled bottles of nonsense, and the punctual discharge of them by railway, road and steamer towards their ultimate goal in the Great Stomach of the People. By all modern standards the business was, as my uncle would say, "absolutely *bona fide.*" We sold our stuff and got the money, and spent the money honestly in lies and clamour to sell more stuff. Section by section we spread it over the whole of the British Isles; first working the middle-class London suburbs, then the outer suburbs, then the home counties, then going (with new bills and a more pious style of "ad") into Wales, a great field always for a new patent-medicine, and then into Lancashire. My uncle had in his inner office a big map of England, and as we took up fresh sections of the local press and our consignments invaded new areas, flags for advertisements and pink underlines for orders showed our progress.

"The romance of modern commerce, George!" my uncle would say, rubbing his hands together and drawing in air through his teeth. "The romance of modern commerce, eh? Conquest. Province by province. Like sogers."

We subjugated England and Wales; we rolled over the Cheviots with a special adaptation containing eleven per cent. of absolute alcohol; "Tono-Bungay: Thistle Brand." We also had the Fog poster adapted to a kilted Briton in a misty Highland scene.

Under the shadow of our great leading line we were presently taking subsidiary specialties into action; "Tono-Bungay Hair Stimulant" was our first supplement. Then came "Concentrated Tono-Bungay" for the eyes. That didn't go, but we had a considerable success with the Hair Stimulant. We broached the subject, I remember, in a little catechism beginning: "Why does the hair fall out? Because the follicles are fagged. What are the follicles? . . ." So it went on to the climax that the Hair Stimulant contained all "The essential principles of that most reviving tonic, Tono-Bungay, together with an emollient and nutritious oil derived from crude Neat's Foot Oil by a process of refinement, separation and deodorization. . . . It will be manifest to any one of scientific attainments that in Neat's Foot Oil derived from the hoofs and horns of beasts, we must necessarily have a *natural* skin and hair lubricant."

And we also did admirable things with our next subsidiaries, "Tono-Bungay Lozenges," and "Tono-Bungay Chocolate." These we urged upon the public for their extraordinary nutritive and recuperative value in cases of fatigue and strain. We gave them posters and illustrated advertisements showing climbers hanging from marvellously vertical cliffs, cyclist champions upon the track, mounted messengers engaged in Aix-to-Ghent rides, soldiers lying out in action under a hot sun. "You can GO for twenty-four hours," we declared, "on Tono-Bungay Chocolate." We didn't say whether you could return on the same commodity. We also showed a dreadfully barristerish barrister, wig, side-whiskers, teeth, a horribly life-like portrait of all existing barristers, talking at a table, and beneath, this legend: "A Four Hours' Speech on Tono-Bungay Lozenges, and as fresh as when he began." That brought in regiments of school-teachers, revivalist ministers, politicians and the like. I really do believe there was an element of "kick" in the strychnine in these lozenges, especially in those made according to our earlier formula. For we altered all our formulæ—invariably weakening them enormously as sales got ahead.

In a little while—so it seems to me now—we were employing travellers and opening up Great Britain at the rate of a hundred square miles a day. All the organisation throughout was sketched in a crude, entangled, half-inspired fashion by my uncle, and all of it had to be worked out into a practicable scheme of quantities and expenditure by me. We had a lot of trouble finding our travellers; in the end at least half of them were Irish-Americans, a wonderful breed for selling medicine. We had still more trouble over our factory manager, because of the secrets of the inner room, and in the end we got a very capable woman, Mrs. Hampton Diggs, who had formerly managed a large millinery workroom, whom we could trust to keep everything in good working order without finding out anything that wasn't put exactly under her loyal and energetic nose. She conceived a high opinion of Tono-Bungay and took it in all forms and large quantities so long as I knew her. It didn't seem to do her any harm. And she kept the girls going quite wonderfully.

My uncle's last addition to the Tono-Bungay group was the Tono-Bungay Mouthwash. The reader has probably read a hundred times that inspiring inquiry of his, "You are Young Yet, but are you Sure Nothing has Aged your Gums?"

And after that we took over the agency for three or four good American lines that worked in with our own, and could be handled with it; Texan Embrocation, and "23—to clear the system" were the chief. . . .

I set down these bare facts. To me they are all linked with the figure of my uncle. In some of the old seventeenth and early eighteenth century prayer-books at Bladesover there used to be illustrations with long scrolls coming out of the mouths of the wood-cut figures. I wish I could write all this last chapter on a scroll coming out of the head of my uncle, show it all the time as unfolding and pouring out from a short, fattening, small-legged man with stiff cropped hair, disobedient glasses on a perky little nose, and a round stare behind them. I wish I could show you him breathing hard and a little through his nose as his pen scrabbled out some absurd inspiration for a poster or a picture page, and make you hear his voice, charged with solemn import like the voice of a squeaky prophet, saying, "George! list'n! I got an ideer. I got a notion, George!"

I should put myself into the same picture. Best setting for us, I think, would be the Beckenham snuggery, because there we worked hardest. It would be the lamplit room of the early nineties, and the clock upon the mantel would indicate midnight or later. We would be sitting on either side of the fire, I with a pipe, my uncle with a cigar or cigarette. There would be glasses standing inside the brass fender. Our expressions would be very grave. My uncle used to sit right back in his armchair; his toes always turned in when he was sitting down and his legs had a way of looking curved, as though they hadn't bones or joints but were stuffed with sawdust.

"George, whad'yer think of T.B. for sea-sickness?" he would say.

"No good that I can imagine."

"Oom! No harm *trying,* George. We can but try."

I would suck my pipe. "Hard to get at. Unless we sold our stuff specially at the docks. Might do a special at Cook's office, or in the Continental Bradshaw."

"It 'ud give 'em confidence, George."

He would Zzzz, with his glasses reflecting the red of the glowing coals.

"No good hiding our light under a Bushel," he would remark. . . .

I never really determined whether my uncle regarded Tono-Bungay as a fraud, or whether he didn't come to believe in it in a kind of way by the mere reiteration of his own assertions. I think that his average attitude was one of kindly, almost parental, toleration. I remember saying on one occasion, "But you don't suppose this stuff ever did a human being the slightest good at all?" and how his face assumed a look of protest, as of one reproving harshness and dogmatism.

"You've a hard nature, George," he said. "You're too ready to run things down. How can one *tell?* How can one venture to *tell?* . . ."

I suppose any creative and developing game would have interested me in those years. At any rate, I know I put as much zeal into this Tono-Bungay as any young lieutenant could have done who suddenly found himself in command of a ship. It was extraordinarily interesting to me to figure out the advantage accruing from this shortening of the process or that, and to weigh it against the capital cost of the alteration. I made a sort of machine for sticking on the labels, that I patented; to this day there is a little trickle of royalties to me from that. I also contrived to have our mixture made concentrated, got the bottles, which all came sliding down a guarded slant-way, nearly filled with distilled water at one tap, and dripped our magic ingredients in at the next. This was an immense economy of space for the inner sanctum. For the bottling we needed special taps, and these, too, I invented and patented.

We had a sort of endless band of bottles sliding along an inclined glass trough made slippery with running water. At one end a girl held them up to the light, put aside any that were imperfect and placed the others in the trough; the filling was automatic; at the other end a girl slipped in the cork and drove it home with a little mallet. Each tank, the little one for the vivifying ingredients and the big one for distilled water, had a level indicator, and inside I had a float arrangement that stopped the slide whenever either had sunk too low. Another girl stood ready with my machine to label the corked bottles and hand them to the three packers, who slipped them into their outer papers and put them, with a pad of corrugated paper between each pair, into a little groove from which they could be made to slide neatly into position in our standard packing-case. It sounds wild, I know, but I believe I was the first man in the city of London to pack patent medicines through the side of the packing-case, to discover there was a better way in than by the lid. Our cases packed themselves, practically; had only to be put into position on a little wheeled tray and when full pulled to the lift that dropped them to the men downstairs, who padded up the free space and nailed on top and side. Our girls, moreover, packed with corrugated paper and matchbox-wood box partitions when everybody else was using expensive young men to pack through the top of the box with straw, many breakages and much waste and confusion.

II

As I look back at them now, those energetic years seem all compacted to a year or so; from the days of our first hazardous beginning in Farringdon Street with barely a

thousand pounds' worth of stuff or credit all told—and that
got by something perilously like snatching—to the days
when my uncle went to the public on behalf of himself and
me (one-tenth share) and our silent partners, the drug
wholesalers and the printing people and the owner of that
group of magazines and newspapers, to ask with honest
confidence for £150,000. Those silent partners were remarkably sorry, I know, that they had not taken larger shares
and given us longer credit when the subscriptions came
pouring in. My uncle had a clear half to play with (including the one-tenth understood to be mine).

£150,000—think of it!—for the goodwill in a string of
lies and a trade in bottles of mitigated water! Do you realise the madness of the world that sanctions such a thing?
Perhaps you don't. At times use and wont certainly blinded
me. If it had not been for Ewart, I don't think I should
have had an inkling of the wonderfulness of this development of my fortunes; I should have grown accustomed to
it, fallen in with all its delusions as completely as my uncle
presently did. He was immensely proud of the flotation.
"They've never been given such value," he said, "for a dozen
years." But Ewart, with his gesticulating hairy hands and
bony wrists, his single-handed chorus to all this as it plays
itself over again in my memory, and he kept my fundamental absurdity illuminated for me during all this astonishing
time.

"It's just on all fours with the rest of things," he remarked; "only more so. You needn't think you're anything
out of the way."

I remember one disquisition very distinctly. It was just
after Ewart had been to Paris on a mysterious expedition
to "rough in" some work for a rising American sculptor.
This young man had a commission for an allegorical figure
of Truth (draped, of course) for his State Capitol, and he
needed help. Ewart had returned with his hair cut *en brosse*
and with his costume completely translated into French. He
wore, I remember, a bicycling suit of purplish-brown, baggy
beyond imagining—the only creditable thing about it was

that it had evidently not been made for him—a voluminous black tie, a decadent soft felt hat and several French expletives of a sinister description. "Silly clothes, aren't they?" he said at the sight of my startled eye. "I don't know why I got 'm. They seemed all right over there."

He had come down to our Raggett Street place to discuss a benevolent project of mine for a poster by him, and he scattered remarkable discourse over the heads (I hope it was over the heads) of our bottlers.

"What I like about it all, Ponderevo, is its poetry. . . . That's where we get the pull of the animals. No animal would ever run a factory like this. Think! . . . One remembers the Beaver, of course. He might very possibly bottle things, but would he stick a label round 'em and sell 'em? The Beaver is a dreamy fool, I'll admit, him and his dams, but after all there's a sort of protection about 'em, a kind of muddy practicality! They prevent things getting at him. And it's not your poetry only. It's the poetry of the customer too. Poet answering to poet—soul to soul. Health, Strength and Beauty—in a bottle—the magic philtre! Like a fairy tale. . . .

"Think of the people to whom your bottles of footle go! (I'm calling it footle, Ponderevo, out of praise," he said in parenthesis.)

"Think of the little clerks and jaded women and overworked people. People overstrained with wanting to do, people overstrained with wanting to be. . . . People, in fact, overstrained. . . . The real trouble of life, Ponderevo, isn't that we exist—that's a vulgar error; the real trouble is th*a*t we *don't* really exist and we want to. That's what this—in the highest sense—muck stands for! The hunger to be—for once—really alive—to the finger tips! . . .

"Nobody wants to do and be the things people are—nobody. *You* don't want to preside over this—this bottling; *I* don't want to wear these beastly clothes and be led about by you; nobody wants to keep on sticking labels on silly bottles at so many farthings a gross. That isn't existing! That's—sus—*substratum*. None of us want to be what we

[156]

are, or to do what we do. Except as a sort of basis. What do we want? *You* know. *I* know. Nobody confesses. What we all want to be is something perpetually young and beautiful—young Joves—young Joves, Ponderevo"—his voice became loud, harsh and declamatory—"pursuing coy, half-willing nymphs through everlasting forests." . . .

There was a just-perceptible listening hang in the work about us.

"Come downstairs," I interrupted, "we can talk better there."

"I can talk better here," he answered.

He was just going on, but fortunately the implacable face of Mrs. Hampton Diggs appeared down the aisle of bottling machines.

"All right," he said, "I'll come." . . .

In the little sanctum below, my uncle was taking a digestive pause after his lunch and by no means alert. His presence sent Ewart back to the theme of modern commerce, over the excellent cigar my uncle gave him. He behaved with the elaborate deference due to a business magnate from an unknown man.

"What I was pointing out to your nephew, sir," said Ewart, putting both elbows on the table, "was the poetry of commerce. He doesn't, you know, seem to see it at all."

My uncle nodded brightly. "Whad I tell 'im," he said round his cigar.

"We are artists. You and I, sir, can talk, if you will permit me, as one artist to another. It's advertisement has—done it. Advertisement has revolutionised trade and industry; it is going to revolutionise the world. The old merchant used to tote about commodities; the new one creates values. Doesn't need to tote. He takes something that isn't worth anything—or something that isn't particularly worth anything—and he makes it worth something. He takes mustard that is just like anybody else's mustard, and he goes about saying, shouting, singing, chalking on walls, writing inside people's books, putting it everywhere, 'Smith's Mustard is the Best.' And behold it *is* the Best!"

"True," said my uncle, chubbily and with a dreamy sense of mysticism; "true!"

"It's just like an artist; he takes a lump of white marble on the verge of a lime-kiln, he chips it about, he makes—he makes a monument to himself—and others—a monument the world will not willingly let die. Talking of mustard, sir, I was at Clapham Junction the other day, and all the banks are overgrown with horseradish that's got loose from a garden somewhere. You know what horseradish is—grows like wildfire—spreads—spreads. I stood at the end of the platform looking at the stuff and thinking about it. 'Like fame,' I thought, 'rank and wild where it isn't wanted. Why don't the really good things in life grow like horseradish?' I thought. My mind went off in a peculiar way it does from that to the idea that mustard costs a penny a tin—I bought some the other day for a ham I had. It came into my head that it would be ripping good business to use horseradish to adulterate mustard. I had a sort of idea that I could plunge into business on that, get rich and come back to my own proper monumental art again. And then I said, 'But *why* adulterate? I don't like the idea of adulteration.' "

"Shabby," said my uncle, nodding his head. "Bound to get found out!"

"And totally unnecessary, too! Why not do up a mixture —three-quarters pounded horseradish and a quarter mustard—give it a fancy name—and sell it at twice the mustard price. See? I very nearly started the business straight away, only something happened. My train came along."

"Jolly good ideer," said my uncle. He looked at me. "That really *is* an ideer, George," he said.

"Take shavin's, again! You know that poem of Longfellow's, sir, that sounds exactly like the first declension. What is it?—'Man's a maker, men say!' "

My uncle nodded and gurgled some quotation that died away.

"Jolly good poem, George," he said in an aside to me.

"Well, it's about a carpenter and a poetic Victorian child, you know, and some shavin's. The child made no end out

[158]

of the shavin's. So might you. Powder 'em. They might be anything. Soak 'em in jipper,—Xylo-tobacco! Powder 'em and get a little tar and turpentinous smell in,—wood-packing for hot baths—a Certain Cure for the scourge of Influenza! There's all these patent grain foods,—what Americans call cereals. I believe I'm right, sir, in saying they're sawdust."

"No!" said my uncle, removing his cigar; "as far as I can find out it's really grain,—spoilt grain. . . . I've been going into that."

"Well, there you are!" said Ewart. "Say it's spoilt grain. It carried out my case just as well. Your modern commerce is no more buying and selling than—sculpture. It's mercy— it's salvation. It's rescue work! It takes all sorts of fallen commodities by the hand and raises them. Cana isn't in it. You turn water—into Tono-Bungay."

"Tono-Bungay's all right," said my uncle, suddenly grave. "We aren't talking of Tono-Bungay."

"Your nephew, sir, is hard; he wants everything to go to a sort of predestinated end; he's a Calvinist of Commerce. Offer him a dustbin full of stuff; he calls it refuse—passes by on the other side. Now *you*, sir—you'd make cinders respect themselves."

My uncle regarded him dubiously for a moment. But there was a touch of appreciation in his eye.

"Might make 'em into a sort of sanitary brick," he reflected over his cigar end.

"Or a friable biscuit. Why *not?* You might advertise: 'Why are Birds so Bright? Because they digest their food perfectly! Why do they digest their food so perfectly? Because they have a gizzard! Why hasn't man a gizzard? Because he can buy Ponderevo's Ashpit Triturating, Friable Biscuit—Which is Better.'"

He delivered the last words in a shout, with his hairy hand flourished in the air. . . .

"Damn clever fellow," said my uncle, after he had gone. "I know a man when I see one. He'll do. Bit drunk, I should say. But that only makes some chaps brighter. If he *wants* to do that poster, he can. Zzzz. That ideer of his about the horseradish. There's something in that, George. I'm going to think over that. . . ."

I may say at once that my poster project came to nothing in the end, though Ewart devoted an interesting week to the matter. He let his unfortunate disposition to irony run away with him. He produced a picture of two beavers with a subtle likeness, he said, to myself and my uncle—the likeness to my uncle certainly wasn't half bad—and they were bottling rows and rows of Tono-Bungay, with the legend "Modern Commerce." It certainly wouldn't have sold a case, though he urged it on me one cheerful evening on the ground that it would "arouse curiosity." In addition he produced a quite shocking study of my uncle, excessively and needlessly nude, but, so far as I was able to judge, an admirable likeness, engaged in feats of strength of a Gargantuan type before an audience of deboshed and shattered ladies. The legend, "Health, Beauty, Strength," below, gave a needed point to his parody. This he hung up in the studio over the oil shop, with a flap of brown paper by way of a curtain over it to accentuate its libellous offence.

CHAPTER THE FOURTH

Marion

I

As I look back on those days in which we built up the great Tono-Bungay property out of human hope and a credit for bottles and rent and printing, I see my life as it were arranged in two parallel columns of unequal width, a wider, more diffused, eventful and various one which continually broadens out, the business side of my life, and a narrow, darker and darkling one shot ever and again with a gleam of happiness, my home-life with Marion. For, of course, I married Marion.

I didn't, as a matter of fact, marry her until a year after Tono-Bungay was thoroughly afloat, and then only after conflicts and discussions of a quite strenuous sort. By that time I was twenty-four. It seems the next thing to childhood now. We were both in certain directions unusually ignorant and simple; we were temperamentally antagonistic, and we hadn't—I don't think we were capable of—an idea in common. She was young and extraordinarily conventional—she seemed never to have an idea of her own but always the idea of her class—and I was young and sceptical, enterprising and passionate; the two links that held us together were the intense appeal her physical beauty had for me, and her appreciation of her importance in my thoughts. There can be no doubt of my passion for her. In her I had discovered woman desired. The nights I have lain awake on account of her, writhing, biting my wrists in a fever of longing! . . .

I have told how I got myself a silk hat and black coat to please her on Sunday—to the derision of some of my fellow-students who chanced to meet me—and how we became engaged. But that was only the beginning of our differences. To her that meant the beginning of a not unpleasant little secrecy, an occasional use of verbal endearments, perhaps even kisses. It was something to go on indefinitely, interfering in no way with her gossiping spells of work at Smithie's. To me it was a pledge to come together into the utmost intimacy of soul and body so soon as we could contrive it. . . .

I don't know if it will strike the reader that I am setting out to discuss the queer, unwise love relationship and my bungle of a marriage with excessive solemnity. But to me it seems to reach out to vastly wider issues than our little personal affair. I've thought over my life. In these last few years I've tried to get at least a little wisdom out of it. And in particular I've thought over this part of my life. I'm enormously impressed by the ignorant, unguided way in which we two entangled ourselves with each other. It seems to me the queerest thing in all this network of misunderstandings and misstatements and faulty and ramshackle conventions which makes up our social order as the individual meets it, that we should have come together so accidentally and so blindly. Because we were no more than samples of the common fate. Love is not only the cardinal fact in the individual life, but the most important concern of the community; after all, the way in which the young people of this generation pair off determines the fate of the nation; all the other affairs of the State are subsidiary to that. And we leave it to flushed and blundering youth to stumble on its own significance, with nothing to guide it but shocked looks and sentimental twaddle and base whisperings and cant-smeared examples.

I have tried to indicate something of my own sexual development in the preceding chapter. Nobody was ever frank and decent with me in this relation; nobody, no book, ever came and said to me thus and thus is the world made, and so and so is necessary. Everything came obscurely, indefinitely, perplexingly; and all I knew of law or convention in the matter had the form of threatenings and prohibitions. Except through the furtive, shameful talk of my coevals at Goudhurst and Wimblehurst, I was not even warned against quite horrible dangers. My ideas were made partly of instinct, partly of a romantic imagination, partly woven out of a medley of scraps of suggestion that came to me haphazard. I had read widely and confusedly "Vathek," Shelley, Tom Paine, Plutarch, Carlyle, Haeckel, William Morris, the Bible, the *Freethinker*, the *Clarion*, "The Woman Who Did,"—I mention the ingredients that come first to mind. All sorts of ideas were jumbled up in me and never a lucid explanation. But it was evident to me that the world regarded Shelley, for example, as a very heroic as well as beautiful person; and that to defy convention and succumb magnificently to passion was the proper thing to do to gain the respect and affection of all decent people.

And the make-up of Marion's mind in the matter was an equally irrational affair. Her training had been one, not simply of silences, but suppressions. An enormous force

[162]

of suggestion had so shaped her that the intense natural fastidiousness of girlhood had developed into an absolute perversion of instinct. For all that is cardinal in this essential business of life she had one inseparable epithet—"horrid." Without any such training she would have been a shy lover, but now she was an impossible one. For the rest she had derived, I suppose, partly from the sort of fiction she got from the Public Library, and partly from the workroom talk at Smithie's. So far as the former origin went, she had an idea of love as a state of worship and service on the part of the man and of condescension on the part of the woman. There was nothing "horrid" about it in any fiction she had read. The man gave presents, did services, sought to be in every way delightful. The woman "went out" with him, smiled at him, was kissed by him in decorous secrecy, and if he chanced to offend, denied her countenance and presence. Usually she did something "for his good" to him, made him go to church, made him give up smoking or gambling, smartened him up. Quite at the end of the story came a marriage, and after that the interest ceased.

That was the tenor of Marion's fiction; but I think the work-table conversation at Smithie's did something to modify that. At Smithie's it was recognised, I think, that a "fellow" was a possession to be desired; that it was better to be engaged to a fellow than not; that fellows had to be kept—they might be mislaid, they might even be stolen. There was a case of stealing at Smithie's, and many tears.

Smithie I met before we were married, and afterwards she became a frequent visitor to our house at Ealing. She was a thin, bright-eyed, hawk-nosed girl of thirty-odd, with prominent teeth, a high-pitched, eager voice, and a disposition to be urgently smart in her dress. Her hats were startling and various, but invariably disconcerting, and she talked in a rapid, nervous flow that was hilarious rather than witty, and broken by little screams of "Oh, my *dear!*" and "You never did!" She was the first woman I ever met who used scent. Poor old Smithie! What a harmless, kindly soul she really was, and how heartily I detested her! Out of the profits on the Persian robes she supported a sister's family of three children, she "helped" a worthless brother, and overflowed in help even to her workgirls, but that didn't weigh with me in those youthfully-narrow times. It was one of the intense minor irritations of my married life that Smithie's whirlwind chatter seemed to me to have far more influence with Marion than anything I had to say. Before all things I coveted her grip upon Marion's inaccessible mind.

In the workroom at Smithie's, I gathered, they always spoke of me demurely as "A Certain Person." I was rumoured to be dreadfully "clever," and there were doubts— not altogether without justification—of the sweetness of my temper.

II

Well, these general explanations will enable the reader to understand the distressful times we two had together when presently I began to feel on a footing with Marion and to fumble conversationally for the mind and the wonderful passion I felt, obstinately and stupidly, must be in her. I think she thought me the maddest of sane men; "clever," in fact, which at Smithie's was, I suppose, the next thing to insanity, a word intimating incomprehensible and incalculable motives. . . .

She could be shocked at anything, she misunderstood everything, and her weapon was a sulky silence that knitted her brows, spoilt her mouth and robbed her face of beauty. "Well, if we can't agree, I don't see why you should go on talking," she used to say. That would always enrage me beyond measure. Or, "I'm afraid I'm not clever enough to understand that."

Silly little people! I see it all now, but then I was no older than she and I couldn't see anything but that Marion, for some inexplicable reason, wouldn't come alive.

We would contrive semi-surreptitious walks on Sunday, and part speechless with the anger of indefinable offences. Poor Marion! The things I tried to put before her, my fermenting ideas about theology, about Socialism, about æsthetics—the very words appalled her, gave her the faint chill of approaching impropriety, the terror of a very present intellectual impossibility. Then by an enormous effort I would suppress myself for a time and continue a talk that made her happy, about Smithie's brother, about the new girl who had come to the workroom, about the house we would presently live in. But there we differed a little. I wanted to be accessible to St. Paul's or Cannon Street Station, and she had set her mind quite resolutely upon Ealing. . . . It wasn't by any means quarrelling all the time, you understand. She liked me to play the lover "nicely"; she liked the effect of going about—we had lunches, we went to Earl's Court, to Kew, to theatres and concerts, but not often to concerts, because, though Marion "liked" music, she didn't like "too much of it," to picture shows—and there was a nonsensical sort of baby-talk I picked up—I forget where now—that became a mighty peacemaker.

Her worst offence for me was an occasional excursion into the Smithie style of dressing, debased West Kensington. For she had no sense at all of her own beauty. She had no comprehension whatever of beauty of the body, and she could slash her beautiful lines to rags with hat-brims and trimmings. Thank Heaven! a natural refinement, a natural timidity, and her extremely slender purse kept her from the real Smithie efflorescence! Poor, simple, beautiful, kindly, limited Marion! Now that I am forty-five, I can look back at her with all my old admiration and none of my old bitterness, with a new affection and not a scrap of passion, and take her part against the equally stupid, drivingly-energetic, sensuous, intellectual sprawl I used to be. I was a young beast for her to have married—a young beast. With her it was my business to understand and control—and I exacted fellowship, passion. . . .

We became engaged, as I have told; we broke it off and joined again. We went through a succession of such phases. We had no sort of idea what was wrong with us. Presently we were formally engaged. I had a wonderful interview with her father, in which he was stupendously grave and *h*-less, wanted to know about my origins and was tolerant (exasperatingly tolerant) because my mother was a servant, and afterwards her mother took to kissing me, and I bought a ring. But the speechless aunt, I gathered, didn't approve —having doubts of my religiosity. Whenever we were estranged we could keep apart for days; and to begin with, every such separation was a relief. And then I would want her; a restless longing would come upon me. I would think of the flow of her arms, of the soft, gracious bend of her body. I would lie awake or dream of a transfigured Marion of light and fire. It was indeed Dame Nature driving me on to womankind in her stupid, inexorable way; but I thought it was the need of Marion that troubled me. So I always went back to Marion at last and made it up and more or less conceded or ignored whatever thing had parted us, and more and more I urged her to marry me. . . .

In the long run that became a fixed idea. It entangled my will and my pride; I told myself I was not going to be beaten. I hardened to the business. I think, as a matter of fact, my real passion for Marion had waned enormously long before we were married, that she had lived it down by sheer irresponsiveness. When I felt sure of my three hundred a year she stipulated for delay, twelve months' delay, "to see how things would turn out." There were times when she seemed simply an antagonist holding out irritatingly against something I had to settle. Moreover, I began to be greatly distracted by the interest and excitement of Tono-Bungay's success, by the change and movement in things, the going to and fro. I would forget her for days together, and then desire her with an irritating intensity. At last, one Saturday afternoon, after a brooding morning, I determined almost savagely that these delays must end.

I went off to the little home at Walham Green, and made Marion come with me to Putney Common. Marion wasn't at home when I got there and I had to fret for a time and talk to her father, who was just back from his office, he explained, and enjoying himself in his own way in the greenhouse.

"I'm going to ask your daughter to marry me," I said. "I think we've been waiting long enough."

"I don't approve of long engagements either," said her father. "But Marion will have her own way about it, anyhow. Seen this new powdered fertiliser?"

I went in to talk to Mrs. Ramboat. "She'll want time to get her things," said Mrs. Ramboat. . . .

I and Marion sat down together on a little seat under some trees at the top of Putney Hill, and I came to my point abruptly.

"Look here, Marion," I said, "are you going to marry me or are you not?"

She smiled at me. "Well," she said, "we're engaged—aren't we?"

"That can't go on for ever. Will you marry me next week?"

She looked me in the face. "We can't," she said.

"You promised to marry me when I had three hundred a year."

She was silent for a space. "Can't we go on for a time as we are? We *could* marry on three hundred a year. But it means a very little house. There's Smithie's brother. They manage on two hundred and fifty, but that's very little. She says they have a semi-detached house almost on the road, and hardly a bit of garden. And the wall to next-door is so thin they hear everything. When her baby cries—they rap. And people stand against the railings and talk. . . . Can't we wait? You're doing so well."

An extraordinary bitterness possessed me at this invasion of the stupendous beautiful business of love by sordid necessity. I answered her with immense restraint.

"If," I said, "we could have a double-fronted, detached house—at Ealing, say—with a square patch of lawn in front and a garden behind—and—and a tiled bathroom——"

"That would be sixty pounds a year at least."

"Which means five hundred a year. . . . Yes, well, you see, I told my uncle I wanted that, and I've got it."

"Got what?"

"Five hundred pounds a year."

"Five hundred pounds!"

I burst into laughter that had more than a taste of bitterness.

"Yes," I said, "really! and *now* what do you think?"

"Yes," she said, a little flushed; "but be sensible! Do you really mean you've got a Rise, all at once, of two hundred a year?"

"To marry on—yes."

She scrutinised me a moment. "You've done this as a surprise!" she said, and laughed at my laughter. She had become radiant, and that made me radiant, too.

"Yes," I said, "yes," and laughed no longer bitterly. She clasped her hands and looked me in the eyes.

She was so pleased that I forgot absolutely my disgust of a moment before. I forgot that she had raised her price two hundred pounds a year and that I had bought her at that.

"Come!" I said, standing up; "let's go towards the sunset, dear, and talk about it all. Do you know—this is a most beautiful world, an amazingly beautiful world, and when the sunset falls upon you it makes you into shining gold. No, not gold—into golden glass. . . . Into something better than either glass or gold." . . .

And for all that evening I wooed her and kept her glad. She made me repeat my assurances over again and still doubted a little.

We furnished that double-fronted house from attic—it ran to an attic—to cellar, and created a garden.

"Do you know Pampas Grass?" said Marion. "I love Pampas Grass . . . if there is room."

"You shall have Pampas Grass," I declared.

And there were moments as we went in imagination about that house together, when my whole being cried out to take her in my arms—now. But I refrained. On that aspect of life I touched very lightly in that talk, very lightly because I had had my lessons.

She promised to marry me within two months' time.

Shyly, reluctantly, she named a day, and next afternoon, in heat and wrath, we "broke it off" again for the last time. We split upon procedure. I refused flatly to have a normal wedding with wedding cake, white favours, carriages and the rest of it. It dawned upon me suddenly in conversation with her and her mother, that this was implied. I blurted out my objection forthwith, and this time it wasn't any ordinary difference of opinion; it was a "row." I don't remember a quarter of the things we flung out in that dispute. I remember her mother reiterating in tones of gentle remonstrance: "But, George dear, you *must* have a cake—to send round." I think we all reiterated things. I seem to remember a refrain of my own: "A marriage is too sacred a thing, too private a thing, for this display." Her father came in and stood behind me against the wall, and her aunt appeared beside the sideboard and stood with folded arms, looking from speaker to speaker, a sternly gratified prophetess. It didn't occur to me then how painful it was to Marion for these people to witness my rebellion.

"But, George," said her father, "what sort of marriage do you want? You don't want to go to one of those there registry offices?"

"That's exactly what I'd like to do. Marriage is too private a thing——"

"I shouldn't feel married," said Mrs. Ramboat.

"Look here, Marion," I said; "we are going to be married at a registry office. I don't believe in all these—fripperies and superstitions, and I won't submit to them. I've agreed to all sorts of things to please you."

"What's he agreed to?" said her father—unheeded.

"I can't marry at a registry office," said Marion, sallow-white.

"Very well," I said. "I'll marry nowhere else."

"I can't marry at a registry office."

"Very well," I said, standing up, white and tense, and it amazed me, but I was also exultant; "then we won't marry at all."

[169]

She leant forward over the table, staring blankly at nothing.

"I don't think we'd better," she said in a low tone; "if it's to be like this."

"It's for you to choose," I said. I stood for a moment watching the cloud of sulky offence that veiled her beauty.

"It's for you to choose," I repeated; and regardless of the others, walked to the door, slammed it behind me and so went out of the house.

"That's over," I said to myself in the road, and was full of a desolating sense of relief. . . .

But presently her half-averted face began to haunt me as she had sat at the table, and her arm and the long droop of her shoulder.

III

The next day I did an unexampled thing. I sent a telegram to my uncle, *"Bad temper not coming to business,"* and set off for Highgate and Ewart. He was actually at work—on a bust of Millie, and seemed very glad for any interruption.

"Ewart, you old Fool," I said, "knock off and come for a day's gossip. I'm rotten. There's a sympathetic sort of lunacy about you. Let's go to Staines and paddle up to Windsor."

"Girl?" said Ewart, putting down a chisel.

"Yes."

That was all I told him of my affair.

"I've got no money," he remarked, to clear up any ambiguity in my invitation.

We got a jar of shandy-gaff, some food, and, on Ewart's suggestion, two Japanese sunshades in Staines; we demanded extra cushions at the boathouse and we spent an enormously soothing day in discourse and meditation, our boat moored in a shady place this side of Windsor. I seem to remember Ewart with a cushion forward, only his heels and sunshade and some black ends of hair showing, a voice and no more, against the shining, smoothly-streaming mirror of the trees and bushes.

"It's not worth it," was the burthen of the voice.

"You'd better get yourself a Millie, Ponderevo, and then you wouldn't feel so upset."

"No," I said decidedly, "that's not my way." . . .

A thread of smoke ascended from Ewart for a while, like smoke from an altar. . . .

"Everything's a muddle, and you think it isn't. Nobody knows where we are—because, as a matter of fact, we aren't anywhere. Are women property—or are they fellow-creatures? Or a sort of proprietary goddesses? They're so obviously fellow-creatures. You believe in the goddess?"

"No," I said, "that's not my idea."

"What is your idea?"

"Well——"

"H'm," said Ewart, in my pause.

"My idea," I said, "is to meet one person who will belong to me—to whom I shall belong—body and soul. No half-gods! Wait till she comes. If she comes at all. . . . We must come to each other young and pure."

"There's no such thing as a pure person or an impure person. . . . Mixed to begin with."

This was so manifestly true that it silenced me altogether.

"And if you belong to her and she to you, Ponderevo—which end's the head?"

I made no answer except an impatient "Oh!"

For a time we smoked in silence. . . .

"Did I tell you, Ponderevo, of a wonderful discovery I've made?" Ewart began presently.

"No," I said, "what is it?"

"There's no Mrs. Grundy."

"No?"

"No! Practically not. I've just thought all that business out. She's merely an instrument, Ponderevo. She's borne the blame. Grundy's a man. Grundy unmasked. Rather lean and out of sorts. Early middle age. With bunchy black whiskers and a worried eye. Been good so far, and it's fretting him! Moods! . . . There's Grundy in a state of sexual panic, for example,—'Fod God's sake cover it up! They get together—they get together! It's too exciting! The most dreadful things are happening!' Rushing about—long arms going like a windmill. 'They must be kept apart!' Starts out for an absolute obliteration of everything—absolute separations. One side of the road for men, and the other for women, and a hoarding—without posters—between them. Every boy and girl to be sewn up in a sack and sealed, just the head and hands and feet out until twenty-one. Music abolished, calico garments for the lower animals! Sparrows to be suppressed—ab-solutely."

I laughed abruptly.

"Well, that's Mr. Grundy in one mood—and it puts Mrs. Grundy—— She's a much-maligned person, Ponderevo—a rake at heart—and it puts her in a most painful state of fluster—most painful! She's an amenable creature. When Grundy tells her things are shocking, she's shocked—pink and breathless. She goes about trying to conceal her profound sense of guilt behind a haughty expression. . . .

"Grundy, meanwhile, is in a state of complete whirlabout. Long lean knuckly hands pointing and gesticulating! 'They're still thinking of things—thinking of things! It's dreadful. They get it out of books. I can't imagine where they get it! I must watch! There're people over there whispering! Nobody ought to whisper! There's something suggestive in the mere act! Then, pictures! In the museum—things too dreadful for words. Why can't we have pure art —with the anatomy all wrong and pure and nice—and pure fiction, pure poetry, instead of all this stuff with allusions—allusions? . . . Excuse me! There's something up behind that locked door! The keyhole! In the interests of public morality—yes, Sir, as a pure good man—I insist—*I'll* look —it won't hurt me—I insist on looking—my duty—M'm'm —the keyhole!' "

He kicked his legs about extravagantly, and I laughed again.

"That's Grundy in one mood, Ponderevo. It isn't Mrs. Grundy. That's one of the lies we tell about women. They're too simple. Simple! Women *are* simple! They take on just what men tell 'em . . ."

Ewart meditated for a space. "Just exactly as it's put to them," he said, and resumed the moods of Mr. Grundy.

"Then you get old Grundy in another mood. Ever caught him nosing, Ponderevo? Mad with the idea of mysterious, unknown, wicked, delicious things. Things that aren't respectable. Wow! Things he mustn't do! . . . Any one who knows about these things, knows there's just as much mystery and deliciousness about Grundy's forbidden things as there is about eating ham. Jolly nice if it's a bright morning and you're well and hungry and having breakfast in the open air. Jolly unattractive if you're off colour. But Grundy's covered it all up and hidden it and put mucky shades and covers over it until he's forgotten it. Begins to fester round it in his mind. Has dreadful struggles with himself about impure thoughts. . . . Then you get Grundy with hot ears,—curious in undertones. Grundy on the loose, Grundy in a hoarse whisper and with furtive eyes and convulsive movements—making things indecent. Evolving—in dense vapours—indecency!

"Grundy sins. Oh, yes, he's a hypocrite. Sneaks round a corner and sins ugly. It's Grundy and his dark corners that make vice, vice! We artists—we have no vices.

"And then he's frantic with repentance. And wants to be cruel to fallen women and decent harmless sculptors of the simple nude—like me—and so back to his panic again."

"Mrs. Grundy, I suppose, doesn't know he sins," I remarked.

"No? I'm not so sure. . . . But, bless her heart! she's a woman. . . . She's a woman.

"Then again you get Grundy with a large greasy smile— like an accident to a butter tub—all over his face, being Liberal Minded—Grundy in his Anti-Puritan moments, 'trying not to see Harm in it'—Grundy the friend of innocent pleasure. He makes you sick with the Harm he's trying not to see in it. . . .

"And that's why everything's wrong, Ponderevo. Grundy,

[173]

damn him! stands in the light, and we young people can't see. His moods affect us. We catch his gusts of panic, his disease of nosing, his greasiness. We don't know what we may think, what we may say. He does his silly utmost to prevent our reading and seeing the one thing, the one sort of discussion we find—quite naturally and properly—supremely interesting. So we don't adolesce; we blunder up to sex. Dare—dare to look—and he may dirt you for ever! The girls are terror-stricken to silence by his significant whiskers, by the bleary something in his eyes."

Suddenly Ewart, with an almost Jack-in-the-box effect, sat up.

"He's about us everywhere, Ponderevo," he said, very solemnly. "Sometimes—sometimes I think he is—in our blood. In *mine*."

He regarded me for my opinion very earnestly, with his pipe in the corner of his mouth.

"You're the remotest cousin he ever had," I said. . . .

I reflected. "Look here, Ewart," I asked, "how would you have things different?"

He wrinkled up his queer face, regarded the water and made his pipe gurgle for a space, thinking deeply.

"There are complications, I admit. We've grown up under the terror of Grundy and that innocent—but docile and—yes—formidable lady, his wife. I don't know how far the complications aren't a disease, a sort of bleaching under the Grundy shadow. . . . It is possible there are things I have still to learn about women. . . . Man has eaten of the Tree of Knowledge. His innocence is gone. You can't have your cake and eat it. We're in for knowledge; let's have it plain and straight. I should begin, I think, by abolishing the ideas of decency and indecency . . ."

"Grundy would have fits!" I injected.

"Grundy, Ponderevo, would have cold douches—publicly —if the sight was not too painful—three times a day. . . . But I don't think, mind you, that I should let the sexes run about together. No. The fact behind the sexes—is sex. It's no good humbugging. It trails about—even in the best

[174]

mixed company. Tugs at your ankle. The men get showing off and quarrelling—and the women. Or they're bored. I suppose the ancestral males have competed for the ancestral females ever since they were both some sort of grubby little reptile. You aren't going to alter that in a thousand years or so. . . . Never should you have a mixed company, never—except with only one man or only one woman. How would that be? . . .

"Or duets only? . . .

"How to manage it? Some rule of etiquette, perhaps." . . . He became portentously grave.

Then his long hand went out in weird gestures.

"I seem to see—I seem to see—a sort of City of Women, Ponderevo. Yes. . . . A walled enclosure—good stone-mason's work—a city wall, high as the walls of Rome, going about a garden. Dozens of square miles of garden—trees—fountains—arbours—lakes. Lawns on which the women play, avenues in which they gossip, boats. . . . Women like that sort of thing. Any woman who's been to a good eventful girls' school lives on the memory of it for the rest of her life. It's one of the pathetic things about women,—the superiority of school and college to anything they get afterwards. And this city-garden of women will have beautiful places for music, places for beautiful dresses, places for beautiful work. Everything a woman can want. Nurseries. Kindergartens. Schools. And no man—except to do rough work, perhaps—ever comes in. The men live in a world where they can hunt and engineer, invent and mine and manufacture, sail ships, drink deep and practise the arts, and fight——"

"Yes," I said, "but——"

He stilled me with a gesture.

"I'm coming to that. The homes of the women, Ponderevo, will be set in the wall of their city; each woman will have her own particular house and home, furnished after her own heart in her own manner—with a little balcony on the outside wall. Built into the wall—and a little balcony. And there she will go and look out, when the

[175]

mood takes her, and all round the city there will be a broad road and seats and great shady trees. And men will stroll up and down there when they feel the need of feminine company; when, for instance, they want to talk about their souls or their characters or any of the things that only women will stand. . . . The women will lean over and look at the men and smile and talk to them as they fancy. And each woman will have this; she will have a little silken ladder she can let down if she chooses—if she wants to talk closer . . ."

"The men would still be competing."

"There perhaps—yes. But they'd have to abide by the women's decisions."

I raised one or two difficulties, and for a while we played with this idea.

"Ewart," I said, "this is like Doll's Island. . . . Suppose," I reflected, "an unsuccessful man laid siege to a balcony and wouldn't let his rival come near it?"

"Move him on," said Ewart, "by a special regulation. As one does organ-grinders. No difficulty about that. And you could forbid it—make it against the etiquette. No life is decent without etiquette. . . . And people obey etiquette sooner than laws . . ."

"H'm," I said, and was struck by an idea that is remote in the world of a young man. "How about children?" I asked; "in the City? Girls are all very well. But boys, for example—grow up."

"Ah!" said Ewart. "Yes. I forgot. They mustn't grow up inside. . . . They'd turn out the boys when they were seven. The father must come with a little pony and a little gun and manly wear, and take the boy away. Then one could come afterwards to one's mother's balcony. . . . It must be fine to have a mother. The father and the son . . ."

"This is all very pretty in its way," I said at last, "but it's a dream. Let's come back to reality. What I want to know is, what are you going to do in Brompton, let us say, or Walham Green *now?*"

"Oh! damn it!" he remarked, "Walham Green! What a chap you are, Ponderevo!" and he made an abrupt end to his discourse. He wouldn't even reply to my tentatives for a time. . . .

"While I was talking just now," he remarked presently, "I had a quite different idea."

"What?"

"For a masterpiece. A series. Like the busts of the Cæsars. Only not heads, you know. We don't see the people who do things to us nowadays . . ."

"How will you do it, then?"

"Hands—a series of hands! The hands of the Twentieth Century. I'll do it. Some day some one will discover it—go there—see what I have done, and what is meant by it."

"See it where?"

"On the tombs. Why not? The Unknown Master of the Highgate Slope! All the little, soft feminine hands, the nervous ugly males, the hands of the flops, and the hands of the snatchers! And Grundy's loose, lean, knuckly affair—Grundy the terror!—the little wrinkles and the thumb! Only it ought to hold all the others together—in a slightly disturbing squeeze. . . . Like Rodin's great Hand—you know the thing!"

IV

I forget how many days intervened between that last breaking off of our engagement and Marion's surrender. But I recall now the sharpness of my emotion, the concentrated spirit of tears and laughter in my throat as I read the words of her unexpected letter—"I have thought over everything, and I was selfish. . . ."

I rushed off to Walham Green that evening to give back all she had given me, to beat her altogether at giving. She was extraordinarily gentle and generous that time, I remember, and when at last I left her, she kissed me very sweetly.

So we were married.

We were married with all the customary incongruities. I gave—perhaps after a while not altogether ungrudgingly—

and what I gave, Marion took, with a manifest satisfaction. After all, I was being sensible. So that we had three livery carriages to the church (one of the pairs of horses matched) and coachmen—with an improvised flavour and very shabby silk hats—bearing white favours on their whips, and my uncle intervened with splendour and insisted upon having a wedding-breakfast sent in from a caterer's in Hammersmith. The table had a great display of chrysanthemums, and there was orange blossom in the significant place and a wonderful cake. We also circulated upwards of a score of wedges of that accompanied by silver-printed cards in which Marion's name of Ramboat was stricken out by an arrow in favour of Ponderevo. We had a little rally of Marion's relations, and several friends and friends' friends from Smithie's appeared in the church and drifted vestryward. I produced my aunt and uncle—a select group of two. The effect in that shabby little house was one of exhilarating congestion. The sideboard, in which lived the table-cloth and the "Apartments" card, was used for a display of the presents, eked out by the unused balance of the silver-printed cards.

Marion wore the white raiment of a bride, white silk and satin, that did not suit her, that made her seem large and strange to me; she obtruded bows and unfamiliar contours. She went through all this strange ritual of an English wedding with a sacramental gravity that I was altogether too young and egotistical to comprehend. It was all extraordinarily central and important to her; it was no more than an offensive, complicated, and disconcerting intrusion of a world I was already beginning to criticise very bitterly, to me. What was all this fuss for? The mere indecent advertisement that I had been passionately in love with Marion! I think, however, that Marion was only very remotely aware of my smouldering exasperation at having in the end behaved "nicely." I had played-up to the extent of dressing my part; I had an admirably cut frock-coat, a new silk hat, trousers as light as I could endure them—lighter, in fact— a white waistcoat, light tie, light gloves. Marion, seeing me

[178]

despondent, had the unusual enterprise to whisper to me that I looked lovely; I knew too well I didn't look myself. I looked like a special coloured supplement to *Men's Wear,* or *The Tailor and Cutter,* Full Dress For Ceremonial Occasions. I had even the disconcerting sensations of an unfamiliar collar. I felt lost—in a strange body, and when I glanced down myself for reassurance, the straight white abdomen, the alien legs confirmed that impression.

My uncle was my best man, and looked like a banker—a little banker—in flower. He wore a white rose in his buttonhole. He wasn't, I think, particularly talkative. At least I recall very little from him.

"George," he said once or twice, "this is a great occasion for you—a very great occasion." He spoke a little doubtfully.

You see I had told him nothing about Marion until about a week before the wedding; both he and my aunt had been taken altogether by surprise. They couldn't, as people say, "make it out." My aunt was intensely interested, much more than my uncle; it was then, I think, for the first time that I really saw that she cared for me. She got me alone, I remember, after I had made my announcement. "Now, George," she said, "tell me everything about her. Why didn't you tell me—*me* at least—before?"

I was surprised to find how difficult it was to tell her about Marion. I perplexed her.

"Then is she beautiful?" she asked at last.

"I don't know what you'll think of her," I parried. "I think——"

"Yes?"

"I think she might be the most beautiful person in the world."

"And isn't she? To you?"

"Of course," I said, nodding my head. "Yes. She *is* . . ."

And while I don't remember anything my uncle said or did at the wedding, I do remember very distinctly certain little things, scrutiny, solicitude, a curious rare flash of intimacy in my aunt's eyes. It dawned on me that I wasn't hiding anything from her at all. She was dressed very smartly, wearing a big-plumed hat that made her neck seem longer and slenderer than ever, and when she walked up the aisle with that rolling stride of hers and her eye all on Marion, perplexed into self-forgetfulness, it wasn't somehow funny. She was, I do believe, giving my marriage more thought than I had done, she was concerned beyond measure at my black rage and Marion's blindness, she was looking with eyes that knew what loving is—for love.

In the vestry she turned away as we signed, and I verily believe she was crying, though to this day I can't say why she should have cried, and she was near crying too when she squeezed my hand at parting—and she never said a word or looked at me, but just squeezed my hand. . . .

If I had not been so grim in spirit, I think I should have found much of my wedding amusing. I remember a lot of ridiculous detail that still declines to be funny, in my memory. The officiating clergyman had a cold, and turned his "n's" to "d's," and he made the most mechanical compliment conceivable about the bride's age when the register was signed. Every bride he had ever married had had it, one knew. And two middle-aged spinsters, cousins of Marion's and dressmakers at Barking, stand out. They wore marvellously bright and gay blouses and dim old skirts, and had an immense respect for Mr. Ramboat. They threw rice; they brought a whole bag with them and gave handfuls away to unknown little boys at the church door and so created a Lilliputian riot; and one had meant to throw a slipper. It was a very warm old silk slipper, I know, because she dropped it out of a pocket in the aisle—there was a sort of jumble in the aisle—and I picked it up for her. I don't think she actually threw it, for as we drove away from the church I saw her in a dreadful, and, it seemed to me, hopeless, struggle with her pocket; and afterwards my eye caught the missile of good fortune lying, it or its fellow, most obviously mislaid, behind the umbrella-stand in the hall. . . .

The whole business was much more absurd, more incoherent, more human than I had anticipated, but I was far too young and serious to let the latter quality atone for its shortcomings. I am so remote from this phase of my youth that I can look back at it all as dispassionately as one looks at a picture—at some wonderful, perfect sort of picture that is inexhaustible; but at the time these things filled me with unspeakable resentment. Now I go round it all, look into its details, generalise about its aspects. I'm interested, for example, to square it with my Bladesover theory of the British social scheme. Under stress of tradition we were all of us trying in the fermenting chaos of London to carry out the marriage ceremonies of a Bladesover tenant or one of the chubby middling sort of people in some dependent country town. There a marriage is a public function with a public significance. There the church is to a large extent the gathering-place of the community, and your going to be married a thing of importance to every one you pass on the road. It is a change of status that quite legitimately interests the whole neighbourhood. But in London there are no neighbours, nobody knows, nobody cares. An absolute stranger in an office took my notice, and our banns were proclaimed to ears that had never previously heard our names. The clergyman, even, who married us had never seen us before, and didn't in any degree intimate that he wanted to see us again.

Neighbours in London! The Ramboats did not know the names of the people on either side of them. As I waited for Marion before we started off upon our honeymoon flight, Mr. Ramboat, I remember, came and stood beside me and stared out of the window.

"There was a funeral over there yesterday," he said, by way of making conversation, and moved his head at the house opposite. "Quite a smart affair it was—with a glass 'earse. . . ."

And our little procession of three carriages with white-favour-adorned horses and drivers, went through all the huge, noisy, indifferent traffic ilke a lost china image in the coal-chute of an ironclad. Nobody made way for us, nobody cared for us; the driver of an omnibus jeered; for a long time we crawled behind an unamiable dust-cart. The irrelevant clatter and tumult gave a queer flavour of indecency to this public coming-together of lovers. We seemed to have obtruded ourselves shamelessly. The crowd that gathered outside the church would have gathered in the same spirit and with greater alacrity for a street accident. . . .

At Charing Cross—we were going to Hastings—the experienced eye of the guard detected the significance of our unusual costume and he secured us a compartment.

"Well," said I, as the train moved out of the station, *"that's all over!"* And I turned to Marion—a little unfamiliar still, in her unfamiliar clothes—and smiled.

She regarded me gravely, timidly.

"You're not cross?" she asked.

"Cross! Why?"

"At having it all proper."

"My dear Marion!" said I, and by way of answer took and kissed her white-gloved, leather-scented hand. . . .

I don't remember much else about the journey, an hour or so it was of undistinguished time—for we were both confused and a little fatigued and Marion had a slight headache and did not want caresses. I fell into a reverie about my aunt, and realised as if it were a new discovery, that I cared for her very greatly. I was acutely sorry I had not told her earlier of my marriage. . . .

But you will not want to hear the history of my honeymoon. I have told all that was needed to serve my present purpose. Thus and thus it was the Will in things had its way with me. Driven by forces I did not understand, diverted altogether from the science, the curiosities and work to which I had once given myself, I fought my way through a tangle of traditions, customs, obstacles and absurdities, enraged myself, limited myself, gave myself to occupations I saw with the clearest vision were dishonourable and vain, **and** at last achieved the end of purblind Nature, the relent-

[182]

less immediacy of her desire, and held, far short of happiness, Marion weeping and reluctant in my arms.

V

Who can tell the story of the slow estrangement of two married people, the weakening of first this bond and then that of that complex contact? Least of all can one of the two participants. Even now, with an interval of fifteen years to clear it up for me, I still find a mass of impressions of Marion as confused, as discordant, as unsystematic and self-contradictory as life. I think of this thing and love her, of that and hate her—of a hundred aspects in which I can now see her with an unimpassioned sympathy. As I sit here trying to render some vision of this infinitely confused process, I recall moments of hard and fierce estrangement, moments of unclouded intimacy, the passage of transition all forgotten. We talked a little language together when we were "friends," and I was "Mutney" and she was "Ming," and we kept up such an outward show that till the very end Smithie thought our household the most amiable in the world.

I cannot tell to the full how Marion thwarted me and failed in that life of intimate emotions which is the kernel of love. That life of intimate emotions is made up of little things. A beautiful face differs from an ugly one by a difference of surfaces and proportions that are sometimes almost infinitesimally small. I find myself setting down little things and little things; none of them do more than demonstrate those essential temperamental discords I have already sought to make clear. Some readers will understand—to others I shall seem no more than an unfeeling brute who couldn't make allowances. . . . It's easy to make allowances now; but to be young and ardent and to make allowances, to see one's married life open before one, the life that seemed in its dawn a glory, a garden of roses, a place of deep sweet mysteries and heart throbs and wonderful silences, and to see it a vista of tolerations and baby-talk; a compromise; the least effectual thing in all one's life.

Every love romance I read seemed to mock our dull intercourse, every poem, every beautiful picture reflected upon the uneventful succession of grey hours we had together. I think our real difference was one of æsthetic sensibility.

I do still recall as the worst and most disastrous aspect of all that time, her absolute disregard of her own beauty. It's the pettiest thing to record, I know, but she could wear curl-papers in my presence. It was her idea, too, to "wear out" her old clothes and her failures at home when "no one was likely to see her"—"no one" being myself. She allowed me to accumulate a store of ungracious and slovenly memories. . . .

All our conceptions of life differed. I remember how we differed about furniture. We spent three or four days in Tottenham Court Road, and she chose the things she fancied with an inexorable resolution,—sweeping aside my suggestions with—"Oh, *you* want such queer things." She pursued some limited, clearly seen and experienced ideal—that excluded all other possibilities. Over every mantel was a mirror that was draped, our sideboard was wonderfully good and splendid with bevelled glass, we had lamps on long metal stalks and cosy corners and plants in grog-tubs. Smithie approved it all. There wasn't a place where one could sit and read in the whole house. My books went upon shelves in the dining-room recess. And we had a piano, though Marion's playing was at an elementary level. . . .

You know, it was the cruelest luck for Marion that I, with my restlessness, my scepticism, my constantly developing ideas, had insisted upon marriage with her. She had no faculty of growth or change; she had taken her mould, she had set in the limited ideas of her peculiar class. She preserved her conception of what was right in drawing-room chairs and in marriage ceremonial and in every relation of life with a simple and luminous honesty and conviction, with an immense unimaginative inflexibility—as a tailor-bird builds its nest or a beaver makes its dam.

Let me hasten over this history of disappointments and

[184]

separation. I might tell of waxings and wanings of love between us, but the whole was waning. Sometimes she would do things for me, make me a tie or a pair of slippers, and fill me with none the less gratitude because the things were absurd. She ran our home and our one servant with a hard, bright efficiency. She was inordinately proud of house and garden. Always, by her lights, she did her duty by me. . . .

Presently the rapid development of Tono-Bungay began to take me into the provinces, and I would be away sometimes for a week together. This she did not like; it left her "dull," she said, but after a time she began to go to Smithie's again and to develop an independence of me. At Smithie's she was now a woman with a position; she had money to spend. She would take Smithie to theatres and out to lunch and talk interminably of the business, and Smithie became a sort of permanent week-ender with us. Also Marion got a spaniel and began to dabble with the minor arts, with poker-work and a Kodak and hyacinths in glasses. She called once on a neighbour. Her parents left Walham Green—her father severed his connection with the gas-works—and came to live in a small house I took for them near us, and they were much with us.

Odd the littleness of the things that exasperate when the fountains of life are embittered! My father-in-law was perpetually catching me in moody moments and urging me to take to gardening. He irritated me beyond measure.

"You think too much," he would say. "If you was to let in a bit with a spade, you might soon 'ave that garden of yours a Vision of Flowers. That's better than thinking, George."

Or in a tone of exasperation, "I *carn't* think, George, why you don't get a bit of glass 'ere. This sunny corner you c'd do wonders with a bit of glass."

And in the summer time he never came in without performing a sort of conjuring trick in the hall, and taking cucumbers and tomatoes from unexpected points of his person. "All out o' *my* little bit," he'd say in exemplary tones. He left a trail of vegetable produce in the most unusual places, on mantelboards, sideboards, the tops of pictures. Heavens! how the sudden unexpected tomato could annoy me! . . .

It did much to widen our estrangement that Marion and my aunt failed to make friends, became, by a sort of instinct, antagonistic.

My aunt, to begin with, called rather frequently, for she was really anxious to know Marion. At first she would arrive like a whirlwind and pervade the house with an atmosphere of hello! She dressed already with that cheerfully extravagant abandon that signalised her accession to fortune, and dressed her best for these visits.

She wanted to play the mother to me, I fancy, to tell Marion occult secrets about the way I wore out my boots and how I never could think to put on thicker things in cold weather. But Marion received her with that defensive suspiciousness of the shy person, thinking only of the possible criticism of herself; and my aunt, perceiving this, became nervous and slangy. . . .

"She says such queer things," said Marion once, discussing her. "But I suppose it's witty."

"Yes," I said; "it *is* witty."

"If I said things like she does——"

The queer things my aunt said were nothing to the queer things she didn't say. I remember her in our drawing-room one day, and how she cocked her eye—it's the only expression—at the India-rubber plant in a Doulton-ware pot which Marion had placed on the corner of the piano.

She was on the very verge of speech. Then suddenly she caught my expression, and shrank up like a cat that has been discovered looking at the milk.

Then a wicked impulse took her.

"Didn't say an old word, George," she insisted, looking me full in the eye.

I smiled. "You're a dear," I said, "not to," as Marion came lowering into the room to welcome her. But I felt extraordinarily like a traitor—to the India-rubber plant, I suppose—for all that nothing had been said. . . .

"Your aunt makes Game of people," was Marion's verdict, and, open-mindedly: "I suppose it's all right . . . for her."

Several times we went to the house in Beckenham for lunch, and once or twice to dinner. My aunt did her peculiar best to be friends, but Marion was implacable. She was also, I know, intensely uncomfortable, and she adopted as her social method, an exhausting silence, replying compactly and without giving openings to anything that was said to her.

The gaps between my aunt's visits grew wider and wider. . . .

My married existence became at last like a narrow deep groove in the broad expanse of interests in which I was living. I went about the world; I met a great number of varied personalities; I read endless books in trains as I went to and fro. I developed social relationships at my uncle's house that Marion did not share. The seeds of new ideas poured in upon me and grew in me. Those early and middle years of one's third decade are, I suppose, for a man the years of greatest mental growth. They are restless years and full of vague enterprise.

Each time I returned to Ealing, life there seemed more alien, narrow, and unattractive—and Marion less beautiful and more limited and difficult—until at last she was robbed of every particle of her magic. She gave me always a cooler welcome, I think, until she seemed entirely apathetic. I never asked myself then what heartaches she might hide or what her discontents might be.

I would come home hoping nothing, expecting nothing. This was my fated life, and I had chosen it. I became more sensitive to the defects I had once disregarded altogether; I began to associate her sallow complexion with her temperamental insufficiency, and the heavier lines of her mouth and nostril with her moods of discontent. We drifted apart; wider and wider the gap opened. I tired of baby-talk and stereotyped little fondlings; I tired of the latest intelligence from those wonderful workrooms, and showed it all too plainly; we hardly spoke when we were alone together. The mere unreciprocated physical residue of my passion remained—an exasperation between us.

No children came to save us. Marion had acquired at Smithie's a disgust and dread of maternity. All that was the fruition and quintessence of the "horrid" elements in life, a disgusting thing, a last indignity that overtook unwary women. I doubt indeed a little if children would have saved us; we should have differed so fatally about their upbringing.

Altogether, I remember my life with Marion as a long distress, now hard, now tender. It was in those days that I first became critical of my life and burthened with a sense of error and maladjustment. I would lie awake in the night, asking myself the purpose of things, reviewing my unsatisfying, ungainly home-life, my days spent in rascal enterprise and rubbish-selling, contrasting all I was being and doing with my adolescent ambitions, my Wimblehurst dreams. My circumstances had an air of finality, and I asked myself in vain why I had forced myself into them.

VI

The end of our intolerable situation came suddenly and unexpectedly, but in a way that I suppose was almost inevitable. My alienated affections wandered, and I was unfaithful to Marion.

I won't pretend to extenuate the quality of my conduct. I was a young and fairly vigorous man; all my appetite for love had been roused and whetted and none of it had been satisfied by my love affair and my marriage. I had pursued an elusive gleam of beauty to the disregard of all else, and it had failed me. It had faded when I had hoped it would grow brighter. I despaired of life and was embittered. And things happened as I am telling. I don't draw any moral at all in the matter, and as for social remedies, I leave them to the social reformer. I've got to a time of life when the only theories that interest me are generalisations about realities.

[188]

To go to our inner office in Raggett Street I had to walk through a room in which the typists worked. They were the correspondence typists; our books and invoicing had long since overflowed into the premises we had had the luck to secure on either side of us. I was, I must confess, always in a faintly cloudily-emotional way aware of that collection of for the most part round-shouldered femininity, but presently one of the girls detached herself from the others and got a real hold upon my attention. I appreciated her at first as a straight little back, a neater back than any of the others; as a softly rounded neck with a smiling necklace of sham pearls; as chestnut hair very neatly done—and as a side-long glance; presently as a quickly turned face that looked for me.

My eye would seek her as I went through on business things—I dictated some letters to her and so discovered she had pretty, soft-looking hands with pink nails. Once or twice, meeting casually, we looked one another for the flash of a second in the eyes.

That was all. But it was enough in the mysterious free-masonry of sex to say essential things. We had a secret between us.

One day I came into Raggett Street at lunch time and she was alone, sitting at her desk. She glanced up as I entered, and then became very still, with a downcast face and her hands clenched on the table. I walked right by her to the door of the inner office, stopped, came back and stood over her.

We neither of us spoke for quite a perceptible time. I was trembling violently.

"Is that one of the new typewriters?" I asked at last for the sake of speaking.

She looked up at me without a word, with her face flushed and her eyes alight, and I bent down and kissed her lips. She leant back to put an arm about me, drew my face to her and kissed me again and again. I lifted her and held her in my arms. She gave a little smothered cry to feel herself so held.

Never before had I known the quality of passionate kisses. . . .

Somebody became audible in the shop outside.

We started back from one another with flushed faces and bright and burning eyes.

"We can't talk here," I whispered with a confident intimacy. "Where do you go at five?"

"Along the Embankment to Charing Cross," she answered as intimately. "None of the others go that way . . ."

"About half-past five?"

"Yes, half-past five . . ."

The door from the shop opened, and she sat down very quickly.

"I'm glad," I said in a commonplace voice, "that these new typewriters are all right."

I went into the inner office and routed out the paysheet in order to find her name—Effie Rink. And I did no work at all that afternoon. I fretted about that dingy little den like a beast in a cage.

When presently I went out, Effie was working with an extraordinary appearance of calm—and there was no look for me at all. . . .

We met and had our talk that evening, a talk in whispers when there was none to overhear; we came to an understanding. It was strangely unlike any dream of romance I had ever entertained.

VII

I came back after a week's absence to my home again—a changed man. I had lived out my first rush of passion for Effie, had come to a contemplation of my position. I had gauged Effie's place in the scheme of things, and parted from her for a time. She was back in her place at Raggett Street after a temporary indisposition. I did not feel in any way penitent or ashamed, I know, as I opened the little cast-iron gate that kept Marion's front garden and Pampas Grass from the wandering dog. Indeed, if anything, I felt as if I had vindicated some right that had been in question. I came back to Marion with no sense of wrong-doing at all

—with, indeed, a new friendliness towards her. I don't know how it may be proper to feel on such occasions; that is how I felt.

I found her in our drawing-room, standing beside the tall lamp-stand that half filled the bay as though she had just turned from watching for me at the window. There was something in her pale face that arrested me. She looked as if she had not been sleeping. She did not come forward to greet me.

"You've come home," she said.

"As I wrote to you."

She stood very still, a dusky figure against the bright window.

"Where have you been?" she asked.

"East Coast," I said easily.

She paused for a moment. "I *know*," she said.

I stared at her. It was the most amazing moment in my life. . . .

"By Jove!" I said at last, "I believe you do!"

"And then you come home to me!"

I walked to the hearthrug and stood quite still there, regarding this new situation.

"I didn't dream," she began. "How could you do such a thing?"

It seemed a long interval before either of us spoke another word.

"Who knows about it?" I asked at last.

"Smithie's brother. They were at Cromer."

"Confound Cromer! Yes!"

"How could you bring yourself——"

I felt a spasm of petulant annoyance at this unexpected catastrophe.

"I should like to wring Smithie's brother's neck," I said. . . .

Marion spoke in dry, broken fragments of sentences. "You . . . I'd always thought that anyhow *you* couldn't deceive me . . . I suppose all men are horrid—about this."

"It doesn't strike me as horrid. It seems to me the most

necessary consequence—and natural thing in the world."

I became aware of some one moving about in the passage, and went and shut the door of the room. Then I walked back to the hearthrug and turned.

"It's rough on you," I said. "But I didn't mean you to know. You've never cared for me. I've had the devil of a time. Why should you mind?"

She sat down in a draped armchair. "I *have* cared for you," she said.

I shrugged my shoulders.

"I suppose," she said, "*she* cares for you?"

I had no answer.

"Where is she now?"

"Oh! does it matter to you? . . . Look here, Marion! This—this I didn't anticipate. I didn't mean this thing to smash down on you like this. But, you know, something had to happen. I'm sorry—sorry to the bottom of my heart that things have come to this between us. But indeed, I'm taken by surprise. I don't know where I am—I don't know how we got here. Things took me by surprise. I found myself alone with her one day. I kissed her. I went on. It seemed stupid to go back. And besides—why should I have gone back? Why should I? From first to last, I've hardly thought of it as touching you. . . . Damn!"

She scrutinised my face, and pulled at the ball-fringe of the little table beside her.

"To think of it," she said. "I don't believe . . . I can ever touch you again."

We kept a long silence. I was only beginning to realise in the most superficial way the immense catastrophe that had happened between us. Enormous issues had rushed upon us. I felt unprepared and altogether inadequate. I was unreasonably angry. There came a rush of stupid expressions to my mind that my rising sense of the supreme importance of the moment saved me from saying. The gap of silence widened until it threatened to become the vast memorable margin of some one among a thousand trivial possibilities of speech that would vex our relations for ever.

Our little general servant tapped at the door—Marion always liked the servant to tap—and appeared.

"Tea, M'm," she said—and vanished, leaving the door open.

"I will go upstairs," said I, and stopped. "I will go upstairs," I repeated, "and put my bag in the spare room."

We remained motionless and silent for a few seconds.

"Mother is having tea with us to-day," Marion remarked at last, and dropped the worried end of ball-fringe and stood up slowly. . . .

And so, with this immense discussion of our changed relations hanging over us, we presently had tea with the unsuspecting Mrs. Ramboat and the spaniel. Mrs. Ramboat was too well trained in her position to remark upon our sombre preoccupation. She kept a thin trickle of talk going, and told us, I remember, that Mr. Ramboat was "troubled" about his cannas.

"They don't come up and they won't come up. He's been round and had an explanation with the man who sold him the bulbs—and he's very heated and upset."

The spaniel was a great bore, begging and doing small tricks first at one and then at the other of us. Neither of us used his name. You see we had called him Miggles, and made a sort of trio in the baby-talk of Mutney and Miggles and Ming.

VIII

Then presently we resumed our monstrous, momentous duologue. I can't now make out how long that duologue went on. It spread itself, I know, in heavy fragments over either three days or four. I remember myself grouped with Marion, talking sitting on our bed in her room, talking standing in our dining-room, saying this thing or that. Twice we went for long walks. And we had a long evening alone together, with jaded nerves and hearts that fluctuated between a hard and dreary recognition of facts and, on my part at least, a strange unwonted tenderness; because in some extraordinary way this crisis had destroyed our mutual apathy and made us feel one another again.

It was a duologue that had discrepant parts, that fell into lumps of talk that failed to join on to their predecessors, that began again at a different level, higher or lower, that assumed new aspects in the intervals and assimilated new considerations. We discussed the fact that we two were no longer lovers; never before had we faced that. It seems a strange thing to write, but as I look back, I see clearly that those several days were the time when Marion and I were closest together, looked for the first and last time faithfully and steadfastly into each other's soul. For those days only, there were no pretences, I made no concessions to her nor she to me; we concealed nothing, exaggerated nothing. We had done with pretending. We had it out plainly and soberly with each other. Mood followed mood and got its stark expression.

Of course there was quarrelling between us, bitter quarrelling, and we said things to one another—long pent-up things that bruised and crushed and cut. But over it all in my memory now is an effect of deliberate confrontation, and the figure of Marion stands up, pale, melancholy, tearstained, injured, implacable and dignified.

"You love her?" she asked once, and jerked that doubt into my mind.

I struggled with tangled ideas and emotions. "I don't know what love is. It's all sorts of things—it's made of a dozen strands twisted in a thousand ways."

"But you want her? You want her now—when you think of her?"

"Yes," I reflected. "I want her—right enough."

"And me? Where do I come in?"

"I suppose you come in here."

"Well, but what are you going to do?"

"Do?" I said with the exasperation of the situation growing upon me. "What do you want me to do?"

As I look back upon all that time—across a gulf of fifteen active years—I find I see it with an understanding judgment. I see it as if it were the business of some one else—indeed of two other people—intimately known yet judged without passion. I see now that this shock, this sudden immense disillusionment, did in real fact bring out a mind and soul in Marion; that for the first time she emerged from habits, timidities, imitations, phrases and a certain narrow will-impulse, and became a personality.

Her ruling motive at first was, I think, an indignant and outraged pride. This situation must end. She asked me categorically to give up Effie, and I, full of fresh and glowing memories, absolutely refused.

"It's too late, Marion," I said. "It can't be done like that."

"Then we can't very well go on living together," she said. "Can we?"

"Very well," I deliberated, "if you must have it so."

"Well, can we?"

"Can you stay in this house? I mean—if I go away?"

"I don't know. . . . I don't think I could."

"Then—what do you want?"

Slowly we worked our way from point to point, until at last the word "divorce" was before us.

"If we can't live together we ought to be free," said Marion.

"I don't know anything of divorce," I said—"if you mean that. I don't know how it is done. I shall have to ask somebody—or look it up. . . . Perhaps, after all, it is the thing to do. We may as well face it."

We began to talk ourselves into a realisation of what our divergent futures might be. I came back on the evening of that day with my questions answered by a solicitor.

"We can't as a matter of fact," I said, "get divorced as things are. Apparently, so far as the law goes you've got to stand this sort of thing. It's silly—but that is the law. However, it's easy to arrange a divorce. In addition to adultery there must be desertion or cruelty. To establish cruelty I should have to strike you, or something of that sort, before witnesses. That's impossible—but it's simple to desert you —legally. I have to go away from you; that's all. I can go on sending you money—and you bring a suit, what is it?—

[195]

for Restitution of Conjugal Rights. The Court orders me to return. I disobey. Then you can go on to divorce me. You get a Decree Nisi, and once more the Court tries to make me come back. If we don't make it up within six months and if you don't behave scandalously—the Decree is made absolute. That's the end of the fuss. That's how one gets unmarried. It's easier, you see, to marry than unmarry."

"And then—how do I live? What becomes of me?"

"You'll have an income. They call it alimony. From a third to a half of my present income—more if you like—I don't mind—three hundred a year, say. You've got your old people to keep and you'll need all that."

"And then—then you'll be free?"

"Both of us."

"And all this life you've hated——"

I looked up at her wrung and bitter face. "I haven't hated it," I lied, my voice near breaking with the pain of it all. "Have you?"

IX

The perplexing thing about life is the irresoluble complexity of reality, of things and relations alike. Nothing is simple. Every wrong done has a certain justice in it, and every good deed has dregs of evil. As for us, young still, and still without self-knowledge, we sounded a hundred discordant notes in the harsh jangle of that shock. We were furiously angry with each other, tender with each other, callously selfish, generously self-sacrificing.

I remember Marion saying innumerable detached things that didn't hang together one with another, that contradicted one another, that were, nevertheless, all in their places profoundly true and sincere. I see them now as so many vain experiments in her effort to apprehend the crumpled confusions of our complex moral landslip. Some I found irritating beyond measure. I answered her—sometimes quite abominably.

"Of course," she would say again and again, "my life has been a failure."

"I've besieged you for three years," I would retort, "asking it not to be. You've done as you pleased. If I've turned away at last——"

Or again she would revive all the stresses before our marriage.

"How you must hate me! I made you wait. Well, now—I suppose you have your revenge."

"Revenge!" I echoed.

Then she would try over the aspects of our new separated lives.

"I ought to earn my own living," she would insist. "I want to be quite independent. I've always hated London. Perhaps I shall try a poultry farm and bees. You won't mind at first my being a burden. Afterwards——"

"We've settled all that," I said.

"I suppose you will hate me anyhow . . ."

There were times when she seemed to regard our separation with absolute complacency, when she would plan all sorts of freedoms and characteristic interests.

"I shall go out a lot with Smithie," she said.

And once she said an ugly thing that I did indeed hate her for, that I cannot even now quite forgive her.

"Your aunt will rejoice at all this. She never cared for me . . ."

Into my memory of these pains and stresses comes the figure of Smithie, full-charged with emotion, so breathless in the presence of the horrid villain of the piece that she could make no articulate sounds. She had long tearful confidences with Marion, I know, sympathetic close clingings. There were moments when only absolute speechlessness prevented her giving me a stupendous "talking-to"—I could see it in her eye. The wrong things she would have said! And I recall, too, Mrs. Ramboat's slow awakening to something in the air, the growing expression of solicitude in her eye, only her well-trained fear of Marion keeping her from speech. . . .

And at last through all this welter, like a thing fated and

altogether beyond our control, parting came to Marion and me.

I hardened my heart, or I could not have gone. For at the last it came to Marion that she was parting from me for ever. That overbore all other things, and turned our last hour to anguish. She forgot for a time the prospect of moving into a new house, she forgot the outrage on her proprietorship and pride. For the first time in her life she really showed strong emotions in regard to me, for the first time, perhaps, they really came to her. She began to weep slow, reluctant tears. I came into her room, and found her asprawl on the bed, weeping.

"I didn't know," she cried. "Oh! I didn't understand!

"I've been a fool. All my life is a wreck!

"I shall be alone! . . . *Mutney!* Mutney, don't leave me! Oh! Mutney! I didn't understand."

I had to harden my heart indeed, for it seemed to me at moments in those last hours together that at last, too late, the longed-for thing had happened and Marion had come alive. A new-born hunger for me lit her eyes.

"Don't leave me!" she said, "don't leave me!" She clung to me; she kissed me with tear-salt lips. . . .

I was promised now and pledged, and I hardened my heart against this impossible dawn. Yet it seems to me that there were moments when it needed but a cry, but one word to have united us again for all our lives. Could we have united again? Would that passage have enlightened us for ever or should we have fallen back in a week or so into the old estrangement, the old temperamental opposition?

Of that there is now no telling. Our own resolve carried us on our predestined way. We behaved more and more like separating lovers, parting inexorably, but all the preparations we had set going worked on like a machine, and we made no attempt to stop them. My trunks and boxes went to the station. I packed my bag with Marion standing before me. We were like children who had hurt each other horribly in sheer stupidity, who didn't know now how to remedy it. We belonged to each other immensely—immensely. The cab came to the little iron gate.

"Good-bye!" I said.

"Good-bye."

For a moment we held one another in each other's arms and kissed—incredibly without malice. We heard our little servant in the passage going to open the door. For the last time we pressed ourselves to one another. We were not lovers nor enemies, but two human souls in a frank community of pain. I tore myself from her.

"Go away," I said to the servant, seeing that Marion had followed me down.

I felt her standing behind me as I spoke to the cabman.

I got into the cab, resolutely not looking back, and then as it started jumped up, craned out and looked at the door.

It was wide open, but she had disappeared. . . .

I wonder—I suppose she ran upstairs.

X

So I parted from Marion at an extremity of perturbation and regret, and went, as I had promised and arranged, to Effie, who was waiting for me in apartments near Orpington. I remember her upon the station platform, a bright, flitting figure looking along the train for me, and our walk over the fields in the twilight. I had expected an immense sense of relief when at last the stresses of separation were over, but now I found I was beyond measure wretched and perplexed, full of the profoundest persuasion of irreparable error. The dusk and sombre Marion were so alike, her sorrow seemed to be all about me. I had to hold myself to my own plans, to remember that I must keep faith with Effie, with Effie who had made no terms, exacted no guarantees, but flung herself into my hands.

We went across the evening fields in silence, towards a sky of deepening gold and purple, and Effie was close beside me always, very close, glancing up ever and again at my face.

Certainly she knew I grieved for Marion, that ours was

now no joyful reunion. But she showed no resentment and no jealousy. Extraordinarily, she did not compete against Marion. Never once in all our time together did she say an adverse word of Marion. . . .

She set herself presently to dispel the shadow that brooded over me with the same instinctive skill that some women will show with the trouble of a child. She made herself my glad and pretty slave and handmaid; she forced me at last to rejoice in her. Yet at the back of it all Marion remained, stupid and tearful and infinitely distressful, so that I was almost intolerably unhappy for her—for her and the dead body of my married love.

It is all, as I tell it now, unaccountable to me. I go back into these remote parts, these rarely visited uplands and lonely tarns of memory, and it seems to me still a strange country. I had thought I might be going to some sensuous paradise with Effie, but desire which fills the universe before its satisfaction, vanishes utterly—like the going of daylight—with achievement. All the facts and forms of life remain darkling and cold. It was an upland of melancholy questionings, a region from which I saw all the world at new angles and in new aspects; I had outflanked passion and romance.

I had come into a condition of vast perplexities. For the first time in my life, at least so it seems to me now in this retrospect, I looked at my existence as a whole.

Since this was nothing, what was I doing? What was I for?

I was going to and fro about Tono-Bungay—the business I had taken up to secure Marion and which held me now in spite of our ultimate separation—and snatching odd week-ends and nights for Orpington, and all the while I struggled with these obstinate interrogations. I used to fall into musing in the trains, I became even a little inaccurate and forgetful about business things. I have the clearest memory of myself sitting thoughtful in the evening sunlight on a grassy hillside that looked toward Sevenoaks and commanded a wide sweep of country, and that I was thinking out my destiny. I could almost write my thoughts down now, I believe, as they came to me that afternoon. Effie, restless little cockney that she was, rustled and struggled in a hedgerow below, gathering flowers, discovering flowers she had never seen before. I had, I remember, a letter from Marion in my pocket. I had even made some tentatives for return, for a reconciliation; Heaven knows now how I had put it! but her cold, ill-written letter repelled me. I perceived I could never face that old inconclusive dulness of life again, that stagnant disappointment. That, anyhow, wasn't possible. But what was possible? I could see no way of honour or fine living before me at all.

"What am I to do with life?" that was the question that besieged me.

I wondered if all the world was even as I, urged to this by one motive and to that by another, creatures of chance and impulse and unmeaning traditions. Had I indeed to abide by what I had said and done and chosen? Was there nothing for me in honour but to provide for Effie, go back penitent to Marion and keep to my trade in rubbish—or find some fresh one—and so work out the residue of my days? I didn't accept that for a moment. But what else was I to do? I wondered if my case was the case of many men, whether in former ages, too, men had been so guideless, so uncharted, so haphazard in their journey into life. In the Middle Ages, in the old Catholic days, one went to a priest, and he said with all the finality of natural law, this you are and this you must do. I wondered whether even in the Middle Ages I should have accepted that ruling without question. . . .

I remember too very distinctly how Effie came and sat beside me on a little box that was before the casement window of our room.

"Gloomkins," said she.

I smiled and remained head on hand, looking out of the window forgetful of her.

"Did you love your wife so well?" she whispered softly.

"Oh!" I cried, recalled again; "I don't know. I don't un-

[201]

derstand these things. Life is a thing that hurts, my dear! It hurts without logic or reason. I've blundered! I didn't understand. Anyhow—there is no need to go hurting you, is there?"

And I turned about and drew her to me, and kissed her ear. . . .

Yes, I had a very bad time—I still recall. I suffered, I suppose, from a sort of *ennui* of the imagination. I found myself without an object to hold my will together. I sought. I read restlessly and discursively. I tried Ewart and got no help from him. As I regard it all now in this retrospect, it seems to me as if in those days of disgust and abandoned aims I discovered myself for the first time. Before that I had seen only the world and things in it, had sought them self-forgetful of all but my impulse. Now I found myself *grouped,* with a system of appetites and satisfactions, with much work to do—and no desire, it seemed, left in me.

There were moments when I thought of suicide. At times my life appeared before me in bleak, relentless light, a series of ignorances, crude blunderings, degradation and cruelty. I had what the old theologians call a "conviction of sin." I sought salvation—not perhaps in the formulæ a Methodist preacher would recognise—but salvation nevertheless.

Men find their salvation nowadays in many ways. Names and forms don't, I think, matter very much; the real need is something that we can hold and that holds one. I have known a man find that determining factor in a dry-plate factory, and another in writing a history of the Manor. So long as it holds one, it does not matter. Many men and women nowadays take up some concrete aspect of Socialism or social reform. But Socialism for me has always been a little bit too human, too set about with personalities and foolishness. It isn't my line. I don't like things so human. I don't think I'm blind to the fun, the surprises, the jolly little coarsenesses and insufficiency of life, to the "humour of it," as people say, and to adventure, but that isn't the root of the matter with me. There's no humour in my blood.

I'm in earnest in warp and woof. I stumble and flounder, but I know that over all these merry immediate things, there are other things that are great and serene, very high, beautiful things—the reality. I haven't got it, but it's there nevertheless. I'm a spiritual guttersnipe in love with unimaginable goddesses. I've never seen the goddesses nor ever shall—but it takes all the fun out of the mud—and at times I fear it takes all the kindliness, too.

But I'm talking of things I can't expect the reader to understand, because I don't half understand them myself. There is something links things for me, a sunset or so, a mood or so, the high air, something there was in Marion's form and colour, something I find and lose in Mantegna's pictures, something in the lines of these boats I make. (You should see X 2, my last and best!)

I can't explain myself, I perceive. Perhaps it all comes to this, that I am a hard and morally limited cad with a mind beyond my merits. Naturally I resist that as a complete solution. Anyhow, I had a sense of inexorable need, of distress and insufficiency that was unendurable, and for a time this aeronautical engineering allayed it. . . .

In the end of this particular crisis of which I tell so badly, I idealised Science. I decided that in power and knowledge lay the salvation of my life, the secret that would fill my need; that to these things I would give myself. I emerged at last like a man who has been diving in darkness, clutching at a new resolve for which he has groped desperately and long.

I came into the inner office suddenly one day—it must have been just before the time of Marion's suit for restitution—and sat down before my uncle.

"Look here," I said, "I'm sick of this."

"Hullo!" he answered, and put some papers aside. "What's up, George?"

"Things are wrong."

"As how?"

"My life," I said, "it's a mess, an infinite mess."

"She's been a stupid girl, George," he said; "I partly

[203]

understand. But you're quit of her now, practically, and there's just as good fish in the sea——"

"Oh! it's not that!" I cried. "That's only the part that shows. I'm sick—— I'm sick of all this damned rascality."

"Eh? Eh?" said my uncle. "*What*—rascality?"

"Oh, *you* know. I want some *stuff*, man. I want something to hold on to. I shall go amok if I don't get it. I'm a different sort of beast from you. You float in all this bunkum. *I* feel like a man floundering in a universe of soap-suds, up and down, east and west. I can't stand it. I must get my foot on something solid or—I don't know what."

I laughed at the consternation in his face.

"I mean it," I said. "I've been thinking it over. I've made up my mind. It's no good arguing. I shall go in for work—real work. No! this isn't work; it's only laborious cheating. But I've got an idea! It's an old idea—I thought of years ago, but it came back to me. Look here! Why should I fence about with you? I believe the time has come for flying to be possible. Real flying!"

"Flying!"

I stuck to that, and it helped me through the worst time in my life. My uncle, after some half-hearted resistance and a talk with my aunt, behaved like the father of a spoilt son. He fixed up an arrangement that gave me capital to play with, released me from too constant a solicitude for the newer business developments—this was in what I may call the later Moggs period of our enterprises—and I went to work at once with grim intensity. . . .

But I will tell of my soaring and flying machines in the proper place. I've been leaving the story of my uncle altogether too long. I wanted merely to tell how it was I took to this work. I took to these experiments after I had sought something that Marion in some indefinable way had seemed to promise. I toiled and forgot myself for a time, and did many things. Science too has been something of an irresponsive mistress since, though I've served her better than I served Marion. But at the time Science, with her order, her inhuman distance, yet steely certainties, saved me from despair.

Well, I have still to fly; but incidentally I have invented the lightest engines in the world. . . .

I am trying to tell of all the things that happened to me. It's hard enough simply to get it put down in the remotest degree right. But this is a novel, not a treatise. Don't imagine that I am coming presently to any sort of solution of my difficulties. Here among my drawings and hammerings *now*, I still question unanswering problems. All my life has been at bottom, *seeking*, disbelieving always, dissatisfied always with the thing seen and the thing believed, seeking something in toil, in force, in danger, something whose name and nature I do not clearly understand, something beautiful, worshipful, enduring, mine profoundly and fundamentally, and the utter redemption of myself; I don't know,—all I can tell is that it is something I have ever failed to find.

XI

But before I finish this chapter and book altogether and go on with the great adventure of my uncle's career, I may perhaps tell what else remains to tell of Marion and Effie, and then for a time set my private life behind me.

For a time Marion and I corresponded with some regularity, writing friendly but rather uninforming letters about small business things. The clumsy process of divorce completed itself. She left the house at Ealing and went into the country with her aunt and parents, taking a small farm near Lewes in Sussex. She put up glass, she put in heat for her father, happy man! and spoke of figs and peaches. The thing seemed to promise well throughout a spring and summer, but the Sussex winter after London was too much for the Ramboats. They got very muddy and dull; Mr. Ramboat killed a cow by improper feeding, and that disheartened them all. A twelvemonth saw the enterprise in difficulties. I had to help her out of this, and then they returned to London, and she went into partnership with Smithie at Streatham, and ran a business that was intimated on the firm's stationery as "Robes." The parents and aunt were stowed away in a cottage somewhere. After that the letters became infrequent. But in one I remember a postscript that had a little stab of our old intimacy: "Poor old Miggles is dead."

Nearly eight years slipped by. I grew up. I grew in experience, in capacity, until I was fully a man, busy with many new interests, living on a larger scale in a wider world than I could have dreamt of in my Marion days. Her letters became rare and insignificant. At last came a gap of silence that made me curious. For eighteen months or more I had nothing from Marion save her quarterly receipts through the bank. Then I damned at Smithie, and wrote a card to Marion.

"Dear Marion," I said, "how goes it?"

She astonished me tremendously by telling me she had married again—"a Mr. Wachorn, a leading agent in the paper-pattern trade." But she still wrote on the Ponderevo and Smith (Robes) notepaper, from the Ponderevo and Smith address.

And that, except for a little difference of opinion about the continuance of alimony which gave me some passages of anger, and the use of my name by the firm, which also annoyed me, is the end of Marion's history for me, and she vanishes out of this story. I do not know where she is or what she is doing. I do not know whether she is alive or dead. It seems to me utterly grotesque that two people who have stood so close to one another as she and I should be so separated, but so it is between us.

Effie, too, I have parted from, though I still see her at times. Between us there was never any intention of marriage nor intimacy of soul. She had a sudden, fierce, hot-blooded passion for me and I for her, but I was not her first lover nor her last. She was in another world from Marion. She had a queer, delightful nature; I've no memory of ever seeing her sullen or malicious. She was—indeed she was magnificently—eupeptic. That, I think, was the central secret of her agreeableness, and, moreover, that she was infinitely kind-hearted. I helped her at last into an opening she coveted, and she amazed me by a sudden display of business capacity. She has now a typewriting bureau in Riffle's Inn, and she runs it with a brisk vigour and considerable success, albeit a certain plumpness has overtaken her. And she still loves her kind. She married a year or so ago a boy half her age—a wretch of a poet, a wretched poet, and given to drugs, a thing with lank fair hair always getting into his blue eyes, and limp legs. She did it, she said, because he needed nursing. . . .

But enough of this disaster of my marriage and of my early love affairs; I have told all that is needed for my picture to explain how I came to take up aeroplane experiments and engineering science; let me get back to my essential story, to Tono-Bungay and my uncle's promotions and to the vision of the world these things have given me.

BOOK THE THIRD

THE GREAT DAYS OF TONO-BUNGAY

CHAPTER THE FIRST

The Hardingham Hotel, and How We Became Big People

I

But now that I resume the main line of my story it may be well to describe the personal appearance of my uncle as I remember him during those magnificent years that followed his passage from trade to finance. The little man plumped up very considerably during the creation of the Tono-Bungay property, but with the increasing excitements that followed that first flotation came dyspepsia and a certain flabbiness and falling away. His abdomen—if the reader will pardon my taking his features in the order of their value—had at first a nice full roundness, but afterwards it lost tone without, however, losing size. He always went as though he was proud of it and would make as much of it as possible. To the last his movements remained quick and sudden, his short firm legs, as he walked, seemed to twinkle rather than display the scissors-stride of common humanity, and he never seemed to have knees, but instead, a dispersed flexibility of limb.

There was, I seem to remember, a secular intensification of his features; his nose developed character, became aggressive, stuck out at the world more and more; the obliquity of his mouth, I think, increased. From the face that returns to my memory projects a long cigar that is sometimes cocked jauntily up from the higher corner, that sometimes droops from the lower;—it was as eloquent as a dog's tail, and he removed it only for the more emphatic modes of speech. He assumed a broad black ribbon for his glasses, and wore them more and more askew as time went on. His hair seemed to stiffen with success, but towards the climax it thinned greatly over the crown, and he brushed it hard back over his ears where, however, it stuck out fiercely. It always stuck out fiercely over his forehead, up and forward.

He adopted an urban style of dressing with the onset of Tono-Bungay and rarely abandoned it. He preferred silk hats with ample rich brims, often a trifle large for him by modern ideas, and he wore them at various angles to his axis; his taste in trouserings was towards fairly emphatic stripes and his trouser cut was neat; he liked his frock-coat long and full, although that seemed to shorten him. He displayed a number of valuable rings, and I remember one upon his left little finger with a large red stone bearing Gnostic symbols. "Clever chaps, those Gnostics, George," he told me. "Means a lot. Lucky!" He never had any but a black mohair watch-chain. In the country he affected grey and a large grey cloth top-hat, except when motoring; then he would have a brown deer-stalker cap and a fur suit of Esquimaux cut with a sort of boot-end to the trousers. Of an evening he would wear white waistcoats and plain gold studs. He hated diamonds. "Flashy," he said they were. "Might as well wear an income tax-receipt. All very well for Park Lane. Unsold stock. Not my style. Sober financier, George."

So much for his visible presence. For a time it was very familiar to the world, for at the crest of the boom he allowed quite a number of photographs and at least one pencil sketch to be published in the sixpenny papers. . . . His voice declined during those years from his early tenor to a flat rich quality of sound that my knowledge of music is inadequate to describe. His Zzz-ing inrush of air became less frequent as he ripened, but returned in moments of excitement. Throughout his career, in spite of his increasing and at last astounding opulence, his more intimate habits remained as simple as they had been at Wimblehurst. He would never avail himself of the services of a valet; at the very climax of his greatness his trousers were folded by a housemaid and his shoulders brushed as he left his house or hotel. He became wary about breakfast as life advanced, and at one time talked much of Dr. Haig and uric acid. But for other meals he remained reasonably omnivorous. He was something of a gastronome, and would eat anything he particularly liked in an audible manner, and perspire upon his forehead. He was a studiously moderate drinker—except when the spirit of some public banquet or some great occasion caught him and bore him beyond his wariness—then he would, as it were, drink inadvertently and become flushed and talkative—about everything but his business projects.

To make the portrait complete one wants to convey an effect of sudden, quick bursts of movement like the jumps of a Chinese-cracker to indicate that his pose, whatever it is, has been preceded and will be followed by a rush. If I were painting him, I should certainly give him for a background that distressed, uneasy sky that was popular in the eighteenth century, and at a convenient distance a throbbing motor-car, very big and contemporary, a secretary hurrying with papers, and an alert chauffeur.

Such was the figure that created and directed the great property of Tono-Bungay, and from the successful reconstruction of that company passed on to a slow crescendo of magnificent creations and promotions until the whole world of investors marvelled. I have already, I think, mentioned how, long before we offered Tono-Bungay to the public, we took over the English agency of certain American specialties. To this was presently added our exploitation of Moggs' Domestic Soap, and so he took up the Domestic Convenience Campaign that, coupled with his equatorial rotundity and a certain resolute convexity in his bearing, won my uncle his Napoleonic title.

II

It illustrates the romantic element in modern commerce that my uncle met young Moggs at a city dinner—I think it was the Bottle-makers' Company—when both were some way advanced beyond the initial sobriety of the occasion. This was the grandson of the original Moggs, and a very typical instance of an educated, cultivated, degenerate plutocrat. His people had taken him about in his youth as the Ruskins took their John, and fostered a passion for history in him, and the actual management of the Moggs' industry had devolved upon a cousin and a junior partner. Mr. Moggs, being of a studious and refined disposition, had just decided—after a careful search for a congenial subject in which he would not be constantly reminded of soap—to devote himself to the History of the Thebaid, when this cousin died suddenly and precipitated responsibilities upon him. In the frankness of conviviality, Moggs bewailed the uncongenial task thus thrust into his hands, and my uncle offered to lighten his burden by a partnership then and there. They even got to terms—extremely muzzy terms, but terms nevertheless.

Each gentleman wrote the name and address of the other on his cuff, and they separated in a mood of brotherly carelessness, and next morning neither seems to have thought to rescue his shirt from the wash until it was too late. My uncle made a painful struggle—it was one of my business mornings—to recall name and particulars.

"He was an aquarium-faced, long, blond sort of chap, George, with glasses and a genteel accent," he said.

I was puzzled. "Aquarium-faced?"

"You know how they look at you. His stuff was soap, I'm pretty nearly certain. And he had a name. And the thing was the straightest Bit-of-All-Right you ever. I was clear enough to spot that . . ."

We went out at last with knitted brows, and wandered up into Finsbury seeking a good, well-stocked looking grocer. We called first on a chemist for a pick-me-up for my uncle, and then we found the shop we needed.

"I want," said my uncle, "half a pound of every sort of soap you got. Yes, I want to take them now.. . . . Wait a moment, George. . . . Now whassort of soap d'you call *that?*"

At the third repetition of that question the young man said, "Moggs' Domestic."

"Right," said my uncle. "You needn't guess again. Come along, George, let's go to a telephone and get on to Moggs. Oh—the order? Certainly. I confirm it. Send it all—send it all to the Bishop of London; he'll have some good use for it—(First-rate man, George, he is—charities and all that) —and put it down to me—here's a card—Ponderevo—Tono-Bungay."

Then we went on to Moggs and found him in a camel-hair dressing-jacket in a luxurious bed, drinking China tea, and got the shape of everything but the figures fixed by lunch time.

Young Moggs enlarged my mind considerably; he was a sort of thing I hadn't met before; he seemed quite clean and well-informed and he assured me he never read newspapers nor used soap in any form at all. "Delicate skin," he said.

"No objection to our advertising you wide and free?" said my uncle.

"I draw the line at railway stations," said Moggs, "south-coast cliffs, theatre programmes, books by me and poetry generally—scenery—oh!—and the *Mercure de France*."

"We'll get along," said my uncle.

"So long as you don't annoy me," said Moggs, lighting a cigarette, "you can make me as rich as you like."

We certainly made him no poorer. His was the first firm that was advertised by a circumstantial history; we even got to illustrated magazine articles telling of the quaint past of Moggs. We concocted Moggsiana. Trusting to our partner's preoccupation with the uncommercial aspects of life, we gave graceful histories of Moggs the First, Moggs the Second, Moggs the Third, and Moggs the Fourth. You must, unless you are very young, remember some of them and our admirable block of a Georgian shop window. My uncle brought early nineteenth-century memoirs, soaked himself in the style, and devised stories about old Moggs the First and the Duke of Wellington, George the Third and the soap dealer ("almost certainly old Moggs"). Very soon we had added to the original Moggs' Primrose several varieties of scented and superfatted, a "special nursery—as used in the household of the Duke of Kent and for the old Queen in Infancy," a plate powder, "the Paragon," and a knife powder. We roped in a good little second-rate black-lead firm, and carried their origins back into the mists of antiquity. It was my uncle's own unaided idea that we should associate that commodity with the Black Prince. He became industriously curious about the past of black-lead. I remember his button-holing the president of the Pepys Society.

"I say, is there any black-lead in Pepys? You know— black-lead—for grates! *Or does he pass it over as a matter of course?*"

He became in those days the terror of eminent historians. "Don't want your drum and trumpet history—no fear," he used to say. "Don't want to know who was who's mistress, and why so-and-so devastated such a province; that's bound to be all lies and upsy-down anyhow. Not my affair. Nobody's affair now. Chaps who did it didn't clearly know. . . . What I want to know is, in the Middle Ages Did they Do Anything for Housemaid's Knee? What did they put in their hot baths after jousting, and was the Black Prince— you know the Black Prince—was he enamelled or painted, or what? I think myself, black-leaded—very likely—like pipe-clay—but *did* they use blacking so early?"

So it came about that in designing and writing those Moggs' Soap Advertisements, that wrought a revolution in that department of literature, my uncle was brought to realise not only the lost history, but also the enormous field for invention and enterprise that lurked among the little articles, the dustpans and mincers, the mouse-traps and carpet-sweepers that fringe the shops of the oilman and domestic ironmonger. He was recalled to one of the dreams of his youth, to his conception of the Ponderevo Patent Flat that had been in his mind so early as the days before I went to serve him at Wimblehurst. "The Home, George," he said, "wants straightening up. Silly muddle! Things that get in the way. Got to organise it."

For a time he displayed something like the zeal of a genuine social reformer in relation to these matters.

"We've got to bring the Home Up to Date? That's my idee, George. We got to make a civilised d'mestic machine out of these relics of barbarism. I'm going to hunt up inventors, make a corner in d'mestic idees. Everything. Balls of string that won't dissolve into a tangle, and gum that won't dry into horn. See? Then after conveniences—beauty. Beauty, George! All these new things ought to be made fit to look at; it's your aunt's idee, that. Beautiful jam-pots! Get one of those new art chaps to design all the things they make ugly now. Patent carpet-sweepers by these greenwood chaps, housemaid's boxes it'll be a pleasure to fall over—rich coloured house-flannels. Zzzz. Pails, f'rinstance. Hang 'em up on the walls like warming-pans. All the polishes and things in such tins—you'll want to cuddle 'em, George! See the notion? 'Sted of all the silly ugly things we got." . . .

We had some magnificent visions; they so affected me that when I passed ironmongers and oil-shops they seemed to me as full of promise as trees in late winter, flushed with the effort to burst into leaf and flower. . . . And really we did do much towards that new brightness these shops display. They were dingy things in the eighties compared to what our efforts have made them now, grey quiet displays. . . .

Well, I don't intend to write down here the tortuous financial history of Moggs' Limited, which was our first development of Moggs and Sons; nor will I tell very much of how from that we spread ourselves with a larger and larger conception throughout the chandlery and minor ironmongery, how we became agents for this little commodity, partners in that, got a tentacle round the neck of a specialised manufacturer or so, secured a pull upon this or that supply of raw material, and so prepared the way for our second flotation, Domestic Utilities;—"Do Ut," they rendered it in the city. And then came the reconstruction of Tono-Bungay, and then "Household Services" and the Boom!

That sort of development is not to be told in detail in a novel. I have, indeed, told much of it elsewhere. It is to be found set out at length, painfully at length, in my uncle's examination and mine in the bankruptcy proceedings, and in my own various statements after his death. Some people know everything in that story, some know it all too well, most do not want the details. It is the story of a man of imagination among figures, and unless you are prepared to collate columns of pounds, shillings and pence, compare dates and check additions, you will find it very unmeaning and perplexing. And after all, you wouldn't find the early figures so much wrong as *strained*. In the matter of Moggs and Do Ut, as in the first Tono-Bungay promotion and in its reconstruction, we left the court by city standards without a stain on our characters. The great amalgamation of Household Services was my uncle's first really big-scale enterprise and his first display of bolder methods; for this we bought back Do Ut, Muggs (going strong with a seven per cent. dividend) and acquired Skinnerton's polishes, the Riffleshaw properties and the Runcorn's mincer and coffee-mill business. To that Amalgamation I was really not a party; I left it to my uncle because I was then beginning to get keen upon the soaring experiments I had taken on from the results then to hand of Lilienthal, Pilcher and the Wright brothers. I was developing a glider into a flyer. I meant to apply power to this glider as soon as I could work out one or two residual problems affecting the longitudinal stability. I knew that I had a sufficiently light motor in my own modification of Bridger's light turbine, but I knew too that until I had cured my aeroplane of a tendency demanding constant alertness from me, a tendency to jerk up its nose at unexpected moments and slide back upon me, the application of an engine would be little short of suicide.

But that I will tell about later. The point I was coming

to was that I did not realise until after the crash how reck-lessly my uncle had kept his promise of paying a dividend of over eight per cent. on the ordinary shares of that hugely over-capitalised enterprise, Household Services.

I drifted out of business affairs into my research much more than either I or my uncle had contemplated. Finance was much less to my taste than the organisation of the Tono-Bungay factory. In the new field of enterprise there was a great deal of bluffing and gambling, of taking chances and concealing material facts—and these are hateful things to the scientific type of mind. It wasn't fear I felt so much as an uneasy inaccuracy. I didn't realise dangers, I simply disliked the sloppy, relaxing quality of this new sort of work. I was at last constantly making excuses not to come up to him in London. The latter part of his business career recedes therefore beyond the circle of my particular life. I lived more or less with him; I talked, I advised, I helped him at times to fight his Sunday crowd at Crest Hill, but I did not follow nor guide him. From the Do Ut time on-ward he rushed up the financial world like a bubble in water and left me like some busy water-thing down below in the deeps.

Anyhow, he was an immense success. The public was, I think, particularly attracted by the homely familiarity of his field of work—you never lost sight of your investment they felt, with the name on the house-flannel and shaving-strop—and its allegiance was secured by the Egyptian solid-ity of his apparent results. Tono-Bungay, after its recon-struction, paid thirteen, Moggs seven, Domestic Utilities had been a safe-looking nine; here was Household Services with eight; on such a showing he had merely to buy and sell Roeburn's Antiseptic fluid, Razor soaks and Bath crys-tals in three weeks to clear twenty thousand pounds. I do think that as a matter of fact Roeburn's was good value at the price at which he gave it to the public, at least until it was strained by ill-conceived advertisement. It was a period of expansion and confidence; much money was seek-ing investment and "Industrials" were the fashion. Prices

[219]

were rising all round. There remained little more for my uncle to do, therefore, in his climb to the high unstable crest of Financial Greatness but, as he said, to "grasp the cosmic oyster, George, while it gaped," which, being translated, meant for him to buy respectable businesses confidently and courageously at the vendor's estimate, add thirty or forty thousand to the price and sell them again. His sole difficulty indeed was the tactful management of the load of shares that each of these transactions left upon his hands. But I thought so little of these later things that I never fully appreciated the peculiar inconveniences of that until it was too late to help him.

III

When I think of my uncle near the days of his Great Boom and in connection with the actualities of his enterprises, I think of him as I used to see him in the suite of rooms he occupied in the Hardingham Hotel, seated at a great old oak writing-table, smoking, drinking, and incoherently busy; that was his typical financial aspect—our evenings, our mornings, our holidays, our motor-car expeditions, Lady Grove and Crest Hill belong to an altogether different set of memories.

These rooms in the Hardingham were a string of apartments along one handsome thick-carpeted corridor. All the doors upon the corridor were locked except the first; and my uncle's bedroom, breakfast-room and private sanctum were the least accessible and served by an entrance from the adjacent passage, which he also used at times as a means of escape from importunate callers. The most external room was a general waiting-room and very business-like in quality; it had one or two uneasy sofas, a number of chairs, a green baize table, and a collection of the very best Moggs and Tono posters; and the plush carpets normal to the Hardingham had been replaced by a grey-green cork linoleum. Here I would always find a remarkable miscellany of people, presided over by a peculiarly faithful and ferocious-looking commissionaire, Ropper, who guarded the door that led a step nearer my uncle. Usually there would be a parson or so, and one or two widows; hairy, eye-glassy, middle-aged gentlemen, some of them looking singularly like Edward Ponderevos who hadn't come off, a variety of young and youngish men more or less attractively dressed, some with papers protruding from their pockets, others with their papers decently concealed. And wonderful, incidental, frowsy people.

All these persons maintained a practically hopeless siege —sometimes for weeks together; they had better have stayed at home. Next came a room full of people who had some sort of appointment, and here one would find smart-looking people, brilliantly dressed, nervous women hiding behind magazines, nonconformist divines, clergy in gaiters, real business men, these latter for the most part gentlemen in admirable morning dress who stood up and scrutinised my uncle's taste in water colours manfully and sometimes by the hour together. Young men again were here of various social origins—young Americans, treasonable clerks from other concerns, university young men, keen-looking, most of them, resolute, reserved, but on a sort of hair trigger, ready at any moment to be most voluble, most persuasive.

This room had a window, too, looking out into the hotel courtyard with its fern-set fountains and mosaic pavement, and the young men would stand against this and sometimes even mutter. One day I heard one repeating in an urgent whisper as I passed, "But you don't quite see, Mr. Ponderevo, the full advantages, the *full* advantages——" I met his eye and he was embarrassed.

Then came a room with a couple of secretaries—no typewriters, because my uncle hated the clatter—and a casual person or two sitting about, projectors whose projects were being entertained. Here and in a further room nearer the private apartments, my uncle's correspondence underwent an exhaustive process of pruning and digestion before it reached him. Then the two little rooms in which my uncle talked; my magic uncle who had *got* the investing public—

to whom all things were possible.

As one came in one would find him squatting with his cigar up and an expression of dubious beatitude upon his face, while some one urged him to grow still richer by this or that.

"Thatju, George?" he used to say. "Come in. Here's a thing. Tell him—Mister—over again. Have a drink, George? No! Wise man! Liss'n."

I was always ready to listen. All sorts of financial marvels came out of the Hardingham, more particularly during my uncle's last great flurry, but they were nothing to the projects that passed in. It was the little brown and gold room he sat in usually. He had had it redecorated by Bordingly and half a dozen Sussex pictures by Webster hung about it. Latterly he wore a velveteen jacket of a golden-brown colour in this apartment that I think over-emphasised its æsthetic intention, and he also added some gross Chinese bronzes. . . .

He was, on the whole, a very happy man throughout all that wildly enterprising time. He made and, as I shall tell in its place, spent great sums of money. He was constantly in violent motion, constantly stimulated mentally and physically and rarely tired. About him was an atmosphere of immense deference; much of his waking life was triumphal and all his dreams. I doubt if he had any dissatisfaction with himself at all until the crash bore him down. Things must have gone very rapidly with him. . . . I think he must have been very happy.

As I sit here writing about all these things, jerking down notes and throwing them aside in my attempt to give some literary form to the tale of our promotions, the marvel of it all comes to me as if it came for the first time, the supreme unreason of it. At the climax of his Boom, my uncle at the most sparing estimate must have possessed in substance and credit about two million pounds'-worth of property to set off against his vague colossal liabilities, and from first to last he must have had a controlling influence in the direction of nearly thirty millions. This irrational muddle of a community in which we live gave him that, paid him at that rate for sitting in a room and scheming and telling it lies. For he created nothing, he invented nothing, he economised nothing. I cannot claim that a single one of the great businesses we organised added any real value to human life at all. Several like Tono-Bungay were unmitigated frauds by any honest standard, the giving of nothing coated in advertisements for money. And the things the Hardingham gave out, I repeat, were nothing to the things that came in. I think of the long procession of people who sat down before us and propounded this and that. Now it was a device for selling bread under a fancy name and so escaping the laws as to weight—this was afterwards floated as the Decorticated Health-Bread Company and bumped against the law—now it was a new scheme for still more strident advertisement, now it was a story of unsuspected deposits of minerals, now a cheap and nasty substitute for this or that common necessity, now the treachery of a too well-informed employee, anxious to become our partner. It was all put to us tentatively, persuasively. Sometimes one had a large pink blusterous person trying to carry us off our feet by his pseudo-boyish frankness, now some dyspeptically yellow whisperer, now some earnest, specially dressed youth with an eye-glass and a buttonhole, now some homely-speaking, shrewd Manchester man or some Scotchman eager to be very clear and full. Many came in couples or trios, often in tow of an explanatory solicitor. Some were white and earnest, some flustered beyond measure at their opportunity. Some of them begged and prayed to be taken up. My uncle chose what he wanted and left the rest. He became very autocratic to these applicants. He felt he could make them, and they felt so too. He had but to say "No!" and they faded out of existence. . . . He had become a sort of vortex to which wealth flowed of its own accord. His possessions increased by heaps; his shares, his leaseholds and mortgages and debentures.

Behind his first-line things he found it necessary at last, and sanctioned by all the precedents, to set up three general trading companies, the London and African Investment Company, the British Traders' Loan Company, and Business Organisations Limited. This was in the culminating time when I had least to do with affairs. I don't say that with any desire to exculpate myself; I admit I was a director of all three, and I will confess I was wilfully incurious in that capacity. Each of these companies ended its financial year solvent by selling great holdings of shares to one or other of its sisters, and paying a dividend out of the proceeds. I sat at the table and agreed. That was our method of equilibrium at the iridescent climax of the bubble. . . .

You perceive now, however, the nature of the services for which this fantastic community gave him unmanageable wealth and power and real respect. It was all a monstrous payment for courageous fiction, a gratuity in return for the one reality of human life—illusion. We gave them a feeling of hope and profit; we sent a tidal wave of water and confidence into their stranded affairs. "We mint Faith, George," said my uncle one day. "That's what we do. And by Jove we got to keep minting! We been making human confidence ever since I drove the first cork of Tono-Bungay."

"Coining" would have been a better word than minting! And yet, you know, in a sense he was right. Civilisation is possible only through confidence, so that we can bank our money and go unarmed about the streets. The bank reserve or a policeman keeping order in a jostling multitude of people, are only slightly less impudent bluffs than my uncle's prospectuses. They couldn't for a moment "make good" if the quarter of what they guarantee was demanded of them. The whole of this modern mercantile investing civilisation is indeed such stuff as dreams are made of. A mass of people swelters and toils, great railway systems grow, cities arise to the skies and spread wide and far, mines are opened, factories hum, foundries roar, ships plough the seas, countries are settled; about this busy striving world the rich owners go, controlling all, enjoying all, confident and creating the confidence that draws us all together into a reluctant, nearly unconscious brotherhood. I wonder and plan my engines. The flags flutter, the crowds cheer, the legislatures meet. Yet it seems to me indeed at times that all this present commercial civilisation is no more than my poor uncle's career writ large, a swelling, thinning bubble of assurances; that its arithmetic is just as unsound, its dividends as ill-advised, its ultimate aim as vague and forgotten; that it all drifts on perhaps to some tremendous parallel to his individual disaster. . . .

Well, so it was we Boomed, and for four years and a half we lived a life of mingled substance and moonshine. Until our particular unsoundness overtook us we went about in the most magnificent of motor-cars upon tangible high roads, made ourselves conspicuous and stately in splendid houses, ate sumptuously and had a perpetual stream of notes and money trickling into our pockets; hundreds of thousands of men and women respected us, saluted us and gave us toil and honour; I asked, and my worksheds rose, my aeroplanes swooped out of nothingness to scare the downland pe-wits; my uncle waved his hand and Lady Grove and all its associations of chivalry and ancient peace were his; waved again, and architects were busy planning the great palace he never finished at Crest Hill and an army of workmen gathered to do his bidding, blue marble came from Canada, and timber from New Zealand; and beneath it all, you know, there was nothing but fictitious values as evanescent as rainbow gold.

IV

I pass the Hardingham ever and again and glance aside through the great archway at the fountain and the ferns, and think of those receding days when I was so near the centre of our eddy of greed and enterprise. I see again my uncle's face, white and intent, and hear him discourse, hear him make consciously Napoleonic decisions, "grip" his nettles, put his "finger on the spot," "bluff," say "snap." He became particularly addicted to the last idiom. Towards the end every conceivable act took the form of saying "snap!" . . .

The odd fish that came to us! And among others came Gordon-Nasmyth, that queer blend of romance and illegality who was destined to drag me into the most irrelevant adventure in my life, the Mordet Island affair; and leave me, as they say, with blood upon my hands. It is remarkable how little it troubles my conscience and how much it stirs my imagination, that particular memory of the life I took. The story of Mordet Island has been told in a government report and told all wrong; there are still excellent reasons for leaving it wrong in places, but the liveliest appeals of discretion forbid my leaving it out altogether.

I've still the vividest memory of Gordon-Nasmyth's appearance in the inner sanctum, a lank, sunburnt person in tweeds with a yellow-brown hatchet face and one faded blue eye—the other was a closed and sunken lid—and how he told us with a stiff affectation of ease his incredible story of this great heap of quap that lay abandoned or undiscovered on the beach behind Mordet's Island among white dead mangroves and the black ooze of brackish water.

"What's quap?" said my uncle on the fourth repetition of the word.

"They call it quap, or quab, or quabb," said Gordon-Nasmyth; "but our relations weren't friendly enough to get the accent right. . . . But there the stuff is for the taking. They don't know about it. Nobody knows about it. I got down to the damned place in a canoe alone. The boys wouldn't come. I pretended to be botanising." . . .

To begin with, Gordon-Nasmyth was inclined to be dramatic.

"Look here," he said when he first came in, shutting the door rather carefully behind him as he spoke, "do you two men—yes or no—want to put up six thousand—for a clear good chance of fifteen hundred per cent. on your money in a year?"

"We're always getting chances like that," said my uncle,

cocking his cigar offensively, wiping his glasses and tilting his chair back. "We stick to a safe twenty."

Gordon-Nasmyth's quick temper showed in a slight stiffening of his attitude.

"Don't you believe him," said I, getting up before he could reply. "*You're* different, and I know your books. We're very glad you've come to us. Confound it, uncle! It's Gordon-Nasmyth! Sit down. What is it? Minerals?"

"Quap," said Gordon-Nasmyth, fixing his eye on me, "in heaps."

"In heaps," said my uncle softly, with his glasses very oblique.

"You're only fit for the grocery," said Gordon-Nasmyth scornfully, sitting down and helping himself to one of my uncle's cigars. "I'm sorry I came. But, still, now I'm here. . . . And first as to quap; quap, sir, is the most radioactive stuff in the world. That's quap! It's a festering mass of earths and heavy metals, polonium, radium, ythorium, thorium, carium, and new things, too. There's a stuff called Xk—provisionally. There they are, mucked up together in a sort of rotting sand. What it is, how it got made, I don't know. It's like as if some young creator had been playing about there. There it lies in two heaps, one small, one great, and the world for miles about it is blasted and scorched and dead. You can have it for the getting. You've got to take it—that's all!" . . .

"That sounds all right," said I. "Have you samples?"

"Well—*should* I? You can have anything—up to two ounces."

"Where is it?" . . .

His blue eye smiled at me and scrutinised me. He smoked and was fragmentary for a time, fending off my questions; then his story began to piece itself together. He conjured up a vision of this strange forgotten kink in the world's littoral, of the long meandering channels that spread and divaricate and spend their burthen of mud and silt within the thunderbelt of Atlantic surf, of the dense tangled vegetation that creeps into the shimmering water with root and sucker. He gave a sense of heat and a perpetual reek of vegetable decay, and told how at last comes a break among these things, an arena fringed with bone-white dead trees, a sight of the hard-blue sea line beyond the dazzling surf and a wide desolation of dirty shingle and mud, bleached and scarred. . . . A little way off among charred dead weeds stands the abandoned station,—abandoned because every man who stayed two months at that station stayed to die, eaten up mysteriously like a leper—with its dismantled sheds and its decaying pier of worm-rotten and oblique piles and planks, still insecurely possible. And in the midst, two clumsy heaps shaped like the backs of hogs, one small, one great, sticking out under a rib of rock that cuts the space across,—quap!

"There it is," said Gordon-Nasmyth, "worth three pounds an ounce, if it's worth a penny; two great heaps of it, rotten stuff and soft, ready to shovel and wheel, and you may get it by the ton!"

"How did it get there?"

"God knows! . . . There it is—for the taking! In a country where you mustn't trade. In a country where the company waits for good kind men to find it riches and then take 'em away from 'em. There you have it—derelict."

"Can't you do any sort of deal?"

"They're too damn stupid. You've got to go and take it. That's all."

"They might catch you."

"They might, of course. But they're not great at catching."

We went into the particulars of that difficulty. "They wouldn't catch me, because I'd sink first. Give me a yacht," said Gordon-Nasmyth; "that's all I need."

"But if you get caught," said my uncle. . . .

I am inclined to think Gordon-Nasmyth imagined we would give him a cheque for six thousand pounds on the strength of his talk. It was very good talk, but we didn't do that. I stipulated for samples of his stuff for analysis, and he consented—reluctantly. I think, on the whole, he would rather I didn't examine samples. He made a motion pocketwards, that gave us an invincible persuasion that he had a sample upon him, and that at the last instant he decided not to produce it prematurely. There was evidently a curious strain of secretiveness in him. He didn't like to give us samples, and he wouldn't indicate within three hundred miles the position of this Mordet Island of his. He had it clear in his mind that he had a secret of immense value, and he had no idea at all of just how far he ought to go with business people. And so presently, to gain time for these hesitations of his, he began to talk of other things.

He talked very well. He talked of the Dutch East Indies and of the Congo, of Portuguese East Africa and Paraguay, of Malays and rich Chinese merchants, Dyaks and negroes and the spread of the Mahometan world in Africa to-day. And all this time he was trying to judge if we were good enough to trust with his adventure. Our cosy inner office became a little place, and all our business cold and lifeless exploits beside his glimpses of strange minglings of men, of slayings unavenged and curious customs, of trade where no writs run, and the dark treacheries of eastern ports and uncharted channels.

We had neither of us gone abroad except for a few vulgar raids on Paris; our world was England, and the places of origin of half the raw material of the goods we sold had seemed to us as remote as fairyland or the forest of Arden. But Gordon-Nasmyth made it so real and intimate for us that afternoon—for me, at any rate—that it seemed like something seen and forgotten and now again remembered.

And in the end he produced his sample, a little lump of muddy clay speckled with brownish grains, in a glass bottle wrapped about with lead and flannel—red flannel it was, I remember—a hue which is, I know, popularly supposed to double all the mystical efficacies of flannel.

"Don't carry it about on you," said Gordon-Nasmyth. "It makes a sore."

I took the stuff to Thorold, and Thorold had the exquisite agony of discovering two new elements in what was then a confidential analysis. He has christened them and published since, but at the time Gordon-Nasmyth wouldn't hear for a moment of our publication of any facts at all; indeed, he flew into a violent passion and abused me mercilessly even for showing the stuff to Thorold. "I thought you were going to analyse it yourself," he said with the touching persuasion of the layman that a scientific man knows and practises all the sciences.

I made some commercial inquiries, and there seemed even then much truth in Gordon-Nasmyth's estimate of the value of the stuff. It was before the days of Capern's discovery of the value of canadium and his use of it in the Capern filament, but the cerium and thorium alone were worth the money he extracted for the gas-mantles then in vogue. There were, however, doubts. Indeed, there were numerous doubts. What were the limits of the gas-mantle trade? How much thorium, not to speak of cerium, could they take at a maximum. Suppose that quantity was high enough to justify our shipload, came doubts in another quarter. Were the heaps up to sample? Were they as big as he said? Was Gordon-Nasmyth—imaginative? And if these values held, could we after all get the stuff? It wasn't ours. It was on forbidden ground. You see, there were doubts of every grade and class in the way of this adventure.

We went some way, nevertheless, in the discussion of his project, though I think we tried his patience. Then suddenly he vanished from London, and I saw no more of him for a year and a half.

My uncle said that was what he had expected, and when at last Gordon-Nasmyth reappeared and mentioned in an incidental way that he had been to Paraguay on private (and we guessed passionate) affairs, the business of the "quap" expedition had to be begun again at the beginning. My uncle was disposed to be altogether sceptical, but I wasn't so decided. I think I was drawn by its picturesque aspects. But we neither of us dreamt of touching it seriously until Capern's discovery. . . .

Nasmyth's story had laid hold of my imagination like

one small, intense picture of tropical sunshine hung on a wall of grey business affairs. I kept it going during Gordon-Nasmyth's intermittent appearances in England. Every now and then he and I would meet and reinforce its effect. We would lunch in London, or he would come to see my gliders at Crest Hill, and make new projects for getting at those heaps again, now with me, now alone. At times they became a sort of fairy-story with us, an imaginative exercise. And then came Capern's discovery of what he called the ideal filament, and with it an altogether less problematical quality about the business side of quap. For the ideal filament needed five per cent. of canadium, and canadium was known to the world only as a newly separated constituent of a variety of the rare mineral rutile. But to Thorold it was better known as an element in a mysterious sample brought to him by me, and to me it was known as one of the elements in quap. I told my uncle, and we jumped on to the process at once. We found that Gordon-Nasmyth, still unaware of the altered value of the stuff, and still thinking of the experimental prices of radium and the rarity value of cerium, had got hold of a cousin named Pollack, made some extraordinary transaction about his life insurance policy, and was buying a brig. We cut in, put down three thousand pounds, and forthwith the life insurance transaction and the Pollack side of this finance vanished into thin air, leaving Pollack, I regret to say, in the brig and in the secret— except so far as canadium and the filament went—as residuum. We discussed earnestly whether we should charter a steamer or go on with the brig, but we decided on the brig as a less conspicuous instrument for an enterprise that was after all, to put it plainly, stealing.

But that was one of our last enterprises before our great crisis, and I will tell of it in its place.

So it was quap came into our affairs, came in as a fairytale and became real. More and more real it grew until at last it was real, until at last I saw with my eyes the heaps my imagination had seen for so long, and felt between my fingers again that half-gritty, half-soft texture of quap, like sanded moist-sugar mixed with clay in which there stirs something——

One must feel it to understand.

v

All sorts of things came to the Hardingham and offered themselves to my uncle. Gordon-Nasmyth stands out only because he played a part at last in the crisis of our fortunes. So much came to us that it seemed to me at times as though the whole world of human affairs was ready to prostitute itself to our real and imaginary millions. As I look back, I am still dazzled and incredulous to think of the quality of our opportunities. We did the most extraordinary things; things that it seems absurd to me to leave to any casual man of wealth and enterprise who cares to do them. I had some amazing perceptions of just how modern thought and the supply of fact to the general mind may be controlled by money. Among other things that my uncle offered for, he tried very hard to buy the *British Medical Journal* and the *Lancet*, and run them on what he called modern lines, and when they resisted him he talked very vigorously for a time of organising a rival enterprise. That was a very magnificent idea indeed in its way; it would have given a tremendous advantage in the handling of innumerable specialties, and indeed I scarcely know how far it would not have put the medical profession in our grip. It still amazes me—I shall die amazed—that such a thing can be possible in the modern state. If my uncle failed to bring the thing off, some one else may succeed. But I doubt, even if he had got both these weeklies, whether his peculiar style would have suited them. The change of purpose would have shown. He would have found it difficult to keep up their dignity.

He certainly did not keep up the dignity of the *Sacred Grove*, an important critical organ which he acquired one day—by saying "snap"—for eight hundred pounds. He got it "lock, stock and barrel"—under one or other of which three aspects the editor was included. Even at that price it didn't pay. If you are a literary person you will remember the bright new cover he gave that representative organ of British intellectual culture, and how his sound business instincts jarred with the exalted pretensions of a vanishing age. One old wrapper I discovered the other day runs:—

"THE SACRED GROVE."

A Weekly Magazine of Art, Philosophy, Science and Belles Lettres.

HAVE YOU A NASTY TASTE IN YOUR MOUTH?
IT IS LIVER.
YOU NEED ONE TWENTY-THREE PILL.
(JUST ONE.)
NOT A DRUG BUT A LIVE AMERICAN REMEDY.

CONTENTS.

A Hitherto Unpublished Letter from Walter Pater.
Charlotte Brontë's Maternal Great Aunt.
A New Catholic History of England.
The Genius of Shakespeare.
Correspondence:—The Mendelian Hypothesis; The Split Infinitive; "Commence," or "Begin"; Claverhouse; Socialism and the Individual; The Dignity of Letters.
Folk-lore Gossip.
The Stage; the Paradox of Acting.
Travel, Biography, Verse, Fiction, etc.

THE BEST PILL IN THE WORLD FOR AN IRREGULAR LIVER.

I suppose it is some lingering traces of the Bladesover tradition in me that makes this combination of letters and pills seem so incongruous, just as I suppose it is a lingering trace of Plutarch and my ineradicable boyish imagination that at bottom our State should be wise, sane and dignified, that makes me think a country which leaves its medical and literary criticism, or indeed any such vitally important criticism, entirely to private enterprise and open to the advances of any purchaser must be in a frankly hopeless condition. These are ideal conceptions of mine. As a matter of fact, nothing could be more entirely natural and representative of the relations of learning, thought and the economic situation in the world at the present time than this cover of the *Sacred Grove*—the quiet conservatism of the one element embedded in the aggressive brilliance of the other; the contrasted notes of bold physiological experiment and extreme mental immobility.

VI

There comes back, too, among these Hardingham memories, an impression of a drizzling November day, and how we looked out of the windows upon a procession of the London unemployed.

It was like looking down a well into some momentarily revealed nether world. Some thousands of needy ineffectual men had been raked together to trail their spiritless misery through the West End with an appeal that was also in its way a weak and unsubstantial threat: "It is Work we need, not Charity."

There they were, half-phantom through the fog, a silent, foot-dragging, interminable, grey procession. They carried wet, dirty banners, they rattled boxes for pence; these men who had not said "snap" in the right place, the men who had "snapped" too eagerly, the men who had never said "snap," the men who had never had a chance of saying "snap." A shambling, shameful stream they made, oozing along the street, the gutter waste of competitive civilisation. And we stood high out of it all, as high as if we looked godlike from another world, standing in a room beautifully lit and furnished, skilfully warmed, filled with costly things.

"There," thought I, "but for the grace of God, go George and Edward Ponderevo."

But my uncle's thoughts ran in a different channel, and he made that vision the text of a spirited but inconclusive harangue upon Tariff Reform.

CHAPTER THE SECOND

Our Progress from Camden Town to Crest Hill

I

So far my history of my aunt and uncle has dealt chiefly with his industrial and financial exploits. But side by side with that history of inflation from the infinitesimal to the immense is another development, the change year by year from the shabby impecuniosity of the Camden Town lodging to the lavish munificence of the Crest Hill marble staircase and my aunt's golden bed, the bed that was facsimiled from Fontainebleau. And the odd thing is that as I come to this nearer part of my story I find it much more difficult to tell than the clear little perspective memories of the earlier days. Impressions crowd upon one another and overlap one another; I was presently to fall in love again, to be seized by a passion to which I still faintly respond, a passion that still clouds my mind. I came and went between Ealing and my aunt and uncle, and presently between Effie and clubland, and then between business and a life of research that became far more continuous, infinitely more consecutive and memorable than any of these other sets of experiences. I didn't witness a regular social progress therefore; my aunt and uncle went up in the world, so far as I was concerned, as if they were displayed by an early cinematograph, with little jumps and flickers.

As I recall this side of our life, the figure of my round-eyed, button-nosed, pink-and-white Aunt Susan tends always to the central position. We drove the car and sustained the car, she sat in it with a magnificent variety of headgear poised upon her delicate neck, and—always with that faint ghost of a lisp no misspelling can render—commented on and illuminated the new aspects.

I've already sketched the little home behind the Wimblehurst chemist's shop, the lodging near the Cobden statue, and the apartments in Gower Street. Thence my aunt and uncle went into a flat in Redgauntlet Mansions. There they lived when I married. It was a compact flat, with very little for a woman to do in it. In those days my aunt, I think, used to find the time heavy upon her hands, and so she took to books and reading, and after a time even to going to lectures in the afternoon. I began to find unexpected books upon her table: sociological books, travels, Shaw's plays.

"Hullo!" I said, at the sight of some volume of the latter.

"I'm keeping a mind, George," she explained.

"Eh?"

"Keeping a mind. Dogs I never cared for. It's been a toss-up between setting up a mind and setting up a soul. It's jolly lucky for Him and you it's a mind. I've joined the London Library, and I'm going in for the Royal Institution and every blessed lecture that comes along next winter. You'd better look out." . . .

And I remember her coming in late one evening with a note-book in her hand.

"Where ye been, Susan?" said my uncle.

"Birkbeck—Physiology. I'm getting on." She sat down and took off her gloves. "You're just glass to me," she sighed, and then in a note of grave reproach: "You old *Package!* I had no idea! The Things you've kept from me!" . . .

Presently they were setting up the house at Beckenham, and my aunt intermitted her intellectual activities. The house at Beckenham was something of an enterprise for them at that time, a reasonably large place by the standards of the early years of Tono-Bungay. It was a big, rather gaunt villa, with a conservatory and a shrubbery, a tennis-lawn, a quite considerable vegetable garden, and a small disused coach-house. I had some glimpses of the excitements of its inauguration, but not many because of the estrangement between my aunt and Marion.

My aunt went into that house with considerable zest, and my uncle distinguished himself by the thoroughness with which he did the repainting and replumbing. He had all the drains up and most of the garden with them, and stood administrative on heaps—administrating whisky to the workmen. I found him there one day, most Napoleonic, on a little Elba of dirt, in an atmosphere that defies print. He also, I remember, chose what he considered cheerful contrasts of colours for the painting of the woodwork. This exasperated my aunt extremely—she called him a "Pestilential old Splosher" with an unusual note of earnestness—and he also enraged her into novelties of abuse by giving each bedroom the name of some favourite hero—Clive, Napoleon, Cæsar, and so forth—and having it painted on the door in gilt letters on a black label. "Martin Luther" was kept for me. Only her respect for domestic discipline, she said, prevented her retaliating with "Old Pondo" on the housemaid's cupboard.

Also he went and ordered one of the completest sets of garden requisites I have ever seen—and had them all painted a hard clear blue. My aunt got herself large tins of a kindlier hued enamel and had everything secretly recoated, and this done, she found great joy in the garden and became an ardent rose grower and herbaceous borderer, leaving her Mind, indeed, to damp evenings and the winter months. When I think of her at Beckenham, I always think first of her as dressed in that blue cotton stuff she affected, with her arms in huge gauntleted gardening gloves, a trowel in one hand and a small but no doubt hardy and promising annual, limp and very young-looking and sheepish, in the other.

Beckenham, in the persons of a vicar, a doctor's wife, and a large proud lady called Hogberry, "called" on my uncle and aunt almost at once, so soon in fact as the lawn was down again, and afterwards my aunt made friends with a quiet gentlewoman next door, à propos of an overhanging cherry tree and the need of repairing the party fence. So she resumed her place in society from which she had fallen with the disaster of Wimblehurst. She made a partially facetious study of the etiquette of her position, had cards engraved and retaliated calls. And then she received a card for one of Mrs. Hogberry's At Homes, gave an old garden party herself, participated in a bazaar and sale of work, and was really becoming quite cheerfully entangled in Beckenham society when she was suddenly taken up by the roots again by my uncle and transplanted to Chiselhurst.

"Old Trek, George," she said compactly, "Onward and Up," when I found her superintending the loading of two big furniture vans. "Go up and say good-bye to 'Martin Luther,' and then I'll see what you can do to help me."

II

I look into the jumbled stores of the middle distance of memory, and Beckenham seems to me a quite transitory phase. But really they were there several years; through nearly all my married life, in fact, and far longer than the year and odd months we lived together at Wimblehurst. But the Wimblehurst time with them is fuller in my memory by far than the Beckenham period. There comes back to me with a quite considerable amount of detail the effect of that garden party of my aunt's and of a little social misbehaviour of which I was guilty on that occasion. It's like a scrap from another life. It's all set in what is for me a kind of cutaneous feeling, the feeling of rather ill-cut city clothes, frock coat and grey trousers, and of a high collar and tie worn in sunshine among flowers. I have still a quite vivid memory of the little trapezoidal lawn, of the gathering, and particularly of the hats and feathers of the gathering, of the parlour-maid and the blue tea-cups, and of the magnificent presence of Mrs. Hogberry and of her clear, resonant voice. It was a voice that would have gone with a garden party on a larger scale; it went into adjacent premises; it included the gardener who was far up the vegetable patch and technically out of play. The only other men were my aunt's doctor, two of the clergy, amiable contrasted men, and Mrs. Hogberry's imperfectly grown-up son, a youth just bursting into collar. The rest were women, except for a young girl or so in a state of speechless good behaviour. Marion also was there.

Marion and I had arrived a little estranged, and I remember her as a silent presence, a shadow across all that sunlit emptiness of intercourse. We had embittered each other with one of those miserable little disputes that seemed so unavoidable between us. She had, with the help of Smithie, dressed rather elaborately for the occasion, and when she saw me prepared to accompany her in, I think it was a grey suit, she protested that silk hat and frock coat were imperative. I was recalcitrant, she quoted an illustrated paper showing a garden party with the King present, and finally I capitulated—but after my evil habit, resentfully. . . . Eh, dear! those old quarrels, how pitiful they were, how trivial! And how sorrowful they are to recall! I think they grow more sorrowful as I grow older, and all the small passionate reasons for our mutual anger fade and fade out of memory.

The impression that Beckenham company has left on my mind is one of a modest unreality; they were all maintaining a front of unspecified social pretension, and evading the display of the economic facts of the case. Most of the husbands were "in business" off stage—it would have been outrageous to ask what the business was—and the wives were giving their energies to produce, with the assistance of novels and the illustrated magazines, a moralised version of the afternoon life of the aristocratic class. They hadn't the intellectual or moral enterprise of the upper-class woman, they had no political interests, they had no views about anything, and consequently they were, I remember, extremely difficult to talk to. They all sat about in the summer-house and in garden-chairs, and were very hatty and ruffley and sunshady. Three ladies and the curate played croquet with a general immense gravity, broken by occasional loud cries of feigned distress from the curate. "Oh! Whacking me about again! Augh!"

The dominant social fact that afternoon was Mrs. Hogberry; she took up a certain position commanding the croquet and went on, as my aunt said to me in an incidental aside, "like an old Roundabout." She talked of the way in which Beckenham society was getting mixed, and turned on to a touching letter she had recently received from her former nurse at Little Gossdean. Followed a loud account of Little Gossdean and how much she and her eight sisters had been looked up to there. "My poor mother was quite a little Queen there," she said. "And such *nice* Common People! People say the country labourers are getting disrespectful nowadays. It isn't so—not if they're properly treated. Here of course in Beckenham it's different. I don't call the people we get here a Poor—they're certainly not a proper Poor. They're Masses. I always tell Mr. Bugshoot they're Masses, and ought to be treated as such." . . .

Dim memories of Mrs. Mackridge floated through my mind as I listened to her. . . .

I was whirled on this roundabout for a bit, and then had the fortune to fall off into a *tête-à-tête* with a lady whom my aunt introduced as Mrs. Mumble—but then she introduced everybody to me as Mumble that afternoon, either by way of humour or necessity.

That must have been one of my earliest essays in the art of polite conversation, and I remember that I began by criticising the local railway service, and that at the third sentence or thereabouts Mrs. Mumble said in a distinctly bright and encouraging way that she feared I was a very "frivolous" person.

I wonder now what it was I said that was "frivolous."

I don't know what happened to end that conversation, or if it had an end. I remember talking to one of the clergy for a time rather awkwardly, and being given a sort of topographical history of Beckenham, which he assured me time after time was "Quite an old place. *Quite* an old place." As though I had treated it as new and he meant to be very patient but very convincing. Then we hung up in a distinct pause, and my aunt rescued me. "George," she said in a confidential undertone, "keep the pot a-boiling." And then audibly, "I say, will you both old trot about with tea a bit?"

"Only too delighted to *trot* for you, Mrs. Ponderevo," said the clergyman, becoming fearfully expert and in his element; "only too delighted."

I found we were near a rustic table, and that the house-maid was behind us in a suitable position to catch us on the rebound with the tea things.

"Trot!" repeated the clergyman to me, much amused; "excellent expression!" And I just saved him from the tray as he turned about.

We handed tea for a while. . . .

"Give 'em cakes," said my aunt, flushed, but well in hand. "Helps 'em to talk, George. Always talk best after a little nushment. Like throwing a bit of turf down an old geyser."

She surveyed the gathering with a predominant blue eye and helped herself to tea.

"They keep on going stiff," she said in an undertone. . . . "I've done my best."

"It's been a huge success," I said encouragingly.

"That boy has had his legs crossed in that position and hasn't spoken for ten minutes. Stiffer and stiffer. Brittle. He's beginning a dry cough—always a bad sign, George . . . Walk 'em about, shall I?—rub their noses with snow?"

Happily she didn't. I got myself involved with the gentle-woman from next door, a pensive, languid-looking little woman with a low voice, and fell talking; our topic, Cats and Dogs, and which it was we liked best.

"I always feel," said the pensive little woman, "that there's something about a dog—— A cat hasn't got it."

"Yes," I found myself admitting with great enthusiasm, "there *is* something. And yet again——"

"Oh! I know there's something about a cat, too. But it isn't the same."

"Not quite the same," I admitted; "but still it's something."

"Ah! But such a different something!"

"More sinuous."

"Much more."

"Ever so much more." . . .

"It makes all the difference, don't you think?"

"Yes," I said, *"all."*

She glanced at me gravely and sighed a long, deep-felt *"Yes."*

A long pause.

The thing seemed to me to amount to a stale-mate. Fear came into my heart and much perplexity.

"The—er—Roses," I said. I felt like a drowning man. "Those roses—don't you think they are—very beautiful flowers?"

"Aren't they!" she agreed gently. "There seems to be something in roses—something—I don't know how to express it."

"Something," I said helpfully.

"Yes," she said, "something. Isn't there?"

"So few people see it," I said; "more's the pity!"

She sighed and said again very softly, *"Yes."* . . .

There was another long pause. I looked at her and she was thinking dreamily. The drowning sensation returned, the fear and enfeeblement. I perceived by a sort of inspiration that her tea-cup was empty.

"Let me take your cup," I said abruptly, and, that secured, made for the table by the summer-house. I had no intention then of deserting my aunt. But close at hand the big French window of the drawing-room yawned inviting and suggestive. I can feel all that temptation now, and particularly the provocation of my collar. In an instant I was lost. I would—— Just for a moment!

I dashed in, put down the cup on the keys of the grand piano and fled upstairs, softly, swiftly, three steps at a time, to the sanctuary of my uncle's study, his snuggery. I arrived there breathless, convinced there was no return for me. I was very glad and ashamed of myself, and desperate. By means of a pen-knife I contrived to break open

[242]

his cabinet of cigars, drew a chair to the window, took off my coat, collar and tie, and remained smoking guiltily and rebelliously, and peeping through the blind at the assembly on the lawn until it was altogether gone. . . .

The clergymen, I thought, were wonderful.

III

A few such pictures of those early days at Beckenham stand out, and then I find myself among the Chiselhurst memories. The Chiselhurst mansion had "grounds" rather than a mere garden, and there was a gardener's cottage and a little lodge at the gate. The ascendant movement was always far more in evidence there than at Beckenham. The velocity was increasing.

One night picks itself out as typical, as, in its way, marking an epoch. I was there, I think, about some advertisement stuff, on some sort of business anyhow, and my uncle and aunt had come back in a fly from a dinner at the Runcorns. (Even then he was nibbling at Runcorn with the idea of our great Amalgamation budding in his mind.) I got down there, I suppose, about eleven. I found the two of them sitting in the study, my aunt on a chair-arm with a whimsical pensiveness on her face, regarding my uncle, and he, much extended and very rotund, in the low arm-chair drawn up to the fender.

"Look here, George," said my uncle, after my first greetings. "I just been saying: We aren't Oh Fay!"

"Eh?"

"Not Oh Fay! Socially!"

"Old *Fly,* he means, George—French!"

"Oh! Didn't think of French. One never knows where to have him. What's gone wrong to-night?"

"I been thinking. It isn't any particular thing. I ate too much of that fishy stuff at first, like salt frog spawn, and was a bit confused by olives; and—well, I didn't know which wine was which. Had to say *that* each time. It puts your talk all wrong. And she wasn't in evening dress, not like the others. We can't go on in that style, George—not a proper ad."

"I'm not sure you were right," I said, "in having a fly."

"We got to do it all better," said my uncle, "we got to do it in Style. Smart business, smart men. She tries to pass it off as humorous"—my aunt pulled a grimace—"it isn't humorous! See! We're on the upgrade now, fair and square. We're going to be big. We aren't going to be laughed at as Poovenoos, see!"

"Nobody laughed at you," said my aunt. "Old Bladder!"

"Nobody isn't going to laugh at me," said my uncle, glancing at his contours and suddenly sitting up.

My aunt raised her eyebrows slightly, swung her foot, and said nothing.

"We aren't keeping pace with our own progress, George. We got to. We're bumping against new people, and they set up to be gentlefolks—etiquette dinners and all the rest of it. They give themselves airs and expect us to be fish-out-of-water. We aren't going to be. They think we've no Style. Well, we give them Style for our advertisements, and we're going to give 'em Style all through. . . . You needn't be born to it to dance well on the wires of the Bond Street tradesmen. See?"

I handed him the cigar-box.

"Runcorn hadn't cigars like these," he said, truncating one lovingly. "We beat him at cigars. We'll beat him all round."

My aunt and I regarded him, full of apprehensions.

"I got idees," he said darkly to the cigar, deepening our dread.

He pocketed his cigar-cutter and spoke again.

"We got to learn all the rotten little game first. See? F'rinstance, we got to get samples of all the blessed wines there are—and learn 'em up. Stern, Smoor, Burgundy, all of 'em! She took Stern to-night—and when she tasted it first—— You pulled a face, Susan, you did. I saw you. It surprised you. You bunched your nose. We got to get used to wine and not do that. We got to get used to wearing

[244]

evening dress—*you*, Susan, too."

"Always have had a tendency to stick out of my clothes," said my aunt. "However—— Who cares?" She shrugged her shoulders.

I had never seen my uncle so immensely serious.

"Got to get the hang of etiquette," he went on to the fire. "Horses even. Practise everything. Dine every night in evening dress. . . . Get a brougham or something. Learn up golf and tennis and things. Country gentleman. Oh Fay. It isn't only freedom from Goochery."

"Eh?" I said.

"Oh!—Gawshery, if you like!"

"French, George," said my aunt. "But *I'm* not old Gooch. I made that face for fun."

"It isn't only freedom from Gawshery. We got to have Style. See! Style! Just all right and one better. That's what I call Style. We can do it, and we will."

He mumbled his cigar and smoked for a space, leaning forward and looking into the fire.

"What is it," he asked, "after all? What is it? Tips about eating; tips about drinking. Clothes. How to hold yourself, and not jes' the few little things they know for certain are wrong—jes' the shibboleth things." . . .

He was silent again, and the cigar crept up from the horizontal towards the zenith as the confidence of his mouth increased.

"Learn the whole bag of tricks in six months," he said, becoming more cheerful. "Eh, Susan? Beat 'em out! George, you in particular ought to get hold of it. Ought to get into a good club, and all that."

"Always ready to learn," I said. "Ever since you gave me the chance of Latin. So far we don't seem to have hit upon any Latin-speaking stratum in the population."

"We've come to French," said my aunt, "anyhow."

"It's a very useful language," said my uncle. "Put's a point on things. Zzzz. As for accent, no Englishman has an accent. No Englishman pronounces French properly. Don't you tell *me*. It's a Bluff. It's all a Bluff. Life's a Bluff

—practically. That's why it's so important, Susan, for us to attend to Style. Le Steel Say Lum. The Style it's the man. Whad you laughing at, Susan? . . . George, you're not smoking. These cigars are good for the mind. . . . What do *you* think of it all? We got to adapt ourselves. We have—so far. . . . Not going to be beat by these silly things."

IV

"What do you think of it, George?" he insisted.

What I said I thought of it I don't now recall. Only I have very distinctly the impression of meeting for a moment my aunt's impenetrable eye. And anyhow he started in with his accustomed energy to rape the mysteries of the Costly Life, and become the calmest of its lords. On the whole, I think he did it—thoroughly. I have crowded memories, a little difficult to disentangle, of his experimental stages, his experimental proceedings. It's hard at times to say which memory comes in front of which. I recall him as presenting on the whole a series of small surprises, as being again and again, unexpectedly, a little more self-confident, a little more polished, a little richer and finer, a little more aware of the positions and values of things and men.

There was a time—it must have been very early—when I saw him deeply impressed by the splendours of the dining-room of the National Liberal Club. Heaven knows who our host was or what that particular little "feed" was about now!—all that sticks is the impression of our straggling entry, a string of six or seven guests, and my uncle looking about him at the numerous bright red-shaded tables, at the exotics in great Majolica jars, at the shining ceramic columns and pilasters, at the impressive portraits of Liberal statesmen and heroes, and all that contributes to the ensemble of that palatial spectacle. He was betrayed into a whisper to me, "This is all Right, George!" he said. That artless comment seems almost incredible as I set it down; there came a time so speedily when not even the clubs of New York could have overawed my uncle, and when he could walk through the bowing magnificence of the Royal

[246]

Grand Hotel to his chosen table in that aggressively exquisite gallery upon the river, with all the easy calm of one of earth's legitimate kings.

The two of them learnt the new game rapidly and well; they experimented abroad, they experimented at home. At Chiselhurst, with the aid of a new, very costly, but highly instructive cook, they tried over everything they heard of that roused their curiosity and had any reputation for difficulty, from asparagus to plover's eggs. They afterwards got a gardener who could wait at table—and he brought the soil home to one. Then there came a butler.

I remember my aunt's first dinner-gown very brightly, and how she stood before the fire in the drawing-room confessing once unsuspected pretty arms with all the courage she possessed, and looking over her shoulder at herself in a mirror.

"A ham," she remarked reflectively, "must feel like this. Just a necklace." . . .

I attempted, I think, some commonplace compliment.

My uncle appeared at the door in a white waistcoat and with his hands in his trouser pockets; he halted and surveyed her critically.

"Couldn't tell you from a duchess, Susan," he remarked. "I'd like to have you painted, standin' at the fire like that. Sargent! You look—spirited, somehow. Lord!—I wish some of those damned tradesmen at Wimblehurst could see you." . . .

They did a lot of week-ending at hotels, and sometimes I went down with them. We seemed to fall into a vast drifting crowd of social learners. I don't know whether it is due simply to my changed circumstances, but it seems to me there have been immensely disproportionate developments of the hotel-frequenting and restaurant-using population during the last twenty years. It is not only, I think, that there are crowds of people who, like we were, are in the economically ascendant phase, but whole masses of the prosperous section of the population must be altering its habits, giving up high-tea for dinner and taking to evening dress, using the week-end hotels as a practise-ground for these new social arts. A swift and systematic conversion to gentility has been going on, I am convinced, throughout the whole commercial upper-middle class since I was twenty-one. Curiously mixed was the personal quality of the people one saw in these raids. There were conscientiously refined and low-voiced people reeking with proud bashfulness; there were aggressively smart people using pet diminutives for each other loudly and seeking fresh occasions for brilliant rudeness; there were awkward husbands and wives quarrelling furtively about their manners and ill at ease under the eye of the waiter; cheerfully amiable and often discrepant couples with a disposition to inconspicuous corners, and the jolly sort, affecting an unaffected ease; plump happy ladies who laughed too loud, and gentlemen in evening dress who subsequently "got their pipes." And nobody, you knew, was anybody, however expensively they dressed and whatever rooms they took.

I look back now with a curious remoteness of spirit to those crowded dining-rooms with their dispersed tables and their inevitable red-shaded lights and the unsympathetic, unskilful waiters, and the choice of "Thig or Glear, Sir?" I've not dined in that way, in that sort of place, now for five years—it must be quite five years, so specialised and narrow is my life becoming.

My uncle's earlier motor-car phases work in with these associations, and there stands out a little bright vignette of the hall of the Magnificent, Bexhill-on-Sea, and people dressed for dinner and sitting about amidst the scarlet furniture-satin and white-enamelled woodwork until the gong should gather them; and my aunt is there, very marvellously wrapped about in a dust cloak and a cage-like veil, and there are hotel porters and under-porters very alert, and an obsequious manager; and the tall young lady in black from the office is surprised into admiration, and in the middle of the picture is my uncle, making his first appearance in that Esquimaux costume I have already mentioned, a short figure, compactly immense, hugely goggled, wearing a sort of brown rubber proboscis, and surmounted by a table-land of motoring cap.

So it was we recognised our new needs as fresh invaders of the upper levels of the social system, and set ourselves quite consciously to the acquisition of Style and *Savoir Faire*. We became part of what is nowadays quite an important element in the confusion of our world, that multitude of economically ascendant people who are learning how to spend money. It is made up of financial people, the owners of the businesses that are eating up their competitors, inventors of new sources of wealth, such as ourselves; it includes nearly all America as one sees it on the European stage. It is a various multitude having only this in common: they are all moving, and particularly their womankind are moving, from conditions in which means were insistently finite, things were few, and customs simple, towards a limitless expenditure and the sphere of attraction of Bond Street, Fifth Avenue, and Paris. Their general effect is one of progressive revolution, of limitless rope.

They discover suddenly indulgences their moral code never foresaw and has no provision for, elaborations, ornaments, possessions beyond their wildest dreams. With an immense astonished zest they begin *shopping,* begin a systematic adaptation to a new life crowded and brilliant with things shopped, with jewels, maids, butlers, coachmen, electric broughams, hired town and country houses. They plunge into it as one plunges into a career; as a class, they talk, think, and dream possessions. Their literature, their Press, turns all on that; immense illustrated weeklies of unsurpassed magnificence guide them in domestic architecture, in the art of owning a garden, in the achievement of the sumptuous in motor-cars, in an elaborate sporting equipment, in the purchase and control of their estates, in travel and stupendous hotels. Once they begin to move they go far and fast. Acquisition becomes the substance of their lives. They find a world organised to gratify that passion.

In a brief year or so they are connoisseurs. They join in the plunder of the eighteenth century, buy rare old books, fine old pictures, good old furniture. Their first crude conception of dazzling suites of the newly perfect is replaced almost from the outset by a jackdaw dream of accumulating costly discrepant old things. . . .

I seem to remember my uncle taking to shopping quite suddenly. In the Beckenham days and in the early Chiselhurst days he was chiefly interested in getting money, and except for his onslaught on the Beckenham house, bothered very little about his personal surroundings and possessions. I forgot now when the change came and he began to spend. Some accident must have revealed to him this new source of power, or some subtle shifting occurred in the tissues of his brain. He began to spend and "shop." So soon as he began to shop, he began to shop violently. He began buying pictures, and then, oddly enough, old clocks. For the Chiselhurst house he bought nearly a dozen grandfather clocks and three copper warming pans. After that he bought much furniture. Then he plunged into art patronage, and began to commission pictures and to make presents to churches and institutions. His buying increased with a regular acceleration. Its development was a part of the mental changes that came to him in the wild excitements of the last four years of his ascent. Towards the climax he was a furious spender; he shopped with large unexpected purchases, he shopped like a mind seeking expression, he shopped to astonish and dismay; shopped *crescendo*, shopped *fortissimo, con molto espressione* until the magnificent smash of Crest Hill ended his shopping for ever. Always it was he who shopped. My aunt did not shine as a purchaser. It is a curious thing, due to I know not what fine strain in her composition, that my aunt never set any great store upon possessions. She plunged through that crowded bazaar of Vanity Fair during those feverish years, spending no doubt freely and largely, but spending with detachment and a touch of humorous contempt for the things, even the "old" things, that money can buy. It came to me suddenly one afternoon just how detached she was, as I saw her going towards the Hardingham, sitting up, as she always did, rather stiffly in her electric brougham, regarding the glittering world with interested and ironically innocent blue eyes from under the brim of a hat that defied comment. "No one," I thought, "would sit so apart if she hadn't dreams— and what are her dreams?"

I'd never thought.

And I remember, too, an outburst of scornful description after she had lunched with a party of women at the Imperial Cosmic Club. She came round to my rooms on the chance of finding me there, and I gave her tea. She professed herself tired and cross, and flung herself into my chair. . . .

"George," she cried, "the Things women are! Do *I* stink of money?"

"Lunching?" I asked.

She nodded.

"Plutocratic ladies?"

"Yes."

"Oriental type?"

"Oh! Like a burst hareem! . . . Bragging of possessions. . . . They feel you. They feel your clothes, George, to see if they are good!"

I soothed her as well as I could. "They *are* Good, aren't they?" I said.

"It's the old pawnshop in their blood," she said, drinking tea; and then in infinite disgust, "They run their hands over your clothes—they paw you."

I had a moment of doubt whether perhaps she had not been discovered in possession of unsuspected forgeries. I don't know. After that my eyes were quickened, and I began to see for myself women running their hands over other women's furs, scrutinising their lace, even demanding to handle jewellery, appraising, envying, testing. They have a kind of etiquette. The woman who feels says, "What beautiful sables?" "What lovely lace?" The woman felt admits proudly: "It's Real, you know," or disavows pretension modestly and hastily, "It's not Good." In each other's houses they peer at the pictures, handle the selvage of hangings, look at the bottoms of china. . . .

I wonder if it *is* the old pawnshop in the blood.

I doubt if Lady Drew and the Olympians did that sort of thing, but here I may be only clinging to another of my former illusions about aristocracy and the State. Perhaps always possessions have been Booty, and never anywhere has there been such a thing as house and furnishings native and natural to the women and men who made use of them. . . .

VI

For me, at least, it marked an epoch in my uncle's career when I learnt one day that he had "shopped" Lady Grove. I realised a fresh, wide, unpreluded step. He took me by surprise with the sudden change of scale from such portable possessions as jewels and motor-cars to a stretch of countryside. The transaction was Napoleonic; he was told of the place; he said "snap"; there were no preliminary desirings or searchings. Then he came home and said what he had done. Even my aunt was for a day or so measurably awe-stricken by this exploit in purchase, and we both went down with him to see the house in a mood near consternation. It struck us then as a very lordly place indeed. I remember the three of us standing on the terrace that looked west-ward, surveying the sky-reflecting windows of the house, and a feeling of unwarrantable intrusion comes back to me.

Lady Grove, you know, is a very beautiful house indeed, a still and gracious place, whose age-long seclusion was only effectively broken with the toot of the coming of the motor-car. An old Catholic family had died out in it, century by century, and was now altogether dead. Portions of the fabric are thirteenth century, and its last architectural revision was Tudor; within, it is for the most part dark and chilly, save for two or three favoured rooms and its tall-windowed, oak-galleried hall. Its terrace is its noblest feature; a very wide, broad lawn it is, bordered by a low stone battlement, and there is a great cedar in one corner under whose level

[252]

branches one looks out across the blue distances of the Weald, blue distances that are made extraordinarily Italian in quality by virtue of the dark masses of that single tree. It is a very high terrace; southward one looks down upon the tops of wayfaring trees and spruces, and westward on a steep slope of beechwood, through which the road comes. One turns back to the still old house, and sees a grey and lichenous façade with a very finely arched entrance. It was warmed by the afternoon light and touched with the colour of a few neglected roses and a pyracanthus. It seemed to me that the most modern owner conceivable in this serene fine place was some bearded scholarly man in a black cassock, gentle-voiced and white-handed, or some very soft-robed, grey gentlewoman. And there was my uncle holding his goggles in a sealskin glove, wiping the glass with a pocket-handkerchief, and asking my aunt if Lady Grove wasn't a "Bit of all Right."

My aunt made him no answer.

"The man who built this," I speculated, "wore armour and carried a sword."

"There's some of it inside still," said my uncle. We went inside. An old woman with very white hair was in charge of the place and cringed rather obviously to the new master. She evidently found him a very strange and frightful apparition indeed, and was dreadfully afraid of him. But if the surviving present bowed down to us, the past did not. We stood up to the dark, long portraits of the extinguished race —one was a Holbein—and looked them in their sidelong eyes. They looked back at us. We all, I know, felt the enigmatical quality in them. Even my uncle was momentarily embarrassed, I think, by that invincibly self-complacent expression. It was just as though, after all, he had *not* bought them up and replaced them altogether; as though that, secretly, they knew better and could smile at him. . . .

The spirit of the place was akin to Bladesover, but touched with something older and remoter. That armour that stood about had once served in tilt-yards, if indeed it had not served in battle, and this family had sent its blood and treasure, time after time, upon the most romantic quest in history, to Palestine. Dreams, loyalties, place and honour, how utterly had it all evaporated, leaving, at last, the final expression of its sprit, these quaint painted smiles, these smiles of triumphant completion! It had evaporated, indeed, long before the ultimate Durgan had died, and in his old age he had cumbered the place with Early Victorian cushions and carpets and tapestry table-cloths and invalid appliances of a type even more extinct, it seemed to us, than the crusades. . . . Yes, it was different from Bladesover.

"Bit stuffy, George," said my uncle. "They hadn't much idee of ventilation when this was built."

One of the panelled rooms was half-filled with presses and a four-poster bed. "Might be the ghost room," said my uncle; but it did not seem to me that so retiring a family as the Durgans, so old and completely exhausted a family as the Durgans, was likely to haunt anybody. What living thing now had any concern with their honour and judgments and good and evil deeds? Ghosts and witchcraft were a later innovation—that fashion came from Scotland with the Stuarts. . . .

Afterwards, prying for epitaphs, we found a marble crusader with a broken nose, under a battered canopy of fretted stone, outside the restricted limits of the present Duffield church, and half buried in nettles. "Ichabod," said my uncle. "Eh? We shall be like that, Susan, some day. . . . I'm going to clean him up a bit and put a railing to keep off the children."

"Old saved at the eleventh hour," said my aunt, quoting one of the less successful advertisements of Tono-Bungay.

But I don't think my uncle heard her.

It was by our captured crusader that the vicar found us. He came round the corner at us briskly, a little out of breath. He had an air of having been running after us since the first toot of our horn had warned the village of our presence. He was an Oxford man, clean-shaven, with a cadaverous complexion and a guardedly respectful manner, a cultivated intonation, and a general air of accommodation to the new order of things. These Oxford men are the Greeks of our plutocratic empire. He was a Tory in spirit, and what one may call an adapted Tory by stress of circumstances; that is to say, he was no longer a legitimist; he was prepared for the substitution of new lords for old. We were pill vendors, he knew, and no doubt horribly vulgar in soul; but then it might have been some polygamous Indian rajah, a great strain on a good man's tact, or some Jew with an inherited expression of contempt. Anyhow, we were English, and neither Dissenters nor Socialists, and he was cheerfully prepared to do what he could to make gentlemen of both of us. He might have preferred Americans for some reasons; they are not so obviously taken from one part of the social system and dumped down in another, and they are more teachable; but in this world we cannot always be choosers. So he was very bright and pleasant with us, showed us the church, gossiped informingly about our neighbours on the countryside —Tux, the banker; Lord Boom, the magazine and newspaper proprietor; Lord Carnaby, that great sportsman, and old Lady Osprey. And finally he took us by way of a village lane—three children bobbed convulsively with eyes of terror for my uncle—through a meticulous garden to a big, slovenly Vicarage with faded Victorian furniture and a faded Victorian wife, who gave us tea and introduced us to a confusing family dispersed among a lot of disintegrating basket chairs upon the edge of a well-used tennis lawn.

These people interested me. They were a common type, no doubt, but they were new to me. There were two lank sons who had been playing singles at tennis, red-eared youths growing black moustaches, and dressed in conscientiously untidy tweeds and unbuttoned and ungirt Norfolk jackets. There were a number of ill-nourished-looking daughters, sensible and economical in their costume, the younger still with long, brown-stockinged legs, and the eldest present—there were, we discovered, one or two hidden away—displaying a large gold cross and other aggressive ecclesiastical symbols; there were two or three fox-terriers, a retrieverish mongrel, and an old, bloody-eyed and very evil-smelling St. Bernard. There was a jackdaw. There was, moreover, an ambiguous, silent lady that my aunt subsequently decided must be a very deaf paying guest. Two or three other people had concealed themselves at our coming and left unfinished teas behind them. Rugs and cushions lay among the chairs, and two of the latter were, I noted, covered with Union Jacks.

The vicar introduced us sketchily, and the faded Victorian wife regarded my aunt with a mixture of conventional scorn and abject respect, and talked to her in a languid, persistent voice about people in the neighbourhood whom my aunt could not possibly know. My aunt received these personalia cheerfully, with her blue eyes flitting from point to point, and coming back again and again to the pinched faces of the daughters and the cross upon the eldest's breast. Encouraged by my aunt's manner, the vicar's wife grew patronising and kindly, and made it evident that she could do much to bridge the social gulf between ourselves and the people of family about us.

I had just snatches of that conversation. "Mrs. Merridew brought him quite a lot of money. Her father, I believe, had been in the Spanish wine trade—quite a lady though. And after that he fell off his horse and cracked his brain pan and took to fishing and farming. I'm sure you'll like to know them. He's *most* amusing. . . . The daughter had a disappointment and went to China as a missionary and got mixed up in a massacre." . . .

"The most beautiful silks and things she brought back, you'd hardly believe!" . . .

"Yes, they gave them to propitiate her. You see, they didn't understand the difference, and they thought that as they'd been massacring people, *they'd* be massacred. They didn't understand the difference Christianity makes." . . .

"Seven bishops they've had in the family!" . . .

"Married a Papist and was quite lost to them." . . .

"He failed some dreadful examination and had to go into the militia." . . .

"So she bit his leg as hard as ever she could and he let go." . . .

"Had four of his ribs amputated." . . .

"Caught meningitis and was carried off in a week."

"Had to have a large piece of silver tube let into his throat, and if he wants to talk he puts his finger on it. It makes him so interesting, I think. You feel he's sincere somehow. A most charming man in every way."

"Preserved them both in spirits very luckily, and there they are in his study, though of course he doesn't show them to everybody."

The silent lady, unperturbed by these apparently exciting topics, scrutinised my aunt's costume with a singular intensity, and was visibly moved when she unbuttoned her dust cloak and flung it wide. Meanwhile we men conversed, one of the more spirited daughters listened brightly, and the youths lay on the grass at our feet. My uncle offered them cigars, but they both declined,—out of bashfulness, it seemed to me, whereas the vicar, I think, accepted out of tact. When we were not looking at them directly, these young men would kick each other furtively.

Under the influence of my uncle's cigar, the vicar's mind had soared beyond the limits of the district. "This Socialism," he said, "seems making great headway."

My uncle shook his head. "We're too individualistic in this country for that sort of nonsense," he said. "Everybody's business is nobody's business. That's where they go wrong."

"They have some intelligent people in their ranks, I am told," said the vicar, "writers and so forth. Quite a distinguished playwright, my eldest daughter was telling me—I forget his name. Milly, dear! Oh! she's not here. Painters, too, they have. This Socialism, it seems to me, is part of the Unrest of the Age. . . . But, as you say, the spirit of the people is against it. In the country, at any rate. The people down here are too sturdily independent in their small way,—and too sensible altogether." . . .

"It's a great thing for Duffield to have Lady Grove occupied again," he was saying when my wandering attention came back from some attractive casualty in his wife's discourse. "People have always looked up to the house—and considering all things, old Mr. Durgan really was extraordinarily good—extraordinarily good. You intend to give us a good deal of your time here, I hope."

"I mean to do my duty by the Parish," said my uncle.

"I'm sincerely glad to hear it—sincerely. We've missed—the house influence. An English village isn't complete——People get out of hand. Life grows dull. The young people drift away to London."

He enjoyed his cigar gingerly for a moment.

"We shall look to you to liven things up," he said,—poor man!

My uncle cocked his cigar and removed it from his mouth.

"Whad you think the place wants?" he asked.

He did not wait for an answer. "I been thinking while you been talking—things one might do. Cricket—a good English game—sports. Build the chaps a pavilion perhaps. Then every village ought to have a miniature rifle range."

"Ye-ees," said the vicar. "Provided, of course, there isn't a constant popping." . . .

"Manage *that* all right," said my uncle. "Thing'd be a sort of long shed. Paint it red. British colour. Then there's a Union Jack for the church and the village school. Paint the school red, too, p'raps. Not enough colour about now. Too grey. Then a maypole."

"How far our people would take up that sort of thing——" began the vicar.

"I'm all for getting that good old English spirit back again," said my uncle. "Merrymakings. Lads and lasses dancing on the village green. Harvest home. Fairings. Yule Log—all the rest of it."

"How would old Sally Glue do for a May Queen?" asked one of the sons in the slight pause that followed.

"Or Annie Glassbound?" said the other, with the huge

[258]

virile guffaw of a young man whose voice has only recently broken.

"Sally Glue is eighty-five," explained the vicar, "and Annie Glassbound is well—a young lady of extremely generous proportions. And not quite right, you know. Not quite right—here." He tapped his brow.

"Generous proportions!" said the eldest son, and the guffaws were renewed.

"You see," said the vicar, "all the brisker girls go into service in or near London. The life of excitement attracts them. And no doubt the higher wages have something to do with it. And the liberty to wear finery. And generally—freedom from restraint. So that there might be a little difficulty perhaps to find a May Queen here just at present who was really young and, er—pretty. . . . Of course I couldn't think of any of my girls—or anything of that sort."

"We got to attract 'em back," said my uncle. "That's what I feel about it. We got to Buck-Up the country. The English country is a going concern still; just as the Established Church—if you'll excuse me saying it, is a going concern. Just as Oxford is—or Cambridge. Or any of those old, fine old things. Only it wants fresh capital, fresh idees and fresh methods. Light railways, f'rinstance—scientific use of drainage. Wire fencing—machinery—all that."

The vicar's face for one moment betrayed dismay. Perhaps he was thinking of his country walks amidst the hawthorns and honeysuckle.

"There's great things," said my uncle, "to be done on Mod'un lines with Village Jam and Pickles—boiled in the country."

It was the reverberation of this last sentence in my mind, I think, that sharpened my sentimental sympathy as we went through the straggling village street and across the trim green on our way back to London. It seemed that afternoon the most tranquil and idyllic collection of creeper-sheltered homes you can imagine; thatch still lingered on a whitewashed cottage or two, pyracanthus, wall-flowers, and daffodils abounded, and an unsystematic orchard or so was white with blossom above and gay with bulbs below. I noted a row of straw beehives, beehive-shaped, beehives of the type long since condemned as inefficient by all progressive minds, and in the doctor's acre of grass a flock of two whole sheep was grazing,—no doubt he'd taken them on account. Two men and one old woman made gestures of abject vassalage, and my uncle replied with a lordly gesture of his great motoring glove. . . .

"England's full of Bits like this," said my uncle, leaning over the front seat and looking back with great satisfaction. The black glare of his goggles rested for a time on the receding turrets of Lady Grove just peeping over the trees.

"I shall have a flagstaff, I think," he considered. "Then one could show when one is in residence. The villagers will like to know." . . .

I reflected. "They will," I said. "They're used to liking to know." . . .

My aunt had been unusually silent. Suddenly she spoke. "He says Snap," she remarked; "he buys that place. And a nice old job of Housekeeping he gives me! He sails through the village swelling like an old Turkey. And who'll have to scoot the butler? Me! Who's got to forget all she ever knew and start again? Me! Who's got to trek from Chiselhurst and be a great lady? Me! . . . You old Bother! Just when I was settling down and beginning to feel at home."

My uncle turned his goggles to her. "Ah! *this* time it is home, Susan. . . . We got there."

VII

It seems to me now but a step from the buying of Lady Grove to the beginning of Crest Hill, from the days when the former was a stupendous achievement to the days when it was too small and dark and inconvenient altogether for a great financier's use. For me that was a period of increasing detachment from our business and the great world of London; I saw it more and more in broken glimpses, and sometimes I was working in my little pavilion above Lady

Grove for a fortnight together; even when I came up it was often solely for a meeting of the aeronautical society or for one of the learned societies or to consult literature or employ searchers or some such special business. For my uncle it was a period of stupendous inflation. Each time I met him I found him more confident, more comprehensive, more consciously a factor in great affairs. Soon he was no longer an associate of merely business men; he was big enough for the attentions of greater powers.

I grew used to discovering some item of personal news about him in my evening paper, or to the sight of a full-page portrait of him in a sixpenny magazine. Usually the news was of some munificent act, some romantic piece of buying or giving or some fresh rumour of reconstruction. He saved, you will remember, the Parbury Reynolds for the country. Or at times it would be an interview or my uncle's contribution to some symposium on the "Secret of Success," or such-like topic. Or wonderful tales of his power of work, of his wonderful organisation to get things done, of his instant decisions and remarkable power of judging his fellow-men. They repeated his great *mot:* "Eight-hour working day—I want eighty hours!"

He became modestly but resolutely "public." They cartooned him in *Vanity Fair.* One year my aunt, looking indeed a very gracious, slender lady, faced the portrait of the King in the great room at Burlington House, and the next year saw a medallion of my uncle by Ewart, looking out upon the world, proud and imperial, but on the whole a trifle too prominently convex, from the walls of the New Gallery.

I shared only intermittently in his social experiences. People knew of me, it is true, and many of them sought to make through me a sort of flank attack upon him, and there was a legend, owing, very unreasonably, partly to my growing scientific reputation and partly to an element of reserve in my manner, that I played a much larger share in planning his operations than was actually the case. This led to one or two very intimate private dinners, to my inclusion in one or two house parties and various odd offers of introductions and services that I didn't for the most part accept. Among other people who sought me in this way was Archie Garvell, now a smart, impecunious soldier of no particular distinction, who would, I think, have been quite prepared to develop any sporting instincts I possessed, and who was beautifully unaware of our former contact. He was always offering me winners; no doubt in a spirit of anticipatory exchange for some really good thing in our more scientific and certain method of getting something for nothing. . . .

In spite of my preoccupation with my experimental work, I did, I find now that I come to ransack my impressions, see a great deal of the great world during those eventful years; I had a near view of the machinery by which our astounding Empire is run, rubbed shoulders and exchanged experiences with bishops and statesmen, political women and women who were not political, physicians and soldiers, artists and authors, the directors of great journals, philanthropists and all sorts of eminent, significant people. I saw the statesmen without their orders and the bishops with but a little purple silk left over from their canonicals, inhaling, not incense, but cigar smoke. I could look at them all the better because, for the most part, they were not looking at me, but at my uncle, and calculating consciously or unconsciously how they might use him and assimilate him to their system, the most unpremeditated, subtle, successful and aimless plutocracy that ever encumbered the destinies of mankind. Not one of them, so far as I could see, until disaster overtook him, resented his lies, his almost naked dishonesty of method, the disorderly disturbance of this trade and that, caused by his spasmodic operations. I can see them now about him, see them polite, watchful, various; his stiff compact little figure always a centre of attention, his wiry hair, his brief nose, his under-lip, electric with self-confidence. Wandering marginally through distinguished gatherings, I would catch the whispers: "That's Mr. Ponderevo!"

"The little man?"

"Yes, the little bounder with the glasses."

"They say he's made——" . . .

Or I would see him on some parterre of a platform beside my aunt's hurraying hat, amidst titles and costumes, "holding his end up," as he would say, subscribing heavily to obvious charities, even at times making brief convulsive speeches in some good cause before the most exalted audiences. "Mr. Chairman, your Royal Highness, my Lords, Ladies and Gentlemen," he would begin amidst subsiding applause and adjust those obstinate glasses and thrust back the wings of his frock-coat and rest his hands upon his hips and speak his fragment with ever and again an incidental Zzzz. His hands would fret about him as he spoke, fiddle his glasses, feel in his waistcoat pockets; ever and again he would rise slowly to his toes as a sentence unwound jerkily like a clockwork snake, and drop back on his heels at the end. They were the very gestures of our first encounter when he had stood before the empty fireplace in his minute draped parlour and talked of my future to my mother.

In those measurelessly long hot afternoons in the little shop at Wimblehurst he had talked and dreamt of the Romance of Modern Commerce. Here, surely, was his romance come true.

VIII

People say that my uncle lost his head at the crest of his fortunes, but if one may tell so much truth of a man one has in a manner loved, he never had very much head to lose. He was always imaginative, erratic, inconsistent, recklessly inexact, and his inundation of wealth merely gave him scope for these qualities. It is true, indeed, that towards the climax he became intensely irritable at times and impatient of contradiction, but that, I think, was rather the gnawing uneasiness of sanity than any mental disturbance. But I find it hard either to judge him or convey the full development of him to the reader. I saw too much of him; my memory is choked with disarranged moods and aspects. Now he is distended with megalomania, now he is deflated, now he is quarrelsome, now impenetrably self-satisfied, but always he is sudden, jerky, fragmentary, energetic, and—in some subtle fundamental way that I find difficult to define —absurd.

There stands out—because of the tranquil beauty of its setting perhaps—a talk we had in the veranda of the little pavilion near my worksheds behind Crest Hill in which my aeroplanes and navigable balloons were housed. It was one of many similar conversations, and I do not know why it in particular should survive its fellows. It happens so. He had come up to me after his coffee to consult me about a certain chalice which in a moment of splendour and under the importunity of a countess he had determined to give to a deserving church in the east-end. I, in a moment of even rasher generosity, had suggested Ewart as a possible artist. Ewart had produced at once an admirable sketch for the sacred vessel surrounded by a sort of wreath of Millies with open arms and wings and had drawn fifty pounds on the strength of it. After that came a series of vexatious delays. The chalice became less and less of a commercial man's chalice, acquired more and more the elusive quality of the Holy Grail, and at last even the drawing receded.

My uncle grew restive. . . . "You see, George, they'll begin to want the blasted thing!"

"What blasted thing?"

"That chalice, damn it! They're beginning to ask questions. It isn't Business, George."

"It's art," I protested, "and religion."

"That's all very well. But it's not a good ad for us, George, to make a promise and not deliver the goods. . . . I'll have to write off your friend Ewart as a bad debt, that's what it comes to, and go to a decent firm." . . .

We sat outside on deck chairs in the veranda of the pavilion, smoked, drank whisky, and, the chalice disposed of, meditated. His temporary annoyance passed. It was an altogether splendid summer night, following a blazing, indolent day. Full moonlight brought out dimly the lines of the receding hills, one wave beyond another; far beyond were the pin-point lights of Leatherhead, and in the fore-ground the little stage from which I used to start upon my gliders gleamed like wet steel. The season must have been high June, for down in the woods that hid the lights of the Lady Grove windows, I remember the nightingales thrilled and gurgled. . . .

"We got here, George," said my uncle, ending a long pause. "Didn't I say?"

"Say!—when?" I asked.

"In that hole in the To'nem Court Road, eh? It's been a Straight Square Fight, and here we are!"

I nodded.

" 'Member me telling you—Tono-Bungay? . . . Well. . . . I'd just that afternoon thought of it!"

"I've fancied at times——;" I admitted.

"It's a great world, George, nowadays, with a fair chance for every one who lays hold of things. The career *ouvert* to the Talons—eh? Tono-Bungay. Think of it! It's a great world and a growing world, and I'm glad we're in it—and getting a pull. We're getting big people, George. Things come to us. Eh? This Palestine thing." . . .

He meditated for a time and Zzzzed softly. Then he became still.

His theme was taken up by a cricket in the grass until he himself was ready to resume it. The cricket too seemed to fancy that in some scheme of its own it had got there. "Chirrrrrup," it said; "chirrrrrup." . . .

"Lord, what a place that was at Wimblehurst!" he broke out. "If ever I get a day off we'll motor there, George, and run over that dog that sleeps in the High Street. Always was a dog asleep there—always. Always . . . I'd like to see the old shop again. I daresay old Ruck still stands between the sheep at his door, grinning with all his teeth, and Marbel, silly beggar! comes out with his white apron on and a pencil stuck behind his ear, trying to look awake. . . . Wonder if they know it's me?. I'd like 'em somehow to know it's me."

"They'll have had the International Tea Company and

all sorts of people cutting them up," I said. "And that dog's been on the pavement this six years—can't sleep even there, poor dear, because of the motor-horns and its shattered nerves."

"Movin' everywhere," said my uncle. "I expect you're right. . . . It's a big time we're in, George. It's a big Progressive On-coming Imperial Time. This Palestine business —the daring of it. . . . It's—it's a Process, George. And we got our hands on it. Here we sit—with our hands on it, George. Entrusted.

"It seems quiet to-night. But if we could see and hear." He waved his cigar towards Leatherhead and London.

"There they are, millions, George. Jes' think of what they've been up to to-day—those ten millions—each one doing his own particular job. You can't grasp it. It's like old Whitman says—what is it he says? Well, anyway it's like old Whitman. Fine chap, Whitman! Fine old chap! Queer, you can't quote him! . . . And these millions aren't anything. There's the millions over seas, hundreds of millions, Chinese, M'rocco, Africa generally, 'Merica. . . . Well, here we are, with power, with leisure, picked out— because we've been energetic, because we've seized opportunities, because we've made things hum when other people have waited for them to hum. See? Here we are—with our hands on it. Big people. Big growing people. In a sort of way,—Forces."

He paused. "It's wonderful, George," he said.

"Anglo-Saxon energy," I said softly to the night.

"That's it, George—energy. It's put things in our grip— threads, wires, stretching out and out, George, from that little office of ours, out to West Africa, out to Egypt, out to Inja, out east, west, north and south. Running the world practically. Running it faster and faster. Creative. There's that Palestine canal affair. Marvellous idee! Suppose we take that up, suppose we let ourselves in for it, us and the others, and run that water sluice from the Mediterranean into the Dead Sea Valley—think of the difference it will make! All the desert blooming like a rose, Jericho lost for ever, all the Holy Places under water. . . . Very likely destroy Christianity." . . .

He mused for a space. "Cuttin' canals," murmured my uncle. "Making tunnels. . . . New countries. . . . New centres. . . . Zzzz. . . . Finance. . . . Not only Palestine.

"I wonder where we shall get before we're done, George? We got a lot of big things going. We got the investing public sound and sure. I don't see why in the end we shouldn't be very big. There's difficulties—but I'm equal to them. We're still a bit soft in our bones, but they'll harden all right. . . . I suppose, after all, I'm worth something like a million, George—cleared up and settled. If I got out of things now. It's a great time, George, a wonderful time!" . . .

I glanced through the twilight at his convexity—and I must confess it struck me that on the whole he wasn't particularly good value.

"We got our hands on things, George—us big people. We got to hang together, George—run the show. Join up with the old order like that mill-wheel of Kipling's. (Finest thing he ever wrote, George;—I jes' been reading it again. Made me buy Lady Grove.) Well, we got to run the country, George. It's ours. Make it a Scientific—Organised—Business—Enterprise. Put idees into it. 'Lectrify it. Run the Press. Run all sorts of developments. All sorts of developments. I been talking to Lord Boom. I been talking to all sorts of people. Great things. Progress. The world on business lines. Only jes' beginning." . . .

He fell into a deep meditation.

He Zzzzed for a time and ceased.

"*Yes,*" he said at last in the tone of a man who has at last emerged with ultimate solutions to the profoundest problems.

"What?" I said after a seemly pause.

My uncle hung fire for a moment and it seemed to me the fate of nations trembled in the balance. Then he spoke as one who speaks from the very bottom of his heart—and I think it was the very bottom of his heart.

"I'd jes' like to drop into the Eastry Arms, jes' when all those beggars in the parlour are sittin' down to whist, Ruck and Marbel and all, and give 'em ten minutes of my mind, George. Straight from the shoulder. Jes' exactly what I think of them. It's a little thing, but I'd like to do it—jes' once before I die." . . .

He rested on that for some time—Zzzz-ing.

Then he broke out at a new place in a tone of detached criticism.

"There's Boom," he reflected.

"It's a wonderful system—this old British system, George. It's staid and stable and yet it has a place for new men. We come up and take our places. It's almost expected. We take a hand. That's where our Democracy differs from America. Over there a man succeeds; all he gets is money. Here there's a system—open to every one—practically. . . . Chaps like Boom—come from nowhere."

His voice ceased. I reflected upon the spirit of his words. Suddenly I kicked my feet in the air, rolled on my side and sat up suddenly on my deck chair with my legs down.

"You don't mean it!" I said.

"Mean what, George?"

"Subscription to the party funds. Reciprocal advantage. Have we got to that?"

"Whad you driving at, George?"

"You know. They'd never do it, man!"

"Do what?" he said feebly; and, "Why shouldn't they?

"They'd not even go to a baronetcy. _No!_ . . . And yet, of course, there's Boom! And Collingshead—and Gorver. They've done beer, they've done snippets! After all Tono-Bungay—it's not like a turf commission agent or anything like that! . . . There have of course been some very gentlemanly commission agents. It isn't like a fool of a scientific man who can't make money!"

My uncle grunted; we'd differed on that issue before.

A malignant humour took possession of me. "What would they call you?" I speculated. "The vicar would like Duffield. Too much like Duffer! Difficult thing, a title." I ran my mind over various possibilities. "Why not take a leaf from a socialist tract I came upon yesterday. Chap says we're all getting delocalised. Beautiful word—delocalised! Why not be the first delocalised peer? That gives you— Tono-Bungay! There is a Bungay, you know. Lord Tono of Bungay—in bottles everywhere. Eh?"

My uncle astonished me by losing his temper.

"Damn it, George, you don't seem to see I'm serious! You're always sneering at Tono-Bungay! As though it was some sort of swindle. It was perfec'ly legitimate trade, perfec'ly legitimate. Good value and a good article. . . . When I come up here and tell you plans and exchange idees —you sneer at me. You *do*. You don't see—it's a big thing. It's a big thing. You got to get used to new circumstances. You got to face what lies before us. You got to drop that tone." . . .

IX

My uncle was not altogether swallowed up in business and ambition. He kept in touch with modern thought. For example, he was, I know, greatly swayed by what he called "This Overman idee, Nietzsche—all that stuff."

He mingled those comforting suggestions of a potent and exceptional human being emancipated from the pettier limitations of integrity with the Napoleonic legend. It gave his imagination a considerable outlet. That Napoleonic legend! The real mischief of Napoleon's immensely disastrous and accidental career began only when he was dead and the romantic type of mind was free to elaborate his character. I do believe that my uncle would have made a far less egregious smash if there had been no Napoleonic legend to misguide him. He was in many ways better and infinitely kinder than his career. But when in doubt between decent conduct and a base advantage, that cult came in more and more influentially: "think of Napoleon; think what the inflexibly-wilful Napoleon would have done with such scruples as yours;" that was the rule, and the end was invariably a new step in dishonour.

My uncle was in an unsystematic way a collector of Napoleonic relics: the bigger the book about his hero the more readily he bought it; he purchased letters and tinsel and weapons that bore however remotely upon the Man of Destiny, and he even secured in Geneva, though he never brought home, an old coach in which Buonaparte might have ridden; he crowded the quiet walls of Lady Grove with engravings and figures of him, preferring, my aunt remarked, the more convex portraits with the white vest and those statuettes with the hands behind the back which threw forward the figure. The Durgans watched him through it all, sardonically.

And he would stand after breakfast at times in the light of the window at Lady Grove, a little apart, with two fingers of one hand stuck between his waistcoat-buttons and his chin sunken, thinking,—the most preposterous little fat man in the world. It made my aunt feel, she said, "like an old Field Marshal—knocks me into a cocked hat, George!"

Perhaps this Napoleonic bias made him a little less frequent with his cigars than he would otherwise have been, but of that I cannot be sure, and it certainly caused my aunt a considerable amount of vexation after he had read *Napoleon and the Fair Sex*, because for a time that roused him to a sense of a side of life he had in his commercial preoccupations very largely forgotten. Suggestion plays so great a part in this field. My uncle took the next opportunity and had an "affair"!

It was not a very impassioned affair, and the exact particulars never of course reached me. It is quite by chance I know anything of it at all. One evening I was surprised to come upon my uncle in a mixture of Bohemia and smart people at an At Home in the flat of Robbert, the R.A. who painted my aunt, and he was standing a little apart in a recess, talking or rather being talked to in undertones by a plump, blond little woman in pale blue, a Helen Scrymgeour who wrote novels and was organising a weekly magazine. I elbowed a large lady who was saying something about them, but I didn't need to hear the thing she said to perceive the relationship of the two. It hit me like a placard on a hoarding. I was amazed the whole gathering did not see it. Perhaps they did. She was wearing a remarkably fine diamond necklace, much too fine for journalism, and regarding him with that quality of questionable proprietorship, of leashed but straining intimacy, that seems inseparable from this sort of affair. It is so much more palpable than matrimony. If anything was wanted to complete my conviction it was my uncle's eyes when presently he became aware of mine, a certain embarrassment and a certain pride and defiance. And the next day he made an opportunity to praise the lady's intelligence to me concisely, lest I should miss the point of it all.

After that I heard some gossip—from a friend of the lady's. I was much too curious to do anything but listen. I had never in all my life imagined my uncle in an amorous attitude. It would appear that she called him her "God in the Car"—after the hero in a novel of Anthony Hope's. It was essential to the convention of their relations that he should go relentlessly whenever business called, and it was generally arranged that it did call. To him women were an incident, it was understood between them; Ambition was the master-passion. A great world called him and the noble hunger for Power. I have never been able to discover just how honest Mrs. Scrymgeour was in all this, but it is quite possible the immense glamour of his financial largeness prevailed with her and that she did bring a really romantic feeling to their encounters. There must have been some extraordinary moments. . . .

I was a good deal exercised and distressed about my aunt when I realised what was afoot. I thought it would prove a terrible humiliation to her. I suspected her of keeping up a brave front with the loss of my uncle's affections fretting at her heart, but there I simply underestimated her. She didn't hear for some time and when she did hear she was extremely angry and energetic. The sentimental situation didn't trouble her for a moment. She decided that my uncle "wanted smacking." She accentuated herself with an unexpected new hat, went and gave him an inconceivable talking-to at the Hardingham, and then came round to "blow-up" me for not telling her what was going on before. . . .

I tried to bring her to a proper sense of the accepted values in this affair, but my aunt's originality of outlook was never so invincible. "Men don't tell on one another in affairs of passion," I protested, and such-like worldly excuses.

"Women!" she said in high indignation, "and men! It isn't women and men—it's him and me, George! Why don't you talk sense?

"Old passion's all very well, George, in its way, and I'm the last person to be jealous. But this is old nonsense. . . . I'm not going to let him show off what a silly old lobster he is to other women. . . . I'll mark every scrap of his underclothes with red letters, 'Ponderevo—Private'—every scrap. . . .

"Going about making love indeed!—in abdominal belts! —at his time of life!" . . .

I cannot imagine what passed between her and my uncle. But I have no doubt that for once her customary badinage was laid aside. How they talked then I do not know, for I who knew them so well had never heard that much of intimacy between them. At any rate it was a concerned and preoccupied "God in the Car" I had to deal with in the next few days, unusually Zzzz-y and given to slight impatient gestures that had nothing to do with the current conversation. And it was evident that in all directions he was finding things unusually difficult to explain.

All the intimate moments in this affair were hidden from me, but in the end my aunt triumphed. He did not so much throw as jerk over Mrs. Scrymgeour, and she did not so much make a novel of it as upset a huge pailful of attenuated and adulterated female soul upon this occasion. My aunt did not appear in that, even remotely. So that it is doubtful if the lady knew the real causes of her abandonment. The Napoleonic hero was practically unmarried, and he threw over his lady as Napoleon threw over Josephine for a great alliance. . . .

It was a triumph for my aunt, but it had its price. For some time it was evident things were strained between them. He gave up the lady, but he resented having to do so, deeply. She had meant more to his imagination than one could have supposed. He wouldn't for a long time "come round." He became touchy and impatient and secretive towards my aunt, and she, I noted, after an amazing check or so, stopped that stream of kindly abuse that had flowed for so long and had been so great a refreshment in their lives. They were both the poorer for its cessation, both less happy. She devoted herself more and more to Lady Grove and the humours and complications of its management. The servants took to her—as they say—she god-mothered three Susans during her rule, the coachman's, the gardener's, and the Up Hill gamekeeper's. She got together a library of old household books that were in the vein of the place. She revived the still-room, and became a great artist in jellies and elder and cowslip wine.

X

And while I neglected the development of my uncle's finances—and my own, in my scientific work and my absorbing conflict with the difficulties of flying,—his schemes grew more and more expansive and hazardous, and his spending wilder and laxer. I believe that a haunting sense of the intensifying unsoundness of his position accounts largely for his increasing irritability and his increasing secretiveness with my aunt and myself during these crowning years. He dreaded, I think, having to explain, he feared our jests might pierce unwittingly to the truth. Even in the privacy of his mind he would not face the truth. He was accumulating unrealisable securities in his safes until they hung a potential avalanche over the economic world. But his buying became a fever, and his restless desire to keep it up with himself that he was making a triumphant progress to limitless wealth gnawed deeper and deeper. A curious feature of this time with him was his buying over and over

[273]

again of similar things. His ideas seemed to run in series. Within a twelve-month he bought five new motor-cars, each more swift and powerful than its predecessor, and only the repeated prompt resignation of his chief chauffeur at each moment of danger, prevented his driving them himself. He used them more and more. He developed a passion for locomotion for its own sake.

Then he began to chafe at Lady Grove, fretted by a chance jest he had overheard at a dinner. "This house, George," he said. "It's a misfit. There's no elbow-room in it; it's choked with old memories. . . . And I can't stand all these damned Durgans!

"That chap in the corner, George. No! the other corner! The man in a cherry-coloured coat. He watches you! He'd look silly if I stuck a poker through his Gizzard!"

"He'd look," I reflected, "much as he does now. As though he was amused."

He replaced his glasses, which had fallen at his emotion, and glared at his antagonists. "What are they? What are they all, the lot of 'em? Dead as Mutton! They just stuck in the mud. They didn't even rise to the Reformation. The old out-of-date Reformation! Move with the times!—they moved against the times. Just a Family of Failure,—they never even tried! . . .

"They're jes', George, exactly what I'm not. Exactly. It isn't suitable. . . . All this living in the Past.

"And I want a bigger place too, George. I want air and sunlight and room to move about and more service. A house where you can get a Move on things! Zzzz. Why! it's like a discord—it jars—even to have the telephone. . . . There's nothing, nothing except the terrace, that's worth a Rap. It's all dark and old and dried up and full of old-fashioned things—musty old idees—fitter for a silver-fish than a modern man. . . . I don't know how I got here."

He broke out into a new grievance. "That damned vicar," he complained, "thinks I ought to think myself lucky to get this place! Every time I meet him I can see him think it. . . . One of these days, George, I'll show him what a

Mod'un house is like!"

And he did.

I remember the day when he declared, as Americans say, for Crest Hill. He had come up to see my new gas plant, for I was then only just beginning to experiment with auxiliary collapsible balloons, and all the time the shine of his glasses was wandering away to the open down beyond. "Let's go back to Lady Grove over the hill," he said. "Something I want to show you. Something fine!"

It was an empty sunlit place that summer evening, sky and earth warm with sundown, and a pe-wit or so just accentuating the pleasant stillness that ends a long clear day. A beautiful peace, it was, to wreck for ever. And there was my uncle, the modern man of power, in his grey top-hat and his grey suit and his black-ribboned glasses, short, thin-legged, large-stomached, pointing and gesticulating, threatening this calm.

He began with a wave of his arm. "That's the place, George," he said. "See?"

"Eh!" I cried—for I had been thinking of remote things. "I got it."

"Got what?"

"For a house!—a twentieth-century house! That's the place for it!"

One of his characteristic phrases was begotten in him. "Four-square to the winds of heaven, George!" he said. "Eh? Four-square to the winds of heaven!"

"You'll get the winds up here," I said.

"A mammoth house it ought to be, George—to suit these hills."

"Quite," I said.

"Great galleries and things—running out there and there —See? I been thinking of it, George! Looking out all this way—across the Weald. With its back to Lady Grove."

"And the morning sun in its eye."

"Like an eagle, George,—like an eagle!"

So he broached to me what speedily became the leading occupation of his culminating years, Crest Hill But all the world has heard of that extravagant place which grew and changed its plans as it grew, and bubbled like a salted snail, and burgeoned and bulged and evermore grew. I know not what delirium of pinnacles and terraces and arcades and corridors glittered at last upon the uplands of his mind; the place, for all that its expansion was terminated abruptly by our collapse, is wonderful enough as it stands,—that empty instinctive building of a childless man. His chief architect was a young man named Westminster, whose work he had picked out in the architecture room of the Royal Academy on account of a certain grandiose courage in it, but with him he associated from time to time a number of fellow professionals, stonemasons, sanitary engineers, painters, sculptors, scribes, metal workers, wood carvers, furniture designers, ceramic specialists, landscape gardeners, and the man who designs the arrangement and ventilation of the various new houses in the London Zoological Gardens. In addition he had his own ideas. The thing occupied his mind at all times, but it held it completely from Friday night to Monday morning. He would come down to Lady Grove on Friday night in a crowded motor-car that almost dripped architects. He didn't, however, confine himself to architects; every one was liable to an invitation to week-end and view Crest Hill, and many an eager promoter, unaware of how Napoleonically and completely my uncle had departmentalised his mind, tried to creep up to him by way of tiles and ventilators and new electric fittings. Always on Sunday mornings, unless the weather was vile, he would, so soon as breakfast and his secretaries were disposed of, visit the site with a considerable retinue, and alter and develop plans, making modifications, Zzzz-ing, giving immense new orders verbally—an unsatisfactory way, as Westminster and the contractors ultimately found.

There he stands in my memory, the symbol of this age for me, the man of luck and advertisement, the current master of the world. There he stands upon the great outward sweep of the terrace before the huge main entrance, a little figure, ridiculously disproportionate to that forty foot arch, with the granite ball behind him—the astronomical ball, brass coopered, that represented the world, with a little adjustable tube of lenses on a gun-metal arm that focussed the sun upon just that point of the earth on which it chanced to be shining vertically. There he stands, Napoleonically grouped with his retinue, men in tweeds and golfing-suits, a little solicitor, whose name I forget, in grey trousers and a black jacket, and Westminster in Jaeger underclothing, a floriferous tie, and peculiar brown cloth of his own.

The downland breeze flutters my uncle's coat-tails, disarranges his stiff hair, and insists on the evidence of undisciplined appetites in face and form, as he points out this or that feature in the prospect to his attentive collaborator.

Below are hundreds of feet of wheeling-planks, ditches, excavations, heaps of earth, piles of garden stone from the Wealden ridges. On either hand the walls of his irrelevant unmeaning palace rise. At one time he had working in that place—disturbing the economic balance of the whole countryside by their presence—upwards of three thousand men. . . .

So he poses for my picture amidst the raw beginnings that were never to be completed. He did the strangest things about that place, things more and more detached from any conception of financial scale, things more and more apart from sober humanity. He seemed to think himself, at last, released from any such limitations. He moved a quite considerable hill, and nearly sixty mature trees were moved with it to open his prospect eastward, moved it about two hundred feet to the south. At another time he caught a suggestion from some city restaurant and made a billiard-room roofed with plate glass beneath the waters of his ornamental lake. He furnished one wing while its roof still awaited completion. He had a swimming bath thirty feet square next to his bedroom upstairs, and to crown it all he commenced a great wall to hold all his dominions together, free from the invasion of common men. It was a ten-foot wall, glass surmounted, and had it been completed as he intended it, it would have had a total length of nearly eleven miles. Some of it towards the last was so dishonestly built that it collapsed within a year upon its foundations, but some miles of it still stand. I never think of it now but what I think of the hundreds of eager little investors who followed his "star," whose hopes and lives, whose wives' security and children's prospects are all mixed up beyond redemption with that flaking mortar. . . .

It is curious how many of these modern financiers of chance and bluff have ended their careers by building. It was not merely my uncle. Sooner or later they all seem to bring their luck to the test of realisation, try to make their fluid opulence coagulate out as bricks and mortar, bring moonshine into relations with a weekly wages-sheet. Then the whole fabric of confidence and imagination totters— and down they come. . . .

When I think of that despoiled hillside, that colossal litter of bricks and mortar, and crude roads and paths, the scaffolding and sheds, the general quality of unforeseeing outrage upon the peace of nature, I am reminded of a chat I had with the vicar one bleak day after he had witnessed a glide. He talked to me of aeronautics as I stood in jersey and shorts beside my machine, fresh from alighting, and his cadaverous face failed to conceal a peculiar desolation that possessed him.

"Almost you convince me," he said, coming up to me, "against my will. . . . A marvellous invention! But it will take you a long time, sir, before you can emulate that perfect mechanism—the wing of a bird."

He looked at my sheds.

"You've changed the look of this valley, too," he said.

"Temporary defilements," I remarked, guessing what was in his mind.

"Of course. Things come and go. Things come and go. But—— H'm. I've just been up over the hill to look at Mr. Edward Ponderevo's new house. That—that is something more permanent. A magnificent place!—in many ways. Imposing. I've never somehow brought myself to go that way

before. . . . Things are greatly advanced. . . . We find—
the great number of strangers introduced into the villages
about here by these operations, working-men chiefly, a little
embarrassing——. It put us out. They bring a new spirit
into the place; betting—ideas—all sorts of queer notions.
Our publicans like it, of course. And they come and sleep
in one's outhouses—and make the place a little unsafe at
nights. The other morning I couldn't sleep—a slight dyspepsia—and I looked out of the window. I was amazed to
see people going by on bicycles. A silent procession. I
counted ninety-seven—in the dawn. All going up to the
new road for Crest Hill. Remarkable I thought it. And so
I've been up to see what they were doing."

"They would have been more than remarkable thirty
years ago," I said.

"Yes, indeed. Things change. We think nothing of it now
at all—comparatively. And that big house——"

He raised his eyebrows. "Really stupendous! . . . Stupendous.

"All the hillside—the old turf—cut to ribbons!"

His eye searched my face. "We've grown so accustomed
to look up to Lady Grove," he said, and smiled in search
of sympathy. "It shifts our centre of gravity."

"Things will readjust themselves," I lied.

He snatched at the phrase. "Of course," he said. "They'll
readjust themselves—settle down again. Must. In the old
way. It's bound to come right again—a comforting thought.
Yes. After all, Lady Grove itself had to be built once upon
a time—was—to begin with—artificial."

His eye returned to my aeroplane. He sought to dismiss
his graver preoccupations. "I should think twice," he remarked, "before I trusted myself to that concern. . . . But
I suppose one grows accustomed to the motion."

He bade me good morning and went his way, bowed and
thoughtful. . . .

He had kept the truth from his mind a long time, but
that morning it had forced its way to him with an aspect
that brooked no denial that this time it was not just changes

that were coming in his world, but that all his world lay open and defenceless, conquered and surrendered, doomed so far as he could see, root and branch, scale and form alike, to change.

CHAPTER THE THIRD

Soaring

I

FOR nearly all the time that my uncle was incubating and hatching Crest Hill I was busy in a little transverse valley between that great beginning and Lady Grove with more and more costly and ambitious experiments in aerial navigation. This work was indeed the main substance of my life through all the great time of the Tono-Bungay symphony.

I have told already how I came to devote myself to this system of inquiries, how in a sort of disgust with the common adventure of life I took up the dropped ends of my college studies, taking them up again with a man's resolution instead of a boy's ambition. From the first I did well at this work. It was, I think, largely a case of special aptitude, of a peculiar irrelevant vein of faculty running through my mind. It is one of those things men seem to have by chance, that has little or nothing to do with their general merit, and which it is ridiculous to be either conceited or modest about. I did get through a very big mass of work in those years, working for a time with a concentrated fierceness that left little of such energy or capacity as I possess unused. I worked out a series of problems connected with the stability of bodies pitching in the air and the internal movements of the wind, and I also revolutionised one leading part at last of the theory of explosive engines. These things are to be found in the *Philosophical Transactions*, the *Mathematical Journal*, and less frequently in one or two other such publications, and they needn't detain us here.

Indeed, I doubt if I could write about them here. One acquires a sort of shorthand for one's notes and mind in relation to such special work. I have never taught nor lectured, that is to say, I have never had to express my thoughts about mechanical things in ordinary everyday language, and I doubt very much if I could do so now without extreme tedium. . . .

My work was, to begin with, very largely theoretical. I was able to attack such early necessities of verification as arose with quite little models, using a turntable to get the motion through the air, and cane, whalebone and silk as building material. But a time came when incalculable factors crept in, factors of human capacity and factors of insufficient experimental knowledge, when one must needs guess and try. Then I had to enlarge the scale of my operations, and soon I had enlarged them very greatly. I set to work almost concurrently on the balance and stability of gliders and upon the steering of inflated bags, the latter a particularly expensive branch of work. I was no doubt moved by something of the same spirit of lavish expenditure that was running away with my uncle in these developments. Presently my establishment above Lady Grove had grown to a painted wood châlet big enough to accommodate six men, and in which I would sometimes live for three weeks together; to a gasometer, to a motor-house, to three big corrugated-roofed sheds and lock-up houses, to a stage from which to start gliders, to a workshop and so forth. A rough road was made. We brought up gas from Cheaping and electricity from Woking, which place I found also afforded a friendly workshop for larger operations than I could manage. I had the luck also to find a man who seemed my heaven-sent second-in-command—Cothope his name was. He was a self-educated man; he had formerly been a sapper and he was one of the best and handiest working engineers alive. Without him I do not think I could have achieved half what I have done. At times he has been not so much my assistant as my collaborator, and has followed my fortunes to this day. Other men came and went as I needed them.

I do not know how far it is possible to convey to any one who has not experienced it, the peculiar interest, the peculiar satisfaction that lies in a sustained research when one is not hampered by want of money. It is a different thing from any other sort of human effort. You are free from the exasperating conflict with your fellow-creatures altogether— at least so far as the essential work goes; that for me is its peculiar merit. Scientific truth is the remotest of mistresses; she hides in strange places, she is attained by tortuous and laborious roads, but *she is always there!* Win to her and she will not fail you; she is yours and mankind's for ever. She is reality, the one reality I have found in this strange disorder of existence. She will not sulk with you nor misunderstand you nor cheat you of your reward upon some petty doubt. You cannot change her by advertisement or clamour, nor stifle her in vulgarities. Things grow under your hands when you serve her, things that are permanent as nothing else is permanent in the whole life of man. That, I think, is the peculiar satisfaction of science and its enduring reward. . . .

The taking up of experimental work produced a great change in my personal habits. I have told how already once in my life at Wimblehurst I had a period of discipline and continuous effort, and how, when I came to South Kensington, I became demoralised by the immense effect of London, by its innumerable imperative demands upon my attention and curiosity. And I parted with much of my personal pride when I gave up science for the development of Tono-Bungay. But my poverty kept me abstinent and my youthful romanticism kept me chaste until my married life was well under way. Then in all directions I relaxed. I did a large amount of work, but I never troubled to think whether it was my maximum nor whether the moods and indolences that came to me at times were avoidable things. With the coming of plenty I ate abundantly and foolishly, drank freely and followed my impulses more and more carelessly.

I felt no reason why I should do anything else. Never at any point did I use myself to the edge of my capacity. The emotional crisis of my divorce did not produce any immediate change in these matters of personal discipline. I found some difficulty at first in concentrating my mind upon scientific work, it was so much more exacting than business, but I got over that difficulty by smoking. I became an inordinate cigar smoker; it gave me moods of profound depression, but I treated these usually by the homœopathic method,—by lighting another cigar. I didn't realise at all how loose my moral and nervous fibre had become until I reached the practical side of my investigations and was face to face with the necessity of finding out just how it felt to use a glider and just what a man could do with one.

I got into this relaxed habit of living in spite of very real tendencies in my nature towards discipline. I've never been in love with self-indulgence. That philosophy of the loose lip and the lax paunch is one for which I've always had an instinctive distrust. I like bare things, stripped things, plain, austere and continent things, fine lines and cold colours. But in these plethoric times when there is too much coarse stuff for everybody and the struggle for life takes the form of competitive advertisement and the effort to fill your neighbour's eye, when there is no urgent demand either for personal courage, sound nerves or stark beauty, we find ourselves by accident. Always before these times the bulk of the people did not over-eat themselves, because they couldn't, whether they wanted to do so or not, and all but a very few were kept "fit" by unavoidable exercise and personal danger. Now, if only he pitch his standard low enough and keep free from pride, almost any one can achieve a sort of excess. You can go through contemporary life fudging and evading, indulging and slacking, never really hungry nor frightened nor passionately stirred, your highest moment a mere sentimental orgasm, and your first real contact with primary and elemental necessities, the sweat of your death-bed. So I think it was with my uncle; so, very nearly, it was with me.

But the glider brought me up smartly. I had to find out how these things went down the air, and the only way to find out is to go down with one. And for a time I wouldn't face it.

There is something impersonal about a book, I suppose. At any rate I find myself able to write down here just the confession I've never been able to make to any one face to face, the frightful trouble it was to me to bring myself to do what I suppose every other coloured boy in the West Indies could do without turning a hair, and that is to fling myself off for my first soar down the wind. The first trial was bound to be the worst; it was an experiment I made with life, and the chance of death or injury was, I supposed, about equal to the chance of success. I believed that with a dawn-like lucidity. I had begun with a glider that I imagined was on the lines of the Wright brothers' aeroplane, but I could not be sure. It might turn over. I might upset it. It might burrow its nose at the end and smash itself and me. The conditions of the flight necessitated alert attention; it wasn't a thing to be done by jumping off and shutting one's eyes or getting angry or drunk to do it. One had to use one's weight to balance. And when at last I did it it was horrible—for ten seconds. For ten seconds or so, as I swept down the air flattened on my infernal framework and with the wind in my eyes, the rush of the ground beneath me filled me with sick and helpless terror; I felt as though some violent oscillatory current was throbbing in brain and backbone, and I groaned aloud. I set my teeth and groaned. It was a groan wrung out of me in spite of myself. My sensations of terror swooped to a climax.

And then, you know, they ended!

Suddenly my terror was over and done with. I was soaring through the air right way up, steadily, and no mischance had happened. I felt intensely alive and my nerves were strung like a bow. I shifted a limb, swerved and shouted between fear and triumph as I recovered from the swerve and heeled the other way and steadied myself.

I thought I was going to hit a rook that was flying

athwart me,—it was queer with what projectile silence that jumped upon me out of nothingness, and I yelled help-lessly, "Get out of the way!" The bird doubled itself up like a partly inverted V, flapped, went up to the right ab-ruptly and vanished from my circle of interest. Then I saw the shadow of my aeroplane keeping a fixed distance be-fore me and very steady, and the turf as it seemed stream-ing out behind it. The turf!—it wasn't after all streaming so impossibly fast. . . .

When I came gliding down to the safe spread of level green I had chosen, I was as cool and ready as a city clerk who drops off an omnibus in motion, and I had learnt much more than soaring. I tilted up her nose at the right mo-ment, levelled again and grounded like a snowflake on a windless day. I lay flat for an instant and then knelt up and got on my feet atremble, but very satisfied with my-self. Cothope was running down the hill to me. . . .

But from that day I went into training, and I kept my-self in training for many months. I had delayed my experi-ments for very nearly six weeks on various excuses because of my dread of this first flight, because of the slackness of body and spirit that had come to me with the business life. The shame of that cowardice spurred me none the less be-cause it was probably altogether my own secret. I felt that Cothope at any rate might suspect. Well,—he shouldn't sus-pect again.

It is curious that I remember that shame and self-accusa-tion and its consequences far more distinctly than I recall the weeks of vacillation before I soared. For a time I went altogether without alcohol, I stopped smoking altogether and ate very sparingly, and every day I did something that called a little upon my nerves and muscles. I soared as fre-quently as I could. I substituted a motor-bicycle for the London train and took my chances in the southward traffic, and I even tried what thrills were to be got upon a horse. But they put me on made horses, and I conceived a perhaps unworthy contempt for the certitudes of equestrian exercise in comparison with the adventures of mechanism. Also I walked along the high wall at the back of Lady Grove garden, and at last brought myself to stride the gap where the gate comes. If I didn't altogether get rid of a certain giddy instinct by such exercises, at least I trained my will until it didn't matter. And soon I no longer dreaded flight, but was eager to go higher into the air, and I came to esteem soaring upon a glider, that even over the deepest dip in the ground had barely forty feet of fall beneath it, a mere mockery of what flight might be. I began to dream of the keener freshness in the air high above the beechwoods, and it was rather to satisfy that desire than as any legitimate development of my proper work that presently I turned a part of my energies and the bulk of my private income to the problem of the navigable balloon.

II

I had gone far beyond that initial stage; I had had two smashes and a broken rib which my aunt nursed with great energy, and was getting some reputation in the aeronautic world when, suddenly, as though she had never really left it, the Honourable Beatrice Normandy, dark-eyed, and with the old disorderly wave of the hair from her brow, came back into my life. She came riding down a grass path in the thickets below Lady Grove, perched up on a huge black horse, and the old Earl of Carnaby and Archie Garvell, her half-brother, were with her. My uncle had been bothering me about the Crest Hill hot-water pipes, and we were returning by a path transverse to theirs and came out upon them suddenly. Old Carnaby was trespassing on our ground, and so he hailed us in a friendly fashion and pulled up to talk to us.

I didn't note Beatrice at all at first. I was interested in Lord Carnaby, that remarkable vestige of his own brilliant youth. I had heard of him, but never seen him. For a man of sixty-five who had sinned all the sins, so they said, and laid waste the most magnificent political début of any man of his generation, he seemed to me to be looking remarkably fit and fresh. He was a lean little man with grey-blue eyes in his brown face, and his cracked voice was the worst thing in his effect.

"Hope you don't mind us coming this way, Ponderevo," he cried; and my uncle, who was sometimes a little too general and generous with titles, answered, "Not at all, my lord, not at all! Glad you make use of it!"

"You're building a great place over the hill," said Carnaby.

"Thought I'd make a show for once," said my uncle. "It looks big because it's spread out for the sun."

"Air and sunlight," said the earl. "You can't have too much of them. But before our time they used to build for shelter and water and the high road." . . .

Then I discovered that the silent figure behind the earl was Beatrice.

I'd forgotten her sufficiently to think for a moment that she hadn't changed at all since she had watched me from behind the skirts of Lady Drew. She was looking at me, and her dainty brow under her broad-brimmed hat—she was wearing a grey hat and loose unbuttoned coat—was knit with perplexity, trying, I suppose, to remember where she had seen me before. Her shaded eyes met mine with that mute question. . . .

It seemed incredible to me she didn't remember.

"Well," said the earl and touched his horse.

Garvell was patting the neck of his horse, which was inclined to fidget, and disregarding me. He nodded over his shoulder and followed. His movement seemed to release a train of memories in her. She glanced suddenly at him and then back at me with a flash of recognition that warmed instantly to a faint smile. She hesitated as if to speak to me, smiled broadly and understandingly and turned to follow the others. All three broke into a canter and she did not look back. I stood for a second or so at the crossing of the lanes, watching her recede, and then became aware that my uncle was already some paces off and talking over his shoulder in the belief that I was close behind.

I turned about and strode to overtake him.

My mind was full of Beatrice and this surprise. I remembered her simply as a Normandy. I'd clean forgotten that Garvell was the son and she the step-daughter of our neighbour, Lady Osprey. Indeed, I'd probably forgotten at that time that we had Lady Osprey as a neighbour. There was no reason at all for remembering it. It was amazing to find her in this Surrey countryside, when I'd never thought of her as living anywhere in the world but at Bladesover Park, near forty miles and twenty years away. She was so alive—so unchanged! The same quick warm blood was in her cheeks. It seemed only yesterday that we had kissed among the bracken stems. . . .

"Eh?" I said.

"I say he's good stuff," said my uncle. "You can say what you like against the aristocracy, George; Lord Carnaby's rattling good stuff. There's a sort of *Savoir Faire*, something—it's an old-fashioned phrase, George, but a good one—there's a Bong-Tong. . . . It's like the Oxford turf, George, you can't grow it in a year. I wonder how they do it. It's living always on a Scale, George. It's being there from the beginning." . . .

"She might," I said to myself, "be a picture by Romney come alive!"

"They tell all these stories about him," said my uncle, "but what do they all amount to?"

"Gods!" I said to myself; "but why have I forgotten for so long? Those queer little brows of hers—the touch of mischief in her eyes—the way she breaks into a smile!"

"I don't blame him," said my uncle. "Mostly it's imagination. That and leisure, George. When I was a young man I was kept pretty busy. So were you. Even then——!"

What puzzled me more particularly was the queer trick of my memory that had never recalled anything vital of Beatrice whatever when I met Garvell again, that had, indeed, recalled nothing except a boyish antagonism and our fight. Now when my senses were full of her, it seemed incredible that I could ever have forgotten. . . .

III

"Oh, Crikey!" said my aunt, reading a letter behind her coffee-machine. *"Here's* a young woman, George!"

We were breakfasting together in the big window bay at Lady Grove that looks upon the iris beds; my uncle was in London.

I sounded an interrogative note and decapitated an egg.

"Who's Beatrice Normandy?" asked my aunt. "I've not heard of her before."

"She the young woman?"

"Yes. Says she knows you. I'm no hand at old etiquette, George, but her line is a bit unusual. Practically she says she's going to make her mother——"

"Eh? Step-mother, isn't it?"

"You seem to know a lot about her. She says 'mother'— Lady Osprey. They're to call on me, anyhow, next Wednesday week at four, and there's got to be you for tea."

"Eh?"

"You—for tea."

"H'm. She had rather—force of character. When I knew her before."

I became aware of my aunt's head sticking out obliquely from behind the coffee-machine and regarding me with wide blue curiosity. I met her gaze for a moment, flinched, coloured, and laughed.

"I've known her longer than I've known you," I said, and explained at length.

My aunt kept her eye on me over and round the coffee-machine as I did so. She was greatly interested, and asked several elucidatory questions.

"Why didn't you tell me the day you saw her? You've had her on your mind for a week," she said.

"It *is* odd I didn't tell you," I admitted.

"You thought I'd get a Down on her," said my aunt conclusively. "That's what you thought," and opened the rest of her letters.

The two ladies came in a pony-carriage with conspicuous punctuality, and I had the unusual experience of seeing my aunt entertaining callers. We had tea upon the terrace under the cedar, but old Lady Osprey, being an embittered Protestant, had never before seen the inside of the house, and we made a sort of tour of inspection that reminded me of my first visit to the place. In spite of my preoccupation with Beatrice, I stored a queer little memory of the contrast between the two other women; my aunt, tall, slender and awkward, in a simple blue homekeeping dress, an omnivorous reader and a very authentic wit, and the lady of pedigree, short and plump, dressed with Victorian fussiness, living at the intellectual level of palmistry and genteel fiction, pink in the face and generally flustered by a sense of my aunt's social strangeness and disposed under the circumstances to behave rather like an imitation of the more queenly moments of her own cook. The one seemed made of whalebone, the other of dough. My aunt was nervous, partly through the intrinsic difficulty of handling the lady and partly because of her passionate desire to watch Beatrice and me, and her nervousness took a common form with her, a wider clumsiness of gesture and an exacerbation of her habitual oddity of phrase which did much to deepen the pink perplexity of the lady of title. For instance, I heard my aunt admit that one of the Stuart Durgan ladies did look a bit "balmy on the crumpet"; she described the knights of the age of chivalry as "korvorting about on the off-chance of a dragon"; she explained she was "always old mucking about the garden," and instead of offering me a Garibaldi biscuit, she asked me with that faint lisp of hers, to "have some squashed flies, George." I felt convinced Lady Osprey would describe her as "a most eccentric person" on the very first opportunity;—"a *most* eccentric person." One could see her, as people say, "shaping" for that.

Beatrice was dressed very quietly in brown, with a simple but courageous broad-brimmed hat, and an unexpected quality of being grown-up and responsible. She guided her step-mother through the first encounter, scrutinised my aunt, and got us all well in movement through the house, and then she turned her attention to me with a quick and half-confident smile.

"We haven't met," she said, "since——"

"It was in the Warren."

"Of course," she said, "the Warren! I remembered it all except just the name. . . . I was eight."

Her smiling eyes insisted on my memories being thorough. I looked up and met them squarely, a little at a loss for what I should say.

"I gave you away pretty completely," she said, meditating upon my face. "And afterwards I gave away Archie."

She turned her face away from the others, and her voice fell ever so little.

"They gave him a licking for telling lies!" she said, as though that was a pleasant memory. "And when it was all over I went to our wigwam. You remember the wigwam?"

"Out in the West Wood?"

"Yes—and cried—for all the evil I had done you, I suppose. . . . I've often thought of it since." . . .

Lady Osprey stopped for us to overtake her. "My dear!" she said to Beatrice. "Such a beautiful gallery!" Then she stared very hard at me, puzzled in the most naked fashion to understand who I might be.

"People say the oak staircase is rather good," said my aunt, and led the way.

Lady Osprey, with her skirts gathered for the ascent to the gallery and her hand on the newel, turned and addressed a look full of meaning—overflowing indeed with meanings—at her charge. The chief meaning no doubt was caution about myself, but much of it was just meaning at large. I chanced to catch the response in a mirror and detected Beatrice with her nose wrinkled into a swift and entirely diabolical grimace. Lady Osprey became a deeper shade of pink and speechless with indignation—it was evident she disavowed all further responsibility, as she followed my aunt upstairs.

"It's dark, but there's a sort of dignity," said Beatrice very distinctly, regarding the hall with serene tranquillity, and allowing the unwilling feet on the stairs to widen their distance from us. She stood a step up, so that she looked down a little upon me and over me at the old hall.

She turned upon me abruptly when she thought her stepmother was beyond ear-shot.

"But how did you get here?" she asked.

"Here?"

"All this." She indicated space and leisure by a wave of the hand at hall and tall windows and sunlit terrace. "Weren't you the housekeeper's son?"

"I've adventured. My uncle has become—a great financier. He used to be a little chemist about twenty miles from Bladesover. We're promoters now, amalgamators, big people on the new model."

"I understand." She regarded me with interested eyes, visibly thinking me out.

"And you recognised me?" I asked.

"After a second or so. I saw you recognised me. I couldn't place you, but I knew I knew you. Then Archie being there helped me to remember."

"I'm glad to meet again," I ventured. "I'd never forgotten you."

"One doesn't forget those childish things."

We regarded one another for a moment with a curiously easy and confident satisfaction in coming together again. I can't explain our ready zest in one another. The thing was so. We pleased each other, we had no doubt in our minds that we pleased each other. From the first we were at our ease with one another. "So picturesque, so very picturesque," came a voice from above, and then: "Beeatrice!"

"I've a hundred things I want to know about you," she said with an easy intimacy, as we went up the winding steps. . . .

As the four of us sat at tea together under the cedar on the terrace she asked questions about my aeronautics. My aunt helped with a word or so about my broken ribs. Lady Osprey evidently regarded flying as a most undesirable and improper topic—a blasphemous intrusion upon the angels. "It isn't flying," I explained. "We don't fly yet."

"You never will," she said compactly. "You never will."

"Well," I said, "we do what we can."

The little lady lifted a small gloved hand and indicated a height of about four feet from the ground. "Thus far," she said, "thus far—*and no farther!* No!"

She became emphatically pink. *"No,"* she said again quite conclusively, and coughed shortly. "Thank you," she said to her ninth or tenth cake. Beatrice burst into cheerful laughter with her eye on me. I was lying on the turf, and this perhaps caused a slight confusion about the primordial curse in Lady Osprey's mind.

"Upon his belly shall he go," she said with quiet distinctness, "all the days of his life."

After which we talked no more of aeronautics.

Beatrice sat bunched together in a chair and regarded me with exactly the same scrutiny, I thought, the same adventurous aggression, that I had faced long ago at the tea-table in my mother's room. She was amazingly like that little Princess of my Bladesover memories, the wilful misbehaviours of her hair seemed the same—her voice; things one would have expected to be changed altogether. She formed her plans in the same quick way, and acted with the same irresponsible decision.

She stood up abruptly.

"What is there beyond the terrace?" she said, and found me promptly beside her.

I invented a view for her.

At the further corner from the cedar she perched herself up upon the parapet and achieved an air of comfort among the lichenous stones. "Now tell me," she said, "all about yourself. Tell me about yourself; I know such duffers of men! They all do the same things. How did you get—here? All my men *were* here. They couldn't have got here if they hadn't been here always. They wouldn't have thought it right. You've climbed."

"If it's climbing," I said.

She went off at a tangent. "It's—I don't know if you'll understand—interesting to meet you again. I've remembered you. I don't know why, but I have. I've used you as a sort of lay figure—when I've told myself stories. But you've always been rather stiff and difficult in my stories—in ready-made clothes—a Labour Member or a Bradlaugh, or something like that. You're not like that a bit. And yet you *are!*"

She looked at me. "Was it much of a fight? They make out it is. I don't know why."

"I was shot up here by an accident," I said. "There was no fight at all. Except to keep honest, perhaps—and I made no great figure in that. I and my uncle mixed a medicine and it blew us up. No merit in that! But you've been here all the time. Tell me what you have done first."

"One thing we didn't do." She meditated for a moment.

"What?" said I.

"Produce a little half-brother for Bladesover. So it went to the Phillbrick gang. And they let it! And I and my stepmother—we let, too. And live in a little house."

She nodded her head vaguely over her shoulder, and turned to me again. "Well, suppose it was an accident. Here you are! Now you're here, what are you going to do? You're young. Is it to be Parliament? I heard some men the other day talking about you. Before I knew you were you. They said that was what you ought to do." . . .

She put me through my intentions with a close and vital curiosity. It was just as she had tried to imagine me a soldier and place me years ago. She made me feel more planless and incidental than ever. "You want to make a flying-machine," she pursued. "And when you fly? What then? Would it be for fighting?" . . .

I told her something of my experimental work. She had never heard of the soaring aeroplane, and was excited by the thought, and keen to hear about it. She had thought all the work so far had been a mere projecting of impossible machines. For her Pilcher and Lilienthal had died in vain. She did not know such men had lived in the world.

"But that's dangerous!" she said, with a note of discovery.

"Oh!—it's dangerous." . . .

"Bee-atrice!" Lady Osprey called.

Beatrice dropped from the wall to her feet.

"Where do you do this soaring?"

"Beyond the high Barrows. East of Crest Hill and the wood."

"Do you mind people coming to see?"

"Whenever you please. Only let me know——"

"I'll take my chance some day. Some day soon." She looked at me thoughtfully, smiled, and our talk was at an end.

IV

All my later work in aeronautics is associated in my memory with the quality of Beatrice, with her incidental presence, with things she said and did and things I thought of that had reference to her.

In the spring of that year I had got to a flying machine that lacked nothing but longitudinal stability. My model flew like a bird for fifty or a hundred yards or so, and then either dived and broke its nose or, what was commoner, reared up, slid back and smashed its propeller. The rhythm of the pitching puzzled me. I felt it must obey some laws not yet quite clearly stated. I became therefore a student of theory and literature for a time; I hit upon the string of considerations that led me to what is called Ponderevo's Principle and my F.R.S., and I worked this out in three long papers. Meanwhile I made a lot of turn-table and glider models and started in upon an idea of combining gas-bags and gliders. Balloon work was new to me. I had made one or two ascents in the balloons of the Aëro Club before I started my gasometer and the balloon shed and gave Cothope a couple of months with Sir Peter Rumchase. My uncle found part of the money for these developments; he was growing interested and competitive in this business because of Lord Boom's prize and the amount of *réclame* involved, and it was at his request that I named my first navigable balloon Lord Roberts Alpha.

Lord Roberts α very nearly terminated all my investigations. My idea both in this and its more successful and famous younger brother, Lord Roberts β, was to utilise the idea of a contractile balloon with a rigid flat base, a balloon shaped rather like an inverted boat that should almost support the apparatus, but not quite. The gas-bag was of the chambered sort used for these long forms, and not with an internal balloonette. The trouble was to make the thing contractile. This I sought to do by fixing a long, fine-meshed silk net over it that was fastened to be rolled up on two longitudinal rods. Practically I contracted my sausage gasbag by netting it down. The ends were too complex for me to describe here, but I thought them out elaborately and they were very carefully planned. Lord Roberts α was furnished with a single big screw forward, and there was a rudder aft. The engine was the first one to be, so to speak, right in the plane of the gas-bag. I lay immediately under the balloon on a sort of glider framework, far away from either engine or rudder, controlling them by wire-pulls constructed on the principle of the well-known Bowden brake of the cyclist.

But Lord Roberts α has been pretty exhaustively figured and described in various aeronautical publications. The unforeseen defect was the badness of the work in the silk netting. It tore aft as soon as I began to contract the balloon, and the last two segments immediately bulged through the hole, exactly as an inner tube will bulge through the ruptured outer cover of a pneumatic tire, and then the sharp edge of the torn net cut the oiled-silk of the distended last segment along a weak seam and burst it with a loud report.

Up to that point the whole thing had been going on extremely well. As a navigable balloon and before I contracted it, the Lord Roberts α was an unqualified success. It had run out of the shed admirably at nine or ten miles an hour or more, and although there was a gentle southwester blowing, it had gone up and turned and faced it as well as any craft of the sort I have ever seen.

I lay in my customary glider position, horizontal and face downward, and the invisibility of all the machinery gave an extraordinary effect of independent levitation. Only by looking up, as it were, and turning my head back could I see the flat aeroplane bottom of the balloon and the rapid successive passages, swish, swish, swish of the vans of the propeller. I made a wide circle over Lady Grove and Duffield and out towards Effingham and came back quite successfully to the starting-point.

Down below in the October sunlight were my sheds and the little group that had been summoned to witness the start, their faces craned upward and most of them scrutinising my expression through field-glasses. I could see Carnaby and Beatrice on horseback, and two girls I did not know with them; Cothope and three or four workmen I employed; my aunt and Mrs. Levinstein, who was staying with her, on foot, and Dimmock, the veterinary surgeon, and one or two others. My shadow moved a little to the north of them like the shadow of a fish. At Lady Grove the servants were out on the lawn, and the Duffield school playground swarmed with children too indifferent to aeronautics to cease their playing. But in the Crest Hill direction—the place looked extraordinarily squat and ugly from above—there were knots and strings of staring workmen everywhere—not one of them working, but all agape. (But now I write it, it occurs to me that perhaps it was their dinner hour; it was certainly near twelve.) I hung for a moment or so enjoying the soar, then turned about to face a clear stretch of open down, let the engine out to full speed and set my rollers at work rolling in the net, and so tightening the gas-bags. Instantly the pace quickened with the diminished resistance. . . .

In that moment before the bang I think I must have been really flying. Before the net ripped, just in the instant when my balloon was at its systole, the whole apparatus was, I am convinced, heavier than air. That, however, is a claim that has been disputed, and in any case this sort of priority is a very trivial thing.

Then came a sudden retardation, instantly followed by an inexpressibly disconcerting tilt downward of the machine. That I still recall with horror. I couldn't see what was happening at all and I couldn't imagine. It was a mysterious, inexplicable dive. The thing, it seemed, without rhyme or reason, was kicking up its heels in the air. The bang followed immediately, and I perceived I was falling rapidly.

I was too much taken by surprise to think of the proper cause of the report. I don't even know what I made of it. I was obsessed, I suppose, by that perpetual dread of the modern aeronaut, a flash between engine and balloon. Yet obviously I wasn't wrapped in flames. I ought to have realised instantly it wasn't that. I did, at any rate, whatever other impressions there were, release the winding of the outer net and let the balloon expand again, and that no doubt did something to break my fall. I don't remember doing that. Indeed, all I do remember is the giddy effect upon the landscape of falling swiftly upon it down a flat spiral, the hurried rush of fields and trees and cottages on my left shoulder and the overhung feeling as if the whole apparatus was pressing down the top of my head. I didn't stop or attempt to stop the screw. That was going on, swish, swish, swish all the time.

Cothope really knows more about the fall than I do. He describes the easterly start, the tilt, and the appearance and bursting of a sort of bladder aft. Then down I swooped, very swiftly, but not nearly so steeply as I imagined I was doing. "Fifteen or twenty degrees," said Cothope, "to be exact." From him it was that I learnt that I let the nets loose again, and so arrested my fall. He thinks I was more in control of myself than I remember. But I do not see why I should have forgotten so excellent a resolution. His impression is that I was really steering and trying to drop into the Farthing Down beeches. "You hit the trees," he said, "and the whole affair stood on its nose among them, and then very slowly crumpled up. I saw you'd been jerked

[298]

out, as I thought, and I didn't stay for more. I rushed for my bicycle."

As a matter of fact, it was purely accidental that I came down in the woods. I am reasonably certain that I had no more control then than a thing in a parcel. I remember I felt a sort of wincing, "Now it comes!" as the trees rushed up to me. If I remember that, I should remember steering. Then the propeller smashed, everything stopped with a jerk, and I was falling into a mass of yellowing leaves, and Lord Roberts α, so it seemed to me, was going back into the sky.

I felt twigs and things hit me in the face, but I didn't feel injured at the time; I clutched at things that broke, tumbled through a froth of green and yellow into a shadowy world of great bark-covered arms, and there, snatching wildly, got a grip on a fair round branch, and hung.

I became intensely alert and clear-headed. I held by that branch for a moment and then looked about me, and caught at another, and then found myself holding to a practicable fork. I swung forward to that and got a leg around it below its junction, and so was able presently to clamber down, climbing very coolly and deliberately. I dropped ten feet or so from the lowest branch and fell on my feet. "That's all right," I said, and stared up through the tree to see what I could of the deflated and crumpled remains that had once been Lord Roberts α festooned on the branches it had broken. "Gods!" I said, "what a tumble!"

I wiped something that trickled from my face and was shocked to see my hand covered with blood. I looked at myself and saw what seemed to me an astonishing quantity of blood running down my arm and shoulder. I perceived my mouth was full of blood. It's a queer moment when one realises one is hurt, and perhaps badly hurt, and has still to discover just how far one is hurt. I explored my face carefully and found unfamiliar contours on the left side. The broken end of a branch had driven right through my cheek, damaging my cheek and teeth and gums, and left a splinter of itself stuck, like an explorer's fartherest-point flag, in the upper maxillary. That and a sprained wrist were all my damage. But I bled as though I had been chopped to pieces, and it seemed to me that my face had been driven in. I can't describe just the horrible disgust I felt at that.

"This blood must be stopped, anyhow," I said, thick-headedly. "I wonder where there's a spider's web"—an odd twist for my mind to take. But it was the only treatment that occurred to me.

I must have conceived some idea of going home unaided, because I was thirty yards from the tree before I dropped.

Then a kind of black disc appeared in the middle of the world and rushed out to the edge of things and blotted them out. I don't remember falling down. I fainted from excitement, disgust at my injury and loss of blood, and lay there until Cothope found me.

He was the first to find me, scorching as he did over the downland turf, and making a wide course to get the Carnaby plantations at their narrowest. Then presently, while he was trying to apply the methodical teachings of the St. John's Ambulance classes to a rather abnormal case, Beatrice came galloping through the trees full-tilt, with Lord Carnaby hard behind her, and she was hatless, muddy from a fall, and white as death. "And cool as a cucumber, too," said Cothope, turning it over in his mind as he told me.

("They never seem quite to have their heads, and never seem quite to lose 'em," said Cothope, generalising about the sex.)

Also he witnessed she acted with remarkable decision. The question was whether I should be taken to the house her step-mother occupied at Bedley Corner, the Carnaby dower house, or down to Carnaby's place at Easting. Beatrice had no doubt in the matter, for she meant to nurse me. Carnaby didn't seem to want that to happen. "She *would* have it wasn't half so far," said Cothope. "She faced us out. . . .

"I hate to be faced out of my opinion, so I've taken a pedometer over it since. It's exactly forty-three yards further.

[300]

"Lord Carnaby looked at her pretty straight," said Cothope, finishing the picture; "and then he give in."

V

But my story has made a jump from June to October, and during that time my relations with Beatrice and the countryside that was her setting had developed in many directions. She came and went, moving in an orbit for which I had no data, going to London and Paris, into Wales and Northampton, while her step-mother, on some independent system of her own, also vanished and recurred intermittently. At home they obeyed the rule of an inflexible old maid, Charlotte, and Beatrice exercised all the rights of proprietorship in Carnaby's extensive stables. Her interest in me was from the first undisguised. She found her way to my worksheds and developed rapidly, in spite of the sincere discouragement of Cothope, into a keen amateur of aeronautics. She would come sometimes in the morning, sometimes in the afternoon, sometimes afoot with an Irish terrier, sometimes riding. She would come for three or four days every day, vanish for a fortnight or three weeks, return.

It was not long before I came to look for her. From the first I found her immensely interesting. To me she was a new feminine type altogether—I have made it plain, I think, how limited was my knowledge of women. But she made me not simply interested in her, but in myself. She became for me something that greatly changes a man's world. How shall I put it? She became an audience. Since I've emerged from the emotional developments of the affair I have thought it out in a hundred aspects, and it does seem to me that this way in which men and women make audiences for one another is a curiously influential force in their lives. For some it seems an audience is a vital necessity, they seek audiences as creatures seek food; others again, my uncle among them, can play to an imaginary audience. I, I think, have lived and can live without one. In my adolescence I was my own audience and my own court of honour. And to have an audience in one's mind is to play a part, to become self-conscious and dramatic. For many years I had been self-forgetful and scientific. I had lived for work and impersonal interests until I found scrutiny, applause and expectation in Beatrice's eyes. Then I began to live for the effect I imagined I made upon her, to make that very soon the principal value in my life. I played to her. I did things for the look of them. I began to dream more and more of beautiful situations and fine poses and groupings with her and for her.

I put these things down because they puzzle me. I think I was in love with Beatrice, as being in love is usually understood; but it was quite a different state altogether from my passionate hunger for Marion, or my keen, sensuous desire for and pleasure in Effie. These were selfish, sincere things, fundamental and instinctive, as sincere as the leap of a tiger. But until matters drew to a crisis with Beatrice, there was an immense imaginative insurgence of a quite different quality. I am setting down here very gravely, and perhaps absurdly, what are no doubt elementary commonplaces for innumerable people. This love that grew up between Beatrice and myself was, I think—I put it quite tentatively and rather curiously—romantic love. That unfortunate and truncated affair of my uncle and the Scrymgeour lady was really of the same stuff, if a little different in quality. I have to admit that. The factor of audience was of primary importance in either case.

Its effect upon me was to make me in many respects adolescent again. It made me keener upon the point of honour, and anxious and eager to do high and splendid things, and in particular, brave things. So far it ennobled and upheld me. But it did also push me towards vulgar and showy things. At bottom it was disingenuous; it gave my life the quality of stage scenery, with one side to the audience, another side that wasn't meant to show, and an economy of substance. It certainly robbed my work of high patience and quality. I cut down the toil of research in my eagerness and her eagerness for fine flourishes in the air, flights that would tell. I shirked the longer road.

And it robbed me, too, of any fine perception of absurdity. . . .

Yet that was not everything in our relationship. The elemental thing was there also. It came in very suddenly.

It was one day in the summer, though I do not now recall without reference to my experimental memoranda whether it was in July or August. I was working with a new and more bird-like aeroplane with wing curvatures studied from Lilienthal, Pilcher and Phillips, that I thought would give a different rhythm for the pitching oscillations than anything I'd had before. I was soaring my long course from the framework on the old barrow by my sheds down to Tinker's Corner. It is a clear stretch of downland, except for two or three thickets of box and thorn to the right of my course; one transverse trough, in which there is bush and a small rabbit warren, comes in from the east. I had started, and was very intent on the peculiar long swoop with which my new arrangement flew. Then, without any sort of notice, right ahead of me appeared Beatrice, riding towards Tinker's Corner to waylay and talk to me. She looked round over her shoulder, saw me coming, touched her horse to a gallop, and then the brute bolted right into the path of my machine.

There was a queer moment of doubt whether we shouldn't all smash together. I had to make up my mind very quickly whether I would pitch-up and drop backward at once and take my chance of falling undamaged—a poor chance it would have been—in order to avoid any risk to her, or whether I would lift against the wind and soar right over her. This latter I did. She had already got her horse in hand when I came up to her. Her woman's body lay along his neck, and she glanced up as I, with wings aspread, and every nerve in a state of tension, swept over her.

Then I had landed, and was going back to where her horse stood still and trembling.

We exchanged no greetings. She slid from her saddle into

,ny arms, and for one instant I held her. "Those great wings," she said, and that was all.

She lay in my arms, and I thought for a moment she had fainted.

"Very near a nasty accident," said Cothope, coming up and regarding our grouping with disfavour. He took her horse by the bridle. "Very dangerous thing coming across us like that."

Beatrice disengaged herself from me, stood for a moment trembling, and then sat down on the turf. "I'll just sit down for a moment," she said.

"Oh!" she said.

She covered her face with her hands, while Cothope looked at her with an expression between suspicion and impatience.

For some moments nobody moved. Then Cothope remarked that perhaps he'd better get her water.

As for me, I was filled with a new outrageous idea, begotten I scarcely know how from this incident, with its instant contacts and swift emotions, and that was that I must make love to and possess Beatrice. I see no particular reason why that thought should have come to me in that moment, but it did. I do not believe that before then I had thought of our relations in such terms at all. Suddenly, as I remember it, the factor of passion came. She crouched there, and I stood over her, and neither of us said a word. But it was just as though something had been shouted from the sky.

Cothope had gone twenty paces perhaps when she uncovered her face. "I shan't want any water," she said. "Call him back."

VI

After that the spirit of our relations changed. The old ease had gone. She came to me less frequently, and when she came she would have some one with her, usually old Carnaby, and he would do the bulk of the talking. All through September she was away. When we were alone together there was a curious constraint. We became clouds

[304]

of inexpressible feeling towards one another; we could think of nothing that was not too momentous for words.

Then came the smash of Lord Roberts α, and I found myself with a bandaged face in a bedroom in the Bedley Corner dower-house with Beatrice presiding over an inefficient nurse, Lady Osprey very pink and shocked in the background, and my aunt jealously intervening.

My injuries were much more showy than serious, and I could have been taken to Lady Grove next day, but Beatrice would not permit that, and kept me at Bedley Corner three clear days. In the afternoon of the second day she became extremely solicitous for the proper aeration of the nurse, packed her off for an hour in a brisk rain, and sat by me alone.

I asked her to marry me.

On the whole I must admit it was not a situation that lent itself to eloquence. I lay on my back and talked through bandages, and with some little difficulty, for my tongue and mouth had swollen. But I was feverish and in pain, and the emotional suspense I had been in so long with regard to her became now an unendurable impatience.

"Comfortable?" she asked.

"Yes."

"Shall I read to you?"

"No. I want to talk."

"You can't. I'd better talk to you."

"No," I said, "I want to talk to you."

She came and stood by my bedside and looked me in the eyes. "I don't—I don't want you to talk to me," she said. "I thought you couldn't talk."

"I get few chances—of you."

"You'd better not talk. Don't talk now. Let me chatter instead. You ought not to talk."

"It isn't much," I said.

"I'd rather you didn't."

"I'm not going to be disfigured," I said. "Only a scar."

"Oh!" she said, as if she had expected something quite different. "Did you think you'd become a sort of gargoyle?"

[305]

"L'Homme qui Rit!—I didn't know. But that's all right. Jolly flowers those are!"

"Michaelmas daisies," she said. "I'm glad you're not disfigured. And those are perennial sunflowers. Do you know no flowers at all? When I saw you on the ground I certainly thought you were dead. You ought to have been, by all the rules of the game."

She said some other things, but I was thinking of my next move.

"Are we social equals?" I said abruptly.

She stared at me. "Queer question," she said.

"But are we?"

"H'm. Difficult to say. But why do you ask? Is the daughter of a courtesy Baron who died—of general disreputableness, I believe—before his father——? I give it up. Does it matter?"

"No. My mind is confused. I want to know if you will marry me."

She whitened and said nothing. I suddenly felt I must plead with her. "Damn these bandages!" I said, breaking into ineffectual febrile rage.

She roused herself to her duties as nurse. "What are you doing? Why are you trying to sit up? Sit down! Don't touch your bandages. I told you not to talk."

She stood helpless for a moment, then took me firmly by the shoulders and pushed me back upon the pillow. She gripped the wrist of the hand I had raised to my face.

"I told you not to talk," she whispered close to my face. "I asked you not to talk. Why couldn't you do as I asked you?"

"You've been avoiding me for a month," I said.

'I know. You might have known. Put your hand back—down by your side."

I obeyed. She sat on the edge of the bed. A flush had come to her cheeks, and her eyes were very bright. "I asked you," she repeated, "not to talk."

My eyes questioned her mutely.

She put her hand on my chest. Her eyes were tormented.

"How can I answer you now?" she said. "How *can* I say anything now?"

"What do you mean?" I asked.

She made no answer.

"Do you mean it must be 'No'?"

She nodded.

"But——" I said, and my whole soul was full of accusations.

"I know," she said. "I can't explain. I can't. But it has to be 'No!' It can't be. It's utterly, finally, for ever impossible. . . . Keep your hands still!"

"But," I said, "when we met again——"

"I can't marry. I can't and won't."

She stood up. "Why did you talk?" she cried. "Couldn't you *see*?"

She seemed to have something it was impossible to say.

She came to the table beside my bed and pulled the Michaelmas daisies awry. "Why did you talk like that?" she said in a tone of infinite bitterness. "To begin like that——!"

"But what is it?" I said. "Is it some circumstance—my social position?"

"Oh, *damn* your social position!" she cried.

She went and stood at the further window, staring out at the rain. For a long time we were absolutely still. The wind and rain came in little gusts upon the pane. She turned to me abruptly.

"You didn't ask me if I loved you," she said.

"Oh, if it's *that*!" said I.

"It's not that," she said. "But if you want to know——" She paused.

"I do," she said.

We stared at one another.

"I do—with all my heart, if you want to know."

"Then, why the devil——?" I asked.

She made no answer. She walked across the room to the piano and began to play, rather noisily and rapidly, with odd gusts of emphasis, the shepherd's pipe music from the

[307]

last act in "Tristan and Isolde." Presently she missed a note, failed again, ran her finger heavily up the scale, struck the piano passionately with her fist, making a feeble jar in the treble, jumped up, and went out of the room. . . .

The nurse found me still wearing my helmet of bandages, partially dressed, and pottering round the room to find the rest of my clothes. I was in a state of exasperated hunger for Beatrice, and I was too inflamed and weakened to conceal the state of my mind. I was feebly angry because of the irritation of dressing, and particularly of the struggle to put on my trousers without being able to see my legs. I was staggering about, and once I had fallen over a chair, and I had upset the jar of Michaelmas daisies.

I must have been a detestable spectacle. "I'll go back to bed," said I, "if I may have a word with Miss Beatrice. I've got something to say to her. That's why I'm dressing."

My point was conceded, but there were long delays. Whether the household had my ultimatum or whether she told Beatrice directly I do not know, and what Lady Osprey can have made of it in the former case I don't imagine. . . .

At last Beatrice came and stood by my bedside. "Well?" she said.

"All I want to say," I said with the querulous note of a misunderstood child, "is that I can't take this as final. I want to see you and talk when I'm better—and write. I can't do anything now. I can't argue."

I was overtaken with self-pity and began to snivel.

"I can't rest. You see? I can't do anything."

She sat down beside me again and spoke softly. "I promise I will talk it all over with you again. When you are well. I promise I will meet you somewhere so that we can talk. You can't talk now. I asked you not to talk now. All you want to know you shall know. . . . Will that do?"

"I'd like to know——"

She looked round to see the door was closed, stood up and went to it.

Then she crouched beside me and began whispering very

softly and rapidly with her face close to me.

"Dear," she said, "I love you. If it will make you happy to marry me, I will marry you. I was in a mood just now—a stupid, inconsiderate mood. Of course I will marry you. You are my prince, my king. Women are such things of mood—or I would have—behaved differently. We say 'No' when we mean 'Yes'—and fly into crises. So now, Yes—yes—yes. I will. . . . I can't even kiss you. Give me your hand to kiss that. Understand, I am yours. Do you understand? I am yours just as if we had been married fifty years. Your wife—Beatrice. Is that enough? Now—now will you rest?"

"Yes," I said, "but why——?"

"There are complications. There are difficulties. When you are better you will be able to—understand them. But now they don't matter. Only you know this must be secret —for a time. Absolutely secret between us. Will you promise that?"

"Yes," I said, "I understand. I wish I could kiss you."

She laid her head down beside mine for a moment, and then she kissed my hand.

"I don't care what difficulties there are," I said, and shut my eyes.

VII

But I was only beginning to gauge the unaccountable elements in Beatrice. For a week after my return to Lady Grove I had no sign of her, and then she called with Lady Osprey and brought a huge bunch of perennial sunflowers and Michaelmas daisies, "just the old flowers there were in your room," said my aunt, with a relentless eye on me. I didn't get any talk alone with Beatrice then, and she took occasion to tell us she was going to London for some indefinite number of weeks. I couldn't even pledge her to write to me, and when she did it was a brief, enigmatical, friendly letter with not a word of the reality between us.

I wrote back a love letter—my first love letter—and she made no reply for eight days. Then came a scrawl: "I can't write letters. Wait till we can talk. Are you better?" . . .

I think the reader would be amused if he could see the papers on my desk as I write all this, the mangled and disfigured pages, the experimental arrangements of notes, the sheets of suggestions balanced in constellations, the blottesque intellectual battlegrounds over which I have been fighting. I find this account of my relations to Beatrice quite the most difficult part of my story to write. I happen to be a very objective-minded person, I forget my moods, and this was so much an affair of moods. And even such moods and emotions as I recall are very difficult to convey. To me it is about as difficult as describing a taste or a scent.

Then the objective story is made up of little things that are difficult to set in a proper order. And love is an hysterical passion, now high, now low, now exalted, and now intensely physical. No one has ever yet dared to tell a love story completely, its alternations, its comings and goings, its debased moments, its hate. The love stories we tell, tell only the net consequence, the ruling effect. . . .

How can I rescue from the past now the mystical quality of Beatrice; my intense longing for her; the overwhelming, irrational, formless desire? How can I explain how intimately that worship mingled with a high, impatient resolve to make her mine, to take her by strength and courage, to do my loving in a violent heroic manner? And then the doubts, the puzzled arrest at the fact of her fluctuations, at her refusal to marry me, at the fact that even when at last she returned to Bedley Corner she seemed to evade me?

That exasperated me and perplexed me beyond measure. I felt that it was treachery. I thought of every conceivable explanation, and the most exalted and romantic confidence in her did not simply alternate, but mingled with the basest misgivings.

And into the tangle of memories comes the figure of Carnaby, coming out slowly from the background to a position of significance, as an influence, as a predominant strand in the nets that kept us apart, as a rival. What were the forces that pulled her away from me when it was so clearly manifest she loved me? Did she think of marrying him? Had I invaded some long-planned scheme? It was evident he did not like me, that in some way I spoilt the world for him. She returned to Bedley Corner, and for some weeks she was flitting about me, and never once could I have talk with her alone. When she came to my sheds Carnaby was always with her, jealously observant. (Why the devil couldn't she send him about his business?) The days slipped by and my anger gathered.

All this mingles with the making of Lord Roberts β. I had resolved upon that one night as I lay awake at Bedley Corner; I got it planned out before the bandages were off my face. I conceived this second navigable balloon in a grandiose manner. It was to be a second Lord Roberts α, only more so; it was to be three times as big, large enough to carry three men, and it was to be an altogether triumphant vindication of my claims upon the air. The framework was to be hollow like a bird's bones, airtight, and the air pumped in or out, as the weight of fuel I carried changed. I talked much and boasted to Cothope—whom I suspected of scepticisms about this new type—of what it would do, and it progressed—slowly. It progressed slowly because I was restless and uncertain. At times I would go away to London to snatch some chance of seeing Beatrice there, at times nothing but a day of gliding and hard and dangerous exercise would satisfy me. And now in the newspapers, in conversation, in everything about me, arose a new invader of my mental states. Something was happening to the great schemes of my uncle's affairs; people were beginning to doubt, to question. It was the first quiver of his tremendous insecurity, the first wobble of that gigantic credit top he had kept spinning so long.

There were comings and goings, November and December slipped by. I had two unsatisfactory meetings with Beatrice, meetings that had no privacy—in which we said things of the sort that need atmosphere, baldly and furtively. I wrote to her several times and she wrote back notes that I would sometimes respond to altogether, sometimes condemn as insincere evasions. "You don't understand. I can't just now explain. Be patient with me. Leave things a little while to me." So she wrote.

I would talk aloud to these notes and wrangle over them in my workroom—while the plans of Lord Roberts β waited.

"You don't give me a chance!" I would say. "Why don't you let me know the secret? That's what I'm for—to settle difficulties!—to tell difficulties to!"

And at last I could hold out no longer against these accumulating pressures.

I took an arrogant, outrageous line that left her no loopholes; I behaved as though we were living in a melodrama.

"You must come and talk to me," I wrote, "or I will come and take you. I want you—and the time runs away."

We met in a ride in the upper plantations. It must have been early in January, for there was snow on the ground and on the branches of the trees. We walked to and fro for an hour or more, and from the first I pitched the key high in romance and made understandings impossible. It was our worst time together. I boasted like an actor, and she, I know not why, was tired and spiritless.

Now I think over that talk in the light of all that has happened since, I can imagine how she came to me full of a human appeal I was too foolish to let her make. I don't know. I confess I have never completely understood Beatrice. I confess I am still perplexed at many things she said and did. That afternoon, anyhow, I was impossible. I posed and scolded. I was—I said it—for "taking the Universe by the throat!"

"If it was only that," she said, but though I heard, I did not heed her.

At last she gave way to me and talked no more. Instead she looked at me—as a thing beyond her controlling, but none the less interesting—much as she had looked at me from behind the skirts of Lady Drew in the Warren when we were children together. Once even I thought she smiled faintly.

"What are the difficulties?" I cried. "There's no difficulty I will not overcome for you! Do your people think I'm no equal for you? Who says it? My dear, tell me to win a title! I'll do it in five years! . . .

"Here am I just grown a man at the sight of you. I have wanted something to fight for. Let me fight for you! . . .

"I'm rich without intending it. Let me mean it, give me an honourable excuse for it, and I'll put all this rotten old warren of England at your feet!"

I said such things as that. I write them down here in all their resounding base pride. I said these empty and foolish things, and they are part of me. Why should I still cling to pride and be ashamed? I shouted her down.

I passed from such megalomania to petty accusations.

"You think Carnaby is a better man than I?" I said.

"No!" she cried, stung to speech. "No!"

"You think we're unsubstantial. You've listened to all these rumours Boom has started because we talked of a newspaper of our own. When you are with me you know I'm a man; when you get away from me you think I'm a cheat and a cad. . . . There's not a word of truth in the things they say about us. I've been slack. I've left things. But we have only to exert ourselves. You do not know how wide and far we have spread our nets. Even now we have a coup—an expedition—in hand. It will put us on a footing." . . .

Her eyes asked mutely and asked in vain that I would cease to boast of the very qualities she admired in me.

In the night I could not sleep for thinking of that talk and the vulgar things I had said in it. I could not understand the drift my mind had taken. I was acutely disgusted. And my unwonted doubts about myself spread from a merely personal discontent to our financial position. It was all very well to talk as I had done of wealth and power and peerages, but what did I know nowadays of my uncle's position? Suppose in the midst of such boasting and confidence there came some turn I did not suspect, some rottenness he had concealed from me? I resolved I had been playing with aeronautics long enough; that next morning I would go to him and have things clear between us.

I caught an early train and went up to the Hardingham.

I went up to the Hardingham through a dense London fog to see how things really stood. Before I had talked to my uncle for ten minutes I felt like a man who has just awakened in a bleak, inhospitable room out of a grandiose dream.

CHAPTER THE FOURTH

How I Stole the Heaps of Quap from Mordet Island

I

"WE got to make a fight for it," said my uncle. "We got to face the music!"

I remember that even at the sight of him I had a sense of impending calamity. He sat under the electric light with the shadow of his hair making bars down his face. He looked shrunken, and as though his skin had suddenly got loose and yellow. The decorations of the room seemed to have lost freshness, and outside—the blinds were up—there was not so much fog as a dun darkness. One saw the dingy outlines of the chimneys opposite quite distinctly, and then a sky of such a brown as only London can display.

"I saw a placard," I said: " 'More Ponderevity.' "

"That's Boom," he said. "Boom and his damned newspapers. He's trying to fight me down. Ever since I offered to buy the *Daily Decorator* he's been at me. And he thinks consolidating Do Ut cut down the ads. He wants everything, damn him! He's got no sense of dealing. I'd like to bash his face!"

"Well," I said, "what's to be done?"

"Keep going," said my uncle.

"I'll smash Boom yet," he said, with sudden savagery.

"Nothing else?" I asked.

"We got to keep going. There's a scare on. Did you notice the rooms? Half the people out there this morning are reporters. And if I talk they touch it up! . . . They didn't used to touch things up! Now they put in character touches —insulting you. Don't know what journalism's coming to. It's all Boom's doing."

He cursed Lord Boom with considerable imaginative vigour.

"Well," said I, "what can he do?"

"Shove us up against time, George; make money tight for us. We been handling a lot of money—and he tightens us up."

"We're sound?"

"Oh, we're sound, George. Trust me for that! But all the same—— There's such a lot of imagination in these things. . . . We're sound enough. That's not it."

He blew. "Damn Boom!" he said, and his eyes over his glasses met mine defiantly.

"We can't, I suppose, run close hauled for a bit—stop expenditure?"

"Where?"

"Well,—Crest Hill."

"What!" he shouted. "Me stop Crest Hill for Boom!" He waved a fist as if to hit his inkpot, and controlled himself with difficulty. He spoke at last in a reasonable voice. "If I did," he said, "he'd kick up a fuss. It's no good, even if I wanted to. Everybody's watching the place. If I was to stop building we'd be down in a week."

He had an idea. "I wish I could do something to start a strike or something. No such luck. Treat those workmen a sight too well. No, sink or swim, Crest Hill goes on until we're under water."

I began to ask questions and irritated him instantly.

"Oh, dash these explanations, George!" he cried; "you only make things look rottener than they are. It's your way. It isn't a case of figures. We're all right—there's only one thing we got to do."

"Yes?"

[315]

"Show value, George. That's where this quap comes in; that's why I fell in so readily with what you brought to me week before last. Here we are, we got our option on the perfect filament, and all we want's canadium. Nobody knows there's more canadium in the world than will go on the edge of a sixpence except me and you. Nobody has an idee the perfect filament's more than just a bit of theorising. Fifty tons of quap and we'd turn that bit of theorising into somethin'—— We'd make the lamp trade sit on its tail and howl. We'd put Ediswan and all of 'em into a parcel with our last year's trousers and a hat, and swap 'em off for a pot of geraniums. See? We'd do it through Business Organisations, and there you are! See? Capern's Patent Filament! The Ideal and the Real! George, we'll do it! We'll bring it off! And then we'll give such a facer to Boom, he'll think for fifty years. He's laying up for our London and African meeting. Let him. He can turn the whole paper on to us. He says the Business Organisations shares aren't worth fifty-two—and we quote 'em at eighty-four. Well, here we are. Gettin' ready for him—loading our gun."

His pose was triumphant.

"Yes," I said, "that's all right. But I can't help thinking where should we be if we hadn't just by accident got Capern's Perfect Filament. Because, you know it was an accident—my buying up that."

He crumpled up his nose into an expression of impatient distaste at my unreasonableness.

"And after all, the meeting's in June, and you haven't begun to get the quap! After all, we've still got to load our gun——"

"They start on Toosday."

"Have they got the brig?"

"They've got a brig."

"Gordon-Nasmyth!" I doubted.

"Safe as a bank," he said. "More I see of that man the more I like him. All I wish is we'd got a steamer instead of a sailing ship——"

"And," I went on, "you seem to overlook what used to

[316]

weigh with us a bit. This canadium side of the business and the Capern chance has rushed you off your legs. After all— it's stealing, and in its way an international outrage. They've got two gunboats on the coast."

I jumped up and went and stared out at the fog.

"And, by Jove, it's about our only chance! . . . I didn't dream."

I turned on him. "I've been up in the air," I said. "Heaven knows where I haven't been. And here's our only chance—and you give it to that adventurous lunatic to play in his own way—in a brig!"

"Well, you had a voice——"

"I wish I'd been in this before. We ought to have run out a steamer to Lagos or one of those West Coast places and done it from there. Fancy a brig in the Channel at this time of year, if it blows southwest!"

"I dessay you'd have shoved it, George. Still—— You know, George. . . . I believe in him."

"Yes," I said. "Yes, I believe in him, too. In a way. Still——"

He took up a telegram that was lying on his desk and opened it. His face became a livid yellow. He put the flimsy paper down with a slow, reluctant movement and took off his glasses.

"George," he said, "the luck's against us."

"What?"

He grimaced with his mouth in the queerest way at the telegram.

"That."

I took it up and read:

"Motor smash compound fracture of the leg gordon nai-smith what price mordet now"

For a moment neither of us spoke.

"That's all right," I said at last.

"Eh?" said my uncle.

"*I'm* going. I'll get that quap or bust."

[317]

II

I had a ridiculous persuasion that I was "saving the situation."

"I'm going," I said quite consciously and dramatically. I saw the whole affair—how shall I put it?—in American colours.

I sat down beside him. "Give me all the data you've got," I said, "and I'll pull this thing off."

"But nobody knows exactly where——"

"Nasmyth does, and he'll tell me."

"He's been very close," said my uncle, and regarded me. "He'll tell me all right, now he's smashed."

He thought. "I believe he will."

"George," he said, "if you pull this thing off——! Once or twice before you've stepped in—with that sort of Woosh of yours——"

He left the sentence unfinished.

"Give me that note-book," I said, "and tell me all you know. Where's the ship? Where's Pollack? And where's that telegram from? If that quap's to be got, I'll get it or bust. If you'll hold on here until I get back with it." . . .

And so it was I jumped into the wildest adventure of my life.

I requisitioned my uncle's best car forthwith. I went down that night to the place of despatch named on Nasmyth's telegram, Bampton S.O. Oxon, routed him out with a little trouble from that centre, made things right with him and got his explicit directions; and I was inspecting the *Maud Mary* with young Pollack, his cousin and aide, the following afternoon. She was rather a shock to me and not at all in my style, a beast of a brig inured to the potato trade, and she reeked from end to end with the faint, subtle smell of raw potatoes so that it prevailed even over the temporary smell of new paint. She was a beast of a brig, all hold and dirty framework, and they had ballasted her with old iron and old rails and iron sleepers, and got a miscellaneous lot of spades and iron wheelbarrows against the loading of the quap. I thought her over with Pollack, one of those tall blond young men who smoke pipes and don't help much, and then by myself, and as a result I did my best to sweep Gravesend clean of wheeling planks, and got in as much cord and small rope as I could for lashing. I had an idea we might need to run up a jetty. In addition to much ballast she held, remotely hidden in a sort of inadvertent way, a certain number of ambiguous cases which I didn't examine, but which I gathered were a provision against the need of a trade.

The captain was a most extraordinary creature, under the impression we were after copper ore; he was a Roumanian Jew, with twitching, excitable features, who had made his way to a certificate after some preliminary naval experiences in the Black Sea. The mate was an Essex man of impenetrable reserve. The crew were astoundingly ill-clad and destitute and dirty; most of them youths, unwashed, out of colliers. One, the cook, was a mulatto; and one, the best-built fellow of them all, was a Breton. There was some subterfuge about our position on board—I forget the particulars now—I was called the supercargo and Pollack was the steward. This added to the piratical flavour that insufficient funds and Gordon-Nasmyth's original genius had already given the enterprise.

Those two days of bustle at Gravesend, under dingy skies, in narrow, dirty streets, were a new experience for me. It is like nothing else in my life. I realised that I was a modern and a civilised man. I found the food filthy and the coffee horrible; the whole town stank in my nostrils, the landlord of the Good Intent on the quay had a stand-up quarrel with us before I could get even a hot bath, and the bedroom I slept in was infested by a quantity of exotic but voracious flat parasites called locally "bugs," in the walls, in the woodwork, everywhere. I fought them with insect powder, and found them comatose in the morning. I was dipping down into the dingy underworld of the contemporary state, and I liked it no better than I did my first dip into it when I stayed with my Uncle Nicodemus Frapp at the bakery at Chatham—where, by-the-by, we had to deal with cockroaches of a smaller, darker variety, and also with bugs of sorts.

Let me confess that through all this time before we started I was immensely self-conscious, and that Beatrice played the part of audience in my imagination throughout. I was, as I say, "saving the situation," and I was acutely aware of that. The evening before we sailed, instead of revising our medicine-chest as I had intended, I took the car and ran across country to Lady Grove to tell my aunt of the journey I was making, dress, and astonish Lady Osprey by an after-dinner call.

The two ladies were at home and alone beside a big fire that seemed wonderfully cheerful after the winter night. I remember the effect of the little parlour in which they sat as very bright and domestic. Lady Osprey, in a costume of mauve and lace, sat on a chintz sofa and played an elaborately spread-out patience by the light of a tall shaded lamp; Beatrice, in a white dress that showed her throat, smoked a cigarette in an armchair and read with a lamp at her elbow. The room was white-panelled and chintz-curtained. About those two bright centres of light were warm dark shadows in which a circular mirror shone like a pool of brown water. I carried off my raid by behaving like a slave of etiquette. There were moments when I think I really made Lady Osprey believe that my call was an unavoidable necessity, that it would have been negligent of me not to call just how and when I did. But at the best those were transitory moments.

They received me with disciplined amazement. Lady Osprey was interested in my face and scrutinised the scar. Beatrice stood behind her solicitude. Our eyes met, and in hers I could see startled interrogations.

"I'm going," I said, "to the west coast of Africa."

They asked questions, but it suited my mood to be vague.

"We've interests there. It is urgent I should go. I don't know when I may return."

After that I perceived Beatrice surveyed me steadily.

The conversation was rather difficult. I embarked upon lengthy thanks for their kindness to me after my accident. I tried to understand Lady Osprey's game of patience, but it didn't appear that Lady Osprey was anxious for me to understand her patience. I came to the verge of taking my leave.

"You needn't go yet," said Beatrice, abruptly.

She walked across to the piano, took a pile of music from the cabinet near, surveyed Lady Osprey's back, and with a gesture to me dropped it all deliberately on to the floor.

"Must talk," she said, kneeling close to me as I helped her to pick it up. "Turn my pages. At the piano."

"I can't read music."

"Turn my pages."

Presently we were at the piano, and Beatrice was playing with noisy inaccuracy. She glanced over her shoulder and Lady Osprey had resumed her patience. The old lady was very pink, and appeared to be absorbed in some attempt to cheat herself without our observing it.

"Isn't West Africa a vile climate?" "Are you going to live there?" "Why are you going?"

Beatrice asked these questions in a low voice and gave me no chance to answer. Then taking a rhythm from the music before her, she said—

"At the back of the house is a garden—a door in the wall—on the lane. Understand?"

I turned over the pages without any effect on her playing.

"When?" I asked.

She dealt in chords. "I wish I *could* play this!" she said "Midnight."

She gave her attention to the music for a time.

"You may have to wait."

"I'll wait."

She brought her playing to an end by—as schoolboys say—"stashing it up."

"I can't play to-night," she said, standing up and meeting my eyes. "I wanted to give you a parting voluntary."

"Was that Wagner, Beatrice?" asked Lady Osprey, looking up from her cards. "It sounded very confused." . . .

I took my leave. I had a curious twinge of conscience as I parted from Lady Osprey. Either a first intimation of middle-age or my inexperience in romantic affairs was to blame, but I felt a very distinct objection to the prospect of invading this good lady's premises from the garden door. I motored up to the pavilion, found Cothope reading in bed, told him for the first time of West Africa, spent an hour with him in settling all the outstanding details of Lord Roberts β, and left that in his hands to finish against my return. I sent the motor back to Lady Grove, and still wearing my fur coat—for the January night was damp and bitterly cold—walked to Bedley Corner. I found the lane to the back of the Dower House without any difficulty, and was at the door in the wall with ten minutes to spare. I lit a cigar and fell to walking up and down. This queer flavour of intrigue, this nocturnal garden-door business, had taken me by surprise and changed my mental altitudes. I was startled out of my egotistical pose and thinking intently of Beatrice, of that elfin quality in her that always pleased me, that always took me by surprise, that had made her for example so instantly conceive this meeting.

She came within a minute of midnight; the door opened softly and she appeared, a short, grey figure in a motor-coat of sheepskin, bareheaded to the cold drizzle. She flitted up to me, and her eyes were shadows in her dusky face.

"Why are you going to West Africa?" she asked at once.

"Business crisis. I have to go."

"You're not going——? You're coming back?"

"Three or four months," I said, "at most."

"Then, it's nothing to do with me?"

"Nothing," I said. "Why should it have?"

"Oh, that's all right. One never knows what people think or what people fancy." She took me by the arm. Let's go for a walk," she said.

I looked about me at darkness and rain.

"That's all right," she laughed. "We can go along the

lane and into the Old Woking Road. Do you mind? Of course you don't. My head. It doesn't matter. One never meets anybody."

"How do you know?"

"I've wandered like this before. . . . Of course. Did you think"—she nodded her head back at her home—"that's all?"

"No, by Jove!" I cried; "it's manifest it isn't."

She took my arm and turned me down the lane. "Night's my time," she said by my side. "There's a touch of the werewolf in my blood. One never knows in these old families. . . . I've wondered often. . . . Here we are, anyhow, alone in the world. Just darkness and cold and a sky of clouds and wet. And we—together. I like the wet on my face and hair, don't you? When do you sail?"

I told her to-morrow.

"Oh, well, there's no to-morrow now. You and I!" She stopped and confronted me.

"You don't say a word except to answer!"

"No," I said.

"Last time you did all the talking."

"Like a fool. Now——"

We looked at each other's two dim faces. "You're glad to be here?"

"I'm glad—I'm beginning to be—it's more than glad."

She put her hands on my shoulders and drew me down to kiss her.

"Ah!" she said, and for a moment or so we just clung to one another.

"That's all," she said, releasing herself. "What bundles of clothes we are to-night. I felt we should kiss some day again. Always. The last time was ages ago."

"Among the fern stalks."

"Among the bracken. You remember. And your lips were cold. Were mine? The same lips—after so long—after so much! . . . And now let's trudge through this blotted-out world together for a time. Yes, let me take your arm. Just trudge, see? Hold tight to me because I know the way—and don't talk—don't talk. Unless you want to talk. . . . Let me tell you things! You see, dear, the whole world *is* blotted out—it's dead and gone, and we're in this place. This dark wild place. . . . We're dead. Or all the world is dead. No! We're dead. No one can see us. We're shadows. We've got out of our positions, out of our bodies—and together. That's the good thing of it—together. But that's why the world can't see us and why we hardly see the world. Sssh! Is it all right?"

"It's all right," I said.

We stumbled along for a time in a close silence. We passed a dim-lit, rain-veiled window.

"The silly world," she said, "the silly world! It eats and sleeps. If the wet didn't patter so from the trees we'd hear it snoring. It's dreaming such stupid things—stupid judgments. It doesn't know we are passing, we two—free of it—clear of it. You and I!"

We pressed against each other reassuringly.

"I'm glad we're dead," she whispered. "I'm glad we're dead. I was tired of it, dear. I was so tired of it, dear, and so entangled."

She stopped abruptly.

We splashed through a string of puddles. I began to remember things I had meant to say.

"Look here!" I cried. "I want to help you beyond measure. You are entangled. What is the trouble? I asked you to marry me. You said you would. But there's something."

My thoughts sounded clumsy as I said them.

"Is it something about my position? . . . Or is it something—perhaps—about some other man?"

There was an immense assenting silence.

"You've puzzled me so. At first—I mean quite early—I thought you meant to make me marry you."

"I did."

"And then——?"

"To-night," she said after a long pause, "I can't explain. No! I can't explain. I love you! But—explanations! To-night—— My dear, here we are in the world alone—and the world doesn't matter. Nothing matters. Here I am in the cold with you—and my bed away there deserted. I'd tell you—— I *will* tell you when things enable me to tell you, and soon enough they will. But to-night—— I won't. I won't."

She left my side and went in front of me.

She turned upon me. "Look here," she said, "I insist upon your being dead. Do you understand? I'm not joking. To-night you and I are out of life. It's our time together. There may be other times, but this we won't spoil. We're— in Hades if you like. Where there's nothing to hide and nothing to tell. No bodies even. No bothers. We loved each other—down there—and were kept apart, but now it doesn't matter. It's over. . . . If you won't agree to that— I will go home."

"I wanted," I began.

"I know. Oh! my dear, if you'd only understand I understand. If you'd only not care—and love me to-night."

"I do love you," I said.

"Then *love* me," she answered, "and leave all these things that bother you. Love me! Here I am!"

"But——!"

"No!" she said.

"Well, have your way."

So she carried her point, and we wandered into the night together and Beatrice talked to me of love. . . .

I'd never heard a woman before in all my life who could talk of love, who could lay bare and develop and touch with imagination all that mass of fine emotion every woman, it may be, hides. She had read of love, she had thought of love, a thousand sweet lyrics had sounded through her brain and left fine fragments in her memory; she poured it out, all of it, shamelessly, skilfully, for me. I cannot give any sense of that talk, I cannot even tell how much of the delight of it was the magic of her voice, the glow of her near presence. And always we walked swathed warmly through a chilly air, along dim, interminable greasy roads—with never a soul abroad it seemed to us, never a beast in the fields.

"Why do people love each other?" I said.

"Why not?"

"But why do I love you? Why is your voice better than any voice, your face sweeter than any face?"

"And why do I love you?" she asked; "not only what is fine in you, but what isn't? Why do I love your dullness, your arrogance? For I do. To-night I love the very rain-drops on the fur of your coat!" . . . .

So we talked; and at last very wet, still glowing but a little tired, we parted at the garden door. We had been wandering for two hours in our strange irrational community of happiness, and all the world about us, and particularly Lady Osprey and her household, had been asleep—and dreaming of anything rather than Beatrice in the night and rain.

She stood in the doorway a muffled figure with eyes that glowed.

"Come back," she whispered. "I shall wait for you."

She hesitated.

She touched the lapel of my coat. "I love you *now*," she said, and lifted her face to mine.

I held her to me and was atremble from top to toe. "O God!" I cried. "And I must go!"

She slipped from my arms and paused, regarding me. For an instant the world seemed full of fantastic possibilities.

"Yes, *go!*" she said, and vanished and slammed the door upon me, leaving me alone like a man new fallen from fairyland in the black darkness of the night.

III

That expedition to Mordet Island stands apart from all the rest of my life, detached, a piece by itself with an atmosphere of its own. It would, I suppose, make a book by itself—it has made a fairly voluminous official report—but so far as this novel of mine goes it is merely an episode, a contributory experience, and I mean to keep it at that.

Vile weather, an impatient fretting against unbearable slowness and delay, sea-sickness, general discomfort and humiliating self-revelation are the master values of these memories.

I was sick all through the journey out. I don't know why. It was the only time I was ever sea-sick, and I have seen some pretty bad weather since I became a boat-builder. But that phantom smell of potatoes was peculiarly vile to me. Coming back on the brig we were all ill, every one of us, so soon as we got to sea, poisoned, I firmly believe, by quap. On the way out most of the others recovered in a few days, but the stuffiness below, the coarse food, the cramped dirty accommodation kept me, if not actually sea-sick, in a state of acute physical wretchedness the whole time. The ship abounded in cockroaches and more intimate vermin. I was cold all the time until after we passed Cape Verde, then I became steamily hot; I had been too preoccupied with Beatrice and my keen desire to get the *Maud Mary* under way at once, to consider a proper wardrobe for myself, and in particular I lacked a coat. Heavens! how I lacked that coat! And, moreover, I was cooped up with two of the worst bores in Christendom, Pollack and the captain. Pollack, after conducting his illness in a style better adapted to the capacity of an opera house than a small compartment, suddenly got insupportably well and breezy, and produced a manly pipe in which he smoked a tobacco as blond as himself, and divided his time almost equally between smoking it and trying to clean it. "There's only three things you *can* clean a pipe with," he used to remark with a twist of paper in hand. "The best's a feather, the second's a straw, and the third's a girl's hairpin. I never see such a ship. You can't find any of 'em. Last time I came this way I did find hairpins anyway, and found 'em on the floor of the captain's cabin. Regular deposit. Eh? . . . Feelin' better?"

At which I usually swore.

"Oh, you'll be all right soon. Don't mind my puffin' a bit? Eh?"

He never tired of asking me to "have a hand at Nap. Good game. Makes you forget it, and that's half the battle."

He would sit swaying with the rolling of the ship and

[327]

suck at his pipe of blond tobacco and look with an inexpressibly sage but somnolent blue eye at the captain by the hour together. "Captain's a Card," he would say over and over again as the outcome of these meditations. "He'd like to know what we're up to. He'd like to know—no end."

That did seem to be the captain's ruling idea. But he also wanted to impress me with the notion that he was a gentleman of good family and to air a number of views adverse to the English, to English literature, to the English constitution, and the like. He had learnt the sea in the Roumanian navy, and English out of a book; he would still at times pronounce the e's at the end of "there" and "here"; he was a naturalised Englishman, and he drove me into a reluctant and uncongenial patriotism by his everlasting carping at things English. Pollack would set himself to "draw him out." Heaven alone can tell how near I came to murder.

Fifty-three days I had outward, cooped up with these two and a shy and profoundly depressed mate who read the Bible on Sundays and spent the rest of his leisure in lethargy, three and fifty days of life cooped up in a perpetual smell, in a persistent sick hunger that turned from the sight of food, in darkness, cold and wet, in a lightly ballasted ship that rolled and pitched and swayed. And all the time the sands in the hour-glass of my uncle's fortunes were streaming out. Misery! Amidst it all I remember only one thing brightly, one morning of sunshine in the Bay of Biscay and a vision of frothing waves, sapphire green, a bird following our wake and our masts rolling about the sky. Then wind and rain close in on us again.

You must not imagine they were ordinary days, days, I mean, of an average length; they were not so much days as long damp slabs of time that stretched each one to the horizon, and much of that length was night. One paraded the staggering deck in a borrowed sou'-wester hour after hour in the chilly, windy, splashing and spitting darkness, or sat in the cabin, bored and ill, and looked at the faces of those inseparable companions by the help of a lamp that gave smell rather than light. Then one would see going up, up, up, and then sinking down, down, down, Pollack, extinct pipe in mouth, humorously observant, bringing his mind slowly to the seventy-seventh decision that the captain was a Card, while the words flowed from the latter in a nimble incessant flood. "Dis England eet is not a country aristocratic, no! Eet is a glorified bourgeoisie! Eet is plutocratic. In England dere is no aristocracy since de Wars of Roses. In the rest of Europe east of the Latins, yes; in England, no.

"Eet is all middle-class, youra England. Everything you look at, middle-class. Respectable! Everything good—eet is, you say, shocking. Madame Grundy! Eet is all limited and computing and self-seeking. Dat is why your art is so limited, youra fiction, your philosophia, why you are all so inartistic. You want nothing but profit! What will pay! What would you?" . . .

He had all those violent adjuncts to speech we Western Europeans have abandoned, shruggings of the shoulders, waving of the arms, thrusting out of the face, wonderful grimaces and twiddlings of the hands under your nose until you wanted to hit them away. Day after day it went on, and I had to keep my anger to myself, to reserve myself for the time ahead when it would be necessary to see the quap was got aboard and stowed—knee deep in this man's astonishment. I knew he would make a thousand objections to all we had before us. He talked like a drugged man. It ran glibly over his tongue. And all the time one could see his seamanship fretting him, he was gnawed by responsibility, perpetually uneasy about the ship's position, perpetually imagining dangers. If a sea hit us exceptionally hard he'd be out of the cabin in an instant making an outcry of inquiries, and he was pursued by a dread of the hold, of ballast shifting, of insidious wicked leaks. As we drew near the African coast his fear of rocks and shoals became infectious.

"I do not know dis coast," he used to say. "I cama hera

because Gordon-Nasmyth was coming too. Den he does not come!"

"Fortunes of war," I said, and tried to think in vain if any motive but sheer haphazard could have guided Gordon-Nasmyth in the choice of these two men. I think perhaps Gordon-Nasmyth had the artistic temperament and wanted contrasts, and also that the captain helped him to express his own malignant Anti-Britishism. He was indeed an exceptionally inefficient captain. On the whole I was glad I had come even at the eleventh hour to see to things.

(The captain, by-the-by, did at last, out of sheer nervousness, get aground at the end of Mordet's Island, but we got off in an hour or so with a swell and a little hard work in the boat.)

I suspected the mate of his opinion of the captain long before he expressed it. He was, I say, a taciturn man, but one day speech broke through him. He had been sitting at the table with his arms folded on it, musing drearily, pipe in mouth, and the voice of the captain drifted down from above.

The mate lifted his heavy eyes to me and regarded me for a moment. Then he began to heave with the beginnings of speech. He disembarrassed himself of his pipe. I cowered with expectation. Speech was coming at last. Before he spoke he nodded reassuringly once or twice.

"E——"

He moved his head strangely and mysteriously, but a child might have known he spoke of the captain.

"E's a foreigner."

He regarded me doubtfully for a time, and at last decided for the sake of lucidity to clench the matter.

"That's what E is—a *Dago!*"

He nodded like a man who gives a last tap to a nail, and I could see he considered his remark well and truly laid. His face, though still resolute, became as tranquil and uneventful as a huge hall after a public meeting has dispersed out of it, and finally he closed and locked it with his pipe.

"Roumanian Jew, isn't he?" I said.

He nodded darkly and almost forbiddingly.

More would have been too much. The thing was said. But from that time forth I knew I could depend upon him and that he and I were friends. It happens I never did have to depend upon him, but that does not affect our relationship.

Forward the crew lived lives very much after the fashion of ours, more crowded, more cramped and dirty, wetter, steamier, more verminous. The coarse food they had was still not so coarse but that they did not think they were living "like fighting cocks." So far as I could make out they were all nearly destitute men; hardly any of them had a proper sea outfit, and what small possessions they had were a source of mutual distrust. And as we pitched and floundered southward they gambled and fought, were brutal to one another, argued and wrangled loudly, until we protested at the uproar. . . .

There's no romance about the sea in a small sailing ship as I saw it. The romance is in the mind of the landsman dreamer. These brigs and schooners and brigantines that still stand out from every little port are relics from an age of petty trade, as rotten and obsolescent as a Georgian house that has sunken into a slum. They are indeed just floating fragments of slum, much as icebergs are floating fragments of glacier. The civilised man who has learnt to wash, who has developed a sense of physical honour, of cleanly temperate feeding, of time, can endure them no more. They pass, and the clanking coal-wasting steamers will follow them, giving place to cleaner, finer things. . . .

But so it was I made my voyage to Africa, and came at last into a world of steamy fogs and a hot smell of vegetable decay, and into sound and sight of surf and distant intermittent glimpses of the coast. I lived a strange concentrated life through all that time, such a life as a creature must do that has fallen in a well. All my former ways ceased, all my old vistas became memories.

The situation I was saving was very small and distant now; I felt its urgency no more. Beatrice and Lady Grove, my uncle and the Hardingham, my soaring in the air and my habitual wide vision of swift effectual things, became as remote as if they were in some world I had left for ever. . . .

IV

All these African memories stand by themselves. It was for me an expedition into the realms of undisciplined nature out of the world that is ruled by men, my first bout with that hot side of our mother that gives you the jungle—that cold side that gives you the air-eddy I was beginning to know passing well. They are memories woven upon a fabric of sunshine and heat and a constant warm smell of decay. They end in rain—such rain as I had never seen before, a vehement, a frantic downpouring of water, but our first slow passage through the channels behind Mordet's Island was in incandescent sunshine.

There we go in my memory still, a blistered dirty ship with patched sails and a battered mermaid to present *Maud Mary*, sounding and taking thought between high ranks of forest whose trees come out knee-deep at last in the water. There we go with a little breeze on our quarter, Mordet Island rounded and the quap, it might be within a day of us.

Here and there strange blossoms woke the dank intensities of green with a trumpet call of colour. Things crept among the jungle and peeped and dashed back rustling into stillness. Always in the sluggishly drifting, opaque water were eddyings and stirrings; little rushes of bubbles came chuckling up light-heartedly from this or that submerged conflict and tragedy; now and again were crocodiles like a stranded fleet of logs basking in the sun. Still it was by day, a dreary stillness broken only by insect sounds and the creaking and flapping of our progress, by the calling of the soundings and the captain's confused shouts; but in the night as we lay moored to a clump of trees the darkness brought a thousand swampy things to life and out of the forest came screaming and howlings, screaming and yells that made us glad to be afloat. And once we saw between the tree stems long blazing fires. We passed two or three villages landward, and brown-black women and children came and stared at us and gesticulated, and once a man came out in a boat from a creek and hailed us in an unknown tongue; and so at last we came to a great open place, a broad lake rimmed with a desolation of mud and bleached refuse and dead trees, free from crocodiles or water birds or sight or sound of any living thing, and saw far off, even as Nasmyth had described, the ruins of the deserted station, and hard by two little heaps of buff-hued rubbish under a great rib of rock, the quap! The forest receded. The land to the right of us fell away and became barren, and far off across a notch in its backbone was surf and the sea.

We took the ship in towards those heaps and the ruined jetty slowly and carefully. The captain came and talked.

"This is eet?" he said.

"Yes," said I.

"Is eet for trade we have come?"

This was ironical.

"No," said I. . . .

"Gordon-Nasmyth would haf told me long ago what it ees for we haf come."

"I'll tell you now," I said. "We are going to lay in as close as we can to those two heaps of stuff—you see them? —under the rock. Then we are going to chuck all our ballast overboard and take those in. Then we're going home."

"May I presume to ask—is eet gold?"

"No," I said incivilly, "it isn't."

"Then what is it?"

"It's stuff—of some commercial value."

"We can't do eet," he said.

"We can," I answered reassuringly.

"We can't," he said as confidently. "I don't mean what you mean. You know so liddle—but—dis is forbidden country."

I turned on him suddenly angry and met bright excited eyes. For a minute we scrutinised one another. Then I said, "That's our risk. Trade is forbidden. But this isn't trade.

[333]

. . . This thing's got to be done."

His eyes glittered and he shook his head. . . .

The brig stood in slowly through the twilight towards this strange scorched and blistered stretch of beach, and the man at the wheel strained his ears to listen to the low-voiced angry argument that began between myself and the captain, that was presently joined by Pollack. We moored at last within a hundred yards of our goal, and all through our dinner and far into the night we argued intermittently and fiercely with the captain about our right to load just what we pleased. "I will haf nothing to do with eet," he persisted. "I wash my hands." It seemed that night as though we argued in vain. "If it is not trade," he said, "it is prospecting and mining. That is worse. Any one who knows anything—outside England—knows that is worse."

We argued and I lost my temper and swore at him. Pollack kept cooler and chewed his pipe watchfully with that blue eye of his upon the captain's gestures. Finally I went on deck to cool. The sky was overcast. I discovered all the men were in a knot forward, staring at the faint quivering luminosity that had spread over the heaps of quap, a phosphorescence such as one sees at times on rotting wood. And about the beach east and west there were patches and streaks of something like diluted moonshine. . . .

In the small hours I was still awake and turning over scheme after scheme in my mind whereby I might circumvent the captain's opposition. I meant to get that quap aboard if I had to kill some one to do it. Never in my life had I been so thwarted! After this intolerable voyage! There came a rap at my cabin door and then it opened and I made out a bearded face. "Come in," I said, and a black voluble figure I could just see obscurely came in to talk in my private ear and fill my cabin with its whisperings and gestures. It was the captain. He, too, had been awake and thinking things over. He had come to explain—enormously. I lay there hating him and wondering if I and Pollack could lock him in his cabin and run the ship without him. "I do not want to spoil dis expedition," emerged from a cloud of protestations, and then I was able to disentangle "a commission—shush a small commission—for special risks!" "Special risks" became frequent. I let him explain himself out. It appeared he was also demanding an apology for something I had said. No doubt I had insulted him generously. At last came definite offers. I broke my silence and bargained.

"Pollack!" I cried and hammered the partition.

"What's up?" asked Pollack.

I stated the case concisely.

There came a silence.

"He's a Card," said Pollack. "Let's give him his commission. I don't mind."

"Eh?" I cried.

"I said he was a Card, that's all," said Pollack. "I'm coming."

He appeared in my doorway a faint white figure and joined our vehement whisperings. . . .

We had to buy the captain off; we had to promise him ten per cent. of our problematical profits. We were to give him ten per cent. on what we sold the cargo for over and above his legitimate pay, and I found in my out-bargained and disordered state small consolation in the thought that I, as the Gordon-Nasmyth expedition, was to sell the stuff to myself as Business Organisations. And he further exasperated me by insisting on having our bargain in writing. "In the form of a letter," he insisted.

"All right," I acquiesced, "in the form of a letter. Here goes! Get a light!"

"And the apology," he said, folding up the letter.

"All right," I said; "apology."

My hand shook with anger as I wrote, and afterwards I could not sleep for hate of him. At last I got up. I suffered, I found, from an unusual clumsiness. I struck my toe against my cabin door, and cut myself as I shaved. I found myself at last pacing the deck under the dawn in a mood of extreme exasperation. The sun rose abruptly and splashed light blindingly into my eyes and I swore at the sun. I found myself imagining fresh obstacles with the men and talking aloud in anticipatory rehearsal of the consequent row.

The malaria of the quap was already in my blood.

V

Sooner or later the ridiculous embargo that now lies upon all the coast eastward of Mordet Island will be lifted and the reality of the deposits of quap ascertained. I am sure that we were merely taking the outcrop of a stratum of nodulated deposits that dip steeply seaward. Those heaps were merely the crumbled out contents of two irregular cavities in the rock; they are as natural as any talus or heap of that kind, and the mud along the edge of the water for miles is mixed with quap, and is radio-active and lifeless and faintly phosphorescent at night. But the reader will find the full particulars of my impression of all this in the *Geological Magazine* for October, 1905, and to that I must refer him. There, too, he will find my unconfirmed theories of its nature. If I am right it is something far more significant from the scientific point of view than those incidental constituents of various rare metals, pitchblende, rutile, and the like, upon which the revolutionary discoveries of the last decade are based. Those are just little molecular centres of disintegration, of that mysterious decay and rotting of those elements, elements once regarded as the most stable things in nature. But there is something—the only word that comes near it is *cancerous*—and that is not very near, about the whole of quap, something that creeps and lives as a disease lives by destroying; an elemental stirring and disarrangement, incalculably maleficent and strange.

This is no imaginative comparison of mine. To my mind radio-activity is a real disease of matter. Moreover, it is a contagious disease. It spreads. You bring those debased and crumbling atoms near others and those too presently catch the trick of swinging themselves out of coherent existence. It is in matter exactly what the decay of our old culture is in society, a loss of traditions and distinctions and assured reactions. When I think of these inexplicable dissolvent centres that have come into being in our globe—these quap heaps are surely by far the largest that have yet been found in the world; the rest as yet mere specks in grains and crystals—I am haunted by a grotesque fancy of the ultimate eating away and dry-rotting and dispersal of all our world. So that while man still struggles and dreams his very substance will change and crumble from beneath him. I mention this here as a queer persistent fancy. Suppose, indeed, that is to be the end of our planet; no splendid climax and finale, no towering accumulation of achievements, but just—atomic decay! I add that to the ideas of the suffocating comet, the dark body out of space, the burning out of the sun, the distorted orbit, as a new and far more possible end—as Science can see ends—to this strange by-play of matter that we call human life. I do not believe this can be the end; no human soul can believe in such an end and go on living, but to it science points as a possible thing, science and reason alike. If single human beings—if one single ricketty infant—can be born as it were by accident and die futile, why not the whole race? These are questions I have never answered, that now I never attempt to answer, but the thought of quap and its mysteries brings them back to me.

I can witness that the beach and mud for two miles or more either way was a lifeless beach—lifeless as I could have imagined no tropical mud could ever be, and all the dead branches and leaves and rotting dead fish and so forth that drifted ashore became presently shrivelled and white. Sometimes crocodiles would come up out of the water and bask, and now and then water birds would explore the mud and rocky ribs that rose out of it, in a mood of transitory speculation. That was its utmost animation. And the air felt at once hot and austere, dry and blistering, and altogether different to the warm moist embrace that had met us at our first African landfall and to which we had grown accustomed.

I believe that the primary influence of the quap upon

[337]

us was to increase the conductivity of our nerves, but that is a mere unjustifiable speculation on my part. At any rate it gave a sort of east wind effect to life. We all became irritable, clumsy, languid and disposed to be impatient with our languor. We moored the brig to the rocks with difficulty, and got aground on mud and decided to stick there and tow off when we had done—the bottom was as greasy as butter. Our efforts to fix up planks and sleepers in order to wheel the quap aboard were as ill-conceived as that sort of work can be—and that sort of work can at times be very ill-conceived. The captain had a superstitious fear of his hold: he became wildly gesticulatory and expository and incompetent at the bare thought of it. His shouts still echo in my memory, becoming as each crisis approached less and less like any known tongue.

But I cannot now write the history of those days of blundering and toil: of how Milton, one of the boys, fell from a plank to the beach, thirty feet perhaps, with his barrow and broke his arm and I believe a rib, of how I and Pollack set the limb and nursed him through the fever that followed, of how one man after another succumbed to a feverish malaria, and how I—by virtue of my scientific reputation—was obliged to play the part of doctor and dose them with quinine, and then finding that worse than nothing, with rum and small doses of Easton's Syrup, of which there chanced to be a case of bottles aboard—Heaven and Gordon-Nasmyth know why. For three long days we lay in misery and never shipped a barrow-load. Then, when they resumed, the men's hands broke out into sores. There were no gloves available; and I tried to get them, while they shovelled and wheeled, to cover their hands with stockings or greased rags. They would not do this on account of the heat and discomfort. This attempt of mine did, however, direct their attention to the quap as the source of their illness and precipitated what in the end finished our lading, an informal strike. "We've had enough of this," they said, and they meant it. They came aft to say as much. They cowed the captain.

Through all these days the weather was variously vile, first a furnace heat under a sky of a scowling intensity of blue, then a hot fog that stuck in one's throat like wool and turned the men on the planks into colourless figures of giants, then a wild burst of thunderstorms, mad elemental uproar and rain. Through it all, against illness, heat, confusion of mind, one master impetus prevailed with me, to keep the shipping going, to maintain one motif at least, whatever else arose or ceased, the chuff of the spades, the squeaking and shriek of the barrows, the pluppa, pluppa, pluppa, as the men came trotting along the swinging high planks, and then at last, the dollop, dollop, as the stuff shot into the hold. "Another barrow-load, thank God! Another fifteen hundred, or it may be two thousand pounds, for the saving of Ponderevo! . . ."

I found out many things about myself and humanity in those weeks of effort behind Mordet Island. I understand now the heart of the sweater, of the harsh employer, of the nigger-driver. I had brought these men into a danger they didn't understand, I was fiercely resolved to overcome their opposition and bend and use them for my purpose, and I hated the men. But I hated all humanity during the time that the quap was near me. . . .

And my mind was pervaded, too, by a sense of urgency and by the fear that we should be discovered and our proceedings stopped. I wanted to get out to sea again—to be beating up northward with our plunder. I was afraid our masts showed to seaward and might betray us to some curious passer on the high sea. And one evening near the end I saw a canoe with three natives far off down the lake; I got field-glasses from the captain and scrutinised them, and I could see them staring at us. One man might have been a half-breed and was dressed in white. They watched us for some time very quietly and then paddled off into some channel in the forest shadows.

And for three nights running, so that it took a painful grip upon my inflamed imagination, I dreamt of my uncle's face, only that it was ghastly white like a clown's, and the throat was cut from ear to ear—a long ochreous cut. "Too late," he said; "too late! . . ."

A day or so after we had got to work upon the quap I found myself so sleepless and miserable that the ship became unendurable. Just before the rush of sunrise I borrowed Pollack's gun, walked down the planks, clambered over the quap heaps and prowled along the beach. I went perhaps a mile and a half that day and some distance beyond the ruins of the old station. I became interested in the desolation about me, and found when I returned that I was able to sleep for nearly an hour. It was delightful to have been alone for so long,—no captain, no Pollack, no one. Accordingly I repeated this expedition the next morning and the next until it became a custom with me. There was little for me to do once the digging and wheeling was organised, and so these prowlings of mine grew longer and longer, and presently I began to take food with me.

I pushed these walks far beyond the area desolated by the quap. On the edges of that was first a zone of stunted vegetation, then a sort of swampy jungle that was difficult to penetrate, and then the beginnings of the forest, a scene of huge tree stems and tangled creeper ropes and roots mingled with oozy mud. Here I used to loaf in a state between botanising and reverie—always very anxious to know what was up above in the sunlight—and here it was I murdered a man.

It was the most unmeaning and purposeless murder imaginable. Even as I write down its well-remembered particulars there comes again the sense of its strangeness, its pointlessness, its incompatibility with any of the neat and definite theories people hold about life and the meaning of the world. I did this thing and I want to tell of my doing it, but why I did it and particularly why I should be held responsible for it I cannot explain.

That morning I had come upon a track in the forest, and it had occurred to me as a disagreeable idea that this was a human pathway. I didn't want to come upon any human beings. The less our expedition saw of the African population the better for its prospects. Thus far we had been singularly free from native pestering. So I turned back and was making my way over mud and roots and dead fronds and petals scattered from the green world above when abruptly I saw my victim.

I became aware of him perhaps forty feet off standing quite still and regarding me.

He wasn't by any means a pretty figure. He was very black and naked except for a dirty loin-cloth, his legs were ill-shaped and his toes spread wide and the upper edge of his cloth and a girdle of string cut his clumsy abdomen into folds. His forehead was low, his nose very flat and his lower lip swollen and purplish-red. His hair was short and fuzzy, and about his neck was a string and a little purse of skin. He carried a musket, and a powder-flask was stuck in his girdle. It was a curious confrontation. There opposed to him stood I, a little soiled, perhaps, but still a rather elaborately civilised human being, born, bred and trained in a vague tradition. In my hand was an unaccustomed gun. And each of us was essentially a teeming, vivid brain, tensely excited by the encounter, quite unaware of the other's mental content or what to do with him.

He stepped back a pace or so, stumbled and turned to run.

"Stop," I cried; "stop, you fool!" and started to run after him, shouting such things in English. But I was no match for him over the roots and mud.

I had a preposterous idea. "He mustn't get away and tell them!"

And with that instantly I brought both feet together, raised my gun, aimed quite coolly, drew the trigger carefully and shot him neatly in the back.

I saw, and saw with a leap of pure exaltation, the smash of my bullet between his shoulder blades. "Got him," said I, dropping my gun, and down he flopped and died without a groan. "By Jove!" I cried with a note of surprise, "I've killed him!" I looked about me and then went forward cautiously, in a mood between curiosity and astonishment, to look at this man whose soul I had flung so unceremoniously out of our common world. I went to him, not as one goes to something one has made or done, but as one approaches something found.

He was frightfully smashed out in front; he must have died in the instant. I stooped and raised him by his shoulder and realised that. I dropped him, and stood about and peered about me through the trees. "My word!" I said. He was the second dead human being—apart, I mean, from surgical properties and mummies and common shows of that sort—that I had ever seen. I stood over him wondering, wondering beyond measure.

A practical idea came into that confusion. Had any one heard the gun?

I reloaded.

After a time I felt securer, and gave my mind again to the dead I had killed. What must I do?

It occurred to me that perhaps I ought to bury him. At any rate, I ought to hide him. I reflected coolly, and then put my gun within easy reach and dragged him by the arm towards a place where the mud seemed soft, and thrust him in. His powder-flask slipped from his loin-cloth, and I went back to get it. Then I pressed him down with the butt of my rifle.

Afterwards this all seemed to me most horrible, but at the time it was entirely a matter-of-fact transaction. I looked round for any other visible evidence of his fate, looked round as one does when one packs one's portmanteau in an hotel bedroom.

Then I got my bearings, and carefully returned towards the ship. I had the mood of grave concentration of a boy who has lapsed into poaching. And the business only began to assume proper proportions for me as I got near the ship, to seem any other kind of thing than the killing of a bird or rabbit.

In the night, however, it took on enormous and portentous forms. "By God!" I cried suddenly, starting wide awake; "but it was murder!"

I lay after that wide awake, staring at my memories. In some odd way these visions mixed up with my dream of my uncle in his despair. The black body which I saw now damaged and partly buried, but which, nevertheless, I no longer felt was dead but acutely alive and perceiving, I mixed up with the ochreous slash under my uncle's face. I tried to dismiss this horrible obsession from my mind, but it prevailed over all my efforts.

The next day was utterly black with my sense of that ugly creature's body. I am the least superstitious of men, but it drew me. It drew me back into those thickets to the very place where I had hidden him.

Some evil and detestable beast had been at him, and he lay disinterred.

Methodically I buried his swollen and mangled carcass again, and returned to the ship for another night of dreams. Next day for all the morning I resisted the impulse to go to him, and played nap with Pollack with my secret gnawing at me, and in the evening started to go and was near benighted. I never told a soul of them of this thing I had done.

Next day I went early, and he had gone, and there were human footmarks and ugly stains round the muddy hole from which he had been dragged.

I returned to the ship, disconcerted and perplexed. That day it was the men came aft, with blistered hands and faces, and sullen eyes. When they proclaimed, through Edwards, their spokesman, "We've had enough of this, and we mean it," I answered very readily, "So have I. Let's go."

VII

We were none too soon. People had been reconnoitring us, the telegraph had been at work, and we were not four hours at sea before we ran against the gunboat that had been sent down the coast to look for us and that would have caught us behind the island like a beast in a trap. It was a

[343]

night of driving cloud that gave intermittent gleams of moonlight; the wind and sea were strong and we were rolling along through a drift of rain and mist. Suddenly the world was white with moonshine. The gunboat came out as a long dark shape wallowing on the water to the east. She sighted the *Maud Mary* at once, and fired some sort of popgun to arrest us.

The mate turned to me.

"Shall I tell the captain?"

"The captain be damned!" said I, and we let him sleep through two hours of chase till a rainstorm swallowed us up. Then we changed our course and sailed right across them, and by morning only her smoke was showing.

We were clear of Africa—and with the booty aboard. I did not see what stood between us and home.

For the first time since I had fallen sick in the Thames my spirits rose. I was sea-sick and physically disgusted, of course, but I felt kindly in spite of my qualms. So far as I could calculate then the situation was saved. I saw myself returning triumphantly into the Thames, and nothing on earth to prevent old Capern's Perfect Filament going on the market in a fortnight. I had the monopoly of electric lamps beneath my feet.

I was released from the spell of that bloodstained black body all mixed up with grey-black mud. I was going back to baths and decent food and aeronautics and Beatrice. I was going back to Beatrice and my real life again—out of this well into which I had fallen. It would have needed something more than sea-sickness and quap fever to prevent my spirits rising.

I told the captain that I agreed with him that the British were the scum of Europe, the westward drift of all the people, a disgusting rabble, and I lost three pounds by attenuated retail to Pollack at ha'penny nap and euchre.

And then you know, as we got out into the Atlantic this side of Cape Verde, the ship began to go to pieces. I don't pretend for one moment to understand what happened. But I think Greiffenhagen's recent work on the effects of radium upon ligneous tissue does rather carry out my idea that emanations from quap have a rapid rotting effect upon woody fibre.

From the first there had been a different feel about the ship, and as the big winds and waves began to strain her she commenced leaking. Soon she was leaking—not at any particular point, but everywhere. She did not spring a leak, I mean, but water came in first of all near the decaying edges of her planks, and then through them.

I firmly believe the water came through the wood. First it began to ooze, then to trickle. It was like trying to carry moist sugar in a thin paper bag. Soon we were taking in water as though we had opened a door in her bottom.

Once it began, the thing went ahead beyond all fighting. For a day or so we did our best, and I can still remember in my limbs and back the pumping—the fatigue in my arms and the memory of a clear little dribble of water that jerked as one pumped, and of knocking off and the being awakened to go on again, and of fatigue piling up upon fatigue. At last we ceased to think of anything but pumping; one became a thing of torment enchanted, doomed to pump for ever. I still remember it as pure relief when at last Pollack came to me pipe in mouth.

"The captain says the damned thing's going down right now," he remarked, chewing his mouthpiece. "Eh?"

"Good idea!" I said. "One can't go on pumping for ever."

And without hurry or alacrity, sullenly and wearily we got into the boats and pulled away from the *Maud Mary* until we were clear of her, and then we stayed resting on our oars, motionless upon a glassy sea, waiting for her to sink. We were all silent, even the captain was silent until she went down. And then he spoke quite mildly in an undertone.

"Dat is the first ship I haf ever lost. . . . And it was not a fair game! It wass not a cargo any man should take. No!"

I stared at the slow eddies that circled above the departed *Maud Mary,* and the last chance of Business Organisations. I felt weary beyond emotion. I thought of my heroics to Beatrice and my uncle, of my prompt *"I'll go,"* and of all the ineffectual months I had spent after this headlong decision. I was moved to laughter at myself and fate.

But the captain and the men did not laugh. The men scowled at me and rubbed their sore and blistered hands, and set themselves to row. . . .

As all the world knows we were picked up by the Union Castle liner, *Portland Castle.*

The hairdresser aboard was a wonderful man, and he even improvised me a dress suit, and produced a clean shirt and warm underclothing. I had a hot bath, and dressed and dined and drank a bottle of Burgundy.

"Now," I said, "are there any newspapers? I want to know what's been happening in the world."

My steward gave me what he had, but I landed at Plymouth still largely ignorant of the course of events. I shook off Pollack, and left the captain and mate in an hotel, and the men in a Sailors' Home until I could send to pay them off, and I made my way to the station.

The newspapers I bought, the placards I saw, all England indeed resounded to my uncle's bankruptcy.

BOOK THE FOURTH

THE AFTERMATH OF TONO-BUNGAY

CHAPTER THE FIRST

The Stick of the Rocket

I

THAT evening I talked with my uncle in the Hardingham for the last time. The atmosphere of the place had altered quite shockingly. Instead of the crowd of importunate courtiers there were just half a dozen uninviting men, journalists waiting for an interview. Ropper the big commissionaire was still there, but now indeed he was defending my uncle from something more than time-wasting intrusions. I found the little man alone in the inner office pretending to work, but really brooding. He was looking yellow and deflated.

"Lord!" he said at the sight of me. "You're lean, George. It makes that scar of yours show up."

We regarded each other gravely for a time.

"Quap," I said, "is at the bottom of the Atlantic. There's some bills—— We've got to pay the men." . . .

"Seen the papers?"

"Read 'em all in the train."

"At bay," he said. "I been at bay for a week. . . . Yelping round me. . . . And me facing the music. I'm feelin' a bit tired."

He blew and wiped his glasses.

"My stomach isn't what it was," he explained. "One finds it—these times. How did it all happen, George? Your Marconigram—it took me in the wind a bit."

I told him concisely. He nodded to the paragraphs of my narrative and at the end he poured something from a medicine bottle into a sticky little wineglass and drank it. I be-

[349]

came aware of the presence of drugs, of three or four small bottles before him among his disorder of papers, of a faint elusively familiar odour in the room.

"Yes," he said, wiping his lips and recorking the bottle. "You've done your best, George. The luck's been against us."

He reflected, bottle in hand. "Sometimes the luck goes with you and sometimes it doesn't. Sometimes it doesn't. And then where are you? Grass in the oven! Fight or no fight."

He asked a few questions and then his thoughts came back to his own urgent affairs. I tried to get some comprehensive account of the situation from him, but he would not give it.

"Oh, I wish I'd had you. I wish I'd had you, George. I've had a lot on my hands. You're clear headed at times."

"What has happened?"

"Oh! Boom!—infernal things."

"Yes, but—how? I'm just off the sea, remember."

"It'd worry me too much to tell you now. It's tied up in a skein."

He muttered something to himself and mused darkly, and roused himself to say—

"Besides—you'd better keep out of it. It's getting tight. Get 'em talking. Go down to Crest Hill and fly. That's *your* affair."

For a time his manner set free queer anxieties in my brain again. I will confess that that Mordet Island nightmare of mine returned, and as I looked at him his hand went out for the drug again. "Stomach, George," he said.

"I been fightin' on that. Every man fights on something—gives way somewhere,—head, heart, liver—something. Zzzz. Gives way somewhere. Napoleon did at last. All through the Waterloo campaign, his stomach—it wasn't a stomach! Worse than mine, no end."

The mood of depression passed as the drug worked within him. His eyes brightened. He began to talk big. He began to dress up the situation for my eyes, to recover what he had admitted to me. He put it as a retreat from Russia. There were still the chances of Leipzig.

"It's a battle, George—a big fight. We're fighting for millions. I've still chances. There's still a card or so. I can't tell all my plans—like speaking on the stroke."

"You might," I began.

"I can't, George. It's like asking to look at some embryo. You got to wait. I know. In a sort of way, I know. But to tell it—— No! You been away so long. And everything's got complicated."

My perception of disastrous entanglements deepened with the rise of his spirits. It was evident that I could only help to tie him up in whatever net was weaving round his mind by forcing questions and explanations upon him. My thoughts flew off at another angle. "How's Aunt Susan?" said I.

I had to repeat the question. His busy whispering lips stopped for a moment, and he answered in the note of one who repeats a formula.

"She'd like to be in the battle with me. She'd like to be here in London. But there's corners I got to turn alone." His eye rested for a moment on the little bottle beside him. "And things have happened.

"You might go down now and talk to her," he said, in a directer voice. "I shall be down to-morrow night, I think."

He looked up as though he hoped that would end our talk.

"For the week-end?" I asked.

"For the week-end. Thank God for week-ends, George!"

II

My return home to Lady Grove was a very different thing from what I had anticipated when I had got out to sea with my load of quap and fancied the Perfect Filament was safe within my grasp. As I walked through the evening light along the downs, the summer stillness seemed like the stillness of something newly dead. There were no lurking workmen any more, no cyclists on the high road.

Cessation was manifest everywhere. There had been, I learnt from my aunt, a touching and quite voluntary demonstration when the Crest Hill work had come to an end and the men had drawn their last pay; they had cheered my uncle and hooted the contractors and Lord Boom.

I cannot now recall the manner in which my aunt and I greeted one another. I must have been very tired then, but whatever impression was made has gone out of my memory. But I recall very clearly how we sat at the little round table near the big window that gave on the terrace, and dined and talked. I remember her talking of my uncle.

She asked after him, and whether he seemed well. "I wish I could help," she said. "But I've never helped him much, never. His way of doing things was never mine. And since— since——. Since he began to get so rich, he's kept things from me. In the old days—it was different. . . .

"There he is—I don't know what he's doing. He won't have me near him. . . .

"More's kept from me than anyone. The very servants won't let me know. They try and stop the worst of the papers—Boom's things—from coming upstairs. . . . I suppose they've got him in a corner, George. Poor old Teddy! Poor old Adam and Eve we are! 'Ficial Receivers with flaming swords to drive us out of our garden! I'd hoped we'd never have another Trek. Well—anyway, it won't be Crest Hill. . . . But it's hard on Teddy. He must be in such a mess up there. Poor old chap. I suppose we can't help him. I suppose we'd only worry him. Have some more soup, George—while there is some? . . ."

The next day was one of those days of strong perception that stand out clear in one's memory when the common course of days is blurred. I can recall now the awakening in the large familiar room that was always kept for me, and how I lay staring at its chintz-covered chairs, its spaced fine furniture, its glimpse of the cedars without, and thought that all this had to end.

I have never been greedy for money, I have never wanted to be rich, but I felt now an immense sense of impending deprivation. I read the newspapers after breakfast—I and my aunt together—and then I walked up to see what Cothope had done in the matter of Lord Roberts β. Never before had I appreciated so acutely the ample brightness of the Lady Grove gardens, the dignity and wide peace of all about me. It was one of those warm mornings in late May that have won all the glory of summer without losing the gay delicacy of spring. The shrubbery was bright with laburnum and lilac, the beds swarmed with daffodils and narcissi and with lilies of the valley in the shade.

I went along the well-kept paths among the rhododendrons and through the private gate into the woods where the bluebells and common orchid were in profusion. Never before had I tasted so completely the fine sense of privilege and ownership. And all this has to end, I told myself, all this has to end.

Neither my uncle nor I had made any provision for disaster; all we had was in the game, and I had little doubt now of the completeness of our ruin. For the first time in my life since he had sent me that wonderful telegram of his I had to consider that common anxiety of mankind,—Employment. I had to come off my magic carpet and walk once more in the world.

And suddenly I found myself at the cross drives where I had seen Beatrice for the first time after so many years. It is strange, but so far as I can recollect I had not thought of her once since I had landed at Plymouth. No doubt she had filled the background of my mind, but I do not remember one definite, clear thought. I had been intent on my uncle and the financial collapse.

It came like a blow in the face now; all that, too, had to end!

Suddenly I was filled with the thought of her and a great longing for her. What would she do when she realised our immense disaster? What would she do? How would she take it? Is filled me with astonishment to realise how little I could tell. . . .

Should I perhaps presently happen upon her?

I went on through the plantations and out upon the downs, and thence I saw Cothope with a new glider of his own design soaring down wind to my old familiar "grounding" place. To judge by its long rhythm it was a very good glider. "Like Cothope's cheek," thought I, "to go on with the research. I wonder if he's been keeping notes. . . . But all this will have to stop."

He was sincerely glad to see me. "It's been a rum go," he said.

He had been there without wages for a month, a man forgotten in the rush of events.

"I just stuck on and did what I could with the stuff. I got a bit of money of my own—and I said to myself, 'Well, here you are with the gear and no one to look after you. You won't get such a chance again, my boy, not in all your born days. Why not make what you can with it?'"

"How's Lord Roberts β?"

Cothope lifted his eyebrows. "I've had to refrain," he said. "But he's looking very handsome."

"Gods!" I said, "I'd like to get him up just once before we smash. You read the papers? You know we're going to smash?"

"Oh! I read the papers. It's scandalous, sir, such work as ours should depend on things like that. You and I ought to be under the State, sir, if you'll excuse me——"

"Nothing to excuse," I said. "I've always been a Socialist —of a sort—in theory. Let's go and have a look at him. How is he? Deflated?"

"Just about quarter full. That last oil glaze of yours holds the gas something beautiful. He's not lost a cubic metre a week." . . .

Cothope returned to Socialism as we went towards the sheds.

"Glad to think you're a Socialist, sir," he said, "it's the only civilised state. I been a Socialist some years—off the *Clarion*. It's a rotten scramble, this world. It takes the things we make and invent and it plays the silly fool with 'em. We scientific people, we'll have to take things over

[354]

and stop all this financing and advertisement and that. It's too silly. It's a noosance. Look at us!"

Lord Roberts β, even in his partially deflated condition in his shed, was a fine thing to stare up at. I stood side by side with Cothope regarding him, and it was borne in upon me more acutely than ever that all this had to end. I had a feeling just like the feeling of a boy who wants to do wrong, that I would use up the stuff while I had it before the creditors descended. I had a queer fancy, too, I remember, that if I could get into the air it would advertise my return to Beatrice.

"We'll fill her," I said concisely.

"It's all ready," said Cothope, and added as an afterthought, "unless they cut off the gas." . . .

I worked and interested myself with Cothope all the morning and for a time forgot my other troubles. But the thought of Beatrice flooded me slowly and steadily. It became an unintelligent sick longing to see her. I felt that I could not wait for the filling of Lord Roberts β, that I must hunt her up and see her soon. I got everything forward and lunched with Cothope, and then with the feeblest excuses left him in order to prowl down through the woods towards Bedley Corner. I became a prey to wretched hesitations and diffidence. Ought I to go near her now? I asked myself, reviewing all the social abasements of my early years. At last, about five, I called at the Dower House. I was greeted by their Charlotte—with a forbidding eye and a cold astonishment.

Both Beatrice and Lady Osprey were out.

There came into my head some prowling dream of meeting her. I went along the lane towards Woking, the lane down which we had walked five months ago in the wind and rain.

I mooned for a time in our former footsteps, then swore and turned back across the fields, and then conceived a distaste for Cothope and went Downward. At last I found myself looking down on the huge abandoned masses of the Crest Hill house.

That gave my mind a twist into a new channel. My uncle came uppermost again. What a strange, melancholy emptiness of intention that stricken enterprise seemed in the even evening sunlight, what vulgar magnificence and crudity and utter absurdity! It was as idiotic as the pyramids. I sat down on the stile, staring at it as though I had never seen that forest of scaffold poles, that waste of walls and bricks and plaster and shaped stones, that wilderness of broken soil and wheeling tracks and dumps before. It struck me suddenly as the compactest image and sample of all that passes for Progress, of all the advertisement-inflated spending, the aimless building up and pulling down, the enterprise and promise of my age. This was our fruit, this was what we had done, I and my uncle, in the fashion of our time. We were its leaders and exponents, we were the thing it most flourishingly produced. For this futility in its end, for an epoch of such futility, the solemn scroll of history had unfolded. . . .

"Great God!" I cried, "but is this Life?"

For this the armies drilled, for this the Law was administered and the prisons did their duty, for this the millions toiled and perished in suffering, in order that a few of us should build palaces we never finished, make billiard-rooms under ponds, run imbecile walls round irrational estates, scorch about the world in motor-cars, devise flying-machines, play golf and a dozen such foolish games of ball, crowd into chattering dinner parties, gamble and make our lives one vast, dismal spectacle of witless waste! So it struck me then, and for a time I could think of no other interpretation. This was Life! It came to me like a revelation, a revelation at once incredible and indisputable of the abysmal folly of our being.

III

I was roused from such thoughts by the sound of footsteps behind me.

I turned half hopeful—so foolish is a lover's imagination, and stopped amazed. It was my uncle. His face was white—

white as I had seen it in my dream.

"Hullo!" I said, and stared. "Why aren't you in London?"

"It's all up," he said. . . .

"Adjudicated?" . . .

"No!" . . .

I stared at him for a moment, and then got off the stile.

He stood swaying and then came forward with a weak motion of his arms like a man who cannot see distinctly, and caught at and leant upon the stile. For a moment we were absolutely still. He made a clumsy gesture towards the great futility below and choked. I discovered that his face was wet with tears, that his wet glasses blinded him. He put up his little fat hand and clawed them off clumsily, felt inefficiently for his pocket-handkerchief, and then, to my horror, as he clung to me, he began to weep aloud, this little, old world-worn swindler. It wasn't just sobbing or shedding tears, it was crying as a child cries. It was—oh! terrible!

"It's cruel," he blubbered at last. "They asked me questions. They *kep'* asking me questions, George."

He sought for utterance, and spluttered.

"The Bloody bullies!" he shouted. "The Blöööödy Bullies."

He ceased to weep. He became suddenly rapid and explanatory.

"It's not a fair game, George. They tire you out. And I'm not well. My stomach's all wrong. And I been and got a cold. I always been li'ble to cold, and this one's on my chest. And then they tell you to speak up. They bait you— and bait you, and bait you. It's torture. The strain of it. You can't remember what you said. You're bound to contradict yourself. It's like Russia, George. . . . It isn't fair play. . . . Prominent man. I've been next at dinners with that chap, Neal; I've told him stories—and he's bitter! Sets out to ruin me. Don't ask a civil question—bellows."

He broke down again. "I've been bellowed at, I been bullied, I been treated like a dog. Dirty cads they ᵃre!

Dirty cads! I'd rather be a Three-Card Sharper than a barrister; I'd rather sell cat's-meat in the streets.

"They sprung things on me this morning, things I didn't expect. They rushed me! I'd got it all in my hands and then I was jumped. By Neal! Neal I've given city tips to! Neal! I've helped Neal. . . .

"I couldn't swallow a mouthful—not in the lunch hour. I couldn't face it. It's true, George—I couldn't face it. I said I'd get a bit of air and slipped out and down to the Embankment, and there I took a boat to Richmond. Some idee. I took a rowing boat when I got there and rowed about on the river for a bit. A lot of chaps and girls there was on the bank laughed at my shirt-sleeves and top hat. Dessay they thought it was a pleasure trip. Fat lot of pleasure! I rowed round for a bit and came in. Then I came on here. Windsor way. And there they are in London doing what they like with me. . . . I don't care!"

"But——" I said, looking down at him, perplexed.

"It's abscondin'. They'll have a warrant."

"I don't understand," I said.

"It's all up, George—all up and over.

"And I thought I'd live in that place, George—and die a lord! It's a great place, reely, an imperial place—if anyone has the sense to buy it and finish it. That terrace——"

I stood thinking him over.

"Look here!" I said. "What's that about a warrant? Are you sure they'll get a warrant? I'm sorry, uncle; but what have you done?"

"Haven't I tole you?"

"Yes, but they won't do very much to you for that. They'll only bring you up for the rest of your examination."

He remained silent for a time. At last he spoke—speaking with difficulty.

"It's worse than that. I done something. . . . They're bound to get it out. Practically they *have* got it out."

"What?"

"Writin' things down—— I done something."

For the first time in his life, I believe, he felt and looked ashamed. It filled me with remorse to see him suffer so.

"We've all done things," I said. "It's part of the game the world makes us play. If they want to arrest you—and you've got no cards in your hand——! They mustn't arrest you."

"No. That's partly why I went to Richmond. But I never thought——"

His little bloodshot eyes stared at Crest Hill.

"That chap Wittaker Wright," he said, "he had his stuff ready. I haven't. Now you got it, George. That's the sort of hole I'm in."

IV

That memory of my uncle at the gate is very clear and full. I am able to recall even the undertow of my thoughts while he was speaking. I remember my pity and affection for him in his misery growing and stirring within me, my realisation that at any risk I must help him. But then comes indistinctness again. I was beginning to act. I know I persuaded him to put himself in my hands, and began at once to plan and do. I think that when we act most we remember least, that just in the measure that the impulse of our impressions translates itself into schemes and movements, it ceases to record itself in memories. I know I resolved to get him away at once, and to use the Lord Roberts β in effecting that. It was clear he was soon to be a hunted man, and it seemed to me already unsafe for him to try the ordinary Continental routes in his flight. I had to evolve some scheme, and evolve it rapidly, how we might drop most inconspicuously into the world across the water. My resolve to have one flight at least in my airship fitted with this like hand to glove. It seemed to me we might be able to cross over the water in the night, set our airship adrift, and turn up as pedestrian tourists in Normandy or Brittany, and so get away. That, at any rate, was my ruling idea. I sent off Cothope with a dummy note to Woking, because I did not want to implicate him, and took my uncle to the pavilion. I went down to my aunt, and made a clean breast of the situation. She became admirably competent. We went into his dressing-room and ruthlessly broke his locks. I got a pair of brown boots, a tweed suit and a cap of his, and indeed a plausible walking outfit, and a little game bag for his pedestrian gear; and, in addition, a big motoring overcoat and a supply of rugs to add to those I had at the pavilion. I also got a flask of brandy, and she made sandwiches. I don't remember any servants appearing, and I forget where she got those sandwiches. Meanwhile we talked. Afterwards I thought with what a sure confidence we talked to each other.

"What's he done?" she said.

"D'you mind knowing?"

"No conscience left, thank God!"

"I think—forgery!"

There was just a little pause. "Can you carry this bundle?" she asked.

I lifted it.

"No woman ever has respected the law—ever," she said. "It's too silly. . . . The things it lets you do! And then pulls you up—like a mad nurse minding a child."

She carried some rugs for me through the shrubbery in the darkling.

"They'll think we're going mooning," she said, jerking her head at the household. "I wonder what they make of us—criminals." . . . An immense droning note came as if in answer to that. It startled us both for a moment. "The dears!" she said. "It's the gong for dinner! . . . But I wish I could help little Teddy, George. It's awful to think of him there with hot eyes, red and dry. And I know—the sight of me makes him feel sore. Things I said, George. If I could have seen, I'd have let him have an omnibusful of Scrymgeours. I cut him up. He'd never thought I meant it before. . . . I'll help all I can, anyhow."

I turned at something in her voice, and got a moonlight gleam of tears upon her face.

"Could *she* have helped?" she asked abruptly.

"*She?*"

"That woman."

"My God!" I cried, *"helped!* Those—things don't help!" . . .

"Tell me again what I ought to do," she said after a silence.

I went over the plans I had made for communicating, and the things I thought she might do. I had given her the address of a solicitor she might put some trust in.

"But you must act for yourself," I insisted. "Roughly," I said, "it's a scramble. You must get what you can for us, and follow as you can."

She nodded.

She came right up to the pavilion and hovered for a time shyly, and then went away.

I found my uncle in my sitting-room in an arm-chair, with his feet upon the fender of the gas stove, which he had lit, and now he was feebly drunken with my whisky, and very weary in body and spirit, and inclined to be cowardly.

"I lef' my drops," he said.

He changed his clothes slowly and unwillingly. I had to bully him, I had almost to shove him to the airship and tuck him up upon its wicker flat. Single-handed I made but a clumsy start; we scraped along the roof of the shed and bent a van of the propeller, and for a time I hung underneath without his offering a hand to help me to clamber up. If it hadn't been for a sort of anchoring trolley device of Cothope's, a sort of slip anchor running on a rail, we should never have got clear at all.

V

The incidents of our flight in Lord Roberts β do not arrange themselves in any consecutive order. To think of that adventure is like dipping haphazard into an album of views. One is reminded first of this and then of that. We were both lying down on a horizontal plate of basketwork; for Lord Roberts β had none of the elegant accommodation of a balloon. I lay forward, and my uncle behind me in such a position that he could see hardly anything of our flight

We were protected from rolling over simply by netting between the steel stays. It was impossible for us to stand up at all; we had either to lie or crawl on all fours over the basket-work. Amidships were lockers made of Watson's Aulite material, and between these it was that I had put my uncle, wrapped in rugs. I wore sealskin motoring boots and gloves, and a motoring fur coat over my tweeds, and I controlled the engine by Bowden wires and levers forward.

The early part of that night's experience was made up of warmth, of moonlit Surrey and Sussex landscape, and of a rapid and successful flight, ascending and swooping, and then ascending again southward. I could not watch the clouds because the airship overhung me; I could not see the stars nor gauge the meteorological happening, but it was fairly clear to me that a wind shifting between north and northeast was gathering strength, and after I had satisfied myself by a series of entirely successful expansions and contractions of the real air-worthiness of Lord Roberts β, I stopped the engine to save my petrol, and let the monster drift, checking its progress by the dim landscape below. My uncle lay quite still behind me, saying little and staring in front of him, and I was left to my own thoughts and sensations.

My thoughts, whatever they were, have long since faded out of memory, and my sensations have merged into one continuous memory of a countryside lying, as it seemed, under snow, with square patches of dimness, white phantoms of roads, rents and pools of velvety blackness, and lamp-jewelled houses. I remember a train boring its way like a hastening caterpillar of fire across the landscape, and how distinctly I heard its clatter. Every town and street was buttoned with street lamps. I came quite close to the South Downs near Lewes, and all the lights were out in the houses, and the people gone to bed. We left the land a little to the east of Brighton, and by that time Brighton was well abed, and the brightly lit sea-front deserted. Then I let out the gas chamber to its fullest extent and rose. I like to be high above water.

I do not clearly know what happened in the night. I think I must have dozed, and probably my uncle slept. I remember that once or twice I heard him talking in an eager, muffled voice to himself, or to an imaginary court. But there can be no doubt the wind changed right round into the east, and that we were carried far down the Channel without any suspicion of the immense leeway we were making. I remember the kind of stupid perplexity with which I saw the dawn breaking over a grey waste of waters below, and realised that something was wrong. I was so stupid that it was only after the sunrise I really noticed the trend of the foam caps below, and perceived we were in a severe easterly gale. Even then, instead of heading south-easterly, I set the engine going, headed south, and so continued a course that must needs have either just hit Ushant, or carry us over the Bay of Biscay. I thought I was east of Cherbourg, when I was far to the west, and stopped my engine in that belief, and then set it going again. I did actually sight the coast of Brittany to the southeast in the late afternoon, and that it was woke me up to the gravity of our position. I discovered it by accident in the southeast, when I was looking for it in the southwest. I turned about east and faced the wind for some time, and finding I had no chance in its teeth, went high, where it seemed less violent, and tried to make a course southeast. It was only then that I realised what a gale I was in. I had been going westward, and perhaps even in gusts north of west, at a pace of fifty or sixty miles an hour.

Then I began what I suppose would be called a Fight against the east wind. One calls it a Fight, but it was really almost as unlike a fight as plain sewing. The wind tried to drive me westwardly, and I tried to get as much as I could eastwardly, with the wind beating and rocking us irregularly, but by no means unbearably, for about twelve hours. My hope lay in the wind abating, and our keeping in the air and eastward of Finisterre until it did, and the chief danger was the exhaustion of our petrol. It was a long and anxious and almost meditative time: we were fairly warm, and only slowly getting hungry, and except that my uncle grumbled a little and produced some philosophical reflections, and began to fuss about having a temperature, we talked very little. I was tired and sulky, and chiefly worried about the engine. I had to resist a tendency to crawl back and look at it. I did not care to risk contracting our gas chamber for fear of losing gas. Nothing was less like a fight. I know that in popular magazines, and so forth, all such occasions as this are depicted in terms of hysteria. Captains save their ships, engineers complete their bridges, generals conduct their battles, in a state of dancing excitement, foaming recondite technicalities at the lips. I suppose that sort of thing works up the reader, but so far as it professes to represent reality, I am convinced it is all childish nonsense. Schoolboys of fifteen, girls of eighteen, and literary men all their lives, may have these squealing fits, but my own experience is that most exciting scenes are not exciting, and most of the urgent moments in life are met by steady-headed men.

Neither I nor my uncle spent the night in ejaculations, nor in humorous allusions, nor any of these things. We remained lumpish. My uncle stuck in his place and grumbled about his stomach, and occasionally rambled off into expositions of his financial position and denunciations of Neal— he certainly struck out one or two good phrases for Neal— and I crawled about at rare intervals in a vague sort of way and grunted, and our basketwork creaked continually, and the wind on our quarter made a sort of ruffled flapping in the wall of the gas chamber. For all our wraps we got frightfully cold as the night wore on.

I must have dozed, and it was still dark when I realised with a start that we were nearly due south of, and a long way from, a regularly-flashing lighthouse, standing out before the glow of some great town, and then that the thing that had awakened me was the cessation of our engine, and that we were driving back to the west.

Then, indeed, for a time I felt the grim thrill of life. I crawled forward to the cords of the release valves, made my uncle crawl forward too, and let out the gas until we were falling down through the air like a clumsy glider towards the vague greyness that was land.

Something must have intervened here that I have forgotten. I saw the lights of Bordeaux when it was quite dark, a nebulous haze against black; of that I am reasonably sure. But certainly our fall took place in the cold, uncertain light of early dawn. I am, at least, equally sure of that. And Mimizan, near where we dropped, is fifty miles from Bordeaux, whose harbour lights I must have seen.

I remember coming down at last with a curious indifference, and actually rousing myself to steer. But the actual coming to earth was exciting enough. I remember our prolonged dragging landfall, and the difficulty I had to get clear, and how a gust of wind caught Lord Roberts β as my uncle stumbled away from the ropes and litter, and dropped me heavily, and threw me on to my knees. Then came the realisation that the monster was almost consciously disentangling itself for escape, and then the light leap of its rebound. The rope slipped out of reach of my hand. I remember running knee-deep in a salt pool in hopeless pursuit of the airship as it dragged and rose seaward, and how only after it had escaped my uttermost effort to recapture it, did I realise that this was quite the best thing that could have happened. It drove swiftly over the sandy dunes, lifting and falling, and was hidden by a clump of wind-bitten trees. Then it reappeared much further off, and still receding. It soared for a time, and sank slowly, and after that I saw it no more. I suppose it fell into the sea and got wetted with salt water and heavy, and so became deflated and sank.

It was never found, and there was never a report of any one seeing it after it escaped from me.

VI

But if I find it hard to tell the story of our long flight through the air overseas, at least that dawn in France stands cold and clear and full. I see again almost as if I saw once more with my bodily eyes the ridges of sand rising behind ridges of sand, grey and cold and black-browed, with an insufficient grass. I feel again the clear, cold chill of dawn, and hear the distant barking of a dog. I find myself asking again, "What shall we do now?" and trying to scheme with a brain tired beyond measure.

At first my uncle occupied my attention. He was shivering a good deal, and it was all I could do to resist my desire to get him into a comfortable bed at once. But I wanted to appear plausibly in this part of the world. I felt it would not do to turn up anywhere at dawn and rest, it would be altogether too conspicuous; we must rest until the day was well advanced, and then appear as road-stained pedestrians seeking a meal. I gave him most of what was left of the biscuits, emptied our flasks, and advised him to sleep, but at first it was too cold, albeit I wrapped the big fur rug around him.

I was struck now by the flushed weariness of his face, and the look of age the grey stubble on his unshaved chin gave him. He sat crumpled up, shivering and coughing, munching reluctantly, but drinking eagerly, and whimpering a little, a dreadfully pitiful figure to me. But we had to go through with it; there was no way out for us.

Presently the sun rose over the pines, and the sand grew rapidly warm. My uncle had done eating, and sat with his wrists resting on his knees, the most hopeless-looking of lost souls.

"I'm ill," he said, "I'm damnably ill! I can feel it in my skin!"

Then—it was horrible to me—he cried, "I ought to be in bed; I ought to be in bed . . . instead of flying about," and suddenly he burst into tears.

I stood up. "Go to sleep, man!" I said, and took the rug from him, and spread it out and rolled him up in it.

"It's all very well," he protested; "I'm not young enough——"

"Lift up your head," I interrupted, and put his knapsack under it.

"They'll catch us here, just as much as in an inn," he grumbled, and then lay still.

Presently, after a long time, I perceived he was asleep. His breath came with peculiar wheezings, and every now and again he would cough. I was very stiff and tired myself, and perhaps I dozed. I don't remember. I remember only sitting, as it seemed, nigh interminably, beside him, too weary even to think in that sandy desolation.

No one came near us, no creature, not even a dog. I roused myself at last, feeling that it was vain to seek to seem other than abnormal, and with an effort that was like lifting a sky of lead, we made our way through the wearisome sand to a farmhouse. There I feigned even a more insufficient French than I possess naturally, and let it appear that we were pedestrians from Biarritz who had lost our way along the shore and got benighted. This explained us pretty well, I thought, and we got most heartening coffee and a cart to a little roadside station. My uncle grew more and more manifestly ill with every stage of our journey. I got him to Bayonne, where he refused at first to eat, and was afterwards very sick, and then took him shivering and collapsed up a little branch line to a frontier place called Luzon Gare.

We found one homely inn with two small bedrooms, kept by a kindly Basque woman. I got him to bed, and that night shared his room, and after an hour or so of sleep he woke up in a raging fever and with a wandering mind, cursing Neal and repeating long, inaccurate lists of figures. He was manifestly a case for a doctor, and in the morning we got one in. He was a young man from Montpellier, just beginning to practise, and very mysterious and technical and modern and unhelpful. He spoke of cold and exposure, and *la grippe* and pneumonia. He gave many explicit and difficult directions. . . . I perceived it devolved upon me to organise nursing and a sick-room. I installed a *religieuse* in the second bedroom of the inn, and took a room for myself in the inn of Port de Luzon, a quarter of a mile away.

And now my story converges on what, in that queer corner of refuge out of the world was destined to be my uncle's deathbed. There is a background of the Pyrenees, of blue hills and sunlit houses, of the old castle of Luzon and a noisy cascading river, and for a foreground the dim, stuffy room whose windows both the *religieuse* and hostess conspired to shut, with its waxed floor, its four-poster bed, its characteristically French chairs and fireplace, its champagne bottles and dirty basins and used towels and packets of *Somatosé* on the table. And in the sickly air of the confined space behind the curtains of the bed lay my little uncle, with an effect of being enthroned and secluded, or sat up, or writhed and tossed in his last dealings of life. One went and drew back the edge of the curtains if one wanted to speak to him or look at him.

Usually he was propped up against pillows, because so he breathed more easily. He slept hardly at all.

I have a confused memory of vigils and mornings and afternoons spent by that bedside, and how the *religieuse* hovered about me, and how meek and good and inefficient she was, and how horribly black were her nails. Other figures come and go, and particularly the doctor, a young man plumply rococo, in bicycling dress, with fine waxen features, a little pointed beard, and the long black frizzy hair and huge tie of a minor poet. Bright and clear-cut and irrelevant are memories of the Basque hostess of my uncle's inn and of the family of Spanish people who entertained me and prepared the most amazingly elaborate meals for me, with soup and salad and chicken and remarkable sweets. They were all very kind and sympathetic people, systematically so. And constantly, without attracting attention, I was trying to get newspapers from home.

My uncle is central to all these impressions.

I have tried to make you picture him, time after time, as the young man of the Wimblehurst chemist's shop, as the shabby assistant in Tottenham Court Road, as the adventurer of the early days of Tono-Bungay, as the confident, preposterous plutocrat. And now I have to tell of him strangely changed under the shadow of oncoming death, with his skin lax and yellow and glistening with sweat, his eyes large and glassy, his countenance unfamiliar through the growth of a beard, his nose pinched and thin. Never had he looked so small as now. And he talked to me in a whispering, strained voice of great issues, of why his life had been, and whither he was going. Poor little man! that last phase is, as it were, disconnected from all the other phases. It was as if he crawled out from the ruins of his career, and looked about him before he died. For he had quite clear-minded states in the intervals of his delirium.

He knew he was almost certainly dying. In a way that took the burthen of his cares off his mind. There was no more Neal to face, no more flights or evasions, no punishments.

"It has been a great career, George," he said, "but I shall be glad to rest. Glad to rest! . . . Glad to rest."

His mind ran rather upon his career, and usually, I am glad to recall, with a note of satisfaction and approval. In his delirious phases he would most often exaggerate this self-satisfaction, and talk of his splendours. He would pluck at the sheet and stare before him, and whisper half-audible fragments of sentences.

"What is this great place, these cloud-capped towers, these airy pinnacles? . . . Ilion. Sky-y-pointing. . . . Ilion House, the residence of one of our great merchant princes. . . . Terrace above terrace. Reaching to the heavens. . . . Kingdoms Cæsar never knew. . . . A great poet, George. Zzzz. Kingdoms Cæsar never knew. . . . Under entirely new management.

"Greatness. . . . Millions. . . . Universities. . . . He stands on the terrace—on the upper terrace—directing—directing—by the globe—directing—the trade." . . .

It was hard at times to tell when his sane talk ceased and his delirium began. The secret springs of his life, the vain imaginations were revealed. I sometimes think that all the life of man sprawls abed, careless and unkempt, until it must needs clothe and wash itself and come forth seemly in act and speech for the encounter with one's fellow-men. I suspect that all things unspoken in our souls partake somewhat of the laxity of delirium and dementia. Certainly from those slimy, tormented lips above the bristling grey beard came nothing but dreams and disconnected fancies. . . .

Sometimes he raved about Neal, threatened Neal. "What has he got invested?" he said. "Does he think he can escape me? . . . If I followed him up. . . . Ruin. Ruin. . . . One would think *I* had taken his money."

And sometimes he reverted to our airship flight. "It's too long, George, too long and too cold. I'm too old a man —too old—for this sort of thing. . . . You know you're not saving—you're killing me."

Towards the end it became evident our identity was discovered. I found the press, and especially Boom's section of it, had made a sort of hue and cry for us, sent special commissioners to hunt for us, and though none of these emissaries reached us until my uncle was dead, one felt the forewash of that storm of energy. The thing got into the popular French press. People became curious in their manner towards us, and a number of fresh faces appeared about the weak little struggle that went on in the closeness behind the curtains of the bed. The young doctor insisted on consultations, and a motor-car came up from Biarritz, and suddenly odd people with questioning eyes began to poke in with inquiries and help. Though nothing was said, I could feel that we were no longer regarded as simple middle-class tourists; about me, as I went, I perceived almost as though it trailed visibly, the prestige of Finance and a criminal notoriety. Local personages of a plump and prosperous quality appeared in the inn making inquiries, the Luzon priest became helpful, people watched our window, and stared at me as I went to and fro; and then we had a raid from a little English clergyman and his amiable, capable wife in severely Anglican blacks, who swooped down upon us like virtuous but resolute vultures from the adjacent village of

Saint Jean de Pollack.

The clergyman was one of those odd types that oscillate between remote country towns in England and the conduct of English Church services on mutual terms in enterprising hotels abroad, a tremulous, obstinate little being with sporadic hairs upon his face, spectacles, a red button nose, and aged black raiment. He was evidently enormously impressed by my uncle's monetary greatness, and by his own inkling of our identity, and he shone and brimmed over with tact and fussy helpfulness. He was eager to share the watching of the bedside with me, he proffered services with both hands, and as I was now getting into touch with affairs in London again, and trying to disentangle the gigantic details of the smash from the papers I had succeeded in getting from Biarritz, I accepted his offers pretty generously, and began the studies in modern finance that lay before me. I had got so out of touch with the old traditions of religion that I overlooked the manifest possibility of his attacking my poor, sinking vestiges of an uncle with theological solicitudes. My attention was called to that, however, very speedily by a polite but urgent quarrel between himself and the Basque landlady as to the necessity of her hanging a cheap crucifix in the shadow over the bed, where it might catch my uncle's eye, where, indeed, I found it had caught his eye.

"Good Lord!" I cried; "is *that* still going on!"

That night the little clergyman watched, and in the small hours he raised a false alarm that my uncle was dying, and made an extraordinary fuss. He raised the house. I shall never forget that scene, I think, which began with a tapping at my bedroom door just after I had fallen asleep, and his voice—

"If you want to see your uncle before he goes, you must come now."

The stuffy little room was crowded when I reached it, and lit by three flickering candles. I felt I was back in the eighteenth century. There lay my poor uncle amidst indescribably tumbled bedclothes, weary of life beyond measure,

[371]

weary and rambling, and the little clergyman trying to hold his hand and his attention, and repeating over and over again:

"Mr. Ponderevo, Mr. Ponderevo, it is all right. It is all right. Only Believe! 'Believe on me, and ye shall be saved'!"

Close at hand was the doctor with one of those cruel and idiotic injection needles modern science puts in the hands of these half-educated young men, keeping my uncle flickeringly alive for no reason whatever. The *religieuse* hovered sleepily in the background with an overdue and neglected dose. In addition, the landlady had not only got up herself, but roused an aged crone of a mother and a partially imbecile husband, and there was also a fattish, stolid man in grey alpaca, with an air of importance—who he was and how he got there, I don't know. I rather fancy the doctor explained him to me in French I did not understand. And they were all there, wearily nocturnal, hastily and carelessly dressed, intent upon the life that flickered and sank, making a public and curious show of its going, queer shapes of human beings lit by three uncertain candles, and every soul of them keenly and avidly resolved to be in at the death. The doctor stood, the others were all sitting on chairs the landlady had brought in and arranged for them.

And my uncle spoilt the climax, and did not die.

I replaced the little clergyman on the chair by the bedside, and he hovered about the room.

"I think," he whispered to me mysteriously, as he gave place to me, "I believe—it is well with him."

I heard him trying to render the stock phrases of Low Church piety into French for the benefit of the stolid man in grey alpaca. Then he knocked a glass off the table, and scrabbled for the fragments. From the first I doubted the theory of an immediate death. I consulted the doctor in urgent whispers. I turned round to get champagne, and nearly fell over the clergyman's legs. He was on his knees at the additional chair the Basque landlady had got on my arrival, and he was praying aloud, "Oh, Heavenly Father,

[372]

have mercy on this thy Child. . . ." I hustled him up and out of the way, and in another minute he was down at another chair praying again, and barring the path of the *religieuse*, who had found me the corkscrew. Something put into my head that tremendous blasphemy of Carlyle's about "the last mew of a drowning kitten." He found a third chair vacant presently; it was as if he was playing a game.

"Good Heavens!" said I, "we must clear these people out," and with a certain urgency I did.

I had a temporary lapse of memory, and forgot all my French. I drove them out mainly by gesture, and opened the window, to the universal horror. I intimated the death scene was postponed, and, as a matter of fact, my uncle did not die until the next night.

I did not let the little clergyman come near him again, and I was watchful for any sign that his mind had been troubled. But he made none. He talked once about "that parson chap."

"Didn't bother you?" I asked.

"Wanted something," he said.

I kept silence, listening keenly to his mutterings. I understood him to say, "They wanted too much." His face puckered like a child's going to cry. "You can't *get* a safe six per cent.," he said. I had for a moment a wild suspicion that those urgent talks had not been altogether spiritual, but that, I think, was a quite unworthy and unjust suspicion. The little clergyman was as simple and honest as the day. My uncle was simply generalising about his class.

But it may have been these talks that set loose some long dormant string of ideas in my uncle's brain, ideas the things of this world had long suppressed and hidden altogether. Near the end he suddenly became clear-minded and lucid, albeit very weak, and his voice was little, but clear.

"George," he said.

"I'm here," I said, "close beside you."

"George. You have always been responsible for the science, George. You know better than I do. Is—— Is it proved?"

"What proved?"

"Either way?"

"I don't understand."

"Death ends all. After so much—— Such splendid beginnings. Somewhere. Something."

I stared at him amazed. His sunken eyes were very grave.

"What do you expect?" I said in wonder.

He would not answer. "Aspirations," he whispered.

He fell into a broken monologue, regardless of me. "Trailing clouds of glory," he said, and "first-rate poet, first-rate . . . George was always hard. Always."

For a long time there was silence.

Then he made a gesture that he wished to speak.

"Seems to me, George——"

I bent my head down, and he tried to lift his hand to my shoulder. I raised him a little on his pillows, and listened.

"It seems to me, George, always—there must be something in me—that won't die."

He looked at me as though the decision rested with me.

"I think," he said; "——something."

Then, for a moment, his mind wandered. "Just a little link," he whispered almost pleadingly, and lay quite still, but presently he was uneasy again.

"Some other world——"

"Perhaps," I said. "Who knows?"

"Some other world."

"Not the same scope for enterprise," I said. "No."

He became silent. I sat leaning down to him, and following out my own thoughts, and presently the *religieuse* resumed her periodic conflict with the window fastening. For a time he struggled for breath. . . . It seemed such nonsense that he should have to suffer so—poor silly little man!

"George," he whispered, and his weak little hand came out. *"Perhaps——"*

He said no more, but I perceived from the expression of his eyes that he thought the question had been put.

"Yes, I think so," I said stoutly.

"Aren't you sure?"

"Oh—practically sure," said I, and I think he tried to squeeze my hand. And there I sat, holding his hand tight, and trying to think what seeds of immortality could be found in all his being, what sort of ghost there was in *him* to wander out into the bleak immensities. Queer fancies came to me. . . . He lay still for a long time, save for a brief struggle or so for breath, and ever and again I wiped his mouth and lips.

I fell into a pit of thought. I did not remark at first the change that was creeping over his face. He lay back on his pillow, made a faint zzzing sound that ceased, and presently and quite quietly he died—greatly comforted by my assurance. I do not know when he died. His hand relaxed insensibly. Suddenly, with a start, with a shock, I found that his mouth had fallen open, and that he was dead. . . .

VIII

It was dark night when I left his deathbed and went back to my own inn down the straggling street of Luzon.

That return to my inn sticks in my memory also as a thing apart, as an experience apart. Within was a subdued bustle of women, a flitting of lights, and the doing of petty offices to that queer, exhausted thing that had once been my active and urgent little uncle. For me those offices were irksome and impertinent. I slammed the door, and went out into the warm, foggy drizzle of the village street lit by blurred specks of light in great voids of darkness, and never a soul abroad. That warm veil of fog produced an effect of vast seclusion. The very houses by the roadside peered through it as if from another world. The stillness of the night was marked by an occasional remote baying of dogs; all these people kept dogs because of the near neighbourhood of the frontier.

Death!

It was one of those rare seasons of relief, when for a little time one walks a little outside of and beside life. I felt as I sometimes feel after the end of a play. I saw the whole business of my uncle's life as something familiar and completed. It was done, like a play one leaves, like a book one closes. I thought of the push and the promotions, the noise of London, the crowded, various company of people through which our lives had gone, the public meetings, the excitements, the dinners and disputations, and suddenly it appeared to me that none of these things existed. It came to me like a discovery that none of these things existed. Before and after I have thought and called life a phantasmagoria, but never have I felt its truth as I did that night. . . . We had parted; we two who had kept company so long had parted. But there was, I knew, no end to him or me. He had died a dream death, and ended a dream; his pain dream was over. It seemed to me almost as though I had died, too. What did it matter, since it was unreality, all of it, the pain and desire, the beginning and the end? There was no reality except this solitary road, this quite solitary road, along which one went rather puzzled, rather tired. . . .

Part of the fog became a big mastiff that came towards me and stopped and slunk round me, growling, barked gruffly, and shortly and presently became fog again.

My mind swayed back to the ancient beliefs and fears of our race. My doubts and disbeliefs slipped from me like a loosely fitting garment. I wondered quite simply what dogs bayed about the path of that other walker in the darkness, what shapes, what lights, it might be, loomed about him as he went his way from our last encounter on earth—along the paths that are real, and the way that endures for ever?

IX

Last belated figure in that grouping round my uncle's deathbed is my aunt. When it was beyond all hope that my uncle could live I threw aside whatever concealment remained to us and telegraphed directly to her. But she came too late to see him living. She saw him calm and still, strangely unlike his habitual garrulous animation, an unfamiliar inflexibility.

"It isn't like him," she whispered, awed by this alien dignity.

I remember her chiefly as she talked and wept upon the bridge below the old castle. We had got rid of some amateurish reporters from Biarritz, and had walked together in the hot morning sunshine down through Port Luzon. There, for a time, we stood leaning on the parapet of the bridge and surveying the distant peaks, the rich blue masses of the Pyrenees. For a long time we said nothing, and then she began talking.

"Life's a rum Go, George!" she began. "Who would have thought, when I used to darn your stockings at old Wimblehurst, that this would be the end of the story? It seems far away now—that little shop, his and my first home. The glow of the bottles, the big coloured bottles! Do you remember how the light shone on the mahogany drawers? The little gilt letters! *Ol Amjig,* and *S'nap!* I can remember it all—bright and shining—like a Dutch picture. Real! And yesterday. And here we are in a dream. You a man—and me an old woman, George. And poor little Teddy, who used to rush about and talk—making that noise he did— Oh!"

She choked, and the tears flowed unrestrained. She wept, and I was glad to see her weeping. . . .

She stood leaning over the bridge; her tear-wet handkerchief gripped in her clenched hand.

"Just an hour in the old shop again—and him talking. Before things got done. Before they got hold of him. And fooled him.

"Men oughtn't to be so tempted with business and things. . . .

"They didn't hurt him, George?" she asked suddenly.

For a moment I was puzzled.

"Here, I mean," she said.

"No," I lied stoutly, suppressing the memory of that foolish injection needle I had caught the young doctor using.

"I wonder, George, if they'll let him talk in Heaven . . ."

She faced me. "Oh! George, dear, my heart aches, and I don't know what I say and do. Give me your arm to lean on—it's good to have you, dear, and lean upon you. . . . Yes, I know you care for me. That's why I'm talking. We've always loved one another, and never said anything about it, and you understand, and I understand. But my heart's torn to pieces by this, torn to rags, and things drop out I've kept in it. It's true he wasn't a husband much for me at the last. But he was my child, George, he was my child and all my children, my silly child, and life has knocked him about for me, and I've never had a say in the matter; never a say; it's puffed him up and smashed him—like an old bag—under my eyes. I was clever enough to see it, and not clever enough to prevent it, and all I could do was to jeer. I've had to make what I could of it. Like most people. Like most of us. . . . But it wasn't fair, George. It wasn't fair. Life and Death—great serious things —why couldn't they leave him alone, and his lies and ways? If *we* could see the lightness of it——

"Why couldn't they leave him alone?" she repeated in a whisper as we went towards the inn.

CHAPTER THE SECOND
Love Among the Wreckage

I

WHEN I came back I found that my share in the escape and death of my uncle had made me for a time a notorious and even popular character. For two weeks I was kept in London "facing the music," as he would have said, and making things easy for my aunt, and I still marvel at the consideration with which the world treated me. For now it was open and manifest that I and my uncle were no more than specimens of a modern species of brigand, wasting the savings of the public out of the sheer wantonness of enterprise. I think that, in a way, his death produced a reaction in my favour, and my flight, of which some particulars now appeared, stuck in the popular imagination. It seemed a more daring and difficult feat than it was, and I couldn't very well write to the papers to sustain my private estimate. There can be little doubt that men infinitely prefer the appearance of dash and enterprise to simple honesty. No one believed I was not an arch plotter in his financing. Yet they favoured me. I even got permission from the trustee to occupy my châlet for a fortnight while I cleared up the mass of papers, calculations, notes of work, drawings and the like, that I left in disorder when I started on that impulsive raid upon the Mordet quap heaps. I was there alone. I got work for Cothope with the Ilchesters, for whom I now build these destroyers. They wanted him at once, and he was short of money, so I let him go and managed very philosophically by myself.

But I found it hard to fix my attention on aeronautics. I had been away from the work for a full half-year and more, a half-year crowded with intense disconcerting things. For a time my brain refused these fine problems of balance and adjustment altogether; it wanted to think about my uncle's dropping jaw, my aunt's reluctant tears, about dead negroes and pestilential swamps, about the evident realities of cruelty and pain, about life and death. Moreover, it was weary with the frightful pile of figures and documents at the Hardingham, a task to which this raid to Lady Grove was simply an interlude. And there was Beatrice.

On the second morning, as I sat out upon the veranda recalling memories and striving in vain to attend to some too succinct pencil notes of Cothope's, Beatrice rode up suddenly from behind the pavilion, and pulled rein and became still; Beatrice, a little flushed from riding and sitting on a big black horse.

I did not instantly rise. I stared at her. *"You!"* I said.

She looked at me steadily. "Me," she said.

I did not trouble about any civilities. I stood up and asked point blank a question that came into my head.

"Whose horse is that?" I said.

She looked me in the eyes. "Carnaby's," she answered·

"How did you get here—this way?"

"The wall's down."

"Down? Already?"

"A great bit of it between the plantations."

"And you rode through, and got here by chance?"

"I saw you yesterday. And I rode over to see you."

I had now come close to her, and stood looking up into her face.

"I'm a mere vestige," I said.

She made no answer, but remained regarding me steadfastly with a curious air of proprietorship.

"You know I'm the living survivor now of the great smash. I'm rolling and dropping down through all the scaffolding of the social system. . . . It's all a chance whether I roll out free at the bottom, or go down a crack into the darkness out of sight for a year or two."

"The sun," she remarked irrelevantly, "has burnt you. . . . I'm getting down."

She swung herself down into my arms, and stood beside me face to face.

"Where's Cothope?" she asked.

"Gone."

Her eyes flitted to the pavilion and back to me. We stood close together, extraordinarily intimate, and extraordinarily apart.

"I've never seen this cottage of yours," she said, "and I want to."

She flung the bridle of her horse round the veranda post, and I helped her tie it.

"Did you get what you went for to Africa?" she asked.

"No," I said, "I lost my ship."

"And that lost everything?"

"Everything."

She walked before me into the living-room of the châlet, and I saw that she gripped her riding-whip very tightly in her hand. She looked about her for a moment, and then at me.

"It's comfortable," she remarked.

Our eyes met in a conversation very different from the one upon our lips. A sombre glow surrounded us, drew us together; an unwonted shyness kept us apart. She roused herself, after an instant's pause, to examine my furniture.

"You have chintz curtains. I thought men were too feckless to have curtains without a woman——. But, of course, your aunt did that! And a couch and a brass fender, and—is that a pianola? That is your desk. I thought men's desks were always untidy, and covered with dust and to-bacco ash."

She flitted to my colour prints and my little case of books. Then she went to the pianola. I watched her intently.

"Does this thing play?" she said.

"What?" I asked.

"Does this thing play?"

I roused myself from my preoccupation.

"Like a musical gorilla with fingers all of one length. And a sort of soul. . . . It's all the world of music to me."

"What do you play?"

"Beethoven, when I want to clear up my head while I'm working. He is—how one would always like to work. Some-times Chopin and those others, but Beethoven. Beethoven mainly. Yes."

Silence again between us. She spoke with an effort.

"Play me something." She turned from me and explored the rack of music rolls, became interested and took a piece, the first part of the Kreutzer Sonata, hesitated. "No," she said, "that!"

She gave me Brahms' Second Concerto, Op. 58, and curled up on the sofa watching me as I set myself slowly to play. . . .

"I say," she said when I had done, "that's fine. I didn't know those things could play like that. I'm all astir . . ."

She came and stood over me, looking at me. "I'm going to have a concert," she said abruptly, and laughed uneasily and hovered at the pigeon-holes. "Now —now what shall I have?" She chose more of Brahms. Then we came to the Kreutzer Sonata. It is queer how Tolstoy has loaded that with suggestions, debauched it, made it a scandalous and intimate symbol. When I had played the first part of that, she came up to the pianola and hesitated over me. I sat stiffly—waiting.

Suddenly she seized my downcast head and kissed my hair. She caught at my face between her hands and kissed my lips. I put my arms about her and we kissed together. I sprang to my feet and clasped her.

"Beatrice!" I said. "Beatrice!"

"My dear," she whispered, nearly breathless, with her arms about me. "Oh! my dear!"

II

Love, like everything else in this immense process of social disorganisation in which we live, is a thing adrift, a fruitless thing broken away from its connexions. I tell of this love affair here because of its irrelevance, because it is so remarkable that it should mean nothing, and be nothing except itself. It glows in my memory like some bright casual flower starting up amidst the *débris* of a catastrophe. For nearly a fortnight we two met and made love together. Once more this mighty passion, that our aimless civilisation has fettered and maimed and sterilised and debased, gripped me and filled me with passionate delights and solemn joys —that were all, you know, futile and purposeless. Once more I had the persuasion "This matters. Nothing else matters so much as this." We were both infinitely grave in such happiness as we had. I do not remember any laughter at all between us.

Twelve days it lasted from that encounter in my châlet until our parting.

Except at the end, they were days of supreme summer, and there was a waxing moon. We met recklessly day by day. We were so intent upon each other at first, so intent upon expressing ourselves to each other, and getting at each other, that we troubled very little about the appearance of our relationship. We met almost openly. . . . We talked of ten thousand things, and of ourselves. We loved. We made

love. There is no prose of mine that can tell of hours transfigured. The facts are nothing. Everything we touched, the
meanest things, became glorious. How can I render bare
tenderness and delight and mutual possession?

I sit here at my desk thinking of untellable things.

I have come to know so much of love that I know now
what love might be. We loved, scarred and stained; we
parted—basely and inevitably, but at least I met love.

I remember as we sat in a Canadian canoe, in a reedy,
bush-masked shallow we had discovered opening out of that
pine-shaded Woking canal, how she fell talking of the
things that happened to her before she met me again. . . .

She told me things, and they so joined and welded together other things that lay disconnected in my memory,
that it seemed to me I had always known what she told me.
And yet indeed I had not known nor suspected it, save perhaps for a luminous, transitory suspicion ever and again.

She made me see how life had shaped her. She told me
of her girlhood after I had known her. "We were poor and
pretending and managing. We hacked about on visits and
things. I ought to have married. The chances I had weren't
particularly good chances. I didn't like 'em."

She paused. "Then Carnaby came along."

I remained quite still. She spoke now with downcast eyes,
and one finger just touching the water.

"One gets bored, bored beyond redemption. One goes
about to these huge expensive houses I suppose—the scale's
immense. One makes one's self useful to the other women,
and agreeable to the men. One has to dress. . . . One has
food and exercise and leisure. It's the leisure, and the space,
and the blank opportunity it seems a sin not to fill. Carnaby
isn't like the other men. He's bigger. . . . They go about
making love. Everybody's making love. I did. . . . And I
don't do things by halves."

She stopped.

"You knew?" she asked, looking up, quite steadily.

I nodded.

"Since when?"

"Those last days. . . . It hasn't seemed to matter really. I was a little surprised——"

She looked at me quietly. "Cothope knew," she said. "By instinct. I could feel it."

"I suppose," I began, "once, this would have mattered immensely. Now——"

"Nothing matters," she said, completing me. "I felt I had to tell you. I wanted you to understand why I didn't marry you—with both hands. I have loved you"—she paused—"have loved you ever since the day I kissed you in the bracken. Only—I forgot."

And suddenly she dropped her face upon her hands, and sobbed passionately—

"I forgot—I forgot," she cried, and became still. . . .

I dabbled my paddle in the water. "Look here!" I said; "forget again! Here am I—a ruined man. Marry me."

She shook her head without looking up.

We were still for a long time. "Marry me," I whispered.

She looked up, twined back a whisp of hair, and answered dispassionately—

"I wish I could. Anyhow, we have had this time. It has been a fine time—has it been—for you also? I haven't grudged you all I had to give. It's a poor gift—except for what it means and might have been. But we are near the end of it now."

"Why?" I asked. "Marry me! Why should we two——"

"You think," she said, "I could take courage and come to you and be your everyday wife—while you work and are poor?"

"Why not?" said I.

She looked at me gravely, with extended finger. "Do you really think that?—of me? Haven't you seen me—all?"

I hesitated.

"Never once have I really meant marrying you," she insisted. "Never once. I fell in love with you from the first. But when you seemed a successful man, I told myself I wouldn't. I was love-sick for you, and you were so stupid, I came near it then. But I knew I wasn't good enough.

What could I have been to you? A woman with bad habits and bad associations, a woman smirched. And what could I do for you or be to you? If I wasn't good enough to be a rich man's wife, I'm certainly not good enough to be a poor one's. Forgive me for talking sense to you now, but I wanted to tell you this somehow——"

She stopped at my gesture. I sat up, and the canoe rocked with my movement.

"I don't care," I said. "I want to marry you and make you my wife!"

"No," she said, "don't spoil things. That is impossible!"

"Impossible!"

"Think! I can't do my own hair! Do you mean you will get me a maid?"

"Good God!" I cried, disconcerted beyond measure, "won't you learn to do your own hair for me? Do you mean to say you can love a man——"

She flung out her hands at me. "Don't spoil it," she cried. "I have given you all I have, I have given you all I can. If I could do it, if I was good enough to do it, I would. But I am a woman spoilt and ruined, dear, and you are a ruined man. When we are making love we are lovers—but think of the gulf between us in habits and ways of thought, in will and training, when we are not making love. Think of it—and don't think of it! Don't think of it yet. We have snatched some hours. We still may have some hours!"

She suddenly knelt forward toward me, with a glowing darkness in her eyes. "Who cares if it upsets?" she cried. "If you say another word I will kiss you. And go to the bottom clutching you. I'm not afraid of that. I'm not a bit afraid of that. I'll die with you. Choose a death, and I'll die with you—readily. Do listen to me! I love you. I shall always love you. It's because I love you that I won't go down to become a dirty familiar thing with you amidst the grime. I've given all I can. I've had all I can. . . . Tell me," and she crept nearer, "have I been like the dusk to you, like the warm dusk? Is there magic still? Listen to the ripple of water from your paddle. Look at the warm evening light in the sky. Who cares if the canoe upsets! Come nearer to me. Oh, my love! come near! So."

She drew me to her and our lips met.

III

I asked her to marry me once again.

It was our last morning together, and we had met very early, about sunrise, knowing that we were to part. No sun shone that day. The sky was overcast, the morning chilly and lit by a clear, cold, spiritless light. A heavy dampness in the air verged close on rain. When I think of that morning, it has always the quality of greying ashes wet with rain.

Beatrice too had changed. The spring had gone out of her movement; it came to me, for the first time, that some day she might grow old. She had become one flesh with the rest of common humanity; the softness had gone from her voice and manner, the dusky magic of her presence had gone. I saw these things with perfect clearness, and they made me sorry for them and for her. But they altered my love not a whit, abated it nothing. And when we had talked awkwardly for half a dozen sentences, I came dully to my point.

"And now," I cried, "will you marry me?"

"No," she said, "I shall keep to my life here."

I asked her to marry me in a year's time. She shook her head.

"This world is a soft world," I said, "in spite of my present disasters. I know now how to do things. If I had you to work for—in a year I could be a prosperous man——"

"No," she said, "I will put it brutally, I shall go back to Carnaby."

"But——!" I did not feel angry. I had no sort of jealousy, no wounded pride, no sense of injury. I had only a sense of grey desolation, of hopeless cross-purposes.

"Look here," she said. "I have been awake all night and every night. I have been thinking of this—every moment when we have not been together. I'm not answering you on an impulse. I love you. I love you. I'll say that over ten thousand times. But here we are——"

"The rest of life together," I said.

"It wouldn't be together. Now we are together. Now we have been together. We are full of memories. I do not feel I can ever forget a single one."

"Nor I."

"And I want to close it and leave it at that. You see, dear, what else is there to do?"

She turned her white face to me. "All I know of love, all I have ever dreamt or learnt of love I have packed into these days for you. You think we might live together and go on loving. No! For you I will have no vain repetitions. You have had the best and all of me. Would you have us, after this, meet again in London or Paris or somewhere, scuffle to some wretched dressmaker's, meet in a *cabinet particulier?*"

"No," I said. "I want you to marry me. I want you to play the game of life with me as an honest woman should. Come and live with me. Be my wife and squaw. Bear me children."

"I looked at her white, drawn face, and it seemed to me I might carry her yet. I spluttered for words.

"My God! Beatrice!" I cried; "but this is cowardice and folly! Are *you* afraid of life? You of all people! What does it matter what has been or what we were? Here we are with the world before us! Start clean and new with me. We'll fight it through! I'm not such a simple lover that I'll not tell you plainly when you go wrong, and fight our difference out with you. It's the one thing I want, the one thing I need —to have you, and more of you and more! This love-making—it's love-making. It's just a part of us, an incident——"

She shook her head and stopped me abruptly. "It's all," she said.

"All!" I protested.

"I'm wiser than you. Wiser beyond words." She turned her eyes to me and they shone with tears.

"I wouldn't have you say anything—but what you're

saying," she said. "But it's nonsense, dear. You know it's nonsense as you say it."

I tried to keep up the heroic note, but she would not listen to it.

"It's no good," she cried almost petulantly. "This little world has made—made us what we are. Don't you see— don't you see what I am? I can make love. I can make love and be loved, prettily. Dear, don't blame me! I have given you all I have. If I had anything more——. I have gone through it all over and over again—thought it out. This morning my head aches, my eyes ache. The light has gone out of me and I am a sick and tired woman. But I'm talking wisdom—bitter wisdom. I couldn't be any sort of helper to you, any sort of wife, any sort of mother. I'm spoilt. I'm spoilt by this rich idle way of living, until every habit is wrong, every taste wrong. The world is wrong. People can be ruined by wealth just as much as by poverty. Do you think I wouldn't face life with you if I could, if I wasn't absolutely certain I should be down and dragging in the first half-mile of the journey? Here I am—damned! Damned! But I won't damn you. You know what I am! You know. You are too clear and simple not to know the truth. You try to romance and hector, but you know the truth. I am a little cad—sold and done. I'm——. My dear, you think I've been misbehaving, but all these days I've been on my best behaviour. . . . You don't understand, because you're a man. A woman, when she's spoilt, is *spoilt*. She's dirty in grain. She's done."

She walked on weeping.

"You're a fool to want me," she said. "You're a fool to want me—for my sake just as much as yours. We've done all we can. It's just romancing——"

She dashed the tears from her eyes and turned upon me. "Don't you understand?" she challenged. "Don't you know?"

We faced one another in silence for a moment.

"Yes," I said, "I know."

For a long time we spoke never a word, but walked on

together, slowly and sorrowfully, reluctant to turn about towards our parting. When at last we did, she broke silence again.

"I've had you," she said.

"Heaven and hell," I said, "can't alter that."

"I've wanted——" she went on. "I've talked to you in the nights and made up speeches. Now when I want to make them I'm tongue-tied. But to me it's just as if the moments we have had lasted for ever. Moods and states come and go. To-day my light is out . . ."

To this day I cannot determine whether she said or whether I imagined she said "chloral." Perhaps a half-conscious diagnosis flashed it on my brain. Perhaps I am the victim of some perverse imaginative freak of memory, some hinted possibility that scratched and seared. There the word stands in my memory, as if it were written in fire.

We came to the door of Lady Osprey's garden at last, and it was beginning to drizzle.

She held out her hands and I took them.

"Yours," she said, in a weary unimpassioned voice; "all that I had—such as it was. Will you forget?"

"Never," I answered.

"Never a touch or a word of it?"

"No."

"You will," she said.

We looked at one another in silence, and her face was full of fatigue and misery.

What could I do? What was there to do?

"I wish——" I said, and stopped.

"Good-bye."

IV

That should have been the last I saw of her, but, indeed, I was destined to see her once again. Two days after I was at Lady Grove, I forget altogether upon what errand, and as I walked back to the station believing her to be gone away she came upon me, and she was riding with Carnaby, just as I had seen them first. The encounter jumped upon us unprepared. She rode by, her eyes dark in her white face, and scarcely noticed me. She winced and grew stiff at the sight of me and bowed her head. But Carnaby, because he thought I was a broken and discomfited man, saluted me with an easy friendliness, and shouted some genial commonplace to me.

They passed out of sight and left me by the roadside. . . .

And then, indeed, I tasted the ultimate bitterness of life. For the first time I felt utter futility, and was wrung by emotion that begot no action, by shame and pity beyond words. I had parted from her dully and I had seen my uncle break and die with dry eyes and a steady mind, but this chance sight of my lost Beatrice brought me to tears. My face was wrung, and tears came pouring down my cheeks. All the magic she had for me had changed to wild sorrow. "Oh God!" I cried, "this is too much," and turned my face after her and made appealing gestures to the beech trees and cursed at fate. I wanted to do preposterous things, to pursue her, to save her, to turn life back so that she might begin again. I wonder what would have happened had I overtaken them in pursuit, breathless with running, uttering incoherent words, weeping, expostulatory. I came near to doing that.

There was nothing in earth or heaven to respect my curses or weeping. In the midst of it a man who had been trimming the opposite hedge appeared and stared at me.

Abruptly, ridiculously, I dissembled before him and went on and caught my train. . . . .

But the pain I felt then I have felt a hundred times; it is with me as I write. It haunts this book, I see, that is what haunts this book, from end to end. . . .

CHAPTER THE THIRD

Night and the Open Sea

I

I HAVE tried throughout all this story to tell things as they happened to me. In the beginning—the sheets are still here on the table, grimy and dog's-eared and old-looking—I said I wanted to tell *myself* and the world in which I found myself, and I have done my best. But whether I have succeeded I cannot imagine. All this writing is grey now and dead and trite and unmeaning to me; some of it I know by heart. I am the last person to judge it.

As I turn over the big pile of manuscript before me, certain things become clearer to me, and particularly the immense inconsequences of my experiences. It is, I see now that I have it all before me, a story of activity and urgency and sterility. I have called it *Tono-Bungay,* but I had far better have called it *Waste.* I have told of childless Marion, of my childless aunt, of Beatrice wasted and wasteful and futile. What hope is there for a people whose women become fruitless? I think of all the energy I have given to vain things. I think of my industrious scheming with my uncle, of Crest Hill's vast cessation, of his resonant strenuous career. Ten thousand men have envied him and wished to live as he lived. It is all one spectacle of forces running to waste, of people who use and do not replace, the story of a country hectic with a wasting aimless fever of trade and money-making and pleasure-seeking. And now I build destroyers!

Other people may see this country in other terms; this is how I have seen it. In some early chapter in this heap

I compared all our present colour and abundance to October foliage before the frosts nip down the leaves. That I still feel was a good image. Perhaps I see wrongly. It may be I see decay all about me because I am, in a sense, decay. To others it may be a scene of achievement and construction radiant with hope. I, too, have a sort of hope, but it is a remote hope, a hope that finds no promise in this Empire or in any of the great things of our time. How they will look in history I do not know, how time and chance will prove them I cannot guess; that is how they have mirrored themselves on one contemporary mind.

II

Concurrently with writing the last chapter of this book I have been much engaged by the affairs of a new destroyer we have completed. It has been an oddly complementary alternation of occupations. Three weeks or so ago this novel had to be put aside in order that I might give all my time day and night to the fitting and finishing of the engines. Last Thursday X 2, for so we call her, was done and I took her down the Thames and went out nearly to Texel for a trial of speed.

It is curious how at times one's impressions will all fuse and run together into a sort of unity and become continuous with things that have hitherto been utterly alien and remote. That rush down the river became mysteriously connected with this book. As I passed down the Thames I seemed in a new and parallel manner to be passing all England in review. I saw it then as I had wanted my readers to see it. The thought came to me slowly as I picked my way through the Pool; it stood out clear as I went dreaming into the night out upon the wide North Sea. . . .

It wasn't so much thinking at the time as a sort of photographic thought that came and grew clear. X 2 went ripping through the dirty oily water as scissors rip through canvas, and the front of my mind was all intent with getting her through under the bridges and in and out among the steamboats and barges and rowing-boats and piers. I lived with

[392]

my hands and eyes hard ahead. I thought nothing then of any appearances but obstacles, but for all that the back of my mind took the photographic memory of it complete and vivid. . . .

"This," it came to me, "is England. That is what I wanted to give in my book. This!"

We started in the late afternoon. We throbbed out of our yard above Hammersmith Bridge, fussed about for a moment, and headed down stream. We came at an easy rush down Craven Reach, past Fulham and Hurlingham, past the long stretches of muddy meadow and muddy suburb to Battersea and Chelsea, round the cape of tidy frontage that is Grosvenor Road and under Vauxhall Bridge, and Westminster opened before us. We cleared a string of coal barges and there on the left in the October sunshine stood the Parliament houses, and the flag was flying and Parliament was sitting. . . .

I saw it at the time unseeingly; afterwards it came into my mind as the centre of the whole broad panoramic effect of that afternoon. The stiff square lace of Victorian Gothic with its Dutch clock of a tower came upon me suddenly and stared and whirled past in a slow half pirouette and became still, I know, behind me as if watching me recede. "Aren't you going to respect me, then?" it seemed to say.

Not I! There in that great pile of Victorian architecture the landlords and the lawyers, the bishops, the railway men and the magnates of commerce go to and fro—in their incurable tradition of commercialised Bladesovery, of meretricious gentry and nobility sold for riches. I have been near enough to know. The Irish and the Labour-men run about among their feet, making a fuss, effecting little; they've got no better plans that I can see. Respect it indeed! There's a certain paraphernalia of dignity, but whom does it deceive? The King comes down in a gilt coach to open the show and wears long robes and a crown; and there's a display of stout and slender legs in white stockings and stout and slender legs in black stockings and artful old gentlemen in ermine. I was reminded of one

[393]

congested afternoon I had spent with my aunt amidst a cluster of agitated women's hats in the Royal Gallery of the House of Lords and how I saw the King going to open Parliament, and the Duke of Devonshire looking like a gorgeous pedlar and terribly bored with the cap of maintenance on a tray before him hung by slings from his shoulders. A wonderful spectacle! . . .

It is quaint, no doubt, this England—it is even dignified in places—and full of mellow associations. That does not alter the quality of the realities these robes conceal. The realities are greedy trade, base profit-seeking, bold advertisement; and kingship and chivalry, spite of this wearing of treasured robes, are as dead among it all as that crusader my uncle championed against the nettles outside the Duffield church. . . .

I have thought much of that bright afternoon's panorama.

To run down the Thames so is to run one's hand over the pages in the book of England from end to end. One begins in Craven Reach and it is as if one were in the heart of old England. Behind us are Kew and Hampton Court with their memories of Kings and Cardinals, and one runs at first between Fulham's episcopal garden parties and Hurlingham's playground for the sporting instinct of our race. The whole effect is English. There is space, there are old trees and all the best qualities of the home-land in that upper reach. Putney, too, looks Anglican on a dwindling scale. And then for a stretch the newer developments slop over, one misses Bladesover and there come first squalid stretches of mean homes right and left and then the dingy industrialism of the south side, and on the north bank the polite long front of nice houses, artistic, literary, administrative people's residences, that stretches from Cheyne Walk nearly to Westminster and hides a wilderness of slums. What a long slow crescendo that is, mile after mile, with the houses crowding closelier, the multiplying succession of church towers, the architectural moments, the successive bridges, until you come out into the second movement of the piece with Lambeth's old palace under your quarter and

[394]

the houses of Parliament on your bow! Westminster Bridge is ahead of you then, and through it you flash, and in a moment the round-faced clock tower cranes up to peer at you again and New Scotland Yard squares at you, a fat beef-eater of a policeman disguised miraculously as a Bastille.

For a stretch you have the essential London; you have Charing Cross railway station, heart of the world, and the Embankment on the north side with its new hotels over-shadowing its Georgian and Victorian architecture, and mud and great warehouses and factories, chimneys, shot towers, advertisements on the south. The northward skyline grows more intricate and pleasing, and more and more does one thank God for Wren. Somerset House is as picturesque as the civil war, one is reminded again of the original Eng-land, one feels in the fretted sky the quality of Restoration lace. . . .

And then comes Astor's strong box and the lawyers' Inns. . . .

(I had a passing memory of myself there, how once I had trudged along the Embankment westward, weighing my uncle's offer of three hundred pounds a year. . . .)

Through that central essential London reach I drove, and X 2 bored her nose under the foam regardless of it all like a black hound going through reeds—on what trail even I who made her cannot tell.

And in this reach, too, one first meets the seagulls and is reminded of the sea. Blackfriars one takes—just under these two bridges and just between them is the finest bridge moment in the world—and behold, soaring up, hanging in the sky over a rude tumult of warehouses, over a jostling competition of traders, irrelevantly beautiful and altogether remote, Saint Paul's! "Of course!" one says, "Saint Paul's!" It is the very figure of whatever fineness the old Anglican culture achieved, detached, a more dignified and chastened Saint Peter's, colder, greyer, but still ornate; it has never been overthrown, never disavowed, only the tall warehouses and all the roar of traffic have forgotten it, every one has forgotten it; the steamships, the barges, go heedlessly by regardless of it, intricacies of telephone wires and poles cut blackly into its thin mysteries, and presently, when in a moment the traffic permits you and you look round for it, it has dissolved like a cloud into the grey blues of the London sky.

And then the traditional and ostensible England falls from you altogether. The third movement begins, the last great movement in the London symphony, in which the trim scheme of the old order is altogether dwarfed and swallowed up. Comes London Bridge, and the great warehouses tower up about you, waving stupendous cranes, the gulls circle and scream in your ears, large ships lie among their lighters, and one is in the port of the world. Again and again in this book I have written of England as a feudal scheme overtaken by fatty degeneration and stupendous accidents of hypertrophy. For the last time I must strike that note as the memory of the dear neat little sunlit ancient Tower of London lying away in a gap among the warehouses comes back to me, that little accumulation of buildings so provincially pleasant and dignified, overshadowed by the vulgarest, most typical exploit of modern England, the sham Gothic casings to the ironwork of the Tower Bridge. That Tower Bridge is the very balance and confirmation of Westminster's dull pinnacles and tower. That sham Gothic bridge; in the very gates of our mother of change, the Sea!

But after that one is in a world of accident and nature. For the third part of the panorama of London is beyond all law, order, and precedence; it is the seaport and the sea. One goes down the widening reaches through a monstrous variety of shipping, great steamers, great sailing-ships, trailing the flags of all the world, a monstrous confusion of lighters, witches' conferences of brown-sailed barges, wallowing tugs, a tumultuous crowding and jostling of cranes and spars, and wharves and stores, and assertive inscriptions. Huge vistas of dock open right and left of one, and here and there beyond and amidst it all are church towers, little patches of indescribably old-fashioned and worn-out houses, riverside pubs and the like, vestiges of townships that were long since torn to fragments and submerged in these new growths. And amidst it all no plan appears, no intention, no comprehensive desire. That is the very key of it all. Each day one feels that the pressure of commerce and traffic grew, grew insensibly monstrous, and first this man made a wharf and that erected a crane, and then this company set to work and then that, and so they jostled together to make this unassimilable enormity of traffic. Through it we dodged and drove, eager for the high seas.

I remember how I laughed aloud at the glimpse of the name of a London County Council steamboat that ran across me. *Caxton* it was called, and another was *Pepys*, and another was *Shakespeare*. They seemed so wildly out of place, splashing about in that confusion. One wanted to take them out and wipe them and put them back in some English gentleman's library. Everything was alive about them, flashing, splashing, and passing, ships moving, tugs panting, hawsers taut, barges going down with men toiling at the sweeps, the water all a-swirl with the wash of shipping, scaling into millions of little wavelets, curling and frothing under the whip of the unceasing wind. Past it all we drove. And at Greenwich to the south, you know, there stands a fine stone frontage where all the victories are recorded in a Painted Hall, and beside it is the "Ship" where once upon a time those gentlemen of Westminster used to have an annual dinner—before the port of London got too much for them altogether. The old façade of the Hospital was just warming to the sunset as we went by, and after that, right and left, the river opened, the sense of the sea increased and prevailed, reach after reach from Northfleet to the Nore.

And out you come at last with the sun behind you into the eastern sea. You speed up and tear the oily water louder and faster, siroo, siroo—swish—siroo, and the hills of Kent —over which I once fled from the Christian teachings of

Nicodemus Frapp—fall away on the right hand and Essex on the left. They fall away and vanish into blue haze, and the tall slow ships behind the tugs, scarce moving ships and wallowing sturdy tugs, are all wrought of wet gold as one goes frothing by. They stand out, bound on strange missions of life and death, to the killing of men in unfamiliar lands. And now behind us is blue mystery and the phantom flash of unseen lights, and presently even these are gone, and I and my destroyer tear out to the unknown across a great grey space. We tear into the great spaces of the future and the turbines fall to talking in unfamiliar tongues. Out to the open we go, to windy freedom and trackless ways. Light after light goes down. England and the Kingdom, Britain and the Empire, the old prides and the old devotions, glide abeam, astern, sink down upon the horizon, pass—pass. The river passes—London passes, England passes. . . .

III

This is the note I have tried to emphasise, the note that sounds clear in my mind when I think of anything beyond the purely personal aspects of my story.

It is a note of crumbling and confusion, of change and seemingly aimless swelling, of a bubbling up and medley of futile loves and sorrows. But through the confusion sounds another note. Through the confusion something drives, something that is at once human achievement and the most inhuman of all existing things. Something comes out of it. . . . How can I express the values of a thing at once so essential and so immaterial. It is something that calls upon such men as I with an irresistible appeal.

I have figured it in my last section by the symbol of my destroyer, stark and swift, irrelevant to most human interests. Sometimes I call this reality Science, sometimes I call it Truth. But it is something we draw by pain and effort out of the heart of life, that we disentangle and make clear. Other men serve it, I know, in art, in literature, in social invention, and see it in a thousand different figures, under a hundred names. I see it always as austerity, as beauty. This thing we make clear is the heart of life. It is the one enduring thing. Men and nations, epochs and civilisation pass, each making its contribution. I do not know what it is, this something, except that it is supreme. It is a something, a quality, an element, one may find now in colours, now in forms, now in sounds, now in thoughts. It emerges from life with each year one lives and feels, and generation by generation and age by age, but the how and why of it are all beyond the compass of my mind. . . .

Yet the full sense of it was with me all that night as I drove, lonely above the rush and murmur of my engines, out upon the weltering circle of the sea. . . .

Far out to the northeast there came the flicker of a squadron of warships waving white swords of light about the sky. I kept them hull-down, and presently they were mere summer lightning over the watery edge of the globe. . . . I fell into thought that was nearly formless, into doubts and dreams that have no words, and it seemed good to me to drive ahead and on and on through the windy starlight, over the long black waves.

IV

It was morning and day before I returned with the four sick and starving journalists who had got permission to come with me, up the shining river, and past the old grey Tower. . . .

I recall the back views of those journalists very distinctly, going with a certain damp weariness of movement, along a side street away from the river. They were good men and bore me no malice, and they served me up to the public in turgid degenerate Kiplingese, as a modest button on the complacent stomach of the Empire. Though as a matter of fact, X 2 isn't intended for the empire, or indeed for the hands of any European power. We offered it to our own people first, but they would have nothing to do with me, and I have long since ceased to trouble much about such questions. I have come to see myself from the outside, my country from the outside—without illusions. We make and pass.

We are all things that make and pass, striving upon a hidden mission, out to the open sea.

THE END

The Best of the World's Best Books
COMPLETE LIST OF TITLES IN

THE MODERN LIBRARY

For convenience in ordering use number at right of title

MODERN LIBRARY GIANTS

A series of full-sized library editions of books that formerly were available only in cumbersome and expensive sets.
THE MODERN LIBRARY GIANTS REPRESENT A
SELECTION OF THE WORLD'S GREATEST BOOKS

These volumes contain from 600 to 1,400 pages each

THE MOST AUTHORITATIVE
DESK DICTIONARY EVER PUBLISHED

• MORE ACCURATE
• MORE UP TO DATE
• MORE USEFUL IN HOME, SCHOOL AND OFFICE

EASIER TO READ
EASIER TO USE

Interior by Melanie Kahane, A. I. D.

No modern library is complete
without THE AMERICAN
COLLEGE DICTIONARY